Scratch the Sky

Book 1 of the
Blood Wild Chronicles

Tamara Brigham

Cover Design by: Tamara Brigham

Published by:
Tamara Brigham
PO Box 151
Clearlake, CA 95422

Printed and bound in the United States of America

First Edition

ISBN # 978-1-7320024-8-7

❧*❧
For
My Dad
❧*❧

Prologue

Through the vacant chasms that had once been city streets, the cries rang out, desperate howls muted by decline, scratching at the feverish night sky with the forlorn frenzy of the lost, the frightened, the panicked. Replies enjoined, separated by urban collapse and the rusted skeletons of civilization, shifting their echoes as each voice raced outward from the center where chaos had been born. Manmade forms that clung to existence despite strangling tendrils of flora, the biting northeast wind, and the gnawing of salty rain blown in from the sea. The familiar tang of it drowned out the bite of decay, cleansing the air of all but the scent of the pursuers from her flared nostrils as she leaped from cracked concrete to the crumbling rusted hood of a metal hulk that had once transported goods through the streets of Queens but had not moved from this spot in more years than she had been alive. The jagged stone wall bore her weight precariously as she scrambled to a higher vantage point from which she could sniff the air, hidden in the shadows of once manicured foliage, in the hopes of spotting the hunters before they spotted her.

"Run, Jia!"

The words reverberated in her head, carried by the November rain that drenched her thick dark pelt and tickled her ears, words that pushed her back into action against her better judgment. But when Roland Marrock spoke, the Pack listened, regardless of his daughter's misgivings about the man's safety. Her last glimpse of him, crouched over Delilah's convulsing, bloody body, trying to drag her out of the open street into the safety of the nearest overgrown passage…the crack and snap of a taut bowstring…his yelp and a howl of warning to the now scattered Pack, an ultimatum that left Jia torn between remaining to help, to fight for his life at his side, and the obedience he demanded.

She knew what she had to do. Against her heart's wishes, duty to the Pack came first. She had to get each of them to safety. She had to warn the others, to lead the hunters away from the den.

She had to lead where her father could not.

Her hesitation on the wall, a moment too long, beneath the radiance of the full moon's silvery fingers, lit a glow in the chartreuse of her irises, a beacon caught in the false beam of a hunter's light. Momentarily blinded by the flare, she froze, but it was the horror of what lay behind the white glare that temporarily robbed her limbs of motion. A glimpse, a visage lost to time, followed by a snap that caught her unaware and the burning in her shoulder that threw her from the wall into the foliage on the other side.

Heart hammering at a furious pace, Jia lurched awake, her hand clutching her shoulder, her head tilted into the drafty air, expecting a threat that was not there as the nightmare's brilliance bled from her memory. Once again, the retreating imagery took with it the hope she had of recollection, the one hope she had of retribution…justice.

Only a nightmare. The Pack slept safe, those around her peaceful and secure in their efforts to remain warm. The wind was still, the air clear of rain, streaks of dark clouds stretched across the half-face moon she could see through the dirty window to her right.

Or maybe they were smudges on the window. It was too far above her head to be certain.

The face behind the traitorous light was gone, taking her father with it, stripping her again of the hopes of finding him. When, she wondered, would this memory-dream cease to frighten her? One time, one objective remembrance of that night, was all she needed to know the truth and put the dream to rest.

But tonight would not be that night. Tonight gave her only the fading glow of adrenalin and the desire to curl up at the side of someone who could relieve the suffocating weight of responsibility she was forced to shoulder.

Eyes squeezed shut, deep brown hair pushed away from her face before her arms wrapped around her torso, she swallowed the sigh. She had always known this duty would come to her. but she had never imagined that it would come like this.

❧Scratch the Sky❧

Chapter 1

H er hand seemed small against Liam's leather-clad arm as he smiled down at the woman beside him, waiting for the nod that prompted him to escort her up the long, wide staircase illuminated by solar-powered squares of light. Anyone who knew Jia Marrock, however, would not be deceived by her stature or the patchwork gown of crimson she wore. Despite her diminutive stature, the round face and large dark eyes that gave her a deceptively child-like appearance, she needed no bodyguard, needed no man beside her to take command of a room, but Liam appreciated the opportunity to play escort and protector, even if she required neither. What she needed this night was a friend, and Liam had been that since before either of them could speak their first words. Most in attendance at this gala, having come to honor the marriage between the Laedan Houses of Channon and Hallister, knew the daughter of Roland Marrock, the heir to the man's position and name, if not by face than by familial reputation. Her attendance was expected.

But none, the lanky blonde with the always disheveled hair thought with a guarded smile of greeting to a dignitary in new leather and Astoria lace, knew Jia the way he did. Tonight it was his duty to be certain, as they skirted the pitfalls of this mainly political assembly, that it stayed that way, that her secrets, her life, were safe.

His crooked sideways smile turned down once more to light on her face, impishly brightening as she returned his affectionate expression, but Jia knew he read the trepidation behind her façade. She did not feel as if she belonged here, did not want to be here, had not wanted to attend what she expected to be a gut-wrenching, horrid affair. As head of the Marrock family, however, a position inherited because Addi, her elder twin by twenty minutes, had a head better suited for medicine than for familial leadership, it was her responsibility to protect the interest of the family name. And something her father had said, something hinted at, words spoken that fateful night when she had lost him, led Jia to believe that somewhere in the maze of LaGuardia's halls, offices, and living quarters, the answer to his disappearance would be found.

Watching Jonni Channon marry, however, was something she preferred to avoid. Despite her conviction that a marriage union between Channons and Marrocks would be a death sentence to herself and those she loved, a corner of her heart continued to wish that this was her marriage this night. It had been talked about by their fathers for so long, it almost felt as something destined to be.

But not if she could resist it.

She did not love him. As a dear friend, yes, but not enough to allow them to overcome society's hurdles. Not in the way Jonni professed his love to her.

Only the steadfastness of Liam at her side, and the affection he bore her, allowed her to be here amongst those she barely trusted to face the duties she knew she must.

"Drink?"

She tore her searching gaze from the crowd, the kaleidoscope of colors they wore speaking of familial status and perceived wealth, amazed by how many had gathered beneath Lowell Channon's roof, and glanced into Liam's grey-green eyes. His offer was tempting, a good, bracing drink to steady her nerves sounding like the balm she required to make it through the evening. But the necessity of remaining clearheaded so as not to make a fool of herself was equally important, and so she shook her head no.

"Water then," Liam agreed, pressing his lips to her forehead and extricating himself from their mutual contact. She would be safe long enough for him to bring her a drink. In this place, with these people, Jia knew how to handle herself far better than Liam ever would. He should not worry about her.

But he did.

৯*৯

Lowell Channon glowered at his son, the icy blue in his eyes enough to freeze the hearts and wills of lesser men when he chose to turn that glare on them. But Jonni held his ground, his fists clenched at his sides now that the formal black suit his father had ordered for this occasion had been draped over a tall stool, its use discarded and rejected against Lowell's wishes.

"I will not do this, Fa. You know I will not. I never agreed to this…I will not marry her…"

"This fixation with Jia has gone on too long! I forbid you to…"

"Forbid?" Jonni ignored the smirk on his nearby brother's otherwise seemingly disinterested face as Donn took the suit before the tailor could retrieve it and held it up to his torso to study himself in the full-length polished metal mirror. Donn should not be here, listening to this argument, but as it was old territory between the eldest Channon heir and their father, an argument Donn had heard more than a dozen times, it had not occurred to Jonni to ask him to leave. "You have no right…"

"I have every right! I am your father! I am Laedan! Have you forgotten how much work has gone into this arrangement? LaGuardia needs this alliance…"

"Then you marry her! I won't do it!" Jia or not, Jonni refused to be bullied into marriage.

Before Lowell could remark on the absurdity of such a solution to the need for a Channon-Hallister union, Donn casually interjected, "You do know what she is, don't you…what all the Marrocks are?" without turning away from the mirror.

Face flushed with fury and stubborn disbelief, Jonni growled, "Rumor and accusation are not proof…"

"Quentin's my most reliable…" began Lowell.

Again, Jonni cut his father short. "Your most reliable," he said, stressing the first word. "I would not trust him with a bucket of…"

Lowell took a step forward, the tension in his body conveying a threat he did not need to make in words. It would not be the first time he struck one of his sons, but if Jonni felt intimidated by the gesture, it did not show on his face, in his eyes, or in his square-shouldered, even-footed stance.

"I trust him!" Lowell snarled. "That is all you need to…"

"I will not marry Oasis Hallister!"

Face to face, eye to eye, balled fists and curled lips pulled tight over snarling teeth, father and son challenged the other to back down from a fight before it could start, the younger man knowing his father never would, the elder realizing again that his control over his sons, at least this one, was no longer what it had been. He had wanted them to be strong, independent, capable men, and yet he was unable to relinquish the position that political necessity had pushed him into. It was a stalemate locked into place by stubbornness, with neither having the will to accept defeat or possessing the strength to facilitate success in this confrontation.

"I'll marry her."

Donn, no longer admiring himself in the mirror, laid the suit, still on its metal hanger, over the back of the stool, and adjusted his blonde hair with his fingers, refusing to look at his father or brother as they broke from their impasse to turn and stare at him. Jonni's eyes, narrowed with distrust, sought the motive behind the middle Channon's declaration but saw none. There was less surprise at that than there was at Donn's offer, for Jonni knew his brother well. Everything Donn did was with calculated purpose, even when others could not see that purpose. Jonni did not trust him, but it was again mistrust born of a gut feeling rather than tangible proof. With his father's ire already raised, Jonni knew better than to hurl accusations at Donn, particularly if the only remedy for their father's mulishness involved Donn's acceptance of a marriage Jonni did not want.

Lowell, on the other hand, expressed no suspicion as he studied his youngest son. Rather, the tint of disbelief on his face morphed gradually into the blush of respect that Jonni had never been able to win from the man, respect he wanted but which he refused to give up his principles and autonomy to gain, respect he had been forced to relinquish as he matured to realize that the future he envisioned for himself was not the one his father wanted for him.

There was no discussing the offer, no debate or argument to be made. Lowell offered one hand as the other clasped Donn's shoulder and turned the young man to face him. Donn showed no hesitation in accepting that handshake on the deal they were making.

"I will see to the arrangements," Lowell grunted with an appreciative nod before striding from the room. There was no thank you, no words of gratitude, but there never were. Donn's reasons for accepting the marriage mattered less than the marriage itself. The future of LaGuardia Borough and the Channon dynasty were more important than anything else. At least one of his sons, Lowell thought with grim determination, had what it took to see that the future was provided for. The disappointments of his other sons could be borne so long as one of the three had what it took to see duty done. This marriage was a political and economic necessity. If Jonni would not step up to the responsibility, and Nik, for all of his charm, was unfit for the task, then it was good and right that Donn assumed the mantle of leadership and duty.

Donn smirked at Jonni and began to undress, a calculating look that turned Jonni's blood to ice. Jonni swallowed the bile in his throat, turned his thoughts to a more pleasant path, and muttered, "You can have her," as he followed their father out of the room.

Watching his brother depart in the reflective metal of the mirror, Donn replied, "I intend to."

The chill up Jonni's spine returned.

⮂*⮂

"Ms. Marrock…a pleasure you could attend. Lovely as ever."

The practiced velvet purr of Thom Quentin's voice produced the usual shudder of distaste, but after more than a year of acquaintance, it was a reaction Jia had learned to hide beneath a schooled, diplomatically courteous smile. If not for the man's position as Lowell Channon's right hand, he and Jia would never have traveled in circles similar enough to cause their paths to cross. Quentin's tastes in life, in food, in dress and company, demanded upper echelon society that Jia flirted with only because the ties that bound Marrocks to Channons required it.

Her dislike of him was also fueled by the fact that her father had not trusted Lowell's choice of business bedfellows. Roland's dislike of Quentin was personal as well as professional, the belief that Quentin had motives meant to undercut the intentions of Lowell's work more than enhance it, but Lowell was caught in the gravity of Quentin's charisma and he refused to entertain the notion that Roland might be right. Though Jia had not yet had the opportunity to work with Quentin, every fiber of her being was rubbed raw in Quentin's company. That was reason enough to avoid him.

"I heard about your father," he continued as she half turned to better look at him. "Has there been any news?"

Trying not to scowl at his crassness in bringing up that topic tonight, ignoring the disgust his company elicited, she diplomatically accepted his outstretched hand. "News? What have you heard?" she asked casually, refusing to admit the truth although she suspected he already knew. Lowell must know what had happened that night, that someone had taken, or possibly killed, Roland Marrock, and if Lowell knew, Quentin undoubtedly did as well.

That did not mean that Jia had to confess to knowing how tightly tied to Lowell's side Quentin actually was.

Thom's lip curled in a knowing smirk and he nodded, appreciating the political dance and Jia's ability to fall adeptly into her father's vacated steps. "The Protectors should be alerted…his absence cannot be a fortuitous thing…"

"There is no need to summon the Protectors."

The truth was, she chose not to go to the Protectors on principle, bowing to the preferences of the Pack in keeping prying law enforcers out of their private affairs. But days had passed without word, without a hint of their patriarch's fate, and each day that slid away added to the likelihood of never finding him, bringing her one step nearer to requesting outside assistance against the Pack's wishes. They could not give up on the man who had dedicated his life to keeping them from destruction. She could not give up on her father.

"I hope not." His tone bore little of the sincerity of his words. "But here is a Tracker on the force, should it be necessary..."

"I have heard of him." Mages, whether Trackers or Healers, were rare, and if any existed in a given area, everyone in the immediate radius knew of them. They were as respected as they were distrusted, their unnatural skills as feared as they were welcomed. Jia did not know the local Tracker by name, had avoided crossing paths with him as most anthro would, but everyone in Queens knew of his proximity. His existence was a threat to the Pack, and so long as they avoided him, they remained safe from the reaches of those prejudice against them.

The growing pressure to find her father, however, was eroding her resolve to continue avoiding the Tracker of LaGuardia.

"I can make introductions...should you wish it..."

The reflective blanching at the suggestion, the hint that the tracker might be an ally or friendly acquaintance of Quentin's, was enough, for now, to dissuade her from seeking the Tracker's aid. Her reply was undermined by Liam's return to her with the glass of requested water.

"There is no need for a Tracker," Liam drawled, his response indicating that he had heard more of their conversation than was expected. "Didn't Jia tell you?"

"Tell me what?" asked Quentin with a raised brow.

"Roland has gone east seeking resources."

Jia nodded with a faint smile at the deception that was indeed plausible where her father was concerned. Since the time of the Undoing, the Marrocks had been the hands-on problem solvers in

LaGuardia, the ones to seek solutions to the needs of the borough's remaining inhabitants. Roland was no exception. More than once during his tenure as co-Laedan at Lowell's side, he had gone into the adjacent territories seeking supplies, resources not already picked clean by scavs, and…for his Pack…the fresh blood of solitary, unaffiliated Cana. The difference this time would be that he had gone without alerting the Channons of his intentions, and the Pack knew the truth. As did Lowell. Hopefully, however, that knowledge did not extend to Quentin. "He should return any day."

Quentin's expression was slightly perplexed. "I was told that HOPE had…" His intended words, a question that revealed details Jia and the Pack feared to be true, were cut short as Laedan Geary Hallister and his entourage of armed retainers strode past, a harsh expression of unsatisfied resolve on the man's world-weary face. The flicker of expectation that lit in Quentin's brown eyes caused Jia to watch the Laedan as well, but there was no trace of why Hallister's passing might have brought Quentin such hope.

Maybe, she thought with a shudder she did not hide, the man was merely pleased that Hallister had taken no notice of him. Avoiding notice by Kennedy Borough's notoriously hard-lined Laedan was something the majority of sane men and women desired.

At least, Jia mused, she and Quentin might share that small morsel of commonality.

On the raised platform at the other end of the room, Lowell Channon cleared his throat, the sound of it, along with the chiseled man's personal charisma, enough to draw the attention of his guests to the formality of covenant signing, and to anticipate the celebration that would follow. At his side, Donnovan waited, head high in arrogant confidence, hands clasped casually before him, well-dressed in a suit of considerable expense, his posture that of a man awaiting his turn to speak. No one made presumptions of his presence at his father's side. Be it as son and brother or legal witness to the union about to take place, Donn's attendance on the platform was of little import beyond the show of political positioning. The Channons and Marrocks, the foundation on which society had been salvaged and rebuilt in their struggling borough, were the makers of tradition. If Lowell preferred to break ritual in favor of change, not one person in the room was likely to challenge him.

Quentin's eyes shifted left to right and he frowned when he failed to find whatever he hoped to see. He straightened his collar, tugging as if to loosen it, and muttered, "Excuse me..." dropping their conversation as the inconsequential thing it was.

Frowning too, Jia made her own visual scan of the people around her. Quentin's behavior and the scent of his tension were enough to rouse her suspicion as the expected hush settled over the night's attendees. "Something's up."

Liam did not doubt Jia's intuition. Of the people in his life, hers was the instinct he trusted most. Her words, a whisper no one else heard as most shuffled nearer the platform, caused Liam to pay closer attention to their surroundings, but beyond the expectation of witnessing a union about to be made, he failed to detect whatever it was that set Jia on edge. It might have been nothing more than the impending marriage of a friend they had both grown up with, a man she had once, as a young girl, considered spending her life with, before the reality of their worlds was forced upon her. She had sworn that period of infatuation was behind her and rarely spoke of, or to, Jonni Channon any longer outside the context of political or social necessity. Perhaps, Liam mused, she had been wrong about the true nature of her feelings for the betrothed Channon.

Oasis Hallister, the sole heir upon which the future of Kennedy Borough rested, climbed the three steps with ease and grace, the only woman on the dais, her father and the present and past he represented following close behind her, prompting her forward with the stone of his determined gaze. Her chestnut brown hair was coiled elegantly, entwined with strands of gold and flowering vines, delicate tendrils of soft brown left to frame her symmetrical face. The gown of creamy golden silk-lace and hemp fiber bore no trace of patching, a new garment that was the truest expression of wealth possible in the world's bleakness. It was fitting that she was so attired, however, for this was her day, a public day on which she represented the promise this union gave as well as the borough from which she hailed. There was no better way for the Hallister dynasty to display their strength and wealth, than to adorn the heiress in all of the finery they could afford. This marriage had taken nearly two years to negotiate and Oasis was the bargaining chip with which Queens would be united and know greater prosperity and peace.

The unexpected, last minute turn of events, being delivered into the hands of the youngest Channon son rather than the eldest, had not been her plan, nor had it been her father's, but so long as marriage was the end result of this day, which Channon she married was largely unimportant. She knew little of the Channon sons beyond their faces, their names, their ages, and their rumored reputations. She had not been permitted to meet them prior to this moment, had been given no opportunity to judge their characters for herself. Holding little stock in rumor, however, and unafraid of what she had heard, she dared to face the future without the trepidation a lesser woman might have carried. Whatever sort of man her soon-to-be husband proved to be, she was confident of her strengths and convinced of the clarity of her future.

When Donnovan Channon stepped forward to greet her, his hot, clammy hand accepting hers from her father's, her chin lifted, her expression set into a determined smile as the Laedans pledged to peace between the boroughs and signed the formal contract which would bind their children and their territories together.

The calculating glance Donnovan made into the audience near the platform passed Oasis unnoticed as she accepted her father-in-law's pen, a moment shared with the elder Channon that passed with nothing beyond a glimpse of shared promise. She put her signature to the pledge in turn. The glance she made into the congregation as well, when Donnovan followed suit, likewise escaped the notice of most, but wherever it had been directed, Donn did not care.

Her intentions did not matter. The deal was struck, the signed contract binding them as husband and wife. In short order there would be an heir, cementing the marriage as indissoluble. If Oasis held up her end of the agreement, playing the part of the dutiful, faithful wife, that was good. If she had any notion of betraying him before that day came, however, Donn would soon break her of it and take every delight in doing so.

≽*≼

Though she pinpointed Yiva Channon by the back of the statuesque woman's head and slightly slumped shoulders, and located Nikolaj Channon slouching against the bar with his back to the proceedings, Jia saw no trace of Jonni amongst the guests. It should have been him on that platform, his blood oath being pledged in marriage to the Hallister heiress. For whatever reason, he was not there. Was he safe, she wondered? Was he healthy? Was he alive?

Remaining out of sight of those who would undoubtedly judge and question him would be the wisest thing he could do, if he lived. That he might refuse an arranged political marriage, might not follow through with the duty imposed on him, had never occurred to Jia, despite her certainty that being head of the Channon family was not the career Jonni desired. Refusal would certainly not ingratiate him to any of the others with political standing. Like her brother Addi, Jonni's interest was pursuing medicine, aiding the people through healing them. Unlike Addi, Jonni's father had never been supportive of that passion. Lowell had accepted his son's medical study as a hobby but he refused to consider that Jonni would reject the position of heir to the Channon legacy in favor of a life of relatively private obscurity, just as Addi had done.

Despite her concern for his welfare, the fear that Jonni could have come to some harm which prevented him from fulfilling this duty, hope for something else gave birth to a momentary flare of warmth in Jia's breast. Movement on the catwalk above drew her gaze upward, and when she made eye contact with the young man there, it was a hope within that she quickly extinguished. Theirs was a union that could never be, not if Jia wanted to protect her Pack. Over the distance between them, she felt Jonni's feelings of betrayal in the way he turned from her as if he had read that extinguishing of hope across a distance he could not possibly have seen it. Undoubtedly, she thought with a stab of regret, he expected her to be elated at his choice not to follow through with this marriage. He had not seen such elation upon her face or in her stance and had faced once again that the feelings he had for her were not reciprocated.

She could not blame him for feeling betrayed, though he had known her choice for more than four years. Idealist and dreamer that he was, however, the hope that she would change her mind if given adequate incentive had remained. Now, with the drying of ink on his brother's marriage contract, that hope slipped once more out of Jonni's fingers and turned to vaporous smoke.

Jia squeezed Liam's hand, finding and taking reassurance from her best friend. "It's gotta be now," she whispered, the sound rough with emotion she did not want to feel or express. The strength to mingle with what passed for society's elite, to risk a confrontation with Jonni before the night ended, was waning faster than the evening's passage. Her real reason for being here had to come first and provided ample reason to avoid the guests.

"Got your back," Liam swore, squeezing her hand in return before letting her go. "Be careful."

The formality of the evening was past. The rest was celebration, a gala he would just as soon escape. But not yet. Not until Jia gave the word. Though he did not watch her disappear into the crowd, he used every other sense he possessed to be certain of her safety as she reached the stairwell that would take her to the chambers from whence LaGuardia was governed. Liam accepted a glass of red berry wine from the tray of a passing serving woman, expected to play the part of elated guest and share a drink in the couple's honor, but he had no intention of imbibing beyond that sip. Like Jia, he needed to keep his senses keen and alert. Whether she found what she sought or not, they might not get out of the party alive if he got careless and inattentive.

≈*≈

"The purity of our blood is what matters most, isn't that so, Ma?" One arm enfolding Oasis possessively against his side, his fingers digging into her hip with enough force to warn her against pulling away, Donn tossed back his second glass of wine and waited for his mother's reply, his tone and gaze challenging her to contradict him...betray him. Lowell heard nothing more than Donn's usual blunt demands for attention, for answers. He could not recall a time when Donn had not spoken to his mother in that demanding tone, and as always, his demands were met with an indulgent smile from the woman who Lowell was certain spoiled the boys with too many favors, too much attention, too much kindness. She was particularly doting with Donnovan, who had suffered the fallout of Nik's condition, Nik the child who, as an infant, demanded a very different sort of attention. Donnovan had been at risk of being ignored, unattended, unloved, but even as a small child, he refused to accept that position within the family.

"Of course it is," Yiva agreed, turning her welcoming smile upon Oasis. "It is an honor to welcome you to our family, dear. I'm sure you'll make one another very happy."

Oasis returned the smile with an easy, natural one of her own, lowering the glass of wine she had barely touched, leaving behind smudges of lip rouge on its sparkling surface. "I'm sure we will," she agreed lightly. Her gaze, and the smile, faltered however as another joined their cluster. Lowell grinned, shook the newcomer's hand, and pulled him into the group as though welcoming family.

"Have you met my aide?"

The younger woman shook her head. "I have not yet had the privilege," she admitted, her full smile returning.

"Nor have I..." Geary Hallister prided himself on knowing everyone of import; that he had not yet become acquainted with the young man so clearly in Lowell's favor was a wrong he was determined to quickly rectify.

"Thomas Quentin...Geary Hallister and his daughter Oasis..." Lowell made no effort to introduce his wife to Hallister. Quentin assumed the two had previously met.

"My wife," Donn corrected, demanding acknowledgment of his claim over the woman who was three years his senior while still making note of his mother's forlorn expression and the expectation with which the blonde woman gazed on her son's new wife.

Quentin smiled, the polite gesture passing over the woman to settle on her father. "Of course," he said, his tone offhanded and glib as the words, as though disdaining her in favor of the political power her father represented. Oasis might be the heiress who bound the future of Kennedy to LaGuardia, but for now, Geary continued to hold the reins of control. The future meant less to Quentin then the present did. This moment was the only one they were guaranteed, and he would make the most of it. "A pleasure, Laedan."

"Likewise." Without looking at their gripped hands, Geary gauged Quentin, his potential, his strengths and flaws, and found him wanting. Oasis saw that judgment in the way her father dropped the handshake and gestured to Lowell, brushing off the newcomer's presence by refusing to acknowledge him further. "We have much to discuss, Channon. If you will all excuse us."

Head bobbing politely, his expression vacant of any understanding of where he stood in the Laedan's eyes, Quentin murmured, "Certainly," as did the others with them before the two leaders moved off to speak alone.

"Ma," Donn said, his voice dripping with a darkly colored note of concern. "Are you feeling well? You look…"

"I'm fine," Yiva quickly replied, her tone reedy and nervous. Without her husband beside her, she appeared to shrink away from her guests, to diminish in charm and posture into a shell of herself. Neither Oasis nor Quentin appeared to notice, however, and whatever Donn saw, he chose to address it by releasing his wife and stepping nearer to his mother's side.

"Nonsense. You look like you could use a drink. Come; sit down. Let me get you something." Expecting Oasis to remain where she was, obediently awaiting his return, he wrapped his arm around his mother's shoulders and steered her toward the bar.

It was their movement that snapped Quentin's attention away from Oasis, while her eyes drifted back from a nearby crowd of guests laughing a little too loudly. "I am not some mindless trophy," she hissed, her face still schooled to neutrality.

"Your husband seems to think you are," Quentin replied casually. "Like father, like son."

"She is not Lowell's trophy." She did not know that to be true of Yiva Channon, as she had just met the woman, but she had to believe that the older woman was more than a pretty face to be dangled at social events or used as a key to unlock the hearts, the minds, the lips of others for her husband's purposes. She had to be more than the mother of the man's sons.

"If you say so." Again Quentin's response was cool, though the perusal with which he studied the dark-haired woman before him was far from casual.

Petulant, her face darkened for a moment before returning to something friendly and happy as she nodded and shook hands with another cluster of important well-wishers. She lost sight of Donn behind a gaggle of dignitaries at the bar, but she was unconcerned. He had chosen this marriage out of duty; he would not so easily turn from it. And what he did, who he did it with, was of little concern to her. They might be held together by a legal contract, but there was nothing else between them. How could there be when they had never met before? "A little respect from you wouldn't hurt either," she muttered without looking at Quentin when the guests moved away.

"We agreed," he scolded. "We don't know each other, remember? Your father…"

"Couldn't care if you lived or died."

Quentin scowled at her apathetic words, although he knew from Geary's nonchalant dismissal that Oasis' assessment was more accurate than his own. "That can change."

"It doesn't matter. You do not need his approval." Her gaze traveled in the direction her father and Lowell had gone. "Neither of us do." She had married out of her father's house, was beholden to him no longer. She did not need to observe Quentin's expression to know her words pleased him. It was to their advantage that Quentin remained below Geary's level of interest…just as it was to their benefit that any past acquaintance they shared remained unnoticed.

"Too true," Quentin agreed. Aware that their extended conversation was drawing stares from the people nearest them, unable to afford the sort of attention that public scrutiny might bring, he bowed, took her hand, and left a lingering kiss on her knuckles. "Again," he said for the benefit of those passing, "I congratulate you on your marriage, ma'am…welcome to LaGuardia. I hope you will find happiness here."

"I intend to…thank you," she said with a nod and a polite smile.

"If you need anything…let me know."

Releasing her hand with a twinkle in his eyes elicited a flush on her cheeks and a quick glance away as she replied, "I certainly will." It was tempting to take him up on that offer tonight, despite her annoyance with his previous standoffish behavior, but she was newly married and knew she was expected to fulfill that conjugal duty, so long as her husband was not too drunk to perform. Still unable to see Donn, however, she wondered if he would even notice her absence.

☙*❧

Yiva accepted the stool as a welcome savior, collapsing upon it with only a glance at her youngest child who slouched over the bar on her other side, one foot hooked beneath his stool as if it would prevent him from falling to the floor. From the flush on his cheeks and the red-rimmed bleariness of his eyes, Nikolaj was well on his way to oblivion already, although, she thought with a sigh, he was never very far from that state. He would be of no comfort, no help to her, and she wondered again, as Donn flagged the tender and ordered two of his favorite drinks, what she could have done differently that might have set Nik on a more productive path.

"So, Little Brother is a trapped man now," Nik slurred, his tone such that it was impossible to judge if he was deriding his twin or congratulating him.

"I am," crowed Donn, sliding one of the drinks to their mother.

Nik raised his nearly empty glass, the pale green liquid within cloudy and thick, suggesting the addition of something more into the alcohol. "Best wishes then, Little Brother. To you!"

"To me," Donn agreed, clacking his glass against Nik's with a smile before downing it in one gulp. Noting that his mother toyed with her glass, traced her finger around its rim with a dazed stare into the dark amber liquid, Donn stroked the back of her head and said, "Drink up, Ma. It is a bad omen not to toast the happy couple."

Would they be happy, Yiva wondered, drawing the small glass slowly to her mouth with little interest in drinking it. She preferred wine, not the bittersweet spiced ale that Donn most often drank, but it was his habit to force his liquor preference on her and anyone else in his company. Refusing it would only raise his ire and that was not an outcome Yiva wanted. She would never wish Donn's dark moods on anyone...particularly his new wife.

She swallowed the defeated sigh with the contents of the glass and squeezed her eyes closed against the burn as she set the empty container back on the bar.

"Another!" Donn called to the tender.

"I shouldn't," Yiva began, making a half-hearted effort to cover her glass with a trembling hand.

Donn grasped her wrist and pulled her hand away. "Nonsense; it will put color in those pale cheeks. It won't do for you to be sickly on such a special night."

Shuddering at the intonation of his words, this time Yiva gave in to the lure of the drink and swallowed it hastily. She turned the glass upside down and slid it away; she would not drink a third, no matter how tempting intoxication was.

Nik, it appeared, had already drunk enough for all of them.

"Have you seen Jonni, Ma?"

She shook her head, giving no thought to why Donn might look for his older brother. He likely intended to gloat and she did not want to be involved in that confrontation between her boys. Eyeing the side stairs behind the bar, she wondered if she could make it to them, escape without Lowell noticing. More than likely, he would be involved in political and economic scheming the rest of the evening. There would be no need for her here. Her duty as accessory, as wife, was over for the night.

Donn's lingering hand on the back of her neck, the fingers that parted her hair to caress the skin beneath, dropped away with the arrival of Oasis at his side, her arm wrapping around his waist as she took her rightful place. Annoyance flashed across his eyes and his jaw clenched until he realized who had disrupted him, but with a look into his new wife's beautiful face, his body's tension eased and he smiled. He had never considered himself to have a way with women. Oasis' attention of her own accord was a welcome change.

"I think we should dance," she purred. "It is expected...."

"True," he agreed smugly. He leaned in to kiss the top of Yiva's head and murmured, "Until later, Ma...take care...be well."

If he noticed the woman's shudder, he did not acknowledge it.

Being ignored was a blessing Yiva was thankful for. The presence of Oasis in Donn's life was another.

He recognized those signatures, the furtive search for escape routes, the muted resistance that always ended in capitulation, the swallowed efforts to speak protests with words that never found voice. Signs of a person cowed by abuse; Walter Ernest had seen it more often in his tenure as Chief of LaGuardia than he could now recall or count. Men, women, young, old, well-to-do or down on their luck, it did not matter. There were invariably people who lived to control others, and some, it seemed, prone to falling victim to it.

The impulse to intervene, to rescue and protect, was tempered by fatigue and the question of who exactly she needed protection from. The Channons owned everything, or at least it seemed to most that they did, for the control of the fuel resources meant the control of the population that needed those resources for heat and cooking, particularly in these increasingly cooler autumn months. Walter had butted heads, working for and alongside Lowell Channon, his father and his sons since the day he had taken the oath of office. Going against them now, when he was so close to retiring from the Protectorate, would be suicide.

He had only to ride out his tenure a few more months, and then the Channons and their problems, the problems of LaGuardia and a world still in the throes of reformation more than ninety-five years since the Undoing, would no longer be his. He would settle into a life of tending his rooftop garden, minding pigeons and chickens, and live as far below public notice as he could manage to achieve. The future he imagined for himself would never come to pass if he stuck his neck out and his nose into things that were none of his business.

But damn it…he hated to see suffering, hated to see bullying, and at this moment hated himself for never having seen Yiva Channon in this light before. She gave every indication of having endured that condition for years. In fairness, Walter rarely crossed paths with the woman except when attending official functions or in passing when duty brought him to these halls to consult with Channon and Marrock. How could he have known?

He scowled and turned on his stool, searching the sea of faces for one he realized he had not seen thus far this evening.

Maybe Marrock had decided there were better things to do than watching his friend's son marry their southern counterpart's daughter. Walter did not know why there had been no marriage unions between Channons and Marrocks, but again, that was no more his concern than why Marrock was not here…and why Yiva appeared so relieved now that the groom had vacated her side in favor of his bride.

He might have to do a little digging to understand what sort of man Donnovan Channon was.

The weakness he felt for beautiful women, this one in particular, finally tipped the scale. He downed the burning clear liquid, set the glass on the counter, and turned with the intention of approaching her, speaking to her, inquiring as to her welfare. But the moment passed as she was now staggering unevenly toward the stairs that led to the level of offices and private Channon quarters. Walter watched her to be sure she made it to the top without incident, which she did despite unsteady steps, and when she was out of sight, his weight settled again onto the stool, his elbows once more on the bar. He should have spoken to her, should have made sure she was well. He should have done his damn job. If anything happened to her, tenure be damned, he would never forgive himself.

It would not be his first unforgiven shortfall, however. And as the day of retirement crept nearer, he knew it would not be his last.

Chapter 2

"My congratulations on your marriage." The sandy-haired man, his face craggy with age and responsibility, clasped Donnovan's shoulder with a grip that demanded attention and respect of everything, everyone, he touched. Donnovan faced him, his expression the nearest Oasis had seen to an honest smile all evening from her new husband. She too knew this man; he had spent many hours in her father's halls throughout her life, practically a favored uncle as he always brought her honeycomb and pretty ribbons whenever he visited. It had been years before she had come to understand who and what he was, how important he was to the stability of Queens, whether one agreed with his politics or not.

He was a useful man to know, to seek favor with. It was good to know her husband also had the man's approval.

Likewise familiar with him, understanding the benefits of currying his favor, Donn accepted the offered hand with a slight bow. "Elder Lord...I believe you know my bride, Oasis..."

"Indeed." Like other men of power, Francis Lord made it a point of knowing anyone of import and influence, including the progeny of such individuals. Those children would be the future leaders. Queens was in their hands. It made sense to groom and court them accordingly. "Please...I am not Elder here...merely Francis." He looked over the couple, perplexed, but not overly so, by the turn of the tide. It had been expected that the eldest Channon would marry the Hallister heiress, not the youngest, but perhaps, he mused behind his neutral congratulatory mask, this was a better match. Both were members of HOPE, the Holy Order of the Pristine Elect, like their fathers and grandfathers before them, and while Francis and Donnovan did not see eye to eye on a few points of dogma, they were points of digression that would not create undue friction between the leadership of HOPE and the Channons.

What did the precise fate of mutes and anthro matter, so long as they were kept from breeding and mixing with the population?

"Francis," Donnovan said politely.

The Elder took Oasis' hand and kissed her knuckles. "I hate to come between you on such a joyous occasion, but would you object terribly if I borrow your husband for a brief matter of business?"

The request was only strange because of the politeness with which he asked permission. As the mayor of one of LaGuardia's three territories, Donnovan was a man of power in his own right and the business of government did not cease just because those in leadership chose to spend a few hours in celebration. It would be necessary to learn the boundaries of Donn's influence, those who served him, the structures in which he ruled, but she already knew that Donn would not be one to easily share power, or the details of it, with his wife. Whatever she wanted to know, she would need to learn through other channels. It would not come to her tonight.

"Of course, Uncle," she said brightly, carefully choosing the often used endearment to inform her husband just how well she knew Elder Lord. If Donnovan believed she held favor with HOPE's highest authority, that would, undoubtedly, grant her favor with him too. She would use it to her advantage. "Husband, I shall be with Gayle when you are finished."

Knowing the name, but not yet having met the woman, Donn nodded with a dismissive wave and fell into step beside the Elder who steered him toward the edge of the crowd with casual steps.

"You usurp your brother's position…"

Donn shrugged. "Jonni was never going to marry her. Nothing Fa could do was going to make it happen. I don't know why he held to that hope so long. She was here, the guests were here…the treaty required a marriage bond…and there was no way under a blood moon that Nik could do this. Whether Fa or Hallister admits it, it was always going to be me…and," he sneered as he watched his wife's retreating back, "there's no finer woman in all of Queens. She will bear many healthy children and bring much wealth to LaGuardia. The Channon line will continue, our hold on Queens tighten…"

"Pleased to hear it." There was the possibility of sons and daughters through the other Channon sons, but currently, that did not appear likely. "And the other matter?"

"Is being tended as we speak. Everything is arranged…it will never come back to either of us unless you betray…"

"Donnovan…son…" The slick, diplomatic smile that settled on the Elder's face was the sort Donn knew all too well as he was proficient in that look himself. "Betrayal between us will benefit no one. After tonight, Queens will be set on a new path…one that I dare say your new alliance will be of great benefit to."

Donn nodded and the Elder moved off after another clasping of hands, slinking, it appeared to Donn, like a thief. He felt certain that Francis Lord was withholding something from him. After tonight, he intended to find out what.

❧*❧

Having grown up in LaGuardia's maze of rooms and corridors, brought here from the time she could walk well enough to follow Roland as he daily strove to keep the borough from collapse, Jia believed she knew every detail, every hiding place, every storage room and office. They had been her playground, safer than the rusting, decaying bits of parkland the survivors had reclaimed from the encroaching overgrowth of nature. Swing sets, see-saws, merry-go-rounds were cobbled together and repaired by wire, hemp rope, bits of wood and any other shred of usable debris to serve some children as play areas, but those corners of land could hardly be deemed safe, not when the threats of gashes, splinters, and irradiated metal were constant, and with the severe shortage of antibiotics and mediplies, such simple wounds might mean the loss of limb or life if left untended. One had to be just as diligent for the threats of natural predators, grubbers, or anyone who wanted a child.

Here, at least, in what remained of the once bustling air terminal, amongst people who valued the promise children held for the borough's future, Jia and Addi, the Channon boys, and a host of other children, had grown up safe together while their parents struggled to ensure they had a future to grow into.

Her father's office, however, was sterile, empty, seemingly untouched at a glance since the day he last sat behind this desk. While Lowell, like the Channons before him, was the public face of leadership, the spokesman, the diplomat, the politician, Roland was the practical-headed doer, the man to offer solutions, to find answers to the dilemmas their people faced in order to subsist in a land where once abundant technology had been lost due to the collapse of infrastructure which had stripped people of easily attainable resources. What mankind now had in abundance was decay, and building a lasting civilization from that was a full-time responsibility that Lowell did not have the head for.

But Lowell did know law; he did know how to sway and manipulate people, how to maintain peace and order. As their forefathers had been after the Undoing, Roland and Lowell were an ideal team, well suited to keeping Queens on a path to endurance and, with luck, prosperity.

Such hopes necessitated the alliance between LaGuardia and Kennedy, although, Jia understood, it left the future of the Marrocks in LaGuardia's government a precarious thing. During the weeks between the marriage announcement of Channon to Hallister and his disappearance, Roland had been ill-at-ease, more cautious than usual, more protective of the Pack. Jia had seen it, they all had, and she suspected it was the new alliance and the future that concerned her father, that he worried for the survival of the Pack and his family should he lose his position as co-Laedan. The union with the Hallisters opened up access to resources both boroughs desperately needed, goods, manpower, and talent. With Quentin ever-increasingly Lowell's right hand and the voice Lowell came more and more to listen to when the need for solutions arose, those in LaGuardia's halls spoke in whispered portents of the day when Lowell would declare himself sole Laedan of LaGuardia, and through the alliance with Kennedy, perhaps Laedan over all of Queens.

Jia never imagined, however, although she feared it more and more with each day of his absence, that it might be death that removed Roland from power. She did not want to believe that Lowell would resort to murder to achieve that end. Surely years of friendship and side by side service meant more than that.

It was something her father said to her early in the morning on the day of his disappearance that brought her to these halls tonight, something that formed the real reason for agreeing to endure what had been meant to be the marriage of one of her closest friends for the sake of political alliance. Roland had spoken of a secret dangerous enough to threaten the lives of everyone in Queens, how the key had to be right in front of his nose, if only he could find it. He had confided in her about the existence of a map and a ledger, but what each contained, Roland claimed he did not know. They were important enough for Lowell to guard them, even from his co-Laedan, and that made Roland suspicious. Jia suspected her father had been seeking both, and that seeking had put his life at risk, but what sort of map and ledger could be worth killing over?

If there had been a falling out between the co-Laedans, Lowell hid it well; the concern he expressed daily when he inquired about Roland's whereabouts seemed genuine. If he knew of the hunt that had taken her father from her, if he had sanctioned it, there were no hints of it in his demeanor. Those questions also, she mused as she closed the door and moved deeper into the unlit office, smelled of desperation. Was Lowell afraid of blame, of the political and legal repercussions accusations of murder might have? Or was he afraid of something Roland had learned that could be turned over to whatever enemies Lowell had, something that Roland might be able to use against him?

Or, she thought bitterly, was Lowell concerned about what Jia might do if she learned there had been a betrayal of trust? It was hard to imagine him being afraid of her, however, given their ages, sizes, and experience. Who was she to think she could follow in Roland's footsteps, let alone have the fortitude to carry out any sort of revenge or retribution for an as yet unproven crime? She knew nothing of the truth; it was premature to consider any course of action.

The first thing she needed to do was find this proof that Roland believed existed, this map and ledger that held some potentially dangerous secret. She needed proof of conspiracy or criminality or treachery, whichever this was.

That proof might be, she feared, something as damning as evidence in Lowell's hands of the double life Roland led. That sort of proof, in the wrong hands, was a death threat hanging over her head too, over all of the Pack. It would be the greatest threat of all.

Only when she reached the desk, her fingers dragging across it, did she notice the subtle differences in the room that indicated someone had been here, someone other than her father. Roland had been frustratingly, compulsively, organized. He had a place for everything, each pen, each piece of paper, each book kept in its precise place when not in use. Only someone who knew him well, who had memorized the details of this room, would notice books out of place between slightly askew bookends. Scrolls of city plans and buildings he had drawn up and charts used to map the city and track food stores, taxation reports, population growth, and climate changes, were no longer in order according to paper size and topic. His pen and inkwell were pushed a little too far from their usual position of easy access and the oil lamp was turned slightly to one side. Perhaps the cleaning staff had moved things, though most knew by now to leave Roland's things the way he placed them.

Suspicious, she grabbed the three topmost scrolls wedged into place on the cubicle shelf and unrolled them one by one on the desk. If someone had been looking for something on one of those scrolls, a co-worker needing information to do their job perhaps, it might behoove her to know what they sought. The placement of the pen and inkwell, the turned position of the books, gave her the ideal amount of space to spread scrolls, hinting that someone had been looking through her father's work.

But the scrolls, a spreadsheet detailing the year's hemp harvest, another with the last census figures tracking the number of workers in a variety of fields, and finally a map of the three LaGuardia districts with delineated borders and known hazards and blockages in what had once been city streets, showed little in common. There was nothing suspicious she could see, nothing worth abducting, or killing, her father for, and nothing that suggested the threat Roland feared was imminent.

If she wanted that, Jia decided, she would need to look in Lowell's office. She left everything in her father's room the way she had found it, despite the temptation to reorganize the desk and scrolls back to the way her father would want them to be. If someone had come here seeking secrets, she did not want them to know she had been here doing the same.

The distant cacophony of music and voices was muted here and faded to a background hum as she listened for closer sounds in the corridor that might suggest she was at risk of discovery. There were none, no footsteps or voices, as those here tonight were more interested in the bounty of uncommon treats and beverages provided by the newly allied Laedans than they were in any business to be found in this wing of offices. She had only to skirt the dark corridor to the next doorway, a locked door easily breached by someone with the talent for it, a talent Jia had developed out of boredom as a child in those hours spent alone here. Barrier penetrated, this door too was closed behind her, locked from within to provide an additional warning should anyone else come. This room, similar in layout but more ostentatious in adornment to her father's, would require more thorough investigation. If her father had found the proofs he sought, he would have been too smart to keep them in his office. Likewise, she presumed, if Lowell had a secret the size of which Roland suspected, he would have kept them somewhere close for protection.

Lowell was a confident man. He would believe such secrets were safest kept within his private reach. He likely believed that anything he wished to hide would best be kept in a room where no one went uninvited. This office would be the first place Roland would search if he had been able.

Several minutes of rummaging, however, through every shelf and drawer, beneath chair cushions and inside the cabinet stocked with abundant alcohol, produced nothing suspicious. Handwritten notes of speeches given or planned, correspondences between the Laedan and business owners, petitions and letters of disputes some felt had been mishandled by the juds who handled their cases brought in turn to the highest authority in LaGuardia for redetermination and hoped for recompense. Little that suggested work, but Lowell's work consisted mainly of meetings and dialogues and face to face negotiations. More tedious details had been relegated to Quentin over the course of the last three years, or else lay in the hands of the three LaGuardia mayors…the three blonde Channon sons. Lowell was the master of delegation, which meant that, while he guided the pieces of government around the board, he rarely had to dirty his hands with day to day problems, giving himself considerable free time to seek more pleasurable pursuits.

It was little wonder his sons had turned out the way they had. Jonni, there was hope for, so long as he maintained the courage to buck his father's political plans for him and gave up his unending pursuit of Jia. Nik, a nice enough fellow at heart, who frequently succumbed to his demons and the constant availability of alcohol in his father's stores, had yet, in many ways, to grow beyond boyhood irresponsibility. And Donn, whose sense of entitlement fostered by his parents' too generous hand, had given in to a sadistic streak that most endeavored to stay away from.

If Jia was forced to take her father's place, she dreaded the day she would be forced to run the borough alongside the three of them.

It was little wonder Roland feared for the future.

The turning of the door handle, a jiggling metallic sound as the deadbolt jarred about in its encasement caused Jia to crouch behind the desk, out of sight of immediate notice as she waited for the following click of a key in the lock and the creek of the door on its hinges. She eyed the windows, calculating how far up she was from the ground, whether she could survive such a leap or not in her current physical form. She believed she could but did not relish being forced into the attempt. Breath held, she listened, but no key turned the tumbler and the knob did not turn again. A drunk guest, perhaps, seeking the toilet, or a couple seeking a private room in which to share intimacy better not displayed downstairs.

Deciding to vacate the room while she could, having found nothing useful or worthwhile in Lowell's office that might warrant her father's concern, she let herself into the corridor after making sure it was safe to do so. The giggling of two women came from further down the hall, supporting her second hunch, but no one was encountered as she hurried away from the offices. If her father had found anything here, he had not left it behind. Heart beating faster as she drew closer to the crowd, she attempted to swallow back the instinct to retreat from the party before she ran into Jonni and was backed into a conversation she was not keen to have.

He had chosen not to move forward with life in the direction his father desired, and that was a good thing. But she suspected his choice not to marry had as much to do with her as it did with rebelling. She did not want to be part of his choices. She wanted their long-standing friendship to survive.

"Party's not up here..."

Jia had not consciously realized she had hesitated near the top of the stairs until that slender arm wrapped around her shoulders. Panic was averted by the recognition of his voice, the press of his hand on her arm, and the familiar combination of personal scent, alcohol, and the blood taint of multiple addictions that made Nik unique. His addictions shifted with time, as one new drug after another was discovered and added to his repertoire of use, but the unhealthy traces left upon his body chemistry never dissipated.

"That's why we're here, and they are there," she pointed out with a relieved smile. She had always liked Nik; she wished he liked himself as well.

He laughed, leaned on the aging metal banister beside her, the red creases upon his forearm indicative of too much leaning this evening. As much as he loved a party, there was only so much of enjoying it in the company of his family he could stomach. "They won't miss me. They won't even notice I'm gone."

"They'll notice." Lowell always noticed where the key players were in any public event, his children and wife included. He would notice Nik's absence and likely be both relieved that his middle child would make no embarrassing public displays, and concerned that Nik might have wandered off to odose and die somewhere private. It had not happened yet, but the longer Nik survived the addictions that were a millstone dragging behind him, the more real and certain that outcome became.

Nik shrugged but chose not to argue or agree. Noticing was not the same thing as caring, and both understood that whether or not his parents cared about his addictions was more a matter of perception than accuracy. "Your excuse?" When she did not immediately reply, he nodded sympathetically. "I haven't seen Jonni…doubt he wants to mingle and answer up for his decision. Shame though…she's a pretty bit. He could have done worse…"

"And she could have done better than Donn," she muttered.

"That's a fate I'd never wish on anyone," he agreed. "Anyone but Donn, that is. Little Brother is not family man material."

"A marriage to himself might have been the best choice for everyone."

Giggling again, wiping his arm across his red, sniffling nose, Nik said, "That would be a wedding I would actually look forward to…and I'd like to witness the wedding night afterward."

Jia shuddered. "Not me." There was only so much of Donn talking about himself she could endure. From the corner of her eye, and with a sniff at the change in the air, she noted the abrupt discoloration on Nik's face and glanced at him with concern.

"You okay?"

"I think…" he slurred with a nod, swaying on his feet as he turned his back to the rail and looked down the corridor in the direction from which she had come. There was a lounge further down the hall, where the staff often congregated around daytime meals, and while that was likely where the effing couple was, it was most likely where Nik had been heading. "I just need a kipple…"

"Need help to get there?" She did not say where, and he did not ask what she meant as he was already staggering toward the lounge, leaning against the wall with one elbow the entire way. Jia watched, worried that he might collapse before he reached his destination. But a scream of surprise from within the lounge accompanied his turn through the doorway, and the pair of women, in disheveled apparel, burst from the room laughing and grumbling in embarrassed annoyance before disappearing through another open door on the other side of the hall. There were no crashes or thumps to suggest that Nik had passed out on the floor or crashed against furniture or shelving, but Jia still snuck to the doorway to see that he was alright. Without entering the room, she could see him sprawled upon a long, plush sofa, hear his loud, labored breathing, proof enough that he lived, for now. She could not be the one to babysit him. It was time, she decided, to escape this party before something went wrong.

ॐ*ॐ

Liam scratched behind his ear, a nervous habit brought out tonight, by the anxiety of waiting for Jia to finish her quest, find whatever it was she believed she sought, and get out of this suffocating crush of snooty people. The Undoing had significantly closed the gap between the haves and the have-nots, had changed the definition of wealth and prosperity, but it had not changed the attitudes of the people on the top tier of society, and Liam was happiest when he was not rubbing elbows with them. Yes, he had grown up in these halls, alongside the Marrocks and Channons and the rest, as his mother and father had been tutors for both families. They had come to that position through Roland, because they were Pack and Pack protected their own, and it was Pack that allowed Liam not to see Jia and Addi as part of the Haves. Their position afforded them favors, but they were favors shared with the whole of the Pack. And as Cana, the Marrocks would always live on the fringes of the Haves, never fully able to participate in that society or let their guards down. They were different in ways that kept their personal lives in the shadows by necessity; whatever the Marrocks were in public, in private they were Pack. They were family.

And Jia was his dearest friend in all the world.

Back against the bar, fingering the rim of the glass he had yet to drink more from, his eyes scanned back and forth over the crowd of maybe five or six dozen people, men and women from LaGuardia and Kennedy, appearing to be people watching when what he was really doing was keeping his eye on the staircase where Jia had ascended too long ago. No one would notice, as his eyes never lingered there or on the catwalk balcony above, and so long as he did not stare, he intended to be the first one to see her there when she started back down.

"Surprised to see you here."

Jerking with a start, the drink in Liam's hand sloshed over his shoes and he hissed, using irritation to blanket the instinctive craving to lash out at the man beside him. It was difficult to startle an anthro, and when one did, the response was rarely good, the need to fight, to protect and preserve self, always lingering just below the surface.

Of course, Jonni Channon did not know that, did not know what Liam was. Or if he did, he had never spoken of it. If he had spoken that knowledge to anyone, the Pack would long ago have been hunted into extinction.

"Sorry…" Jonni grabbed a hemp cloth napkin from the bar and stooped to wipe the liquid from Liam's leather shoes.

"Likewise." Muttering in his awkwardness, Liam sidestepped Jonni's reach and added, "To seeing you here…not the sorry part."

"Saw you and figured Jia can't be far…"

Liam did not allow any degree of affront to register on his face. Of course Jonni was looking for Jia. She was his entire reason for being here...for not marrying the Hallister girl as his father intended. "I haven't seen her for some time...probably mingling..."

"Probably." Jonni knew her almost as well as Liam, however, at least he believed he did. Jia was not the mingling sort unless forced into it. "Any news about Roland?" It was easier to believe Jia had come tonight in the hopes for news about her father than to believe she had come to talk Jonni out of marrying Oasis Hallister...even though Jonni's secret hope was that Jia had come for him and him alone. Bringing Liam could mean that she wanted moral support to attend because she had not wanted to see Jonni married.

"He's east." It was the same lie given to Lowell and Quentin, a consistent tale the Pack clung to as they waited for proof of life or death. The Pack had to believe the best for their Alpha. None wanted to consider the consequences of his death. "Supply run."

The far eastern reaches of the land were wild, largely uninhabited as far as the residents of Queens knew. There had been no need to press east for livable space or resources yet, but it was not inconceivable that Roland would choose to brave that frontier in search of resources LaGuardia could use.

It was only inconceivable that he might have done so without telling Lowell.

"Then you expect him back soon."

Liam shrugged. There were dangers in the life of a scav; everyone in Queens knew it. It was a necessary job, salvaging anything of use that decay had not devoured, and many made their living doing so. But the mortality rate of scavs was high; undertaking retrievals in wild, unknown territory made the risk higher still. Liam knew it made little sense for Roland to have undertaken such a mission alone, but for all anyone knew, he was not alone but had gone salvaging amongst friends.

Jonni's head bobbed in understanding. "So she came tonight in Roland's stead." It made sense. As close as Jia was to her father, as familiar as she was with what he did for the Channons and for LaGuardia, it was logical that she would come in his stead, lend the Marrock blessing to the union of Kennedy and LaGuardia. Like Jonni, she was reluctant to be part of the political game their fathers played, but unlike Jonni, she was a little more willing to fill Roland's shoes when the need arose, at least for appearance sake.

"And you came as her bodyguard."

"Couldn't let her travel the night alone." Liam knew she could take care of herself, as she was an alpha Cana with good instincts, but those were details that Jonni did not need to know. No one outside of Pack did.

"Waiting to escort her home." Again Jonni's head bobbed, though now there was disappointment on his face. Waiting for her with Liam had seemed like a good idea, a sure way of bumping into her, but he realized now that, should she join them, she would use Liam as an excuse to evade conversation. "She's lucky to have you."

Lips twisting into a grin, though he felt a bit of pity for the other man, Liam said, "Don't I know it." Okay, he thought. Maybe he was bragging. But since Jia told him that more than once in the years they had known each other, he felt it acceptable to say it now, especially since he knew it would rankle Jonni.

Movement caught his eye and he scolded himself for faltering in his duty to watch for her. But it was only Nik at her side, the one Channon least likely to hurt or betray her. Wanting to keep Jonni from spotting her, he downed the portion of drink that had not spilled on his shoes and faced the bar. "Another," he muttered to the bartender. Glancing at Jonni, he asked, "Drink with me?"

After a moment of ponderous hesitation, Jonni shook his head. "Not tonight. I should go…" Before my father or Donn notices me here, he thought bitterly. "Let her know I'm looking for her, please?"

"I will." Liam would let her know, but he was not going to attempt to persuade her to seek Jonni out. Her decision to come here tonight had hinged on avoiding Jonni as much as possible.

He waited until he was alone, Jonni's brooding aura lingering in the air, before turning again with a full drink in his hand. Hopefully, he had kept her safe long enough. And hopefully, he thought, as she started down the stairs, she had found what she was looking for and they could head home. Liam reached back, set the drink upon the counter, and pushed away from the bar. They would meet at the main door. The wedding debacle would soon be a memory left behind.

The dark mass wrapped in a cloak that covered the lower portion of its face watched them retreat, arm in arm, from one of many places he could not go. He would not be welcome there. He was not welcome anywhere. But the thickly muscled man with sharp eyes and sharper fangs had sworn an oath and he would follow through with that until his final breath was robbed from him.

If either of them knew they were followed, they did not show it. Keeping to the shadows, a survival strategy he had been forced to adopt years ago in order to live and stay near the Pack, he leaped from collapsing building to collapsing building, silent and sure of his footing. She was his responsibility, his more than anyone else's. Particularly now that Roland Marrock was gone.

Chapter 3

"**V**anya, get down from there."

Kato grabbed for her scarred bare ankle but the thin woman scrambled out of his reach, giggling like a school girl despite the danger her precarious position put her in. The crumbling concrete mountain, once an inner support wall of the old office building in which the pair took refuge when the rains began late that afternoon, no longer held the weight of the ceiling above. Whatever materials it was made of had buckled, leaving a hole gaping in the second floor above them. The collapsing support wall now created an unsteady, impractical staircase to the second story where the pigeons cooed and the cold rain dripped incessantly into dark, dirty sunken pools that caused the floor to sag as it sought passage to the level beneath. There were fewer drafts on the first floor, and without material for a fire, and the uncertainty of building one without attracting unwanted attention, they would have to make due with body warmth and shelter from the wind and rain. The second story of the building held no value to them, save as the playground Vanya thought it should be, but how to distract his sister from a self-destructive path was a challenge Kato constantly faced.

It was not her fault. He could never blame her. Radiation…too many chemicals in the drinking water, in the air, the food…their mother's ill health…any or all of those things could be contributors to

Vanya's perpetually child-like state. She did not understand danger, not in the way most people did, nor did she easily remember lessons learned from one day to the next. Keeping his older sister safe was a full-time duty, but it was never one he resented. How could he; she was the only family he had. If she could accept him and his differences, surely he could accept hers.

There were ways, however, tried and proven, to distract Vanya from something he did not want her to do, and so he rummaged in her light pack for the instrument of distraction. As they made their way west, he carried the majority of their supplies, anything he found that could be of use, so as not to hear her complain that her burden was too heavy. A blanket, once bright red but now a dull, stained crimson, the hairbrush that had belonged to their mother, a toothbrush from an abandoned home, an extra sweater of blue and gold...too big and now growing threadbare with age, eleven mismatched socks that she had discovered and tucked away, and finally, the treasure he sought.

"Peppermint is cold. You should come keep him warm."

At the mention of Peppermint, Vanya leaped from her elevated perch, scurried to the closet where her brother was building a temporary nest, and snatched the dirty yellow bear from his hands. For all of her grace and agility, she should have been Fela, he mused once again, like he was, but perhaps whatever kept her mind from maturing had conspired to keep her from developing the full breadth of Fela traits.

It was better that way, for gods only knew what might have become of her if her already fractured mind had been further segregated between human and feline.

Crouched in the corner with her back against the wall where she could watch the closet door, a safe lookout as her brother had taught her, she clutched the stuffed bear and began to rock front and back, one hand stroking the top of the animal's head. Her lips moved as she mumbled, incoherent words meant only for the bear's ears, so caught in her imaginary dialogue and the taking care of Peppermint that she would likely be in that position until she fell asleep if nothing else disturbed her. It meant she would be quiet, so long as he made no effort to take the bear and no one found them here, and quiet was good, necessary for survival.

The building was abandoned, and from what he had determined as they entered this lonely length of overgrown structures, there was no one else living amongst the nearby ruins. What scents he had detected, human and not, were long faded, just a taint on moldering shreds of window shades and etched into walls and floors where traces of once overcrowded civilization had accumulated after decades of rain and wind and snow. But just because he detected no one living here, it did not mean that others might not patrol these streets from nearby settlements or might pass through as he and Vanya were doing, others who might think nothing of killing them for what supplies they carried, possibly as a food source or, more likely, for no reason at all other than out of fear for their safety. People could not be trusted; Kato had learned that the hard way. There was no reason others should trust him or Vanya either.

He pried open a metal tin, not knowing what he would find within but believing it would be food, and after inspecting the contents, which turned out to be carrots, he slid the can across the cold concrete floor to Vanya who did not seem to notice. Then he tore into the tight paper wrapping he had bound around a length of dried sausage he had traded someone for in passing. The tilt of Vanya's head as the wrapping came away and perfumed the air with the scent of spiced meat was followed by the cautious but deliberate movement of her foot which slid the can back in his direction. When she held her hand to him without raising her head or looking at him, he scowled and looked at the meal in his hands.

He was not a selfish man. He gave the best of everything he found for his sister's comfort and care. Blankets and clothing so she would not be cold, food so she would not be hungry, water so she would not thirst. Often he went without those things himself because keeping Vanya alive, keeping her satisfied, meant keeping her happy and keeping them both safe. But the beast in his belly demanded meat, could not effectively manage without it, and it had been too many days since he had consumed any as it was. If he gave in to her demanding hand, he was going to need to hunt, risk leaving her alone, but if he did not give her what she asked for, he risked a screaming fit that would draw all manner of predators to their shelter. In the end, after one small bite, he growled in defeated annoyance and gave her the sausage, and with ivory chopsticks procured from an empty restaurant on the day he and Vanya had been forced to leave home, he dug into the contents of the can. That small groan was the only complaint he made. Vanya's silence was more important than his immediate need for protein. Once she slept, he would find some way to satiate the roaring beast in his core.

Absently he pulled a dog-eared leather-bound book from his pack, a photo album he had found from which he had removed most of the original photos of a family he had never known. He had wondered, as he used the photos for fuel in some past night's fire, what had become of them. Had they perished among the earliest victims of the Undoing? Had they abandoned their home and everything they knew for somewhere potentially safer? Had they been home, or away on a much deserved holiday, in the days when the world had ended? Had they been one of the lucky families taken into the fabled water cities, cities meant to preserve the best of humanity while the rest were left to whatever fate the world hurled at them? No clues in that house revealed their fate, but as that day had come more than ninety-five years ago, Kato felt no guilt in seizing the album for his own purposes or in burning the images of a life long past. He kept one picture, a family image of a husband and wife, son and daughter, standing in front of a towering statue that held a torch high in the air. He kept it less in honor of the people now lost, then in remembrance of the location in which they had stood.

That image, like so many others accumulated before and since, was now stuffed into the stained plastic sleeves, a fading collection of cards depicting images of places that had once been. Paris, London, Rome. New Orleans, the Grand Canyon, the snowy mountains of Vermont. Hawaiian beaches, plains of majestic bison, waterfowl on Lake Michigan. There were many more cards saved from the ravages of the elements, places that might no longer exist for all he knew. His education, such as it was, had not included the geography and history of the world that had been, but he understood that these images, these places, had once been real. If they had existed before, they might exist now. Maybe someday, they would be real again. He intended to see them. All of them.

His mother had seen no need for such useless information. When she had been healthy, sober enough, to educate him at all, it had been in the rudimentary basis of reading, writing, and counting. There had been no one else, no father or neighbors, to supplement that learning, and Vanya had never learned anything beyond her letters, her numbers, and how to write both her name and his. It had been much more important to learn to survive in a hostile, abandoned world, and survival had become something, as he fought day and night to provide for his mother and sister, that he was very good at.

He substituted dreaming for learning, creating in his head what he would never see with his eyes as he collected these picture cards from the places his wanderings took him. He assumed people had lived in these places, real people. Someone had built these monuments and stadiums and marvels that he suspected the Undoing had devoured, just as it was devouring everything in the neighborhood where he had grown up and everything he had passed in the last three months of slow, laborious travel. They had not come far, not as far as he would like, but he had to keep Vanya's safety and low stamina in mind.

Besides, there was no hurry to reach somewhere else. They did not know if somewhere else existed. All they knew that existed were the boundaries of collapsing civilization they saw each day, their world limited by how far their feet could carry them. What lay ahead, what now lay behind, were unknowns.

As far as he knew, what was left behind was no longer there.

But he had dreams and a plan, the hope of somewhere warmer, somewhere drier, somewhere with open land where the threat of toppling buildings, decaying machinery, and hidden grubbers dogged their heels. He could maneuver those things, survive them. Vanya could not, and if anything happened to Kato, Vanya would not survive long. He needed her to be somewhere safe…if such a place existed.

He believed, from the proof of the cards he carried, that such places had to be real, but he had no idea how to find them, or how to reach them from where they rested tonight.

"Kato."

The whisper came to him from far away, not penetrating his thoughts until it was followed by a tapping on his knee that he expected had begun before she said his name. She did not often speak, not to him or other people at least. He glanced at her, swallowing the scowl he felt for his own daydreaming...a potentially deadly thing in a world of hidden dangers...to see her holding out an uneaten half of sausage to him. Precisely half, he knew, minus the nibble he had taken, as Vanya had an inherent knack for that sort of detail. With Peppermint stuffed between her thighs and belly as she continued to crouch in the corner, she now picked up the partially eaten can of carrots and drank the juice from it as she watched him.

Looking directly at people was another thing she rarely did, as if it frightened her to see people's eyes. In the moments when she did look at him this way, there seemed a rare level of lucidity, an awareness of the world and her surroundings that almost never came to the surface.

But as he took the offering with a grateful smile, closing the card book with his other hand, that clarity faded and her brown eyes shifted from his face to stare into the darkness beyond the closet.

"Are we going to see mother soon?"

Kato frowned, thankful she was not looking at him to see it. It made her sad to see him frown, frightened her to see him scowl, so he had learned to school his expressions when near her. It did no good to remind her of the truth, of their mother, in a drunken stupor, passed out in the small vegetable garden she had kept, found and devoured there in the fading twilight by the trio of grubbers who had stumbled through their yard in their never-ending shuffling quest for food. Vanya had been the first to respond to the woman's agonizing screams as she was ripped apart by the bony fingers and rotting teeth of those who had once been human but were no longer. It had been Vanya to first see her that way, to shriek in horror at the sight. The sound distracted the grubbers, drew them from their still-conscious meal, and Kato had reached both in time to snatch Vanya from their grasp. He fled with her into the brick house that had been their home for as long as Kato could remember. Up to the second floor, for grubbers could not effectively maneuver stairs, where brother and sister hid behind a closed closet door, listening to the shuffling of feet throughout the level below them, the continual chirping shrieks and groans and growls the grubbers made as they tried to drag themselves up the back porch steps in search of fresh, living prey.

At least, in that moment, they had forgotten about the dying woman in the garden.

With his hand clasped over Vanya's mouth to mute her screams, they listened together until Vanya, terrified to the point of fainting, collapsed into Kato's arms.

Hours later, when darkness fully settled, while Vanya slept, the continuity of sound louder now as other grubbers followed the noises of their kind and joined those three at the base of the stairs, it was obvious that the grubbers were not going to leave soon and were not likely to enter the house. There were too many for Kato to kill, and so he made a plan. As silently as he could, he snuck about the house, stuffing three canvas satchels his mother kept for foraging supplies, with as much food and warm clothes and blankets as he could. The grubbers would not leave their position at the back porch steps until some other sound or food scent drew them away. He could be that distraction, but leaving Vanya alone with the lingering memory of what she had witnessed, alone to fend for herself, was not an option. The inevitable day his mother had warned of had come.

They could not stay in this house any longer.

Packs secured on his broad back, Vanya in his arms, Kato got her down the stairs and out the front door without her waking. There had been a moment's hesitation, the choice about what to do about their mother looming over him, tugging him back toward the carnage they were leaving behind. But he had seen grubber victims before; the no longer living creatures, at least not living in the true sense of the word, always tore into the fleshiest parts of a victim first, tearing the insides out as they gorged. Most likely, the woman was dead, and if by some miracle she was still alive, she would not be much longer. There was nothing Kato could have done besides put her out of her misery and risk putting Vanya in harm's way to do so. His mother had instilled in him very early that his sister's safety came first. He had to think of Vanya and no one else.

Hours later, after they had holed up in an abandoned shed so that Vanya could sleep peacefully, the young woman had awakened with the rebirth of the sun and no apparent memory of what had come in the hours before. For the next several days she asked about their mother multiple times a day, accepting that they were going to meet her in a new house as their old one was no longer safe. Over time, the questions had come less frequently, now she asked maybe two or three times a week instead of four or five times a day. She seemed neither to remember his reminders that they would meet their mother soon nor the trauma that had set them on the run.

Kato viewed that as a good thing. The less Vanya remembered about that day, the easier the task of controlling her was.

"Soon, yes," he promised again, before ripping off a hunk of sausage, sighing with involuntary relief to eat something more substantial than canned vegetables. "A few more days."

"Few more days." She nodded and swallowed a mouthful of carrots.

Not believing that Vanya had any grasp of the passage of days, he was again thankful she accepted his words, the lies he hated telling but were necessary for their mutual safety. Why remind her of things her memory saw fit to purge, just for the sake of honesty? Why traumatize her all over again?

With their meal complete, but the beast coiled within far from satisfied, Kato stood and stretched, raking his black curls away from his face as he listened to the sounds of the night. He needed to hunt. It would be the only thing that would settle him. The broken off closet door was dragged from where it lay and propped on its side in front of the closet. Other objects, heavier ones, chunks of concrete and broken furniture, were placed in front of it. Vanya watched with sleepy eyes, curling on her side, Peppermint clutched to her chest. This was one routine she remembered after so many nights of traveling with him in unfamiliar places. He barricaded her in somewhere safe whenever he had to find supplies, and when she awoke, he would be there with whatever goodies he had been lucky enough to find.

"Sweets?" she murmured.

"If I can find them, they are yours." The odds of finding anything in such an area of isolated abandonment were small, but he always looked. "Stay quiet…stay safe."

Her head bobbed yes, but her eyes were closed now, and before he was out of the building, he knew she would be asleep.

❧*❧

Once he knew she was safely back amidst the protection of the others, the shorn man known as Deuce to the Pack he shadowed, slunk into the darkness of the streets barely aware that the rain had soaked through his too thin clothing. The elements barely bothered him, a genetic anomaly that set him apart from most. Barefoot, he clambered over slippery stone, concrete and asphalt, his toes and fingers finding their hold in the moss and vines growing there, going through the motions of his life as he did every night before he would be content and able to settle somewhere to lay his head to sleep. He knew he was not welcome at the warmth of their fire, despite the secret hope that, with the absence of Roland, his situation would change. They did not trust him, however, had no reason to since most knew him only by reputation and rumor, and he had spent so many years on the fringes he doubted he would feel comfortable amongst them even if he was embraced by the Pack once more.

Until they settled on a new Pack Alpha or found Roland, his hopes and wishes were little more than dreamy speculation.

Unable to sleep until he knew the borders were secure, saving his rest for the daylight hours when the Pack was less vulnerable, he began one more circle of the streets and buildings surrounding the one they called home, an abandoned clinic they had originally raided for mediplies and then turned into a dwelling sixteen years prior. That was a long time for a Pack to be settled into an area, or into a building within a territory, and Deuce could not help feeling anxious about the Pack being discovered here. The Marrocks had been a staple of this region since the Undoing, but they rarely stayed in one building for more than four or five years. To Deuce, the Pack needed to move, despite Roland's insistence that they needed stability more.

But Deuce was omega. The choice was not his to make.

Shouts, crashes of wood and metal, the tell-tale sounds of confrontation, carried through the mostly empty, overgrown streets on the tail-end of the rainstorm. Deuce lifted his head, smelled the traces of the fight on the wind, and ran with the strides of a man use to distance on uneven, overgrown terrain. His sure steps halted before they brought him within sight of the disturbance, and he climbed, using thick ivy vines to hoist himself, through the broken second story window above a mechanic's garage to get a better vantage point to see what lay ahead. From there he was able to approach the skirmish unseen, and watch as one group of darkly clothed individuals overpowered another and, taking possession of the three carts and their cargo, hauled their score down the cleared but bumpy street.

He did not know who were the attackers, who were the victims. He could not tell what the wagons contained, beyond noting that the sound of the wagon's creaking groan denoted significant weight. Nor did he want to know. Such pirating was a common threat to scavs, as someone always wanted what someone else had worked hard to find, and many had no compunction about using violence to take from others. The what, and the who, were none of Deuce's concern.

Odds were, someone else would try to steal that cargo before the sun broke the horizon. Some things never changed.

ॐ*ॐ

The Pack slept, but Jia did not. Pensive, head and heart full of the evening's events, she circled the perimeter of their den once, despite knowing that the sentries would keep everyone safe, and then she climbed to the roof to be alone. Only Maz was there, perched on the cement ledge with the garden's camouflage at his back, eyes steadily scanning through the rain to the north-west, to the direction of LaGuardia's Fortress and the bulk of 'civilization' the Flushing Pack was familiar with. East, wild and untamed, was less of a threat than the controlled districts of LaGuardia and Kennedy. And the Hallister influence, the borders of Kennedy borough, ran far to the south. If inclined, the Laedan could order raids conducted into the Flushing Wilds, but the new contract between Hallister and Channon made such action less likely. With Pain watching to the east, and Uncle to the south-west from other vantage points within the multi-leveled structure, there was nowhere safer to be, Jia believed, then where they were.

That her father had begun to feel differently, begun to exhibit an unusual level of wariness, continued to concern her, even though she had been unable to find any proof or hints to support Roland's fears.

Arms encircled her and a kiss was pressed into the hair at the top of her head. She sighed and leaned back against her brother's chest, welcoming his quiet understanding. Hands made for healing, for tending the ills and injuries of others, squeezed her arms, a replacement for words he did not speak. Their father's disappearance had brought the already close siblings closer, and their Cana instincts kept them well aware of the other's moods. Addi did not need to ask to know that his twin was troubled, nor did he need to ask why.

"He's still out there."

Perhaps he was referring to their father, or perhaps to the hunched gargoyle-like shadow on the rim of the building opposite their position. Preferring not to discuss their father again, though she too believed he was alive and waiting for rescue or escape, Jia chose to apply Addi's words to the Omega who stayed always near the Pack but rarely came close enough for any to see without looking for him.

"I think we should welcome him into the Pack."

Addi shook his head, his chin moving back and forth on the top of her head. "Until you're ordained…there are still those who do not trust him."

"Or me," she said, completing his unspoken thought. The belief in Roland's return was strong enough within the Pack that none were yet ready to admit the need for a new Alpha, not even a temporary one. Despite her intelligence and the training given by Roland, specifically for the day he could no longer guide them, there were doubts about her youthful suitability for the position. Untested as a leader, her small stature suggested weakness to some, even though physical strength had never been a condition for leading the Flushing Pack. While physical strength was a desirable attribute, blood had been the deciding factor in all Flushing Pack leaders, Marrock blood. Addi was no fighter, was no leader, which left the position to her. While Roland had not been a fighter either, how many in the Pack would have been able to beat him in a fight? Had any ever tried?

She had never witnessed any struggles to know, but she wagered that Maz, at least, could have beaten him, Uncle and Pain as well. But they respected the force of charisma, the family name, and Roland's intellect, and supported his leadership. She hoped she could likewise prove herself, was not sure why some lacked faith in her, and prayed that winning the doubters over would not require fighting others for her place.

"Give it time. They will come around…and when they do…" The shadow crabbed sideways and jumped from the roof's edge out of their line of sight. "That will be the time to debate bringing Deuce into the Pack. For now…"

For now, so long as hope for her father's return existed, so long as his irrational…to her…dislike for the man accused of crimes never proven was believed, the Pack would side against Deuce.

Now out of sight, it seemed to Jia that Deuce knew it as well.

❧*❧

His hands rubbed up and down her bare arms, the firmness of their youth and the way she looked at him with a hint of wonder and lust lit a fire in his core that Lowell had not felt in a long time. He loved his wife; no other woman compared to Yiva's beauty in his eyes, and she had proven her loyalty time and again in the years they had known one another. But over the last few years, she had changed, faded, subtly at first but now to the point where he no longer recognized the shell of a woman he had married. Try as he did, he could not reach her, could not penetrate the walls she had erected when he had not been looking. He did not understand the need for those defenses, did not know how to break through them or convince her to talk, and so, gradually, he drifted further away from her just as she was drifting away from him. If she did not love him any longer, she never said it. And as the mother of his children, his political ally in a world he knew he could make better, he would never discard her. It was not the way of the world any longer.

Not that his love for her had ever kept him from pursuing fertile young blood. Lowell wanted more children, though he had yet to father more, to his knowledge, than the three sons he shared with Yiva. More than that, however, he craved the thrill of newness, of the forbidden, and he was Laedan: why should anything he wanted, particularly an exquisite young woman, be denied him? What he wanted, Lowell took. Yiva had known that from the day they had met. Believing she had her secret lovers as well, now that she could no longer bear him children and no longer showed interest in sharing his bed, Lowell had never made an effort to hide his wandering libido from his wife, his sons, or those with whom he worked.

This, however, as he trailed his nose through this nubile beauty's brown hair, was another matter entirely. She was his son's new wife. There was risk in such a tryst, but not enough risk to make her forbidden.

Finger's slipped into the waistband of his trousers where they had drawn up the fabric of his tucked in shirt, she caressed the still firm flesh of his stomach and drew her tongue slowly over her lips. He was a handsome man, more so to her, despite the age difference between them, then her youthful new husband. Fit in the way her father no longer was, his dirty blonde hair untouched by gray and his face barely touched by the lines of age, it was only those crinkles at the corners of his eyes and the world-weariness within them that spoke of his maturity. What difference did years make, she reminded herself as she toyed with the top button of his trousers, when he could give her everything she wanted?

She had few doubts that Donnovan would try, but it was his father she needed, his father who held LaGuardia's true power now that Roland Marrock seemed to no longer be part of the equation.

Neither of them spoke; she took her cues from his rapid breathing and the heat coiling off his body, the quivering of the pulse point at the side of his neck. Talking would make the moment awkward. He knew that as well as she did. He had craved bedding her since the moment they met, when her father introduced her across a conference room table as a pawn to be bartered in marriage, and in every moment alone with her since, as the negotiations to secure her marriage to his son had progressed. He had made that craving clear to her. Until today, however, she refused to express any reciprocated feelings or distaste for his attention.

Seeking him out in his office now, in the pre-dawn hours of her first day as a wife, told Lowell enough.

Why settle for a boy when she could taste an experienced man? What woman would not want that?

There was a knock on the door, an echoing hollow sound that interrupted her fingers as the second button of his pants popped open, and Lowell groaned as he forced himself to step away. He untucked his shirt to cover both the open buttons and the proof of his arousal and dropped into the chair behind the desk. She slid off her perch, her face neutral. Both picked up the drinks Lowell poured when she had come in and Lowell propped his feet up on his desk.

"Yes?" he called, his voice tight with the caged tension that tightened every fiber of his body. It had been unusual enough that she had found him here at this hour. A second visitor seemed highly suspect and peculiar.

"Sir…it is Thomas…may I come in?"

The corners of Oasis' mouth twitched, an indication to Lowell that she was as disappointed by the interruption as he was, as he replied, "By all means, Thom…enter."

Less disheveled in appearance than Lowell, still dressed in the dark blue suit he had worn to the previous evening's celebration, Quentin hesitated in the entryway when the open door revealed the man and woman within. Nothing in their proximity to one another spoke of anything untoward, Only Oasis' long flimsy robe, the sort more suited to a private bedchamber than the Laedan's office, suggested anything unusual. She stood at the window, her back to the door, seemingly gazing at the ocean, but she turned to look at him and smiled when he entered, a drink in her hand, her expression light and innocent. If was the smile, more than Lowell's place at his desk where Thom often found him, that undercut his suspicions.

"Couldn't sleep either?" Lowell asked casually. "Care to join us for a drink?"

"No sir, I need to..."

Business. Lowell sighed and put down his barely touched tumbler. Any hopes he possessed of spreading Oasis upon his desk and claiming her were now unraveled.

Oasis too set her glass down, intentionally too close to his though it seemed innocent to Thom, the glass having been drained quickly as Thom watched, meant to convince him further of her innocence in being here. "I can tell when I'm not wanted," she said with a purr, her movement around Lowell, the desk, and Thom as she went to the door, bringing her body close to each. Eyes intently following the sway of her hips as she departed, neither man noticed the other's reaction to her.

"It's too early for business, Thom..."

"The shipment..." he grunted, tearing his eyes away from the door now that his worried employer had noticed his gaze lingering a little too long on Lowell's new daughter-in-law.

"What about it?" Lowell did not need to ask which shipment. There was only one that mattered today, the relocation of highly prized stock that he did not want to fall into the hands of Hallister or any other self-professed overlord or power-hungry Protector in LaGuardia who might wish to use the contents against him. He had another, more personal reason for moving it, but that was part of a plan, of two plans, that he dared not discuss with anyone.

"It is gone."

"Gone...?" Eyes narrowing, he ignored the burning in his belly that told him he had known what Thom's words would be before they were spoken. Swiveling in his chair, he went to the window to stare at the graying sky over the equally gray sea, comfortable that the previous secret hidden by his untucked shirt no longer needed to be kept as he stood in the same spot Oasis had stood. That matter was buried under the avalanche created by his now chaotic thoughts, but her perfume lingered in the air and threatened to bring it back. "Do you think he's responsible?"

Quentin did not ask who. "How could he be?" He's been out of the picture for days; there's no way he could have known about..."

"But what if he did?" Lowell's balled fists clenched behind his back. "It is him, isn't it? He did this. You promised me..."

"He's dead...I swear to you. Laedan, this wasn't him." Thom had not done the deed himself, but those he bought off to carry out his order had sworn to him the problem was taken care of. Taken care of meant dead.

"Then who?"

That was the question on both men's minds as they stood shoulder to shoulder at the window, unable to feel the warming sun's rays despite the brightening sky. To Lowell's knowledge, the only people who had known about the movement of goods conducted under the security of the wedding and reception and cold autumn rain had been the men doing the moving and the two standing in this room now. There had been those who had loaded the wagon, of course, but what could they have known?

"The escorts? The warehouse workers?"

Thom shook his head. "The escorts are dead." If one of them had been the traitor, then that one had died to keep the secret, and Thom could think of no one so disloyal to the Laedan, or to Quentin himself, who would have taken such a step. He had chosen those escorts carefully, to guarantee the shipment's safety. They had sworn an oath. But that did not mean they had kept it. "Jia?"

It was Lowell's turn to shake his head. No. The young woman was still clinging to the notion that her father was missing, had traveled east for supplies and discoveries. She had not yet stepped into Roland's shoes, had not accepted responsibilities for his duties, and was thus unlikely to know his business. Lowell was hoping she would leave her father's post vacant, although he knew that the tactical advantage of her assuming the co-Laedanship, of keeping her close, outweighed his wishes that she stayed out of the dangerous game her father had played. Lowell liked her, faults and all. There was no duplicity in her, no mistrust or wariness, and it seemed likely that Roland had kept whatever suspicions he harbored to himself. Jia knew nothing of such matters; Lowell was sure of it.

Briefly, he wondered if Roland had been suspicious at all, or if it had been his own paranoia that allowed him to believe his best friend might be capable of plotting treason against him. There had been no proof beyond Roland digging his heels in against Lowell's desire to better arm and equip a fighting force within LaGuardia's territorial boundaries. Roland had always favored peaceful solutions. Lowell would have been more concerned if Roland had responded to his desire for military might any differently than he had.

Quentin, however, had been less certain of Roland's loyalties, and Quentin's level-headed discourse had prevailed in swaying Lowell's choices. Lowell was not so blind as to miss Quentin's envy of Roland's position, not so naïve as to believe Quentin did not have his heart set on the position of co-Laedan. Lowell might have let himself be swayed against Roland, but only because it suited the agenda he had set into motion long ago.

Besides, there was no way one inexperienced woman would have had the resources to kill highly trained, well-armed, escorts.

"Scavs then." Thom spoke the only conclusion they could logically make. A large enough group of scavs, fortunate enough to cross paths with a protected cargo, would have made the effort to take it if they thought they could succeed. But a group large enough to succeed was a threat to the established order. Such a group had to be led, and Lowell would have the head of the man or woman bold enough to strike against him.

"Get Donnovan in here…and get me that mage. We're getting that shipment back before this day is over or there will be hell to pay…" And someone, Thom or the escorting agent or his son as the mayor of District 3 where the cargo had been lost, was going to pay.

Chapter 4

Belly full, the great black beast slept where it often did, curled protectively around the sleeping woman he would do anything to protect. Her arms about his lean muscled neck, her face pressed into fur without notice of the dampness of rain it still bore or the wet smell she would be left with for the upcoming day, she rested peacefully, discarding the small yellow bear in favor of a much warmer sleep-buddy. When she awoke to find her brother beside her, when they finished their dried biscuit breakfast and began pressing west again, this time without the rain, she would speak of the mysterious bipedal feline with awe and wonder and longing, never realizing, it seemed, that the tailless cat rarely left her side. Catlike or human, Kato was always there, would always be there. One day he might even tell her the truth, show her the truth.

But only if he believed he would not drive her mad by doing so.

In the distance, a wild cock greeted the arriving sun with a throaty, trumpeting call. Unwilling to take the risk of telling her today, Kato accepted the return of his human form, rolled free of Vanya's embrace, and hurried to dress before she awoke. Weary from the night's hunt, but with his restless belly full of fresh meat and his muscles temporarily purged of the impulse to run, he glanced at Vanya's innocent sleeping face and sighed.

It was going to be another very long day. But he was determined, as always, for her sake, that it would be a good one.

⮞*⮜

Protector Valentine, known as Vance to those he served with, was a lot of things, but normal had never been one of them. As he squatted over the three mutilated bodies lying before the podium in this rarely used remnant of a church, the tails of his long black leather coat dragging in the dust behind him, he listened, not only to the sounds the old building made as the wind pushed against the walls and the straining rafters, but also to the sounds that the other Protectors could not hear, whispers of things that had gone before, past voices which left their imprint on the atmosphere, just as his companions boots left behind a muddy trail on the stone floor.

Most often the sounds left a distinct pattern, more traceable than a man's footprints, but here the sounds were muddled, muffled, muted by the accumulation of voice prints left throughout the building's long history as a place of congregation and worship. From amidst the freshest auditory vibrations, the infant's cries stood out, but the cries told him less about the child then examining her tiny gray body did. Hairless, with narrow slits for nostrils where her nose should be, the child's wide, lidless red eyes were dim and cloudy, her spindly body too emaciated to have survived long. Vance was certain the girl had starved to death as she showed no marks, no signs of injury, only a crusty white flaky substance around the edges of her lopsided mouth that might have been the product of suffocation, might have been the symptom of strangulation if her neck had borne bruises, or might, he mused, be the product of someone's attempt to feed her. There was a tin lying open on the stone steps nearby, its white contents spilled across the floor; a finger dabbed into the still slightly damp puddle indicated powdered milk and potato mashed into a thin, watery pulp. Powdered milk was a rare commodity, something existing now only in abandoned storerooms and basements, but someone had given the precious gift to this poor mutant creature in the hopes of saving its life.

A selfless act that deserved better than either of these victims had gotten.

One, a pudgy fellow, squat and balding, lay splayed as if he had been thrown against the wall with more force than a normal man could have mustered, a broken doll of a man with stringy blonde hair and slightly crossed blue eyes. Not far from his tobacco-stained outstretched hand, a handgun, another rare and expensive commodity, lay spent, its surface charred as if the weapon had discharged in reverse. That, Vance noted, would explain the burns to the side of the man's face, the appearance of being too close to the source of an explosion. It did not, however, explain the claw marks ripped deep into his chest and across his other sleeveless arm.

Those gouges were explained by something else, the body of the frail-looking man that had fallen as if in an attempt to protect the child. As scrawny as the dead man was, equally malnourished, he did not have the appearance of a man of strength, but his bloody fingertips and the red spreading down his arms like rain trails on window glass told a different tale.

"Anthro?"

Vance shuddered at the tone with which that word was spoken but he chose not to be baited. "Ursa...judging by the marks left."

One of the other Protectors with him, still sketching quick images of the pudgy dead man, muttered, "Bet this poor sod was trying to stop him from eating that..."

"No one was trying to eat anyone." Such ignorance, Vance thought bitterly. He pointed to the white powder sprinkled across the skinny man's chest. "He was feeding her...or trying to..."

"Little too late I'd say," snorted another Protector, the only woman among them, her hair cropped close to her head in a boyish fashion. Sal was the only Protector Vance could tolerate working with, the only one he remotely liked, the only one who did not rub all of his senses in entirely wrong ways.

"He found her here...tried to save her." He did not know how he knew that; it was a mage gift to know such things at times, with no explanation necessary. It was that gift that set him apart, kept Vance from fitting in with others on the force, but it was also a gift that made him the most sought-after Protector in LaGuardia. If there were other Mages, he did not know them. How he had gone from being the misfit to Chief Ernest's favorite son was a thing of wonder.

Sal, at least, rarely seemed bothered by his oddities. She went with his premonitions without question most of the time. It was another reason Vance could stomach working with her when duty required a partner at his side.

It was the mage gift that, while most other Protectors looked at one another skeptically, unwilling or unable to believe that the anthro had been the victim here, also forced them to take Vance at his word. The mage's premonitions were rarely wrong.

"No point in looking for its mother," a third Protector said, pointing at the infant with disgust. "Guess we're done here."

Vance had to agree. Mutani children were often abandoned, left in boxes, in mounds of waste, drowned in dirty pools, left exposed to wind and rain and sun and cold, left to whatever fates had in store. Sometimes, when the children were found alive, they were taken to the nearest foundling home to be raised until they were old enough to fend for themselves. Many were taken to the mutani zone, where others of their kind could raise them, but this child had not been so lucky. Vance could trace her mother if given time and opportunity, but to what end? No one would fine or punish the woman for abandoning the unwanted thing. The child was mutani…that was considered punishment enough to its parents. As precious and desperately needed as children were, few wanted those malformed, ill-fated children, not when the future of humanity was at stake.

A sound, breathing and the creak of timbers caused by the shifting of weight, drew Vance's gaze upward into the drafty, hole-ridden eaves, revealing the form of a man present only long enough to be noticed before he was gone, like a ghost or a bit of smoke dissipated by the wind. A third culprit, he wondered? Was this little fellow not the anthro after all, but merely a good doer who happened to be in the wrong place at the wrong time?

Again Vance sniffed the air. The ghost was anthro alright, the scent on the air Cana rather than Ursa. He glanced at the dead shooter on the other side of the room; those scratches were definitely not Cana. He would have to be the biggest Cana Vance had ever encountered to make slashes as wide apart and deep as the fellow bore, and Cana were more inclined to use their jaws, not their claws, if pressed into a fight. Bending over the thin man, making note of the bullet hole torn into his chest near his armpit, Vance took a better scenting of him and stood only when he was satisfied. The Cana had not been the killer, but that did not explain why he had been here.

Unless the child was his.

"Protector Segara."

The formal tone commanded attention, and Vance recognized the blocky fellow who entered the church. One of the Laedan's lackeys, which meant that he was here on official business for either the Laedan or someone in the Laedan's family or employ. With an internal, silent groan of annoyance, as he would prefer to leave this grizzly site and go for a drink…or several…instead of head directly into another case, Vance got to his feet and wiped his hands on his trousers. "Yes?"

"Laedan Channon requests your attendance at the Hall." He said no more; Vance doubted the fellow knew anything about the summons. The Channon staff was well trained to keep whatever they knew behind closed lips, trained not to see what went on before their eyes within the Fortress; even if the fellow did know why Channon wanted the mage, he was not going to say.

"You guys wrap it up here," Vance instructed, making eye contact with each of the Protectors in the room before settling on Sal's round face. The sounds above indicated that, while unseen, their observer had remained to listen but was going his way now, a relief as it was one less thing Vance had to worry about. An altercation between Protectors and an anthro was not a report he wanted to write up, nor did he want unnecessary casualties on either side. "And make sure," he chastised, "that the bodies get decent, proper treatment."

Not burial; land was scarce, protected for growing things now for all but the most well-to-do families. There were other ways to settle the dead, preferred ways, and that pudgy fellow on the far side of the room would have to be treated accordingly lest the grubber virus manifested.

"Yes, sir," Sal said with a nod. Any dissent with the mage's orders went unspoken. He would have to rely on Sal's word, and the written reports they would give later, for proof that they obeyed his command and followed usual protocols. At least he trusted Sal to do the right thing.

There were shaggy horses outside of the church, three ridden by the Laedan Guard, their bulky leather armor fitted with protective metal plates that identified them, and two empty animals that seemed bored and inattentive of their surroundings. The growl and mutter of grubbers rose and fell on the air, indicating a hive nearby, but Vance knew this sector, knew them not to be a threat, and apparently, the horses agreed with his assessment. Vance swung up onto the back of the dun-colored animal his escort pointed to, adjusted himself in the saddle, and accompanied them to the Fortress.

Most could not ride a horse. Vance only knew how because his mother had once been stable hand for the Laedans. It was why Channon knew Vance so well, knew where to find him even when he would rather not be found.

Not for the first time, he considered moving far beyond the reaches of the Channons. Also not for the first time, Vance realized he had nowhere else to go.

⮞*⮜

"Isn't that Marrock's pack?"

Jonni froze in the corridor, out of sight of the open doorway ahead, where the muffled voices rose and fell in the hushed tones of secrecy. He knew his youngest brother's voice without seeing the newly married man, and the sound of it, accompanied by the thought of Donn engaged in honeymoon activities with the woman who had almost been Jonni's bride, made him shudder and gag. Oasis seemed like a nice enough woman, intelligent and well-schooled, and she was certainly beautiful, but none of those temptations had been enough, in addition to the duty expected of him, to persuade him to marry. He pitied her now, however, for being forced to endure his less than gentle, less than kind, brother, and hoped she had the fortitude to stand up to the fate Jonni's decision had forced on her.

"Is it?" That was Quentin's voice, the flippant, nonchalant tone one that Jonni had heard in men feigning ignorance, and hearing it made Jonni inch closer to the door, years of practiced stealth allowing him to draw near without being heard. Having never seen Donn exchange more than dutiful pleasantries with their father's assistant when the brothers and Quentin met with the elder Channon for district business, and knowing that Quentin was a man Donn had expressed loathing for on multiple occasions, a private conversation between the two warranted investigation.

Particularly since the name Marrock had been mentioned, and once again the anthro accusation was thrust into the spotlight.

Quentin first brought up the accusation against Roland to their father less than two months ago and Lowell, disgusted by the possibility that his best friend and co-Laedan of so many years could have hidden something like that from him their whole lives, had secretly begun to have the man and his family investigated, while denying, to Quentin at least, that the accusations could be true. Donn had sworn to the accuracy of Quentin's claim, however, citing a reliable source he refused to name, although Jonni suspected now that the information had been tortured out of someone, possibly Erilyn Bardeau, one of their previous caregivers who had gone missing just prior to Quentin's first accusation. Rumors had circulated about the Bardeaus for years, but if that suspicion had been proven, there had been, to Jonni's knowledge, no public claims made, no discussion of it within the family, and no effort to apprehend any of the other Bardeau family members. If one parent had been anthro, the odds were high that the children were as well. With her husband dead for over ten years, there were no means of proving whether he had been guilty of the same genetic fault as his wife, but one member tainted was enough to condemn an entire family.

Perhaps someone, Donn, Quentin, or Lowell, was waiting to build a solid case against them, although what reason there could be to wait was beyond Jonni's grasp. Most of the time, suspicions were enough to warrant arrest and conviction. Perhaps they were hoping to use that knowledge to build a solid case against Roland, and that had led to his disappearance. If he suspected mistrust in those around him, a wise man like Roland would have disappeared rather than risk his family. As close as Jia was to Liam Bardeau, Erilyn's nephew, and with whispered misgivings now circulating behind closed doors about both her father and her best friend, it was no wonder Lowell had insisted that a marriage between a Marrock and a Channon was out of the question. What did they know that Jonni did not?

He could not see his brother's smirk, but Jonni could imagine it, the youngest Channon reading Quentin's words and tone as easily as Jonni had. "So I have heard…at least I heard tell there is family near there…" Donn's voice was as tellingly casual as Quentin's. "I suppose we shall learn soon enough. When will you…?"

There was the long hesitation of a man weighing his options, weighing trust against ambition, Donn's usefulness against his reputation. When Quentin did reply, it was in a low, serious tone. "Tonight…barring complications."

"Do you require anything?" As the iron-fisted mayor of District 3, Donn had all of the territory's resources and manpower at his disposal, and if Quentin's claims were true, if there was a Cana pack in the Flushing wildlands, then because those lands bordered District 3, Donnovan wanted in on any attempt to exterminate them. He wanted his share of the prestige, credit, and power that a successful raid could bring with his father and with HOPE. If Quentin intended to move any the Channon Guard, or even private hires, for the task, into Flushing, they would need to travel through the Zone, where the mutani were segregated, up and around through District 1 to come into the wildlands from the east, or else they were going to have to take the shortest route…directly through District 3. That would necessitate cooperation of the Mayor if Quentin wanted his men undisturbed, which Donn suspected was why his father's aide had casually mentioned his intentions. Rather than asking for permission outright, the man had maneuvered Donn into doing the asking. Well played, Donn thought without a trace of bitterness.

They had never collaborated before, and in general, Donn chose not to tangle his affairs with the man who held his father's ear, choosing to prove his aptitude for leadership on his own. But the benefits on this occasion outweighed the risk of mutual cooperation.

"Unhindered passage will be enough." Quentin did not technically need permission, the men at his disposal were the Laedan's forces and had the freedom to travel anywhere within LaGuardia. Travel throughout the borough was not restricted, save by the blockage of streets by hazardous debris, fallen buildings, and overgrown foliage. If the Channon's personal guards, LaGuardia soldiers, or the Protectorate were on official business, none of those personally responsible to any of the three mayors were permitted to hinder them, and it was men from all of those forces that Quentin had at his disposal. But as he did not have authority to conduct the raid he intended, and had not gained clearance for it from Lowell, having Donnovan's unilateral permission meant that, should Lowell raise issue with the sweeper raid or how it was conducted, the responsibility would become Donn's. Donn, Quentin knew, would woo his father's support with ease. It was the mayor's protection Quentin needed if he was going to proceed with his plan.

They both knew it.

Donn nodded his head slowly. "You shall have it. Anything you need...men to assist if you wish...protection for as long as you require...however I may assist you...come to me."

The creaking of furniture announced that the two were now on their feet, heading toward the door, and so Jonni hastily retreated into the nearest room with an open door, in the hopes that neither would notice or detect him there. As it was an empty meeting room, and he wanted to appear casual in case either or both men passed by, Jonni hurriedly took a seat at the long central table, opened the folder of documents he carried that were destined for his father's approval and signature, and yanked out a blank page. Hunched there, one handwritten document seemingly being copied or referred to on the blank page, Jonni hoped he would appear natural enough, relaxed enough to the man who called, "Hello, old man," in passing.

The gesture Jonni made in response to the intended insult, ring finger and pinky finger flipped from his otherwise closed fist, brought the expected laugh from Donn. It was not the first time they had shared that obscenity between them. The familiar shared gesture kept the youngest Channon from inquiring about Jonni's business. Whatever Jonni was doing, Donn neither knew nor cared. He had his own business to tend to.

The message was hastily written despite the questions that balled and burned in Jonni's belly. Was it true? Was this the reason Jia had pushed him away, refused to consider marriage. Had she wanted to protect him from incrimination as well as protect her family, herself?

Was she Cana?

Did she love him after all, enough to sacrifice happiness to protect him?

Fastening the message closed with the wax kit and seal he carried throughout his daily duties, it occurred to Jonni that he had suspected this truth longer than his father had, and though it perturbed him that Jia did not trust him with the truth, he understood her caution and realized that the possibility made little difference to him. He did not believe the anthro condition to be contagious, to be spread through casual or intimate contact, and had never considered anthro to be the threat that HOPE and many others claimed, the threat his own father believed they were. Nor could he consider it an unnatural state, for if, as was medically theorized, it was a genetic condition present at birth, then it was as natural to humanity now as hair and eye color. Yes, marriage to a Marrock 'monster' would have pushed him out of the family business, but it was not a business Jonni wanted. He would have been content to leave the Fortress and join Addi's medipractice in the poorer regions of the borough. A simple life, a life of helping others, without political scheming and his family's emotional baggage. It was the future Jonni had dreamt of most often growing up. A future spent with her.

Addi. That was the answer. Jonni did not know where Jia called home, had no idea where the Marrocks went when they were not staying in one of the Fortress' suites as Roland and Jia had done three or four nights a week all of her life. Many in the boroughs were secretive about where they lived, about which small corner of the post-Undoing world they had carved out for themselves and the survival of their family. Such privacy was a means of protecting meager resources, the food they raised, the goods they scavenged or made. Odds were that Lowell had their residence on file somewhere, as it might have been where Quentin had gotten the information from, but for Jonni to go looking for it would raise questions and might alert Donn and Quentin to the discovery of the planned sweep.

Jonni could not get a message directly to Jia, but he could get it to Addi. That was the next best thing. The locations of the clinics were well known, as were the identities of much-needed doctors and healers, and the cluster of doctors with whom Addi worked were no exception. Jonni could not deliver a message himself, could not risk drawing attention to the Marrocks by traveling through the borough in search of a man he called friend, but his personal assistant could do so without question for her own father served in the same clinic.

The message was sent, the envoy instructed to deliver it without delay, Jonni claiming that it was a private health matter for which he would only see Doctor Marrock. Nothing about that request was out of the ordinary, the two men having shared training and medivice over the years. Addi was the doctor Jonni most often sought when he felt ill, regardless of the distance needed to travel between them.

Afterward, Jonni was left with no option but to pray that whatever higher power might still care about the fate of people in this ruined world, cared for the safety of Jia Marrock. That, and he prayed that he was wrong about Thomas Quentin's intentions.

⮞*⮜

The long, dim corridors that once linked air terminals, that had been filled with travelers day and night, never seemed to change, no matter how many times he passed through them. He imagined the dull gray walls had once gleamed white, and that many of the boarded over panels above had contained glass, allowing the warmth of the sun to brighten the lives of those hurried travelers. But he had never seen them that way, had never seen photos of those long lost days, and so the notion was pure speculation, a vision, gleaned from the whispers in the walls, of what the world should have been like before the perpetual clouds set in, blanketing the world in cold, suffocating Queens from the sun.

Was all the world this way, he wondered? He had never met anyone from outside of Queens, either from the north or the south, who could tell him. To the west, LaGuardia's borough stretched to the East River's edge, a silly name since the river was west and not east, and though Vance had never journeyed to those far reaches of the borough, he knew people who had, who told him that the weather there was no less gray and dismal, the world no less shrouded in decay and destruction.

He had seen blue sky once, as a boy, perched on his father's shoulders atop the tallest building they could find in order to see as far as the mist would allow. Their treacherous climb through rubble and dust had been rewarded with that hint of azure, a patch no bigger than his small hand when he stretched his fingers out to touch it. He had kept his hand there, squinting at the rays of unfiltered sunlight that pierced the gray veil, watching the treasure until the charcoal clouds devoured it. It was the one memory of his childhood, of his father, that he clung to whenever the darkness of the world and people's souls became more than he wished to endure.

More and more of late, that memory was not proving to be enough. He was tired. So tired. He wanted only to drink and forget.

It was no wonder Walter was planning to retire. How any one man had done this job for so long was a mystery.

And Walter was not even a mage.

"This way, Protector."

His escort gestured him through a door he opened into an empty anteroom with another closed door beyond it, a room with no window and only those two doors as routes of escape. Vance tugged his fingers beneath the too tight fabric around his neck and wished he had foregone the uniform today. Unlike other Protectors, his status as mage meant leniency in attire and his own choice of work hours, but the meeting of chiefs had been conducted over breakfast before the work day began and he had been asked to attend. Such a meeting called for the formality of uniform, and Vance had not had the opportunity to change before being called to the homicide scene. Now here he was, trying not to pace this windowless box that lacked not only a view of the outside world but also a proper ventilation system. If he had to wait much longer, he believed he would lose what little sanity he had left.

"Segara...my apologies for keeping you waiting." The voice accompanied the opening of the second door, bringing with it a rush of cool air and a glimpse of the sea through the window which silhouetted the Laedan who greeted him with an outstretched hand. "Please...come in."

This was not Lowell's business office. That was where the two met most frequently, a formal setting that maintained a level of professionalism Vance preferred. The day he was viewed as a political pawn or lackey of the Channons was the day he quit his job; he had decided that before he was appointed Mage of LaGuardia. The warm beige of the walls, the cushioned chairs and short table set with breakfast suggested this was a private office, a personal space that had little to do with the usual business of running LaGuardia.

The intimacy made Vance frown.

"Have you eaten?" Lowell gestured to the bountiful meal as he sat on the sofa and poured himself a cup of steaming tea. Coffee was a rare and precious commodity, but tea, particularly ivy tea, was bountiful and inexpensive.

The damned stuff covered nearly every wall in Queens.

"I have. Thank you."

"Then you've had an early start. Please, sit." The Laedan pushed an open cigarette tin across the table, perfuming the air with tobacco and marijuana. Vance declined that offer as well, this time with a shake of his head and a wave of his hand. He did not like to smoke; smoke inhibited the senses that allowed him to do his duties. Despite his seeming calm, Vance recognized the tension around the other man's eyes. There was a problem afoot, one the Laedan expected him to solve. Vance sat in a single chair, rather than on the sofa where Lowell was, and waited for his host to speak.

"I need your help."

"I surmised that much."

Lowell chuckled darkly. Hiding things from a mage was nearly impossible. He wondered for a moment if asking Segara to undertake this task was the right thing to do. "Yes…well…you would. Of course you would. Why else would I invite you here?" He swallowed a long sip of tea and with closed eyes, breathed in the aromatic steam rising from the cup. It soothed his agitation, agitation that would be too easily detected by the shorter man. "Roland is missing."

"Marrock, sir? How long?"

"A few days…a week…I don't know. He did not arrive one day…has not been seen since. His daughter says he journeyed east in search of resources, else I would have reported this sooner…"

"And you doubt her?" Vance knew Marrock had children, a son and a daughter, but oddly, for all of his times in the Fortress, he had never crossed paths with either of them.

"I think there's more than what she's telling me. There were documents…" The cup clattered against its saucer as he hastily set it down, the sound deliberately jarring as it cut off whatever he had been about to say and served to distract them both from the uncompleted statement. "Last night there were three wagons of goods stolen from me. I want them back."

Expression skillfully blank, Vance asked, "You believe Marrock's disappearance and the theft of the wagons to be related?"

Relieved that the Mage did not press him about the mentioned documents, though he knew the man would not likely let that mistakenly made statement go, Lowell nodded over his bite of toast. "They can't be a coincidence…"

"What was in the wagons?"

Eyes slightly narrowed, Lowell muttered, "What the hell difference does that make?"

"What makes you think the theft and Marrock's absence are connected?" Vance countered. "Was it food? Tools? Mediplies?"

"Mediplies." If the response was spoken too hastily, the mage did not appear to hear it as such. "It was being transported through District 3 to a District 1 checkpoint for dispersal to the clinics."

"What happened to suggest…?"

"It left the warehouse…never arrived…and all of those escorting it are dead!" Exasperated, Lowell forced himself not to erupt off of the sofa or to reach across the table to strike the other man. The mage was doing his job, was the best Tracker there was; if anyone could find his wagons, and his co-Laedan, it would be Valentine Segara; he had to be thorough, but thorough meant too many probing questions that Lowell could not legitimately answer. It also meant following every mistaken word Lowell uttered.

"Did Roland know about the shipment? Why do you think…?"

"Yes…no…no. The arrangements were made after his disappearance, but his son is a d3 doctor…it has to be connected."

Again it took effort not to scowl at the deliberate misdirection of information. Vance nodded once. "So, you believe that the matters are connected but have no information or supporting proof beyond Marrock's doctor son? Do you believe Doctor Marrock would have cause to steal this shipment?"

The corners of Lowell's mouth tightened. He liked Addison well enough, except that the young man's life choices had steered Jonni away from his duty to family and borough…and the fact that, if Roland was Cana, both of his children likely were as well. For that reason alone, though he had not previously planned it this way, Lowell nodded his agreement to the mage's question.

Allowing Addison to take the blame for the theft, or at least orchestrating it, would steer the mage away from the truth. Lowell had planned this 'theft' for weeks, before Roland Marrock went missing, it was why he believed the two things were connected, but he had not planned for the shipment to actually be stolen and he could not admit to any of it now. So long as suspicion swirled around the Marrocks, be it father, son, or daughter, it gave Lowell time to find that shipment on his own and find proof that Roland had been dealt with as he had asked.

"I will look into it," Vance promised, rising and adjusting his uniform jacket to hang properly over his slight frame. "I will let you know as soon as I have news…and if you think of any detail…"

"See Quentin on the way out…he will get you the names of the escorts we lost…and an inventory of stolen commodities. Perhaps someone in their families will know who did this and why. Please do hasten with this…" He would rather the man took his time, but mages were known for being thorough and swift. Lowell was going to have to prepare a backup plan to implement the moment the mage began to uncover the truth. "People need those supplies."

"You will know what I know as soon as I do."

His statement was already true. Lowell Channon knew he was lying, hiding the truth, and Vance knew that too. Sometimes lies were a political necessity, but rarely were they a good pretext on which to hire a mage.

Chapter 5

The Flushing Pack, as it was known amongst the other Cana packs scattered around Queens, suffered, as did everyone else since the Undoing, from a dangerous lack of children. Conditions left behind by the series of cataclysms that rocked the old world had taken their toll on successful procreation and marred humanity with a mortality rate that made those children who did survive precious gifts to be guarded, treasured, and given every advantage so that they could thrive and reach adulthood. Too many were born to die, or died before birth, and of those who lived, starvation, atmospheric conditions, dangers of the crumbling world in which they lived, disease and the threat of predators proved equally fatal. Despite those threats and the odds, however, nine children filled the Pack's ranks, nine children kept under supervision at all times by the older members in order to enhance their likelihood of maturing to contribute to the Pack's survival, to reproduce and grow the Pack further. Four were Maz' children, three daughters and a son, ranging in ages from six to ten, motherless since the cold had robbed them of Maz's wife three winters past. Three others, the Morgan siblings, and the burly, hairless Sola, had come into the Pack through the foundling system via Addi's wife Trill. Pregnant herself with the couple's second child, Trill continued her work at one of District 3's foundling homes, and did her best to channel anthro children into families outside of the system where they had a higher chance of survival. Like the mutani, anthro did not fare well in the foundling system, where they were either bullied into attempting life on their own in the streets or were occasionally killed by the other children's, or even other staff members', cruelty. Finding appropriate homes was no easy task, as anyone adopting an anthro child ran the risk of being accused of being one, and Trill too ran a similar risk.

It had not stopped her from bringing those four children into the Pack, however. With them under Pack guardianship, cared for along with their own two-year-old son, it kept Addi, Trill, and Maz as the child-producing core of the Pack. The oldest of the nine, also in their charge, was Reif, the only child of Roland's sister, a girl of fifteen nearing the age of entering the Pack as more than a pup. With initiation rapidly approaching, her birthday less than two months away, Reif already bore much of the responsibility for supervising the younger children, as did fourteen-year-old Randi Morgan.

This morning, as they did most days when the formal education of reading, writing, and numbers did not fill their time, the children tended the collection of potted vegetables on the rooftop of their medifac home, helping Ilba and Zen provide food for the Pack in the most efficient ways possible. It was vital that the knowledge of growing things, of tending to the goats, rabbits, and chickens the Pack raised, was never lost. Such a loss meant starvation, something none of them could afford. Once the products of their growing labors, the vegetables and fruits, eggs and milk there for the gleaning, were gathered for the morning, the children would cluster around Liam to learn other skills that would, it was hoped, prevent civilization from slipping entirely into ignorance.

Liam grinned at Jia from where he leaned against the doorway that gave egress back into the building from the roof as she passed, her morning survey of the gardens and the children's well-being complete. She had seen to the welfare of the adults before those who worked outside of the Pack left their shelter for the day. With Addi and Trill working elsewhere, serving the community as a whole, and the Pack needing adult protection from threats that always lingered beyond the perimeter of their senses, either Maz, Pain, or Uncle remained each day while the others scavenged the ruined streets for goods worth selling or trading for supplies or for use by the Pack. Some things they could not make themselves. Today it was Uncle who paced the corridors of the clinic, who listened, who watched, who remained vigilant over the children's welfare, as Liam did likewise in waiting for their attention. The women were equally responsible for their safety and would never shirk that duty, but the more bodies available to protect the pups, the better.

A whistle from below, from inside the clinic, a tone each pack member recognized, beckoned Jia to the main entrance. Unofficially the Pack's leader as Roland's daughter, she was the one deferred to when it came to interactions with outsiders. She knew the workings of the Laedan's Fortress, the ways of government and law, the ways the Protectorate functioned. She knew best who to go to for favors and supplies. She knew the world in a way that most of the Pack never would. That made her a valuable asset, even if she had no leadership experience.

It was not leadership Uncle was seeking, however, as he blocked the door with his broad, stalwart frame, his fists clenched at his side in warning to whoever was outside. She could not see past him, but she could smell the other, the strange tang on the air giving rise to a prickle across her neck that made the tiny hairs there stand on end. Rather than announce her arrival with words, knowing that Uncle heard her, scented her, felt her the moment she came into the antechamber, she placed her hand on his shoulder and bid him step aside with a gentle squeeze. He growled in acknowledgment and turned only enough so she could squeeze past to speak to the visitor. Uncle refused to move from his post, keeping the stranger, and anyone else, from getting inside.

"Protector."

She did not know the slender man of Hispanic descent, had never seen him before and was sure she would have remembered him if she had. He had an air about him of someone familiar, as if they had met in a previous life, in a time and place much different than the dismal surroundings in which they lived. The uniform, the silver and red epaulets on his dark blue breast pocket and lapel told her who he was, what he was, but as a gust of wind doused her with his scent again, she knew that the uniform did not tell her everything she should know. Friend or foe, she felt she needed to know him better. Such knowledge, however, was normally beyond her grasp, as her people did not associate with his sort. The risks were too high. Her gaze settled onto one rank pin in particular and her brow furrowed. "Mage," she corrected with wary suspicion, pushing down every instinct within her other than those needed for survival.

"Ms. Marrock." It was not like Vance to shift uncomfortably beneath anyone's gaze, not Lowell's or Chief Ernest's. Well-centered in himself, well-trained and confident, there were few who could make him uncomfortable in his own skin. Maybe it was because this tiny woman with doll-like features, round and seemingly innocent to the eye, was undeniably Cana, as was the dark-skinned man behind her. He had not known that before coming here, had no reason to suspect he was stepping into pack territory on the Laedan's behalf. Having never met Roland Marrock except in passing, he had never paid enough attention to the other Laedan to make note of that important fact, and he had heard no rumors about the brilliant man to have drawn such a conclusion on his own.

He wondered if Channon knew.

Vance knew Lowell. He knew of the man's dislike for all things anthro. He knew of the HOPE rallies held within the Fortress, knew that every Channon born had attended those rallies and had likely been recruited into the shadowy, semi-religious organization. So many purebloods in power turned that way. If this young woman was Cana, it was likely Roland was as well. Had Channon known all along? Had he recently learned the truth?

It was an important detail Vance would have to uncover without divulging this pack to the repercussions of exposure. Digging beneath those particular Channon rocks was a risk for Vance as well, but he was beginning to feel the nagging realization that he would be faced with no other choice.

Or maybe his discomfort arose because she was so damned pretty...and he rarely fared well with beautiful women. His efforts at relationships seldom lasted more than three weeks; being a tracker mage in a relationship did not work in Vance's favor. Women did not appreciate his ability to see through them.

Not many people did.

"May we speak somewhere?" Vance glanced at the other man, feeling less awkward and uncomfortable with him then he did with her. As an anthro of significant size, the man could rip his throat out if provoked, Vance had little doubt, but he feared the man doing so less then he feared this doe-eyed creature with long waves of the richest brown hair he had ever noticed on a woman. Given the chance, she could rip through more than his throat. "Privately?"

Uncle growled again, but a glance and a brush of Jia's hand across his permitted him to back down without losing face and allowed her to step away unhindered. A mage was a danger to pack survival, a danger to any anthro, but Jia showed no visible concern as she moved into the empty gray street. "Of course." Another growl, this time showing his displeasure with her choice, but Uncle did not attempt to stop her from crossing the cleared section of street. He continued to watch, but the mage was alone and Uncle's duty was protecting the Pack. He would remain where he was until her return.

Jia would have to protect herself if the need arose, at least long enough for help to reach her.

Her eyes scanned the block as far as she could see, noting that even the vines looked gray this morning and the air smelled of rain and the ozone of lightning, though none currently fell and no hint of an electrical storm swirled above them. Knowing that mages rarely went on official business without at least one regular Protector to accompany them, as mages were often less proficient as fighters or marksmen as they were trackers, she expected his partner to be hidden nearby, close enough to watch but not near enough to interfere unless trouble arose. But Jia sensed no one except those of her own Pack in the building behind her, and the restless sleeping form somewhere above in the nondescript building she motioned the mage into. It was not entirely out of Uncle's earshot, but it was as much privacy as she was willing to give the unfamiliar mage. If he was brave enough to enter a pack's territory alone, he deserved respect. Mages were not known to be foolhardy.

Of course, maybe he had no inkling of where he would end up before he arrived.

"What is it, mage?" Respect, in her opinion, equated to politeness. And today, respect was going to have to be earned.

"Segara…Vance Segara." Training and an upbringing in which manners were important when interacting with others if he wanted to make a good impression, bid him offer his hand. The effort was also presented to show her that he was unarmed, as he knew she did not trust him. He carried a standard issue long dagger on his hip, the nearly foot-long engraved blade that all Protectors carried on duty, a thing of beauty as much as it was a weapon, but a scrutinizing glance of the leather loop and belt which held it would reveal a noticeable lack of use. He might have trained to use it upon entering the Protectorate, might have demonstrated a maintained proficiency every year, but it was obvious he rarely resorted to using it.

Why threaten anyone with a weapon when what he was could be seen as threat enough?

"Mage Segara." He was pleasing to the eye, his shaggy black locks and a few days' worth of stubble giving him a more boyish countenance than his position demanded, a youthfulness offset by the world-weariness of his warm brown eyes. But Jia was not going to fall into familiarity merely because he had a handsome, friendly face.

"What do you know of your brother's whereabouts last night?"

Her relaxed stance did not change. Her neutral, inquisitive expression did not change. But the mage sensed the tension that raced through her on the rush of her blood, tightening every muscle. He could hear the increased speed of fluid through her veins, feel the strengthened pounding of her heart as if his hand lay on her chest with the organ beating beneath it. And he noted the narrowing of her pupils, a telltale clue of discomfort.

"He was home…with his children and wife."

"You were with him? All night?"

Her lips pursed. "After the wedding, yes, until he left this morning."

"That would be the wedding of the Laedan's son to the Hallister heiress?"

"Was there another worth attending?" Her tone, clipped and cool, dripped with more sarcasm than intended. Others of the Protectorate had been present, mingling in last night's crowd, but to her knowledge, he had not been one of the guests. She would have detected the strangeness of his mage blood over the normalcy of everyone else's. "What is this about?"

Vance shook his head dismissively. "A shipment of mediplies was pirated not far from his Center; there is reason to suspect..."

"You think because he is a doctor, he is also a thief?" She huffed, crossed her arms, but then allowed them to fall to her sides again. She could not afford to coil protectively into herself, not if fight or flight was to become a necessity.

Movement in the rafters suggested that the Omega was aware of them, stirred by their voices and her agitated mood. If the mage sensed the additional entity in the area, he did not show it.

"I am exploring the possibilities, nothing more. As I said, the pirating..."

"How did you find us?"

Vance refused to move as she began to circle him with measured, stalking steps. Wondering if this was the way an animal felt when a predator circled before the kill, he widened his stance and chose not to follow her movement with his eyes. "One of the Center's staff..."

"If you were already there, you could have spoken with Addi yourself...saved you the trouble of coming here..."

"He was not there; it was early," Vance admitted. "And in truth, I came more specifically to ask about your father..."

"What about my father?"

Her footsteps stopped behind him and he struggled against the impulse to crouch, to turn, to react to the sudden certainty that she would lunge and snap his neck between her jaws.

He was also struggling to conceal the more intimate effect that excitement was producing. He did not have a death wish…but damn if the thought of her mouth at his neck and throat, even if a mouth of ripping sharp fangs, had not gone straight to his groin.

"Who sent you? Who hired you?"

Undaunted, Vance swallowed and continued, "He has been missing for more than seven days; is that correct?"

"Lowell." Maybe Jonni, in his unending quest to prove his worth to her, maybe even Nik as the middle Channon son was prone to irrational actions for no reason other than they seemed good choices in the moment he made them. But it was more likely that the Laedan had finally taken it upon himself to begin an investigation into his partner's whereabouts. Jia could not blame Lowell for it; the two co-Laedans had been friends their entire lives and she knew Lowell was concerned about Roland's absence…or at least he feigned concern…but she had not expected Lowell to hire the mage.

Or maybe, she thought with a flutter in her belly, the decision to bring in outside help was Liam's. Jia had talked enough about doing so, had been discouraged from it by the majority of the Pack, but it would be just like Liam to take the matter into his own hands so that she did not have to go against the wishes of the Pack. Liam, gentle soul that he was, had sworn long ago to support her in any way he could, even to the point of taking heat from the Pack on her behalf and risking becoming an outcast, just as Deuce had done long ago.

"What do you know of his absence?"

Lifting her chin, Jia sniffed the air and her nose wrinkled in response. Fear. At last. This mage was as afraid of what she could do to him as she was of what he could to do her. She had never known a man, a normal, to be directly afraid of her. Other than the standard fears people carried about anthro, she had never given another person cause to fear her. The rush such a power gave her was intoxicating, and though she did not want this man to be afraid of her, fear was something she could use to her advantage until she knew whether she could trust his motives. There was no scent of dishonesty about him, no hint of underhandedness or intention to bring HOPE down on the

Pack, but innocent of intention or not, his being here was a threat. Above them, Deuce obviously shared her concern as he shuffled around to find a better position from which to listen.

It was a threat she was going to have to address as soon as he went his way.

She took a few more steps until she again stood in front of him, face to face, no more than six inches between them, so that she could judge if his eyes spoke of the same honesty as his scent. So close, the perfume of his truths became hopelessly entangled with the traces of mage that set him apart, entangled with the heady intoxication of his masculinity. She needed distance, she thought abruptly. This was not safe. This would never do.

Aware that they were not alone, that the Cana he had sensed that morning, at the site of the triple homicide, was moving above them, Vance flexed his fingers, wondering if he was going to need to fight his way out of this building in order to stay alive. Not that he would get far, if the remainder of her Pack was nearby. They would either fall on him in the street or run him until he dropped of exhaustion and then rip him apart where he fell. He cleared his throat and focused on her face, shutting out the distractions that were preventing him from doing his job. At least if he died on duty, he would have a decent memory service…if his body was ever found.

"He did not go scavving in the east." He knew it then, in the tiny lines at the corners of her mouth and eyes, in the weight that burdened her shoulders and echoed through the hollow halls of her heart, knew it with a certainty that only a mage could know things. Not all truths came so plainly, so clearly, but this one struck with a force that could only be matched by his having experienced that loss himself. "He had no hand in this theft." It did not matter what the Laedan had said. Vance was certain of his deductions.

His temples throbbed and his eyes narrowed at the pain.

In spite of her intentions, urged by the turn of his lips and the softening of his features that hinted at an understanding and empathy she had not expected him to possess, she sighed, the sound long and forlorn in defeat.

"An ambush…he was…shot…taken…"

That was not the explanation Vance had anticipated. A death, perhaps, illness or injury that his family was hiding in an effort to avoid quarantine, but not an abduction. Nor had he expected that fleeting moment when he wanted nothing more than to capture her face between his hands and kiss her. What the hell was wrong with him? Blinking in surprise at her words and his reaction to her proximity and perceived vulnerability, he asked in a rough voice, "Taken by whom?"

The change of expression snapped her out of the spell-like trance he had held over her and Jia took a guarded step back with a snarl, a sound directed as much at herself as it was at him. "I don't know," she snapped. Of course he was empathetic; he was a tracker mage. It was how they worked. "Isn't that your job? To know these things?"

Startled again, this time by the unexpected change between them, the moment of desire thankfully put behind him, Vance forced his shoulders to shrug while he straightened his stance and forced his emotions deep into his belly. "Why didn't you report this?"

He knew why. Without a word, without a touch to relay a thought, an image, or a sound, he saw it. Saw the man bent over a fallen comrade, saw a glint of shine from a bolt gun before its taut line snapped, a sound that he heard even as the victim commanded his daughter to run.

He saw the insignia caught in a glimmer of moonlight that revealed every fear for the man that this woman shouldered. She had seen it too, the memories he was viewing being hers, but she had yet to consciously recall that split second image to mind.

"HOPE."

That complicated his search more than Vance had bargained for, but the revelation did not surprise him. If HOPE had any inkling of the truth now confirmed for Vance, or had even a trace of suspicion that the co-Laedan was not of pure human lineage, the order for capture, for proof, for justice, would have been swift and complete.

But as one of the borough's oldest and most elite families, having loyally served LaGuardia from the time of the Undoing alongside the

Channons, how could such a secret have been held for so long…and what could have changed to expose it? Would Lowell have turned on his best friend if such a secret came to light?

To Vance, that answer was, 'undoubtedly'.

"I will help you find him."

"We will find him." Jia charged back into the street, aware now that her unsettled state had agitated the restless Omega in the rooms above and that he was preparing for a fight. Maybe Deuce would take care of the problem of Vance Segara so that she would not have to. She wanted to trust this mage, knew what sort of invaluable service such an individual could provide both in the search, in the finding, and, if they were lucky, in the retrieval of her father. But the Pack's wishes swayed her choices, even when each of her instincts pushed her toward the opposite conclusion.

Again Vance shrugged. Her choice was no surprise. Anthro had no reason to trust a stranger who could easily betray them to the Protectorate, to the Laedan, or even to HOPE. HOPE employed mages to hunt anthro and hidden mutani: Jia had no reason to trust him to either do as he promised or to keep her and her Pack's secret safe. He was not going to stop his search because Jia and her family were already seeking Roland's whereabouts. Vance had Laedan Channon, and his own conscience, to answer to. But proving himself to her by finding her father was suddenly a significant driving impulse. "If I find anything…"

The crunch and splash of boots stamping through disintegrating concrete puddles prevented Vance from saying more and kept Jia from verbally refusing or rebuking him for interference. Addison, his coat collar drawn up and held closed around his neck with a gloved hand, hesitated in his approach upon recognizing the uniform of the man who followed his sister from the dilapidated structure. His hesitation was brief, however, and he pulled his hair from his face as he stopped beside and slightly behind his sister. He might have situated himself behind her, but it was a protective stance. Addi had his sister's back against whatever threat the Protector represented.

Had Roland been the Pack's Alpha? Was this sprite of a Cana before him the Alpha now?

Vance's respect for her blossomed.

"Good, the man I was looking for." Addison had not given his name, but his behavior, the familial likeness they shared, and the similarity in their auras were clues enough for a mage. Vance ignored Jia's growl, choosing not to reveal the deduction he had made about her position within this Cana pack or the physical reaction he had to the growl. He saw no useful reason to prove that he understood her world. This was not the first Cana pack he had come across, but it was, he suspected, the strongest. He had come here on duty, not to cause trouble where there was none. He was not going to allow an overzealous, overprotective sibling, even the possible pack alpha, to keep him from it.

"Don't answer him."

Addi scowled at his sister before dutifully facing the other man, his face set into an amenable smile. "Protector. What can I do for you?" His expression already bore traces of worry as he toyed with the scrap of paper hidden in his jacket pocket. He did not think the Protector's presence was a coincidence. Normally he would have heeded Jia's request, but if there was a connection between the Protector and what Addi already knew, he wanted to hear it.

Wondering if he had misjudged her strength and position if even her brother would disobey her, Vance nodded once. Undoubtedly, the doctor's line of work brought him into daily contact with the Protectorate, as the wounded, the lost, the ill were brought to his clinic for care, frequently enough in the custody of a Protector that their uniformed presence did not unsettle him as it did his sister. It was obvious in the easy way Addi offered his hand, unwary, unpresuming of the man's status as mage…if he even made the effort to identify him as such by the badges on his lapel. Maybe he consciously chose to answer the questions to protect his pack, to protect his sister.

Not all members of a pack were anthro, for some children born into that life were as human as any pureblood could be, but Addison Marrock was as Cana as his sister. Vance saw it, but the clues in

Addi's aura were less obvious to the mage than they were in Jia. He wondered why that was.

"Were any wounded scavs brought into your facility during the night…or this morning? Did you treat any of them?"

Addi's furrowed brow lasted only for a brief moment of thought. "None I'm aware of," he replied, "but we do not normally make a habit of inquiring after a person's line of work."

"You were on duty overnight?"

"No…no, I was home…" Now Addi did glance at his sister, a flash of concern about where this line of inquiry was going giving rise to further hesitation. A missing person, perhaps, or the suspect in another crime, but it felt as if Addi was being viewed as a suspect and that concerned him. Perhaps he should not have volunteered information as his sister had demanded, but too much was at stake for him not to take the risk.

"Were you expecting any deliveries yesterday? Today? Mediplies? Provisions? Did you receive anything like that?"

"I wish we had, but no," he chuckled, the sound more forced than relaxed. "We're operating on a shortfall of everything these days. The last promised distribution was three weeks ago…"

It was Vance's turn to scowl, making note of the man's word choice. Promised…with the implication that no such distributions had been made. "You receive distributions from the Laedans' warehouses?" He sidestepped casually away from the discomfiting proximity of Jia's rising annoyance.

"Supposed to…but the sleet storm caused the last to be deferred; there's been no reschedule, despite petitions to the Laedan."

The shadow that ghosted across Jia's face indicated she had not been aware of this critical development. Addi could not see it, but he knew the look was there. He would be grilled for that oversight of truth later, but later would not be today. His petition had been made through their father, however, and not for the first time had Roland resisted his son's requests. Making another petition through Jia, who had not officially accepted her father's duties within the Fortress, would mean forcing her into those duties, and Addi was not the sort of man to make such demands on his twin. He would get what he needed some other way or the Center would make do without.

That did not, however, mean he would resort to theft. The possibility that someone on his staff might have, however, was a very real one.

The Protector was also troubled, but there was no hint of the cause of his concern or expression of it beyond the nod of his head.

"Would it be much trouble if I inspected your stores?" It would mean retracing his steps to the medifac, but he had not considered taking an inventory before when his focus had been on finding Addison. If the doctor had participated in, or been responsible for, the theft of a wagon of mediplies, he would surely be smart enough not to stash them where they could easily be counted. Vance did not believe he would find anything now but felt he had to make a show of the search to support his questions.

There was no trace of falsehood in the doctor; he was an open volume of honesty and kindness. Vance had rarely known his instincts to be wrong, but there was a reason the Laedan suspected Addi of theft. If this mission was less about recovering stolen property...or if the property had not been stolen...but rather Vance had been sent here to gain proof that the Marrocks were anthro, enemies of the state...then the mage first had to learn what had been taken and from where...and what that had to do with the Marrocks.

What had begun as a simple enough duty now appeared as if it would take longer than expected, straying into darker corners than anticipated. Vance was going to need help.

"Of course," Addi agreed quickly. He wanted that inventory now too. If one of the other doctors was guilty of such a theft, he wanted to know. He did not know what he would do if it was discovered to be true. Doctors, like supplies, were in great demand. Such a theft would not be fair to other Centers, but did it really matter as long as the supplies were used to help those who needed them?

It was a moral dilemma Addi did not have an answer for.

"You'll have to go without me, however...my wife's condition demands attention..."

"Condition?"

"She is with child."

Vance nodded. Pregnancies since the Undoing were precarious things. It was understandable that the doctor would be concerned about her welfare. If Vance had been in his position, he too would have been checking on her well-being multiple times a day.

"I understand. Thank you. Ms. Marrock." Vance had not forgotten the woman was there. In fact, he seemed unable to forget she was nearby even after putting distance between them. The nerves on the right side of his body tingled as though rubbed raw by her company. "I will be in touch, let you know what I find."

"Suit yourself." She tucked her arm through her brother's and steered Addi away, ending the encounter with the mage rather like a petulant child might end an unpleasant moment, before the man asked any more questions or learned anything more about her. She could feel his eyes following her briefly before he trekked off in the direction of the Center, his hands stuffed into the pockets of his coat and his head bowed to plow through the rising cold wind. She could sense Deuce's powerful presence on that chilling breeze and wondered for a moment if she should send the Omega after the mage to prevent him from disclosing the Pack's location to anyone.

Not knowing what other skills the mage might possess, however, might mean sending Deuce to his death. The rest of the Pack might be little concerned with the Omega's fate, but Jia did not want him to die. He had been a fixture with the Pack since the day she had drawn breath and long before. She could not imagine him absent there on the fringes of her life.

Addi wrapped one arm around Jia's shoulders and pulled her against him with a kiss on her temple. He was relieved that, on the surface at least, the Protector's visit had nothing to do with the message he carried. "He's only doing his…"

"He's asking questions about Father."

The amusement dropped from Addi's demeanor and he stopped, forcing Jia to do so as well in the middle of the street. "It had to happen," he muttered, twisting his fingers around the note in his pocket. "Someone other than us is going to miss him. Did he say who put him on the trail?"

"He would not confirm it…but it has to be Lowell. Who else has the resources to employ a mage…"

"Mage?" Addi's features now turned to worry. He had never encountered a mage amidst the Protectors who passed through the medifac's doors and was not familiar with the variety of rank insignia those in uniform wore. It was commonly believed that mages did not wear the standard uniform of the Protectorate, another reason such individuals were considered so dangerous. They could be anyone passed on the street. With this man being in uniform, it had not occurred to Addi that he could be a mage.

And if Lowell had been the one to send him, then there might be more of a tie to his unshared message than Addi had at first feared. Voice heavy with near panic, he drew the piece of hemp paper from the inner breast pocket of his coat and offered it to Jia. "Then we've…here…read this…it was delivered not long ago. I was on my way to the Center…stopped to aide a child with a fractured arm when the messenger found me…I came straight home."

Hence his absence from the Center when the mage had been there. It was a surprise the two had not crossed paths on the way.

Recognizing Jonni's crisp scripting of her name upon the page, and also that the Channon seal had been broken on the folded edge, presumably by her brother, Jia read the contents hastily, feeling no need to berate Addi for a breach of privacy. She had no secrets from him, not even Jonni's affection or her reasons for choosing not to reciprocate the feelings. She expected the note to be a request to meet, or a plea to be given another chance to court her from a young man who refused to accept her rebuff. What she read, however, made her blood curdle in her veins.

His voice low, as if it would hide his words from Uncle in the doorway of their home and the other man hidden in the shadows across the street, Addi dropped his head closer to hers so that their foreheads pressed together. They had often talked this way as children, as if the contact would aid in the sharing of thoughts between them. "Why would Quentin…?"

"I don't know." She drew comfort from her brother's touch and allowed it to ease the eruption of chaos within. What she did know was that the Pack could not remain where it was, could not risk being caught here, captured or killed outright, by those Jonni claimed were due to arrive. The percolating need to relocate that had begun to brew as a result of being tracked here by the mage was now at a rolling boil. If his visit here was meant as proof to Quentin of the Pack's location, Jia was going to hunt that mage down and rip his throat out herself.

Pulling away from her brother, she lifted her head, decision made, and shouted, 'Uncle!" She waved the other man over, aware that he had probably heard every word that had been said after she and Segara had come out of the opposite building, or most of them until the moment the mage departed. When he was close enough, she made no effort to disguise the situation, believing he knew the truth already, and thrust the neatly handwritten page into his hands. "We need to move. Now. Do you know where Pain and Maz…?"

"I know the quadrant." The Pack's territory was sectioned into four roughly equal locales; by knowing the quadrant the scavs would be in each day, or the quadrant where a hunt might be underway, it was easier to get messages to those away from the den in order to summon them.

"Call them back. We need them to help…"

Without bothering to read the message, Uncle asked, "Relocate? Where? Your father…"

Her growl silenced him, his expression now one of pained displeasure. "Is not here, and would want what is best for the Pack. If Jonni…"

"The Channons cannot be trusted…"

"Jonni is not like that." Whatever his faults, Jonni loved her. He would not express such a threat on a whim, not if it meant going against his father and bringing down more of the man's wrath upon him. Nor had she ever believed Nik to be a threat, not even in his most intoxicated moments. If any in that family were a threat, it was the

Channon mentioned in the note, Jonni's powerful father, and the other man mentioned whom Jia had never trusted.

If Quentin, the Laedan right-hand, was directing a raid against the Flushing Pack, the odds were the order had come from Lowell.

What did such an order mean to any efforts he was making to find Roland?

"He is his father's son." To Uncle, that should be enough to plant suspicion on every Channon boy. He grunted with a glance at the doorway where he had stood, then up to the rooftop where the echoes of children reciting their letters originated. He was loathe to believe the note to be anything other than a trap, but if by some twist it was an honest warning, ignoring it put the Pack at risk. He would never forgive himself if he did nothing and caused the Pack harm. If they relocated and nothing happened, at most it was an inconvenience.

"Where should we go?"

"I'll think of something." There was no ready answer for that question, no clear direction that would guarantee the Pack's safe retreat. Some Packs held three or more safe houses at the ready and often moved between them through the year in an effort to remain undetected by HOPE or any other entity that might wish them harm. But Roland had been, for most of his life, adamant about remaining settled, only uprooting his children by ferrying them back and forth between the Pack home and the Laedans' Fortress. If the Flushing Pack had any such safe houses or retreats, beyond those where they sometimes stored supplies and necessities to be used during or after hunts, Jia did not know of them, nor, apparently, did Uncle. She wondered if any of the others would.

"We should discuss our options…"

But despite his protest, the hastily read message was pushed back into her hand when her chastising gaze hardened and Uncle sprinted in the direction opposite where the Protector had gone, quickly disappearing around the corner. He could put out the call, and would if the men he sought were not easily tracked, because Jia was right. There was no time for discussion. With no given hour, only the day's date as the proposed timing of the raid, Pack debate about the future would create delays. The future would have to wait for discussion until their next moment of security in whatever shelter they could find or make.

"I will ready the others." Addi was already dashing into the den. If their belongings could be packed by the time Maz and Pain returned with the scav wagon, they could hastily load it and be on the move. The Pack had few possessions to transport, but the potted plants, rabbit hutch, goats and chickens would have to be moved or else abandoned.

No one would want to abandon the hard work for survival they had managed to eke out in this place Roland had called home.

"Alpha."

The tone of contrition belonging to the large man squatting behind her, though out of her easy reach, was unfamiliar as she had never heard Deuce speak. He never came near enough to the Pack, or to her, to allow conversation, and there was some belief amongst the Pack that the Omega could only form animal sounds, the deep howl that often joined with the rest of the Pack, not the language of a civilized, learned man. If any of the others in the Pack, or most of them at least, saw him with her, near enough to touch Jia if he stretched out his hand but making no effort to do so, they would rally an assault to drive him away. Some might choose to kill him for no more than rumors whispered about him. Jia's first instinct was retreat as well, an instinct based on a lifetime of indoctrination that he might attack. But never in all of his watchful days had Deuce threatened her, or anyone else in the Pack, and that knowledge overwrote the impulsive fear, allowing her to squat to his level when the gesture of her hand would not encourage him to rise.

"Deuce."

He looked at her warily and skittered backward in order to keep distance between them, and he endeavored to lower himself further without lying flat on the ground. Not even her gentle smile and the use of his name could reassure him into coming nearer, and for that Jia felt a moment of guilt. There were times as a small child when she, like the other children, had taunted him with thrown rocks and hurled insults, always from a safe distance and under at least partial adult supervision, behavior that few of the adults except for her mother had tried to discourage. When she began to understand her mother's admonitions, to understand the cruelty of her actions, Jia had stopped participating in the bullying, and gradually, as the months passed, she changed the behavior of the other children as well. Despite the efforts to rectify her wrongs, however, it had not been enough to undo the damage done by hurtful words and actions.

"What do you wish?"

Deuce shook his head in refusal, not asking for anything for himself. That was not his place. "I know somewhere, a safe place…"

Jia would have glanced at her brother for a second opinion, or gotten one from Liam if he had been beside her, but she was alone now, alone with Deuce, and as she had indicated to Uncle, there was no time for a lengthy discussion about the Pack's future. The choice to trust Deuce's offer or reject it had to be made on her own.

But did she dare trust the outcast Cana enough to accept an unknown haven?

He had never attempted to cause the Pack harm despite their cruelties. Perhaps he saw this as his moment of revenge, his chance to lead them into greater peril then the impending raid portended. He followed Jia whenever she left the shelter of the Pack's company, perhaps to protect her, perhaps with the hopes of harming her, but for all of the opportunities he had been given, he had never tried, and his actions had never been those of retaliation. Instead, he stayed, always there, always watchful, when it would have been easier for him to have broken off, form his own pack or find shelter in another or settle into the life of a lone wolf.

All of those details, the choices he had made, and the eager eyes he kept trained on her face without looking directly at her, spoke to Jia of the mettle from which Deuce was made. It was upon that knowledge that she likewise chose to act.

"Where?"

His face brightened and his body quivered; if he had a tail, she imagined it would be wagging.

"Across the Flushing Wilds…"

A scowl ghosted across her round face but did not settle. The territory on the eastern side of the Flushing Wilds was largely unexplored, claimed by neither LaGuardia or Kennedy but instead by smaller territorial warlords, weaker than the Laedans of the boroughs but, when rallied together in coalition with the clusters of anthro and mutani living there, enough to keep the Laedans from pressing for eastern land. Both the Channons and the Hallisters, and thus to a degree the Marrocks, had focused their people's efforts on westward expansion, clearing streets of debris and resources, repairing what structures they could to use as livable space for each new generation born. They had never pressed east.

By taking the Pack East, she would be leading them into lands where the intended raiding party would not likely follow. It would take them out of harm's way, likely leave them safe so long as they could negotiate with whatever leaders they met on the other side.

Accepting his suggestion as the best possible, short-term, option, the safety of the Pack mattering more than whether they remained in LaGuardia borough or not, she nodded and offered her hand to shake on the deal. "When we are ready...lead me." It would not take the rest of the Pack long to determine her intentions, to realize the Omega was leading them, but Jia intended for them to be well on their journey to safety before anyone offered significant objection.

Hesitantly, Deuce's hand came forward. He touched his palm to hers, his expression hinting at what he expected her reaction to be. When instead she closed her small hand around his larger one, accepting his handshake with a smile, he smiled warily in return.

The first one, Jia wagered, he had made in many years.

≈Scratch the Sky≈

Chapter 6

The shelves in the storeroom of LaGuardia's Southeast Medifac were picked over, gaping holes between opened, partially empty containers speaking of the lack of which Addison had spoken. The room smelled of spilled antiseptic alcohol, stale hemp-board packaging, and too many bodies having come and gone over time. Soft echoes of voices remained within the walls, common medical chatter amongst co-workers, whistling snatches of tune, mutters to oneself, but nothing that hinted at a crime. The only crime here was the failure of the Laedans to provide the provisions promised to their people. Whatever the cause of the previously aborted shipment, there had been plenty of opportunity in the weeks hence to rectify the matter, to send the mediplies as agreed.

If this stolen shipment had been the Laedan's effort to make good on the agreement, it was even more imperative that Vance found it quickly.

Since the Undoing, mediplies of any sort were low as it was, humanity forced to fall back to older, more invasive, less reliable means of treating ailment and injury. There were more than a few circulating the boroughs who claimed medical knowledge and miracle cures, and the all too rare healer-mages, but facilities such as this, which gave training as well as aid, gave hope. Roland had vetted each Center thoroughly, as had his father and grandfather before him, before adding each Center to the roster of those sanctioned to receive mediplies from the government's protected stash. Without official approval, the only means of procuring mediplies and provisions was to scavenge them from homes, ruined clinics, discovered warehouses, or to create their own...or, for the less scrupulous, steal it from sanctioned locations. Such theft was rare and had been what Vance expected to find when Channon sent him on this hunt.

But if anyone on the staff of LaGuardia Southeast was guilty of theft, they had not brought that supply here. On the off chance that one of the staff was involved in the alleged heist, Vance questioned everyone in the building, patients included, and took down the name of staff who were not present this day with the intention of questioning them as well. What supplies they did have appeared to have been there for some time, and every individual Vance spoke with who had access to that storage room spoke honestly of their lack, of their wait for promised materials that had never come, of the strain that shortage created on their ability to treat their patients. There was no hint of falsehood in any of them, just as there had been none in Addison.

His failure to find anything of use, save for the expanding proof that no theft had been committed by Dr. Marrock or his co-workers, compounded with the questions raised during his visit with the Marrock siblings, encouraged Vance to go back to the beginning, to find the location of the piracy, the origins and intended destination of the cargo, and brought him back to the borough's headquarters with his head throbbing and a deep frown on his face.

"Bad one?" asked Sal who, seated on the bench in front of her locker, had already changed out of her uniform for the day and was lacing up her boots. She watched Vance out of the corner of her eye, knowing he felt uncomfortable when people stared and having no desire to draw his unnecessary focus.

Vance grunted and began to tug off the uniform shirt, grateful that his skin could breathe and not itch beneath the stiff, formal fabric any longer. "The three bodies were...?"

"Disposed of accordingly," she answered, neither surprised nor put off by his avoidance of her question. Vance had never liked to talk about work outside of work, and as both were going off duty, that was off duty enough for him to keep his thoughts on work to himself. "Report's been submitted."

"Good." It was one less detail in a sea of details he had to worry about. He was grateful Sal had none of a Protector's usual aversion to reports and paperwork. "Gonna need your help tomorrow."

She lifted one eyebrow but rather than ask what he intended, what he wanted, she remained silent, waiting for him to continue.

"Stolen mediplies. Once I get some addresses, I'll need you to head over to one or the other…try to track down their path…where it went wrong…what's missing."

Because there was nothing unusual in such a case, except for the fact that it was not the sort Vance was typically assigned to, Sal nodded in agreement. "Let me know when and where." There might be more skilled or qualified individuals in the Protectorate, but none he trusted more. His trust in her was why she agreed to his request without asking for further details.

"Got your usual beat tomorrow?"

She nodded and slung her dirty beige hemp and leather jacket over her shoulder. "As of this moment, yeah."

"Then I'll find you." First, he was going to have to learn from the Laedan the details of the warehouses involved on the shipping and receiving ends…and perhaps the locations of all other Channon warehouses as well. His suspicions that he was being lied to demanded the truth from the Laedan and his mayor-sons, as well as his staff. Vance did not, however, believe he was going to get cooperation from any of them.

ᚥ*ᚥ

In their haste to return the scav wagon to the clinic, a wheel was lost with a loud crack that sank the right rear corner into a muddy hole deeper than the men had anticipated. The goods they had scavenged that morning had been hastily unloaded, left on the street where the wagon collapsed, an unfortunate loss but one less important than the impending threat to home and Pack. With no spare wheel on hand for repair, for which Pain and Maz blamed each other, it was up to the three men to maneuver the wagon through the streets to home, two supporting the disabled rear of the wagon while the third pulled the front by the tongue. Though designed to be pulled by a pack animal, a mule, ox, or something equally strong enough to manage a wagon of its size, the Pack had no such animal in its care; it had meant refashioning the wagon to be pulled by one or two men, modifications that proved to be their saving grace now.

But it also meant the wasted passage of time and meant arriving at the clinic later than Uncle intended, much later than the Pack could graciously accept. Furthermore, it meant time spent replacing the broken wheel while the adults sniped at each other, and then a hasty loading of plants, animals, their water-collection system, cooking utensils and hoarded weapons, as well as the books the Alpha had spent years collecting on the Pack's behalf. Clothing, bedding, and personal items were stuffed into packs and sacks to be carried by the individuals who owned them. With Addi, Ilba, Zen and Liam acting as sentries at the head of each of the three most likely paths a raiding force could take to reach them, and the seven-month pregnant Trill supervising the youngest children, loading fell to the older children and to the men who had spent the bulk of their energy dragging the wagon home and repairing it as quickly as possible. From the clinic roof, Jia scanned the horizon, overseeing the moving of the garden while she watched for movement that might not be noticeable from the ground positions of her packmates.

Time was fleeting, slipping away too quickly now that the sun, hidden behind the perpetual blanket of clouds, was beginning its descent below the city skyline. Hindered by the limitation of the human eye, the four distant sentries would now have taken a more capable, agile form, but it was a form that, if they were spotted, would prove what their purported hunters expected them to be. Night monsters, animals, uncivilized and dangerous inhuman creatures, worthy of capture and experimentation if possible, or death if necessary. Each would be hidden, more familiar with their surroundings then their hunters would be, but the risk was still present, greater than Jia was comfortable exposing them to.

But it was a risk some of them had to take if the Pack was to be saved, and those taking it were the best ones for the task. Two had volunteered, two she had been forced to appoint, and though the Pack had accepted her judgment, she knew that, should anything go wrong tonight, the burden of failure was going to fall on her shoulders for the choices she had made.

Just as they would have fallen upon Roland's shoulders if he had been here to make the decisions instead.

Furtive movement in the distance, along the perimeter of the heavily forested curb, obscured the long shadows cast by the bent fingers of empty buildings, drew Ilba's attention from the point on the street she had focused on for the past several minutes. More the movement of prey, she thought, of those leery of being captured, then those who were hunting, and so she crept closer, mimicking their movements as she darted from one rusted hulk to another, obstacles that provided shelter but no longer obstructed this particular roadway. Her own actions made her scowl as she waited for the creeping wraiths to reappear. If she mirrored their movements in stalking them, it was possible that they too were stalking. Hunting.

Uncertain, she held her breath and waited.

Zen noted the gesture, the waving of an arm by the lone figure traveling at a seemingly casual pace down the center line of the maze-like path through the fog-drenched street. Beneath the cracked, mossy pavement, the tunnels were full of rainwater and sewage, the lowest collection point from the neighboring streets, and for reasons she did not understand, the ambient temperature mix of the street air and the runoff created a nearly perpetual fog between this stretch of buildings. It was an ideal location for an ambush, a favored place for the Pack to hunt and play beneath the light of a full moon, but as this evening spread thicker, this was no place for play.

She could not see the movement on either side of the road, but the turn of the traveler's head, as slight as it was, with each gesture of its arm, suggested that the brazen explorer was not alone. And the cut of its black leather coat, the tight-fitting cowl that covered all but the individual's nose and mouth, and eyes hidden behind goggles, were a recognizable thing to anyone in the borough. Zen scurried back to a more hidden vantage point and tipped back her head.

Her howl of warning, when it came, was not the first to shatter the twilight's muffled silence. Several streets to her left, through the darkest path passable to any large beast or man that chose to journey to this corner of the borough, Addi's deep-throated howl ended in a yip in time for Zen's to join it, a tandem warning to those nearly a mile behind that the hunters they feared had arrived. Those that Addi saw, however, were less secretive in their movement, a steady pounding of marching feet that foretold their coming before he actually saw them. He did not wait for visual confirmation of their presence; Cana hearing recognized the sounds at a significant distance, untangled their direction of origin from the myriad of other early evening sounds the borough was prone to, and guessed at their position from the sounds and the scent of them. Their steady pace would put them in range of home, and the pups, in less than twenty minutes; without knowing if the wagon was repaired and loaded, without knowing if the Pack had yet to get underway, twenty minutes was a risk Addi could not allow. Trill had to get the children away. She had to be safe, and it was his responsibility to assure that the Pack had every possible moment to make it to safety.

Rearing up on his hind legs, his tailless Cana form of dusty brown silhouetted by the glow of a single torch burning in the doorway of some other resident on this street, Addi threw his head back, pointed his muzzle at the starless sky, and howled again before charging forward to greet the hunters.

He intended to disappear into the shadows, safe out of range of any bolts or spears the hunters carried, before any of them had the chance to take aim. It would set off a hunt for the too bold Cana, but better they hunt for him than the pups.

He hoped the other sentries chose to take the same initiative.

A howl, a sound more animal than human, echoed from a street to the east, her brother's howl, followed in short order by two more voices, Zen and Ilba, the indicator that their hunters had chosen to encroach from multiple directions, the three least traveled, more difficult paths to take instead of the easiest, most direct route from LaGuardia's Fortress garrison to the southeast corner of District 3. Gathered around the wagon, the men and women there, as well as the children, looked at one another in distress as they realized that the majority of their escape routes were cut off. There were other routes, known only to the Pack, which would afford them escape into LaGuardia's inner heart, but each would be slow going with their wagon of necessities in tow and young children to protect.

By the time Jia reached the street, her heart thundered faster as she listened to the four distinct howls communicate changes in position as they wove through abandoned buildings and alleys, the echoes created by that seemingly random movement designed to confuse their hunters as to their location and number but easily understood by the Pack. The wagon had been turned in the street to face the only passage north out of their territory left to them.

"Turn around!" Jia shouted, pointing south in the direction the wagon had previously faced.

"There's nowhere to go!" barked Pain, his lean features set in defiance despite Maz's hesitancy at the head of the wagon. One of the three men stopping meant that the wagon ground to a halt and the others stumbled as the metal forked tongue lurched against them.

"East! We go east!" They could travel south, into the wasteland between LaGuardia and Kennedy, but that was not the recommendation Deuce had given. They would go east, back in the direction where Pain and Maz had been scavenging earlier that day, in the direction of freedom.

"There's nothing there," wailed Trill, her hands covering her son's ears although it was not enough to keep out the angry shouts or the distant yips and howls of their packmates. It was terror Trill would spare the children, if she could. "We cannot risk…"

Maz nodded, a hand reaching into the wagon bed to still the woman's hysteria, reading Jia's intention in her eyes now that she was near enough to be visible in the twilight. There was merit in her plan, if a plan it was, and if it was a spur of the moment decision, well, he mused with a clearing of his throat, there was merit in that as well. "Into the Wilds."

"Beyond the Wilds," she corrected with an appreciative flicker in her eyes. Where beyond the wilds they could go, she did not know, and there was no way to force the Pack to follow the Omega to safety without Jia appearing to have formed the notion on her own. They would flee along routes they knew as a Pack, into the Flushing Wilds where they could lose their hunters long enough to regroup and formulate a more solid plan.

"We go north."

Eyes blazing red as the metamorphosis began to spread through her veins, a necessity she could not resist if she was to keep her father's Pack safe, Jia lunged at Pain with a snarl that stopped mere inches from his nose, daring him to challenge her. "They mean to drive us into a trap. Why do you think they cut us off on three routes…left us only one known road back into the borough? They want us to go that way."

Liam had given no report of hunters being within visual range on that main road, but the odds were a blockade or ambush had been set far enough out that he had not detected it, far enough out that anyone fleeing in terror would not know it was there until it was too late to turn the wagon around. By that time, the raiders would have circled behind and cut off their retreat.

"They won't follow us into the Wilds or beyond…they have no authority there…"

"Nor do we…."

"Better chances there," Maz said with a note of deep affection for the protesting Middle-eastern dissenter, "then against them." He thumbed over his shoulder toward the chaos which was growing steadily closer. The zig-zagging calls of the Cana were slowing the approach, but none had faith that it would hold off the raid for long. If they wasted many more minutes arguing, they would lose any advantage to the escape their packmates were giving them.

Uncle knew it too, and although he was not comfortable with the risk Jia suggested, moving the children into the unfamiliar, potentially hostile territory of the Wilds, it was a better risk than remaining where they were and hoping to fight off what was likely at least two dozen or more Channon guards.

"We go east," he grunted, taking the decision out of Pain's hands by working with Maz to turn the wagon. With a limited turn radius, however, and continued reluctance from Pain, the effort took longer than it should have…until Deuce erupted from the shadows across the street, grabbed the wagon tongue with both hands, and yanked the wagon the rest of the way around with a strength that surprised everyone. The newly repaired wheel creaked against the strain, and the load on the bed shuddered against the sideboards, but the repair held, the load remained secure, and Deuce jumped clear of any fists that might have been aimed at him by the startled men left to maneuver the wagon.

A different sound, a yelp of injury, pulled Jia's attention away from the wagon, away from Deuce. Addi's yelp. The hair sprouting across her skin stood on end as she arched her neck from side to side to ease the tension of the shift from human to something other. The three men could manage the wagon. Her efforts were better spent aiding her brother, working with those who might well sacrifice their lives in an effort to see the pups and their supplies to safety. "I'll buy time! Keep the children safe!"

"Jia!" shrieked Rief, her tear-streaked face set in horror at the realization that she might lose one or all of the few living blood relatives she had remaining. She stretched forth her arm as if to pull her cousin back, but it was too late. Her hand came back filled with nothing but air and empty promise.

"You can't…" Trill's cry rang simultaneous to that of the girl who sat near her clinging to two of the younger children as they held on to the sideboards of the bouncing wagon beginning its hasty journey east. The deep brown of fur, the snarl of fangs and the flick of sharp ears had already replaced Trill's sister-in-law, however, as Jia bounded northwest into the darkness, the bipedal Cana form affording her speed and agility that would ensure survival and that of those she ran to assist better than her human form could.

"Go!" If the three pulling the wagon at their top speed considered hesitating, considered following Jia into battle, the Omega's deep growl, which ended in a more familiar Cana howl, spurred them to continue. None were prone to obeying the outcast, saw him as anything more than a tolerated shadow on the edges of their life, but at this moment they knew he had the Pack's best interest at heart. Of one mind now in the interest of protecting the pups, the three shifted in unison so that their Cana strength enabled them to run through the night with their precious cargo at a speed the approaching hunters would find difficult to match.

Two blocks to go and they would be engulfed by whatever safety the Wilds would bring. Two long blocks of praying to whatever fates bound the universe that Jia's decisions would prove to their benefit.

Behind them, the Omega leaped after the brown Cana he would give his life to protect…whether Roland had ever believed it or not.

By the time Jia located her brother, the hunters, now running to find and capture their prey, were less than a dozen blocks from the building the Pack called home. Addi's bicep bled, the gash there evidence of a metal bolt's grazing bite, but he was otherwise unharmed, his steps, his leaps from wall to vehicle to low tree branch were sure and steady, keeping him far enough ahead of his pursuers that none hit him a second time. Others shots were fired, but none came close, and as the twins were joined by Zen's pale blonde Cana form, and a bolt buzzed by Jia's ear, the cry that erupted behind was that of a man, not a wolf. It was joined by the gurgling of a blood cry that could only have come from one source.

Deuce.

Jia looked back, certain that, whatever the Omega's strengths were, he could not fend off a host of hunters equipped with weapons on his own. Claws dug into her arm, Addi's tight grip holding her back from a potentially vain pursuit. If Deuce was sacrificing himself for her, for the Pack, it was better to let him, better for them to join forces with Ilba and Liam and regroup with the rest of the Pack. They trusted the strengths of the Pack's older males, but three would never be enough to withstand the forces mounted against them if the hunters were to catch up.

Her duty was Pack. Though part of it, Deuce was an expendable pawn to be used as necessary in favor of the Pack's survival.

Her mournful howl of gratitude and farewell was joined by the strangled echo of Deuce's roar. A trio of black-clad Channon Guards erupted through the fog of this street and the massive dark-furred Cana skirted a fallen tree to disappear into the mist.

Jia's attention now shifted to the frenzied yapping and snarling somewhere ahead of them, the frantic sounds of a wolf pinned into a corner without means of escape, an angry, frightened sound that pulled her heart into her throat. Four Guards, net and shock sticks in hand, had followed the blonde male Cana into a street that, thanks to the recent collapse of an ivy weakened wall, was now a dead-end. Having not anticipated this change in what had been a reliable vein of travel, not having enough maneuvering room to poise and leap onto what may or may not have been a stable foothold, Liam was left with nowhere to run. Frightened, the Cana cried, the sound turning into one of relief as his four packmates leaped over the blockage from the other side. Ilba landed atop the debris, the foreboding shape of her black Cana towering and frightening enough with its sudden appearance to force the hunters to retreat a few steps. Zen, coming to her little brother's defense, launched herself from fallen stone, her paws barely touching the ground, to drop one hunter beneath her weight. Addi did likewise, feeling no remorse when his jaws closed around the wrist of the man he felled.

With one side of the net now dropped, those holding the other corners dropped theirs as well in favor of the long knives and club sticks they carried on their belts. Rather than aide their fallen comrades, confident that their training and weaponry would enable them to put down the anthro who dared assault them, the two stalked forward, unheeding the smaller she-wolf now snarling and pacing between them and the prize they had cornered. It did not matter to them which Cana they subdued. Their orders were to bring one or two back alive and kill the others. With no way to tell what human face each monster wore, it made no difference to them which Cana volunteered for death and which became the required prize.

With the other Guards now unhindered from pursuing the likely fleeing Pack, their element of surprise blown long before their objective came into sight, the men in this alley were free to act as they saw fit and necessary.

One heavy stick was thrown, its trajectory seemingly haphazard as it ricocheted off of the nearest wall on what should have been a harmless path. The handle struck Ilba's leg, tumbling her from her perch, causing her to roll down the mound of sharp concrete edges and broken spikes of rebar to land on her feet in the alley…but not without knocking Zen off of her adversary and into a scattering of glass shards. The flying stick, meanwhile, its course altered by the strike, flew sideways, and despite its slowed momentum, it still possessed enough force that, when it caught Jia across the temple, she crumpled to the dirt like a decapitated grubber.

Though no longer protected, her sheltering presence had served Liam well enough that now, furious with her injury, he yowled and leaped over her body, straight onto the nearest adversary's chest, his fangs slashing and snapping across the man's unprotected face. The Guard who wiggled free of Zen's aborted attack snatched up his shocker from where it had dropped, ignited the blue glow at the unshielded end, and charged at the Cana disfiguring his friend. Ilba pulled Zen to her feet and Addi's victim lay unconscious at his, but any intention the three had at subduing the Guard with the shocker was aborted by the arrival of another six Guards at the alley's end. With his sister down, and as far as Addi knew dead, he was not prepared to go down with her. The Pack needed each of them alive, as many of them as could make it out of this fight in one piece.

Her eyesight was blurred, the blow to her temple robbing her of clarity of sight and mind and the ability to hear anything except a loud ringing buzz in her skull, but Jia was aware enough of the incoming shocker and managed to bark a weak warning to Liam. The sound was drowned out beneath the thunderous howl of another, a bloody bulk of a being who cleared the cluster of debris without touching it, and after knocking two assailants aside with his forearm, snatched her immobile body from the melee and led the others to safety. With the others following, leaving Liam to crumple beneath the electronic sting of the shocker, Jia screamed out to him once more, her eyes locking onto his stunned, disbelieving blue ones' moments before the world went dark for them both.

≈Scratch the Sky≈

Chapter 7

It was a losing battle to trudge through unfamiliar landscape against the brutal north squall that forced its way between buildings in a pattern that created random whirlwinds in their path, hindered as he was by a woman more interested in exploring the nooks and crannies along the way or else complaining about the cold and the sting of the wind against her exposed red cheeks and nose. The obstacles that arose before them, where buildings had collapsed into roadways or abandoned automobiles had been left to the overthrow of nature, had to be scouted, judged each time to determine the ease of getting over or around, further slowing their progress. Most obstacles he could clear easily if he was alone. Vanya, however, would not be so lucky, and so Kato forced himself to find alternate routes time and again, pushing them further south than he intended to travel.

He had only been able to scout the trail a short distance during his hunt the night before, as he had not wished to stray far from his sister's side, and that ground had been covered before their pause for the midday meal. Not midday, he judged, but Vanya had been hungry and so they found a ledge of what had once been a vehicle overpass, facing south, which afforded them shelter from the wind though not the cold. Vanya wore nearly every article of clothing they possessed, and yet still she bemoaned the temperature and Kato, discouraged again by a roadblock which forced them to turn back and take a different street in order to bypass the destruction, was nearing the point of defeat for the day.

The autumn sun sank lower in the west, nearly lost now over the horizon, bringing with it the end of the increasingly shorter daylight, and soon it would be too dark for Vanya to travel safely. The pink tint in the western clouds and the silver grey of the moon peeping through the covering to the east was the only light to be had. There were no lights in windows here, no sounds of life in this dismal swath of city as they trudged north, providing protection from the detection and attack of most others, but there were always dangers to be found in the darkness, and Vanya could not fight them alone. It was better, he decided, to choose shelter for the night and hope for better weather and progress once daylight returned.

"Just a few more blocks," he promised Vanya with a playful boop on her nose to lighten her flagging spirits. "We'll find somewhere safe for the night."

Vanya nodded and yawned, her expression less than hopeful but entirely trusting of her brother's leadership. Hugging Peppermint close to her chest 'because he was cold', she mumbled, "Okay..." through too cold lips. She tried to quicken her pace to reach the end of that few more blocks more quickly, to please him. The faster she walked, the sooner she could sleep.

The distant echo of shouting, loud panicked voices, the stifled crying of frightened children and the rattle of wooden wheels carrying a too heavy burden on uneven roads, erupted from the silence, whether just now given voice or coming into hearing range as the distance between source and listeners grew shorter. Too distant, he realized, for Vanya to hear, as the woman continued to mutter to the bear against her chest and showed no recognition of external sounds, not even the crunch of his boots on the gravelly surface they walked on or the crunch of fallen autumn leaves. Kato grabbed his sister's arms and pulled her against him, listening to the night, determining where the threat hailed, where it was heading, and whether or not it was worth investigating.

He had little doubt there was a threat. The sounds of fleeing in haste were ones heard often before, this family or that dragging belongings behind as they fled whatever horrors their life had become, sometimes real, sometimes imagined, but always horrors nonetheless. Whatever those threats might have been, it had been the wisest choice, he had told himself each time, to stay away from it. The troubles of others were not his concern. He had troubles of his own, a sister to protect as he searched for some elusive future he could not define. He and Vanya could not afford to involve themselves in the difficulties of others, not even when she begged him in order to share company for a few hours upon the road.

Kato did not trust others. With Vanya's too trusting nature, he could not afford to. Thus he chose again to ignore the sounds and push north in search of the night's haven.

But as they hiked, facing into the icy wind, there was a rising scent in the air, the sweetness of dense foliage and clean, fresh water untainted by salt and the waste left behind by man. It was a new scent, reminiscent of his mother's garden, but stronger, more pungent, a certain sanctuary that would protect them from those who hunted ones like him…and hurt ones like Vanya. The pull was strong to run in the direction of the scents, to seek this shelter and drink deep of unpolluted waters, but the wariness of experience and the need to stay with Vanya held him back. Whatever that miracle place was, it would still be there come dawn, once Vanya had rested and the refugees he could still hear, whoever they were, were gone. He had made her a promise after all; he would not drag her into the path of danger to satisfy the call of his feral spirit.

In an effort to refuse the lure, he pulled Vanya into the next viable shelter he found, a corner structure that had once served as a convenience store, its shelves long ago pilfered of anything edible or of other marginal value. The windows were broken out, the glass stolen for some other use, allowing the elements to gradually erode the walls within, but the mechanical latch on the ice room door still functioned, and without power to operate the compressor unit, it would be warm enough, the tight seal providing a shelter protected from the wind and the cold as well as from passersby who had no reason to suspect someone might hide within it. It was the ideal place to settle Vanya for the night, the perfect place to protect her from the rise and fall of the continuing crash and clatter of refugees, an easy place for the Fela to protect her while she munched on honeycomb and berries and slept contentedly in the company of Peppermint. There was barely even the taint of spoiled milk or meat there any longer, smells that made the corners of Kato's lips curl but which Vanya did not notice.

Though confident she would be safe, Kato stepped out of the room, closed the door and latched it behind him, and gave rein to the stronger side of his nature. Long, powerful legs allowed him to leap easily onto the gradually sinking roof of the convenience store, where he settled on the domed front edge to keep watch. It was not the highest vantage point to be had, but it was adequate for his purpose; nothing was likely to drop down on him from the nearest buildings, and anything approaching from any of the four intersecting streets would be seen and dealt with, all threats negated before they knew Vanya was here.

Licking his paws clean of the day's travel, the Fela watched.

≫*≪

From the balcony he could not believe still supported weight, even after every repair he had made to ensure that it did, Vance guzzled his second metal tin of hemp beer, listening to the howls in the distance, howls that ricocheted between the borough's remaining structures in such a way that it was impossible to tell from which direction they originated. Nor could he tell, as he worked his way toward the night's alcoholic stupor, whether the howls belonged to the many wolves and wild dogs now freely roaming the lands mankind had once ruled, or whether the sounds belonged to Cana. Did Cana howl? Did they sound the same as wolves?

He knew no one who had ever compared the two.

What Vance did know, as he retreated out of the wind and the cold for the comfort of his lumpy, accommodating sofa, was the sound that bled in through the dirty glass panes of the balcony doors was desperate and terrifyingly afraid…and that knowing tore the mage's heart in two and kept him from his desired sleep for a very long time…in spite of the self-induced lethargy he intended to hide within as he did every night.

⊷*⊷

Lowell stared at the window, his expression long and grave, the frown etched there born of a dozen secrets he could never tell, secrets that not even the hidden flashes of desire given from the young woman across the table could ease. At Oasis' side, the new husband her father had abandoned her to cast long, ponderous looks at another, who only smiled the smile of a man too pleased with his own accomplishments and said, "The wolves are restless tonight."

Another howl, long and mournful, gave rise to a shiver across Yiva's shoulders. Donnovan's hand over hers in an apparent gesture of comfort gave rise to another.

"Indeed," Donn said, equally pleased to interpret the wild cries as proof of the success of Quentin's plan. "I wonder what has disturbed them so…"

Nik, toying with the green beans on his plate, fitting them into the outline of a house on a mountainside replied, "Full moon," in a sickly tone that stank of the weariness of addiction and intoxication.

Yanking Oasis to her feet suddenly and dragging her, off balanced, to the window, Donn craned his head from side to side as if seeking something outside before finally remarking, "Why so it is, Nik…come see…it is spectacular."

But as quickly as the words were spoken, a heavier shroud of clouds moved in front of the silver sphere, erasing all but a pale glow from sight, only the after image burning within Donn's mind. "Did you see, darling? Did you see it?"

The grip on her arm was a little too tight, his words too stern to be purely those of excitement over a rare viewing of the moon, but Oasis attributed that to the secret she knew he shared with Quentin, a secret that she was not privy to, a secret she felt she deserved to know. She needed his trust; it was unrealistic to expect to receive it so quickly after marriage, but she remained hopeful.

So it would take more time. She was patient. She had waited this long. She could wait a little longer.

"I wish they would stop," Yiva whispered, staring at her barely touched plate, hands clutched in her lap. "Lowell…make them stop."

A scowl of determination settled over her husband's face and he looked up after stabbing a cube of pork with his fork. "We shall," he promised. "A hunt…what we need is a hunt."

"Yes, a good old fashioned hunt," Quentin agreed, imagining a horse and foot chase through the streets on the quest for wolves, either four-legged or two-legged ones. The notion of spilling blood made him smile behind the cloth used to dab his mouth. "How long has it been? Shall I see to the arrangements?"

Lowell nodded, unaware, as he decided to eat with gusto and ignore the grating howls of the wolves, that a similar hunt had already been sanctioned and was underway as they dined.

Looking over his shoulder at Quentin, Donn smiled, a wicked smile Quentin graciously returned. If anyone other than Jonni noticed that exchange, they did not question its meaning. Fearing that his message had reached Addison and Jia too late to save them, that it might not have reached the woman he loved at all, Jonni swore that he would find some way to bring his brother, and Quentin, to whatever form of justice he was able to mete out if any harm had come to the Marrocks.

≈*≈

There was no stopping to rest, no opportunity to circle back in the hopes of finding Liam alive, unharmed, safe. When Jia swam back to her senses, became aware and clearheaded enough to desire the risk, she knew that truth even before Deuce planted her feet on the ground and bid her run with the rest.

The Guards pursued them still, but were less willing to veer off the straight path that brought them to the now empty shell which had housed the Flushing Pack for so many years. They would not destroy objects that could be confiscated and used; commodities were too rare and valuable to be wantonly destroyed. But they were making certain that, should the Pack return, there would be nothing left for them except the building's shell.

The five Cana paused only long enough to witness the methodical demolition of their home begin as men used hands, boots, and whatever weapons and tools they carried to turn over furnishings, break open empty crates or tear through obviously repaired walls with the hopes of finding their quarry hiding within. It was a long enough pause by the Cana, however, for the five to catch their breath. When the majority of the Guards, save for six selected to remain to explore the clinic and another four sent back to collect their dead and injured, broke away to push in the only directions the Pack could have gone, the five began to run again, this time intentionally fleeing to the southeast with howls meant to lead their hunters away from the Pack. The Guard divided, some choosing to follow the easterly path toward the Wilds, a few choosing to comb alleys north and west which the Pack might have chosen to hide in or sneak through, and the other, larger unit remaining on the trail of the five fleeing Cana stragglers.

They did not know how many the Pack held. They did not know if the five were all that remained.

The trail for anyone transporting children through the Wilds would grow steadily more difficult and unsafe, surely, in the uncontrolled, uncivilized eastern lands. An adult pack might chance it, assuming hybrid wolf form in order to disappear in the thick overgrowth of the Wilds which separated LaGuardia borough from that untamed chaos. It seemed likely the Pack would choose to keep their young safe so the easterly path into the Wilds seemed the least likely one for the Pack to take. It was not worth ruling out entirely, hence the contingent of Guards sent to push as far east as they dared in search of evidence that the pack had fled that way. If the Guards were lucky, perhaps the pack would be trapped at the fringes of the Wilds and could be exterminated there as their orders commanded.

The wasteland between LaGuardia and Kennedy, while uncontrolled by any significant ruling power, was known to be home to at least three Cana packs. Taking sanctuary among them, seeking safety in numbers, was surely the more logical direction for any frightened animal to choose. More easily traveled and free to be swept by teams from both LaGuardia and Kennedy when the need arose, so long as each side was mindful of traps and landmines planted by previous generations in an effort to protect their precious borough boundaries, anyone taking refuge there had to rely on those living in the region just to avoid losing life or limb to the hidden explosives. Maybe the guards would not need to kill their quarry. Maybe their reckless flight into the minefield would solve that problem for them.

Jia ran as the others ran, urged on by her brother and the unexpected service of the Omega at their side. The others chose not to question his company or his aid. He had saved Jia's life, had saved all of their lives, and was continuing to fight beside them in spite of the injuries he had sustained. Thick crimson dripped into his eyes from multiple head wounds, matted the patchy gray tipped fur across his torso and limbs, and he left crimson prints on the ground from the blood which dripped down his legs, a trail easily followed by those in pursuit. It pained him to continue, his eyes ran with tears of discomfort and exertion, but still he ran, his body shielding Jia's as best as he was able. The need that pushed him drew the others in his wake so that they struggled to keep up with his relentless pace.

Did the ache of his efforts match the gnashing pain that burned and tore her heart asunder with each step that drew Jia further away from Liam? Twice in so short a time, she had been forced to flee while those she loved were ripped from her life, twice she had been helpless to save them. Zen had left behind a brother, a pain Jia easily understood; if it had been her brother, only someone forcibly carrying her away, as Deuce had done, would have torn her from his side. But Jia had lost both her father, forced to leave him because his sense of duty demanded nothing less, and her dearest friend. She realized, as the sobbing growl forced tears into her red eyes and drove her to sprint past Deuce with a burst of furious speed in order to take the lead, that she had never given proper consideration to exactly what Liam Bardeau meant to her.

With the others unable to see her grief, she gave a baying howl to the barely visible moon, beseeching the universe to keep Liam safe and return him to her. If those external forces that controlled life and death could do that for her, she swore she would give Liam every thought and attention he deserved. Whatever that meant.

The Fela heard the sounds of running feet, a sound barely perceptible over the wind to human ears, a sound that carried with it the baying of wolves, a sound that made the cat's black fur prickle along the length of his spine. Behind those sounds, an even more uncomfortable set followed...the sound of men bearing the bitter stench of gunpowder and an electrical sting...men radiating with the reek of fear and hatred and dutiful fury.

Men hunting beasts.

Crouched, ears flat against his head as he poised in waiting, expecting to seek refuge in the building below where his sister safely slept, oblivious to the approaching bedlam outside, the cat watched the five Cana, most of them showing signs of injury, burst into the open intersection and fan out, giving the eighteen black-clad wraiths behind more difficult targets to hit. The hunters were far enough back that they did not immediately see where their quarry had gone, meaning that they too spread their force thinner, some peeling off to investigate each of the other three streets, some in pairs forcing their way into the structures that surrounded the intersection which might best serve as hiding places for their prey.

Kato growled, a sound lost in the howling gale, as one of the Cana disappeared into the building below. He was unfamiliar with Cana, had only known a few in brief passing acquaintance, but he trusted them no more than he trusted anyone else. He knew them to be rarely solitary, choosing to operate in swarms that were a threat to a lone individual like himself, and he had seen more than once the way they hunted, using the strength of numbers to take down even the strongest prey. This hunt, obvious as it was, did not concern him, and the odds were that, if he made his presence known, these hunters would not hesitate to capture or kill him as well.

Those that hunted anthro rarely cared which sub-species was caught in their net. Their ultimate goal was to exterminate them all, Cana, Fela, and Ursa alike.

He listened to the sounds beneath him for the telltale click of the freezer room door that would expose Vanya to the battle about to be waged in the intersection, but it never came, the brown Cana who had chosen the convenience store as refuge seemingly content to remain hidden behind shelves or the checkout counter, or was perhaps considering sanctuary beyond the open restroom door or escape through the broken window that room possessed. It might have intended to sneak out through the back delivery door, but when three hunters, their black leather garb tight to their skin and slickened now by the moisture in the cold air, stalked into the building, Kato understood there was no choice. It was either fight the hunters, as was being done now in buildings all around the intersection, or do nothing and trust fate to keep Vanya safe.

Kato trusted fate even less then he trusted other people.

He leaped from his vantage point, landing softly on the quiet pads of all four feet, and crept back into the building, his nose twitching as he sorted the scents that assailed him.

It seemed the smarter plan when it had come to her, divide the hunters, pick them off one by one, keep them engaged long enough to prevent any survivors from locating the Pack. With luck, the wagon had crossed into the Wilds by now and the Guards who had followed it had either been killed or had given up pursuit. If forced to, she knew Maz, Pain, and Uncle would fight to the death to protect the pups, and that the three would likely be able to overpower the few Guards who had chosen to follow the east road. If lost, Trill and Reif and the older children would forge a new pack, would care for the younger pups, would find a way to survive on their own for as long as they must. It was not an ideal choice, leaving the pregnant she-wolf to manage all of the Pack's children alone, but Jia had faith in her brother's wife to do what needed to be done.

Just as she had faith in those with her now.

From every corner of the intersection, she could hear the fighting as, one by one, her Pack slaughtered every hunter who crossed their paths. She worried for Deuce, already weakened from too many untended injuries, but from the echoes of battle that reached her, perhaps she did not need to worry about him. His years of solitary survival had made him the most formidable member of the Flushing Pack. Should they survive this day, he would be an outcast no more.

It was her own pursuers she needed to focus on, Guards with shocker sticks and long-poled blades that would keep her at bay if she attempted to confront them head-on. In the near darkness, however, she had the advantage, so long as she remained beyond the field of their night goggles, and here there were empty shelves that reached nearly to the collapsing ceiling, and the metal girders crisscrossing the decaying panels were still strong enough to bear her weight, providing places to hide. The guards swept the room, weapons and gazes remaining low as they expected her to appear behind one empty display or the next, and she awaited her first opportunity to remove any one of the three from the hunt.

When one reached a gloved hand to twist the long handle of a heavy metal door, an angry growl filled the store. From downwind of her, the only reason Jia had not sensed the newcomer sooner, the Fela leaped and with a swipe of its wide black paw tore through the leather to expose the fleshy neck beneath. The man's scream as he fell beneath the Fela's weight, brought his companions scrambling over debris to come to his aid. Seeing her chance, Jia dropped, feet knocking a display case over in front of one of the two before she pinned the last individual against the wall, her fangs at his throat before his attempt to jab the Fela with his shocker succeeded. He fell, blood gushing from a wound that would quickly take his life, and beside her, the Fela's prey dropped as well, his head dangling limply to one side, his neck snapped at the base of his skull.

There was a momentary glance between them, Cana and Fela, before the Guard threw his blade in the hopes of hitting either of them. It grazed the cat's side, eliciting a shriek of outrage, providing the wolf with the opportunity to charge, head down, into the hunter's stomach. The injury was not enough to drop the Fela, however, and he sprung over the fallen corpse at his feet. Front paws caught the Guard at the shoulders in the same moment the Cana rammed her snout low into the hunter's belly, and the man fell, torn asunder by two sets of fangs that, without weapons, he was helpless to fight.

With no desire to feast on the flesh of such a beast, the Fela retreated to a sentry stance before the metal door the Guard had attempted to open…a door where now a faint pounding could be heard accompanying a frightened voice calling her brother's name.

"Kato! Kato! Are they here? Answer me! Kato!"

Fela and Cana faced one another, the cat snarling in warning, the wolf's ears flickering back and forth as she listened to the sounds behind the door and those in the street outside. Many of the hunters were dead, it seemed, or else dying, but those who had run down the cardinal directions of the other three streets would be returning soon, their shouts to their company already signaling their race back to help the fallen. There were no howls, no way to know if any of her pack had been injured, as each would remain silent in their chosen positions until the battle was over, the Guards defeated, the Pack saved. She wondered if she should go to them, finish the fight, end the brutality that this night had thrust upon her.

But she felt an obligation to the Fela who aided in their fight, even if it had been to protect whoever was behind this door. The child, for that was what the voice sounded like to her, would not still without reassurance, but opening the door meant exposing her to the blood of a battle not yet complete. A child would not be safe outside of that enclosure yet, and as long as she cried out, she would be little safer inside. The Fela was in an obvious quandary, duty bound to protect the child but here, in the open, with the faint sound of wailing and shouting punctuating the night, he too was at risk.

Jia growled, a sound meant to bid him stay and attend to his own duty, before she turned and bounded from the building into an area about to be compromised by the rapidly approaching Guards. Whether the Fela did not understand her intent, thought her growl a threat or challenge, or whether because he felt his charge's needs were better met by engaging in the eradication of the threat, he bounded after Jia into the center of the intersection.

With her action noted by the other Cana, apparently under pursuit by the larger Fela, the others in the Pack emerged from their hidden positions to join her, their convergence upon her position one of wary threat as they glowered with gold or red eyes at the now stationary Fela who should not, in their opinion, be part of this battle.

With the imminent threat, however, nine Guards thrusting blades and shockers to herd them into a tight circle, they stood back to back with the Fela, each gauging their nearest opponents for weakness instead of fretting about the lone cat in their midst.

Jia glanced sidelong at the Fela, held back from an impulsive leap into battle by his paw on her forearm, annoyed at the hindrance but giving in to it when their gazes met. There were no verbal means of relaying his intentions, but she knew. It had worked for them once, and if they operated in tandem again, there was no reason a joint effort would not succeed a second time. No reason, she thought grimly, except that the five Cana and one Fela were outnumbered by Guards with weapons the anthro lacked.

Her head nodded a fraction, but it was enough of a movement, an agreement he hoped, to what he intended, that when he made the high, flat-footed leap that only a cat could make, Kato had to trust that she too would act. Again she charged, keeping her body low so that her movement kept her below the angle of the shocker. Her snarling jaws aimed at the Guard's groin, the Fela's paws aimed at the Guard's shoulders and his jaws at the man's face, broke the stalemate and gave birth to a frenzied fight that was over minutes after it began. Yowls and howls and the cries and moans of dying men filled the streets until they faded into silence beneath a gently falling rain which washed the blood from the muzzles of those now crouched on weary haunches, listening for Guards they may have missed, watching one another with the expectation of another fight.

It was often the way it was between Cana and Fela. Not because of blood animosity between cat and dog, but because trust was a commodity hard earned between naturally solitary creatures and naturally pack related ones. This Fela was an outsider, not one of them, and now that the fight, which he had entered for reasons unknown, was over, there was little reason for that trust to remain.

No reason except that he had fought, and killed, beside them when he could just as easily have remained hidden.

And no reason, Kato thought as he slunk slowly backward in the direction of the convenience store, that a pack of Cana, likely hungry now from the exertion of the fight, should not fall on him and make a quick meal of one lone Fela who could not overpower so many, even if they were each wounded and more battle-weary then he.

But the other Cana deferred to the smaller, bloody brown she-wolf who watched his retreat with curious eyes and made no effort to stop him or pursue. Her ears pricked forward, listening to the even fainter cries of the child trapped in the freezer room. The child, his child she presumed, would be safe now. These Guards were no longer a threat. Elsewhere, however, others might still be in pursuit of a wagon loaded with everything the Pack held precious.

Saving one child, she hoped, made up for the tremendous loss of life she had contributed to this night. One father and child protected, as now her Pack must be. She waited until the Fela was nearly at the building's door, still creeping backward as if expecting an ambush, and then gave one soft woofing bark before leading her injured companions in the direction of fresh wild earth and water. North to where the wagon sounds had gone earlier.

She looked at the Fela one more time, over her shoulder, as the Cana bolted in the direction of their cubs. Kato was sure her gaze met his. He waited, listening to their retreat, devouring their scent on the wind until it was washed away by distance and the misting rain, until he was assured that they would not come back for him. Waited diligently until he knew that Vanya was no longer in harm's way, to go to her and reassure her that, though he was wounded, he would live, and the monsters in the night would never harm either of them.

Chapter 8

The midnight hour had passed before the Pack reunited in the dingy, dilapidated outbuilding near the eastern edge of the Wilds, having evaded the last of the Guards by pushing deeper into the forest than the Guards were comfortable traveling. There were real dangers here, wolves, wildcats, grubbers, and more, and the unfamiliar terrain made them ill-equipped to continue with the wagon. Where they went, however, when Jia and her companions failed to find a trace of them, was unknown, and that unknown meant that two of their number remained on watch through the remainder of the night. She had wanted a third, but the Pack's exhaustion was real, so rather than assign others to the duty, she and Addi volunteered, knowing as they scouted the perimeter that Deuce was also there, injured and equally weary, but watching from the shadows, diligent as always to the Pack's need for security despite his personal suffering. He refused any invitation to nest with the Pack by separating from Jia's small group as soon as the proximity of the wagon and the welfare of the pups was achieved. Instead of leaving, however, he remained nearby.

Jia intended to ask him about that watchfulness when the opportunity arose. Finding shelter for the Pack tonight, a place they could call home however temporary, was her foremost priority.

Finding Liam and bringing him home, Liam and her father, was her second. What the future held beyond that, she could not foresee.

But she could not remain here, still and on duty, without trying to bring them back. Perhaps Liam had been fortunate enough to escape. Perhaps he had made it to the clinic in the hopes that his Pack would return. Or perhaps he was tracking their scent and would join them soon. And what if, she mused with burning panic, her father returned home to find no trace of the Pack? How could she not leave him some clue that might help him find his way to them?

Entrusting the Pack to the Omega's watchful eye and Addi's capable hands, she elected to abandon her post. Her father had often left the Pack when duty necessitated it, trusting the others to maintain order until his return. Duty to her father, and to Liam, demanded this action, duty to Liam's sister. Believing the Pack was safe where they were, that wild predators and grubbers were no threat and the Guards would not follow them here, was the only reason she was able to leave them in Addi and Deuce's care. Addi was Roland Marrock's son. He would do right by them, just as she would. And Deuce had proven himself many times over tonight.

Not only the survivors depended on her. The missing did as well…and the dead…a responsibility she could lay at no one else's feet. She watched Deuce through the foliage, gauging his watchfulness, and when satisfied that he would keep the Pack safe until her return, she ran again, the Cana galloping along the trail they had taken east, toward the world she had left behind.

There were duties in LaGuardia that only she could attend to. On this night, and throughout the day to come, the Pack would rest, hunt, recover their strength. Come the hour of her return, the future would be reshaped. In this new, uncertain time, the Pack needed to be led. Jia would not know, until the day's end, whether she had the fortitude to be their leader or not.

⮞*⮜

With the alcohol burn still flooding his system, blurring his vision but disallowing sleep, Vance threw on his overcoat and boots and began the long, solitary walk through the borough's sleeping streets, following the direction his hazy instincts were pulling him without giving thought to where he would eventually end up. Many feared the night, the darkness, and with good reason. Nocturnal animals ruled what remained of the harsh, once man-made jungle, animals that had reclaimed what humanity had once stolen and had just as surely destroyed with their arrogance and folly.

Some clung to the beliefs that the world, or whatever deity they still believed in, had turned against humankind, sending destruction via a host of catastrophes, earthquakes, storms, solar and interstellar radiation pulses, and the global eruption of volcanic hotspots, all of which had inhibited communication, the transport of commodities, and the direct ability of man to survive in harsh conditions. But it had been man turning against himself, riots and fear and prejudice against those who were different that had rained down the specter of war, atomic and otherwise, that in Vance's understanding was the ultimate cause of where the world had ended up. Humanity could surely have bounced back from whatever holocaust the natural world had thrown at them if they had banded together for survival instead of turning on one another like a host of feral, rabid beasts.

Worse than the beasts, actually, for man killed out of hatred. Beasts knew no such emotion.

It was no wonder the natural world had seen fit to reclaim the land. The dregs of humanity, he mused as he stumbled upon a cluster of hibernating grubbers bumping into one another at the end of the empty alley he passed, had no more rights to this world than did the wildlife that strove to take it back.

The grubbers did not notice his cautious passing, and in the cold, he knew he could easily outrun them.

If humanity survived it would be a miracle, particularly, he thought with a grimace when he eventually stopped, his feet halting at their destination to find the debris of life discarded through no longer shielded windows, if they continued to commit atrocities such as this against one another.

There was blood on the grassy pavement, barely retaining its hold beneath the onslaught of the falling misty rain that Vance had not noticed as he walked, but there were no bodies to be found. As the light of dawn clawed its way into the sky, he scoured every room, every corridor, every level of what yesterday had been a haven for a host of families bound together by a pact of blood and genetics. Today it was nothing but one more unlivable building in a borough filled with unlivable buildings. Had they been captured, he wondered with a sick, sinking feeling. Had they been slaughtered? Had any of them, however many had once lived here, made it out alive and free?

Had Jia Marrock survived?

He had done this. Though his first thought was to storm the Fortress, to demand an explanation from Laedan Channon as to why this had been done, to refuse to work for the man any longer in a world where those with power resorted to the butchery of their own people, Vance believed his coming here yesterday, his finding where the Pack resided in order to confront them about the alleged theft, had been the key that allowed this regrettable act to occur. The likelihood that he had been sent on this errand, that the accusations against Addison and the fears Lowell had offered concerning Laedan Marrock's absence were part of some scheme to locate the suspected anthro pack and eradicate them, was so high that Vance could barely believe he had not taken the notion seriously sooner. It was HOPE's way, after all, to use mages to track anthro in order to capture or kill them. Though to his knowledge the Channons were not active members of HOPE, the family had political ties to the organization. No public accusations of being anthro had ever been leveled against the Marrocks, had ever crossed Lowell's lips within Vance's hearing, but Vance's suspicions had been there from the moment Lowell gave him this job, from the moment he first came to this place.

Fates, he muttered as he toed the potting soil on the stones at his feet, feeling eyes on him and expecting it to be a remnant of whoever had dealt this blow, proved her to be wiser than me.

"Mage."

Emerging from the shadows, Jia had to admit she was not surprised to find him there. The likelihood that he had contributed to the assault on the Pack was high, although the remorse and guilt on his weary features assured her that the destruction of lives before them had come as an unexpected shock to him. Whether he had known this could happen as a result of his visit or not, whether he was at fault for leading the Guard here or the raid had already been deployed before his involvement, he had never intended to be an instrument of death and destruction.

He might be a Protector, but his soul was too gentle to wish that sort of malice on anyone.

"You survived…" He breathed an honest sigh of relief, a sound that put her at ease as she scanned the area for signs of life. If Liam or her father had come during the night, they had left no trace.

Had she been the one watching him, Vance wondered. Had she been here all along?

Did she blame him for this as he blamed himself?

"I'm sorry…"

"You did not do this." Her voice was heavy, sad, and colored with defeat. She had been here long enough to find tattered clothing amongst the discarded debris into which she had changed once her human form was reclaimed; it was barely suitable to protect her from the elements and she wrapped her arms close to her chest for both comfort and an extra bit of warmth. Subtle clues had been left for her father and Liam, symbols that few others would recognize, in the belief that the men were wise enough to interpret them, to find their Pack if they returned. They would return, she reminded herself repeatedly. But there were no traces of Liam, save for his name, along with hers, Zen's, and Addi's etched into the concrete lip of the roof that had been put there when they were children, and the faint traces of his scent that remained in the places where he slept, where he sat to eat, where he taught the pups. To find him, Jia was going to have to return to the last place he was seen.

She had been resisting doing that when the mage arrived, and discreetly following him as he investigated the crime scene had provided enough of a distraction to put off the inevitable.

"No? But I could have. I didn't consider I might be followed."

"It wasn't you." Jonni's message was lost, destroyed in the chaos of the hunt, and she would not have given it to the mage if she still had it. Allegations made against the powerful and connected Laedan were dangerous things, as her father's disappearance proved. It was possible, as Uncle believed, that the fault lay with HOPE rather than the Channons, or that some random act of violence by anthro hunting vigilantes was responsible…in spite of the Channon Guard uniforms some of the hunters had worn…but things Roland had said before his disappearance suggested otherwise. Somehow, some way, she would deal with Quentin, Donnovan and Lowell Channon herself, but only after she had proof and her father and Liam were safe.

Vance scrutinized her bruised face and nodded, accepting her words as truth based on whatever details she was withholding from him. He could have probed for the answers, but he honestly did not want them. What he wanted most was for this day to be over when it had only just begun, to lose himself in another bottle or two of hemp beer and forget he had ever woken up to this.

He had not, he thought with irony. He had never woken up at all. That would have required going to sleep.

"Do you still intend to find my father?"

His head bobbed once. Giving up was tempting, as it would cut ties to the Laedan, ties he wanted to resist with every fiber of his life. But giving up on this willful young woman was not an option, particularly if it went against her wishes. "Is that what you want?"

Rather than answer the question with unnecessary words, she summoned him with a gesture and murmured, "Come with me."

He nodded again, wiped the rain from his face, and traced her footsteps in the direction opposite the rising sun.

⧞*⧟

"It's early." Her voice, submissively annoyed and disappointed, broken by hiccupping snuffles, made it tempting to shed the clothes he had just pulled on to rejoin her in the warmth of the marriage bed, but if he was to meet Quentin before his father summoned the other man to his first duty of the day, Donn had to do it now, while the sun barely colored the sky, while it was likely his father was still sleeping off the effects of last night's drink. Plying him with ale had been an easily accomplished necessity as the howls during the night had dragged on longer than intended, their untraceable echoes spread thin across the landscape so that it was impossible to locate their origins or their point of ending. But end they had, and Donn presumed the end had come as ordered, bloody and final.

"Don't fret, wife…there shall be more of me for you upon my return." He rubbed one hand over his aching groin, a pleasant ache that came from the force of the joining they had just shared. Oasis' face was red, tear-streaked, expressing just enough discomfort in her pout to set his core throbbing with longing again. Hurting her was a necessity, as it proved his position in their marriage. The fact that she did not shrink from it and chose to welcome his return satisfied his need for brutality.

He would certainly be back for her, as soon as his business with Quentin was complete.

He expected her to be waiting when he came.

The door closed, locked to ensure her obedience without thought as to the inequity of that action. He did not care if she heard it or not, although his heart secretly thrilled over the likelihood that she had.

"If you've hurt her, so help me fates…"

Spun around and thrust against the wall with force enough to knock the wind from his lungs, Donn's first instinct was a mixture of surprise and the desire to lash out in careless retaliation. The inability to breathe precluded the second instinct, however, and finding Jonni's face inches from his, his icy blue eyes dark with indignation gave fuel to the first. Donn's mouth opened and closed several times, the effort to breathe, to speak, giving the appearance of a fish taken from the sea. As breath seeped back into his lungs, he began to laugh, a wheezing sound that eventually grew into a delighted chortle that added fury to his brother's outrage.

"I haven't hurt anyone," he said with calm innocence, knowing that was not technically true and knowing his inability to quash his amusement at Jonni's expense did not support the words he uttered. Jonni growled and the flash of emotion brought enough warning that, instead of suffering the blow from Jonni's incoming fist, Donn was able to block it with one forearm in the same instant his own fist caught Jonni across the jaw. Less of a fighter than Donn, Jonni stumbled back to crash into the opposite wall. Any further words Donn intended, any further indignant attack he wanted to make to prove his superiority and strength to his older brother was aborted by the voice at the other end of the corridor.

"Donnovan!"

Expecting their father to be asleep, finding him awake and dressed as if he had been about business for some time already in spite of his obvious hangover, Donn froze and then hid his shock by straightening his shirt and drawing back his shoulders.

"Fa."

Jonni's eyes narrowed, the effort forcing his lips into a scowl. Donn never showed his disdain for their father, the disdain Jonni knew to be there regardless of Donn's skill in masking it. As usual, perhaps because he was too far away to recognize it or because he carried a blind spot where his youngest son was concerned, Lowell again failed to detect what Jonni did not believe he was imagining.

"What is this?"

"Donn's an ass."

Donn snorted, offering his hand to his brother for aid to his feet. "Brotherly row; starting the day with a little adrenalin, eh, Jonni?"

Again Jonni scowled and muttered, "You're still an ass," as he reluctantly accepted the offered hand. It was tempting to call out his brother on the raid conducted during the night, but with neither proof that it had happened, nor certainty that their father did not already know, Jonni decided it was wiser to keep his suspicions and accusations to himself.

"Everyone knows that." Donn had never hidden from such name calling. The more he heard it, Jonni mused, the more determined Donn seemed to prove such names accurate.

"Well, no more of it. Jonni," Lowell dismissed Donn with a wave and turned his attention to his eldest son. "Do you have the reports I requested?"

"They were finished…accurate up to yesterday's figures…"

"My apologies for that…but I have time to review them now, if you will bring them to my office." Lowell was already walking away as the request was made, expecting to be heard and obeyed without maintaining eye contact or receiving acknowledgment of the request.

Casting a daggerous look at his brother while simultaneously responding, "I will bring them at once," Jonni caught his brother's boastful grin. Deciding any delight in tormenting his brother further would have to wait, Donn let him go without a word. His father would be occupied long enough for Donn to meet with Quentin; he had his own business to take care of and Jonni was not part of it.

⮞*⮜

He watched her, kneeling with her fingers, then her nose, to the empty spot of fractured asphalt; the scars in the moss and grass there deep and fresh enough to hint at the skirmish she suggested, without words, had occurred here the night before. The chunks of concrete brick that had tumbled from the top of the collapsed wall and scattered at the base supported a mad scramble over it, to flee the scene, but the rain had washed away any blood evidence. The memory-voices that had seeped into the facades of the buildings around them, into the buckled wall that blocked the passage, and into the worn street beneath their feet were jumbled and chaotic, some faded some fresh, a difficult cacophony to untangle into individual threads yet clearly detectable.

Jia's proximity, as Vance remained vigilant to protect her, managed to draw her imprint free of the jumble, presenting him with a tarnished image of combat, of claws and fangs and a blow to the head that had removed her from this fight and left one of her company vulnerable to the enemy.

She had not spoken during their skulking journey, had revealed nothing of where they were going or what had happened the night before, but the ghosts of this place, as fresh as they were, sang of hunter and prey, of fear and a frantic struggle for survival. Someone important had been lost here, but as she knelt where the ghosts told Vance someone had fallen, she shook her head and sighed.

"He did not die here."

"No…he did not." Vance did not know who 'he' was, but he felt no presence of death, only pain and terror and the ache of regret.

"We were protecting the others…giving them time to…this was no small hunt…this was to have been a slaughter." Her head lifted and she met his gaze. "They blocked all of the paths out save one…thought to drive us into their trap. They did not expect us to know…to have time…to retreat."

He nodded and glanced back in the direction they had come; there were too many streets and buildings between where they stood and the place she had, until yesterday, called home. Her words suggested an escape south or east, but he chose not to ask which. He could follow her trail, find her if he needed to, but speaking the question and answer aloud would make her vulnerable again. He wanted her to be safe.

"Were any of the others taken?"

"No." He did not know how many had called that place home, how large her pack might be, and she was grateful he did not ask. Asking something she could not answer would mean lying to him, something she was loath to do. "They're safe…only Liam…"

The way she spoke the name, heartbroken and colored with regret, made Vance's chest tighten. Of course, her affections were spoken for. A woman like her, intelligent, strong, lovely…the child of a Laedan, in the fertile years of life, was most likely married. Perhaps she was already a mother. As usual, Vance's heart pulled him down an unproductive path of inevitable disappointment. But he hid that from her as he shrugged off his jacket and wrapped it around her trembling shoulders. Better she think he believed her cold than think he was saddened or jealous of the missing Cana.

"If he did not die here, he was likely taken," he agreed. The things rumored to be done to captive anthro made death preferable to some, but at least it offered hope of life, hope that rescue or escape was possible. Hands on her shoulders as he adjusted the coat, he asked, "There were too many to have been a community hunt, yes?" He could not see the shadows that had pursued the pack, found their forms peculiarly hidden from his view, but a raid of the magnitude Jia suggested meant that this had not been carried out by a rabble of common folk on a Frankenstein-monster hunt to erase anthro from their community. That sort of thing did happen on occasion, usually against single Ursa or Fela, or lone families who could be overpowered by a dozen or so armed individuals.

But few such mobs took on a full Cana pack. Whatever the truths were about anthro, the myths, rumors, and fears about them rarely allowed the average people to willingly take on such a large group. Self-preservation typically kept the status quo between human and anthro. If a pack or pride was felt to be too large, believed to be a community threat, the possibility of their location being given to HOPE agents soared. In Vance's experience, however, HOPE conducted surgical strikes with small teams designed to capture as many anthro as possible. Some were invariably killed in such strikes but most were caught to be used for labor or for experimentation. Full-scale slaughter was not normally HOPE's style.

Why was the Flushing Pack treated as a threat dangerous enough to require a large-scale incursion? And if not HOPE-based, not a community effort, then why would the Laedan order such a strike? It had to have been the Laedan…or else some local Protectorate office. Who else could have controlled and organized so many hunters? Perhaps Laedan Hallister had organized it as a favor to Channon, but then the attack teams would have approached from the south instead of the north and west.

More questions to nag at him without any hint of answer yet. Scowling, he asked, "Where was Roland when he was taken?"

"I…" Jia hesitated, debating with herself the merits and complications of sharing such information. Forced outside of the borough, her access to helpful resources would be limited now if she wished to keep the location of the Pack a secret. She could think of only one other, possibly two, who might be able to help her learn the truth, who might be able to find Liam and her father, but the mage was her best bet, regardless of what the Pack believed about his kind.

"They will not want you involved," she began, leading north, reluctant to leave this dead-end place. "They won't trust you."

Vance snorted. "I wouldn't trust me either if I were them." When she side-eyed him, he shrugged.

"But I can find them…Roland and your…"

A melancholy smile pulled at her lips, the first one she had felt since last night. Involving herself with a mage was an insane notion, but it felt nice to have drawn the notice of someone outside of the Pack…someone who was not a Channon. "Best friend," she finished the sentence for him. Liam was definitely that. Anything more would be discussed at length as soon as he was home and safe.

Her expression brightened a little at the boyish twinkle that sprung into his eyes, a twinkle that was quickly extinguished with an embarrassed flush of his cheeks. This was not the occasion for this, he reminded himself. He was working. Afterward, after he upheld his promise and found the two missing men…preferably alive so that she continued to see him favorably, then, perhaps, he would take another step. He would be a fool to do anything else now.

Their trek led them through a populated section of the borough, dawn and a new day's struggle for survival drawing people from their homes. These were streets Vance knew, a few long blocks away from the Protectorate's headquarters and nearly a dozen more away from the Fortress, streets where the majority of his work kept him amongst people he knew. Most of the time his days revolved around finding property stolen by neighbors, thugs or scavs, finding children who had wandered too far from home, putting down nests of grubbers, or investigating deaths that could be anything from accidental in their dangerous world to brutal murder as people fought over the necessities of life. The same sort of duties he had been asked to do by Laedan Channon this time, find the stolen, find the missing, investigate the potentially deceased, but the gravity of this job was already taking its toll. His fears, as Jia's, were that the two men sought were beyond saving, but he never gave up on a subject or suspect until they were found.

Unlike his normal cases, however, if the wrongdoings centered around HOPE, if they were the hands guilty of this, recompense would be impossible. Nobody, not even the Laedans, could subvert the heavy hand of HOPE. Lowell, Vance suspected, might attempt it, however, and he feared the woman with him would try as well.

Jia ignored the curious eyes from windows or passersby or people on their stoops; they had no reason to know who or what she was, only her walking in the company of the mage…if they knew him…and her dirty clothing marked her as a curiosity, but even that was not so unusual. The luxury of clean clothes often relied on the mercy of collected rainwater that had not already been earmarked for drinking, cooking, and use in tending the needs of one's food sources. These dusty, muddy trousers, too big at the waist and hips, and torn pullover tunic-like shirt that hung mid-thigh were men's clothing, Liam's or Addi's most likely though she did not recognize either article; while too large, torn, and dirty, they were more acceptable in public then her natural fur and skin would have been.

The open space she led Vance too, lined on one side by an eight-foot-high wall and a twisted, rusted metal fence on two others, still contained the element-eaten skeletons of vehicles abandoned there as the Undoing sank its fangs deeper into the survivability of the world's remaining population. Most had been pushed toward the wall, support to keep it from crumbling, to allow it to serve as protection to those who lived on the other side. This was a poor section of the borough, with few intact buildings and bands of nearly feral individuals who did their best to resist the leadership of the Laedans. People with secrets, a place where Vance often found stolen goods and missing individuals…individuals who had fled 'civilized' life in favor of something more primal. People who, for the most part, respected the mage because he respected them. It made a logical destination for a pursued anthro to run to, to take up temporary shelter, because few probed into the personal details of their neighbors and most protected each other's' right to privacy.

It was also, Vance mused, within a reasonable path of flight for one coming from the Fortress and heading toward the southeastern sector of District 3 where Jia had lived...or vice versa. Jia had given him few details of that pursuit, and of course, Lowell had said nothing, but the echoes in this place were loud and demanding, no mere whisper left by distant voices. Having heard Marrock speak many times, both being proponents of progress and change, of improving the day to day life for everyone in the borough, Vance knew the voice well. Harsh and demanding as it bid his daughter to flee, soft and strained as it clung to hope for the injured woman he knelt over, and finally vicious and stoic when the stingers came and beat him into submission and, eventually, into unconsciousness.

"He was taken from here alive." The mage was certain of that. Jia watched as he stared, glassy-eyed, to the south-east. In the direction of HOPE. The scowl that settled over his face as his focus returned to his surroundings bore traces of confusion on top of the regret most would feel where HOPE's involvement was concerned. "Did he have enemies? Anyone who wished him harm? Anyone who might have known...what he is?"

Still staring where Vance had been looking, hoping to see any clue along that line of sight that her father might have left for her, Jia shrugged. "No obvious enemies that I am aware of...but he did not bring his work home with him...at least he didn't until the end..."

"What happened at the end? What changed?"

Side-stepping closer to him, dropping her voice in case there was anyone nearby to overhear, she replied, "I do not know the details. He said Lowell was planning something significant for the borough. If he knew what, he did not say...but it was something he was unhappy about, something he wanted proof of. He said on the last day that there were maps, a ledger. But if he saw them, copied them, took them, I do not know."

Inside of Vance's skull, small clickings echoed off subconscious details and connections that he could not yet put into words as he listened. Lowell had spoken of documents, and had just as quickly sidestepped that matter. Where they the same documents of which Marrock had spoken to his daughter? "So Lowell…"

"Lowell was his friend…" That fact was true and made it difficult to believe that the man would turn against his childhood playmate and co-Laedan. What was also true, what Vance likely already knew, was that Lowell, and at least one of his sons, had an unquenchable lust for power. Lowell would be just as happy, Jia knew, to govern the borough alone.

Donnovan Channon certainly desired to control his surroundings without anyone to second guess him.

"And," she added hastily, to avert a potential argument or suggestion that she was blind to the Laedan's faults, "it is no secret in the Fortress that Thomas wants my father's position."

"Thomas Quentin?" Jia nodded but did not elaborate and so Vance prompted, "Whatever this was, that Roland suspected, might it be something Lowell would kill to protect?" Again she did not speak, perhaps out of sympathy for Lowell or because the possibility was too chilling to admit. "The Channons…do they know about…?"

Though she waited, he did not complete the sentence. It was enough to make her look at him, his sympathetic eyes studying her face then quickly looking away when their gazes met.

"That we are Cana?" It was an obvious question the mage had been unable to tactfully verbalize. First Jia shook her head no, but then she shrugged. "We have been Cana since the first generation after…Marrocks working side by side with Channons…the secret kept all this time. He was careful, we all are, but…" She sighed and stuffed her cold hands into the pockets of the long coat Vance had lent to her. "It was only a matter of time, I suppose. Jonni wanted…wants…to marry me, but, of course, that could not happen, knowing the family's connections within HOPE…maybe…"

"Perhaps he took action…retaliation…for rejection?"

"He would never…" But perhaps another Channon had on his behalf. Or perhaps Lowell's continued discouraging of their union had been due to suspicion of the truth. Maybe, two minds at once thought as their eyes met, a suspicion of the truth had been enough to initiate the hunt…and arrest. Some of the Pack had been in Cana form when the capture occurred, but Roland had not been one of them. He had relied on the Pack to protect him, and each other, had thought to outwit his pursuers…and had paid the price for it. If only he had changed, Jia thought again with a hint of bitterness in her eyes for the first time, he might have escaped.

But he still would have returned for the fallen, and as Cana, leaning over the body of a packmate, it would have been enough to warrant immediate arrest and prosecution of the whole pack.

Not arrest by the Laedan's troops, however, or else the Channons would have suspected her the night of the wedding.

Unless they were pretending to be ignorant to allow her to condemn herself, allow her to lead them back to the pack.

Perhaps their loss of home had been her fault.

A stab of pain behind her eyes made her blink and look away from Vance. Too many questions. How could the mage find the truth when Jia's information only presented more questions and precious few answers?

"I will talk to the Channons." Sniffing the air and pinpointing the location of the sun behind still pink and mauve and orange clouds, he nodded. "I have somewhere to be this morning…another lead to follow…" And he had to meet Sal at the Protectorate office before doing that. Hopefully, Sal would wait for him as they had discussed the previous evening. "But after…"

"I'm going to the Fortress."

Vance shook his head. "I wouldn't do that if…you'll be…"

"I'll be okay."

"If someone there ordered last night's…"

She acknowledged his intent with a nod as she interrupted him. "Then I will be letting them know they failed. But I am not going to hide. I have a right to be there, to go where I choose, and I might be able to learn something in talking to them."

He could not prevent her from going, only strongly advise against the risk. But she was right; under normal conditions, as the Marrock representative in her father's stead, a right established by her attendance at previous meetings when obligations prevented Roland from being there, she had much freer rein to rooms, to documents, to people. Vance would have to petition for access to such things or else gain dispensation from Chief Ernest to force permission. Such petitions or privileges would raise Channon ire. Jia was the logical choice for infiltration, but Vance did not like it.

"You can't go like this." He indicated her attire, which she had not given consideration to before making her decision to act. "Come to the Protectorate…we should have something…"

She shook her head. "I'll manage." The thought of being surrounded by so many Protectors, being visually dissected by every set of eyes within that place where word might leak back to the Fortress before she was ready to make herself known, made her skin crawl. Vance understood that reaction too well. He felt that way almost every time he walked into the building.

"Shall we meet later? This evening? Compare our days' findings?" The request sounded unexpectedly more hopeful than he intended, and so Vance struggled to keep his expression as casual and unassuming as he could.

"Not today…tomorrow…or the next…" Regardless of what she discovered in the Fortress, she had to return to the Pack, face whatever allegations were made for her absence, perhaps endure the shame of not being permitted pack leadership. Whether she wished to be or not, she was Roland's daughter. With Addi refusing leadership, it left only her, but she might not be welcomed as leader after what had transpired during the night, after what she had done this morning. If she was challenged for leadership by any of those she respected, she did not know if she had what it would take to win a contest…or to endure the leadership of another.

"Where?"

"I will find you."

Lips parting to give protest, Vance caught his breath in time to swallow the objections he was about to make. There was no pressing need to meet with her sooner, unless either learned something significant. Wanting to see her again was not, he chastised himself, reason enough. Of course, she would not want to let him know where to find her; she had others to protect, and finding him was merely a matter of seeking him at the Protectorate. It was safer for her, practical. Acceptable.

"Be careful." He took back his coat when she offered it, treasuring the inadvertent benefit of wrapping himself in her scent when he pulled it on again.

"And you, mage…thank you." This sort of thing might be his duty, but the risks, facing both Laedan and HOPE for answers, were huge. He would need his wits to come through this case alive. Jia did not envy him anymore, she imagined, then he envied her.

He watched her climb the mountain of destroyed vehicles with inhuman adeptness, perch briefly on the wall to look back at him, and then leap down on the other side, beyond Vance's field of sight. If he had been in pursuit, he would have lost her at that moment. But his pursuit now was more mundane and required Sal's help to complete. When the day's quest was over, he expected to have a few answers to share.

He could daydream, meanwhile, that they could then share so much more.

Chapter 9

Chief Ernest hated these mandatory meetings almost as much as he had grown to hate the business he had chosen as his life's work. Such meetings got him out of his drafty office without exposing him to the blood, piss, and mud of street work, but the grinding of political machinery grated on his nerves. An unauthorized hunt, recounted to the Protectorate by nearly two dozen varying sources, required a report to the Laedan; the law requiring it had stood since first put in effect after the Undoing, when mutani and anthro first began to appear in the borough. Often, Walter felt the report was for show more than because of any governing interest in those particular sub-groups of humanity. The Laedans had to at least appear attentive to everyone's survival, even if they were not.

It was no surprise, therefore, that Laedan Channon claimed no knowledge of the District 3 hunt, and the promise to look into it, to discuss it with the son who was mayor of that district, sounded like so much political lip-service. But it was out of Walter's hands now, reported as required, and unless the Laedan put the matter back into the hands of the Protectorate, there was nothing for the Chief to do. Unless someone reported others missing, abducted, or killed in the hunt, Ernest had nothing else to go on. He should be concerned about the Cana, he knew, but mainly he was too damned tired to care.

The request to keep an eye on Protectorate Mage Segara, however, was something he did care about, worrisome despite the Laedan's reassurance that it was no matter of urgency. It was of little concern to the Chief when Lowell hired the mage; many hired mages for private work outside of the Protectorate. Segara worked his own hours, seemed to Ernest to always be working, but so long as he fulfilled the duties of his post, what other jobs he took were of little concern to Walter. Segara had worked for the Laedans in the past; this should be no different.

Except that this time, Lowell told Ernest about the 'special assignment' and asked him to report the mage's activities as he learned them. Unable to pinpoint why such a covert, behind the back maneuver irritated him, Walter furrowed his brow as he reached the immobile escalating staircase and started down to the ground level.

He did not notice the woman at the bottom until too late, as the two rounded the corner there and bumped into one another. The flowers she carried, pink and gold and white chrysanthemums on long, freshly cut stems, scattered across the floor.

"I'm sorry," he muttered, bending to help retrieve them, and only then, when his hand brushed hers and they looked at one another, did he see the swelling, bruising imprint of a palm across her cheek and the slight reddening around her eye. "Mrs. Channon…" he started, appalled as he lifted his fingers to her cheek. She shrank from his touch, turning her face to the side to hide the evidence as well as to prevent potential further abuse. "Who…?"

"It is nothing. I rolled off the bed in my sleep."

It was a weak excuse, one that did not account for the shape of the mark she bore, but having seen such evidence on others, Walter doubted he could get her to turn evidence against the guilty. Fear? Shame? Mindfulness of family status? Misguided love? Whatever bound her in silence would be a bond she would not break. He was reminded of the timid, frightened reflex he had seen in her after the wedding and wondered again who was responsible. The Laedan, surely, for if it was anyone else, Lowell would likely have had their hand for the offense. Or both hands and their head.

With the flowers gathered, Walter caught her free hand and drew her to her feet as he stood. She began to flinch away from him, but when his gesture was understood and recognized as helpful rather than hurtful, she relaxed a little. "Please, if you need anything, come to me. Or summon me and I will come to you. You should not have to tolerate this…no one should."

Something in her eyes, a glimmer of hope, softened her expression for a moment before she muttered hastily, "I have to go…Lowell is expecting these." Two by two, she bounded up the stairs, aware that the Chief was watching her. At the top, she hesitated long enough to look back at him, a dozen things she wanted to say pushing into her mouth but were stopped by her teeth only to be swallowed down into an acidic ball of fear and regret in the pit of her stomach. She did manage a faint, "Thank you," before disappearing down the corridor to the left.

Thank you for the assistance with the flowers, Walter wondered, or thank you for the offered aid, the generosity of caring? There was no good way to find out. But Walter felt a strong, tugging conviction that he needed to try.

⮟*⮜

"Jia?" Shocked, disbelieving of what his glazed red eyes saw, Nik sprang from the lobby bench where he had been dozing away the heaviness of his most recent high, pulled the tiny woman into his embrace, and layered the top of her head with kisses of relief. She was real. Sometimes in this state, it was difficult to tell between hallucination and reality. She smelled of exertion, a wet fur smell that made him giggle, of morning dew and a sweet musk that he associated with her from the time he was old enough to notice such details about other people. All clues were enough to convince him that she was no figment of the drug's design. "You're safe!"

Jia stiffened, not because of the hug but because, whatever had precipitated the night's hunt, Nik had apparently known something of it. Were all of the Channons involved, she wondered, extracting herself from his embrace carefully, never knowing what manner of high he might be experiencing, whether he might be happy or melancholy or belligerent. Today, at this moment, he appeared frightened, although increasingly less so by looking at her again, gripping her arms in his hands when he could no longer hug her, not to hurt her but to keep her from getting away.

"What do you know, Nik?" she asked, her voice a whisper because she knew how well voices carried in this cavern of a room.

"They know," he muttered, shaking his head in denial. "They know...they know...they all know..."

"Who knows? What do they know?"

"All of them. All of them know. Everything." Obviously not fully aware of his surroundings and not in full control of his senses, his arms flung out to the side and he danced in a limp circle with his head thrown back and a loud "Aaaaarroooo!" that reverberated from wall to wall around them.

She tried to grab him without hurting him, hoping to silence him, but he danced just beyond her reach and stayed that way as she tried to move close enough to capture his hand. "I heard them...sneaking in their closet room voices...but I don't know why..."

The last word dragged out into a mournful sound as he collapsed dizzily onto the bench where he had sprawled before, his head in his hands now shaking from side to side as the words turned into a long moan of despair. Around his feet, the paraphernalia of drug use was scattered, needles and spoons and a spilled paper package of rainbow-hued pills. He had probably mixed his poisons, she thought with regret, wishing again she held the key to making him stop.

"Why would anyone want to hurt you?" Nik whined, though without tears to support his remorse. "You're one of the good ones."

She sat, an arm around his shoulder, holding him close as she glanced about, cautious of anyone who might be near. No one could be seen, no one heard, only the whirr of the ever turning fan system that kept fresh air circulating through the Fortress complex. Nik scooted closer, burrowed his face against her neck like a child seeking comfort from his mother, and continued to groan.

"Who wants to hurt me, Nik?"

Whatever Nik knew, however, was lost to the incoherence of substance abuse that pulled him from semi-lucidity into a sleep-like daze that finally stilled the sounds of despair. Gently she settled him, propping him against the raised arm of the bench and turning his head so he would not choke on his vomit in his sleep if it came to that. It was impossible to be angry with him, the boy who had battled the clutches of addiction as far back as he had been able to seek substances to strangle whatever demons he shouldered. Frustrated that he could not give her answers, yes, but never angry with him.

Besides, she already knew the answers to the questions she asked. Jonni's message was further testimony. What she needed to know, however, was what part Jonni had played in the decisions that precipitated the hunt and what part Lowell shouldered.

Leaving Nik there in spite of the urge to sit with him until he was coherent again, Jia tugged down the dark blue sweater she had obtained and smoothed out the similarly blue trousers. The color had been selected specifically because it matched the formal uniform Roland wore on business days, the same color Lowell wore when speaking before the throngs, rallying them to his most recent cause or public agenda. Wearing it, she hoped, would suggest that she was in the Fortress on business, thus no one would restrict her movements or question her being here.

The ploy worked well enough to allow her through corridor after corridor, nods of greeting and short, cordial words exchanged with those she had known all of her life. There were few young faces here, little fresh blood or thought in LaGuardia's governing mechanism. What there was belonged to four young men, three brothers and one relative newcomer handpicked by Laedan Channon. She should stay, Jia thought reluctantly as she turned the last corner to her father's office without hindrance. Someone needed to balance the Channon influence, someone who could speak as the voice of the people instead of a voice catering to the wheels of power. Her father wanted that of her, as much as she had wanted it for herself. But at what cost, if the Channons knew the Marrock secret?

Could she consider governing the borough, even co-governing, when she had yet to accept or master the governing of the Pack?

The latch twisted in her hand, the door popping open to undercut the echo of footsteps further down the corridor. Four sets, recognizable ones that caused her to straighten, her shoulders taut, and face them with resolve.

"Jia! It is good to see you!"

There was no denying the relief in Jonni's voice as he rushed forward and embraced her as his brother had done, though instead of a shower of kisses to the top of her head, a single one fell on her cheek, innocent and yet near enough to her mouth to intimate the kiss he would have preferred to give. For a moment, the breadth of his body blocked the others from view, but not before she made note of the other three expressions. Each was sufficiently surprised to see her, and a look shared between the younger two suggested a query, a secret shared, a failure questioned. The third bore a trace of guilt and concern that did not speak of fear but clearly covered something she was not meant to see. By the time Jonni pulled back, trying to hold onto her hands but relenting to her pulling away, the other faces were neutral and calm.

Correction. Donn's face could never be neutral. Jia often imagined that, even in his sleep, his expression was overshadowed with a sheen of menace.

"I was not expecting you," Lowell said when he reached her, taking her hands in an affectionate, almost fatherly way that sent a shiver up her spine. It was not a new level of affection, but today it felt to come with strings attached, strings that felt to Jia as if they threatened to wrap around her throat. "If I had, I would have averted heat to Roland's office…" he added, thinking her responding shiver was due to cold rather than due to him. The corridors were often chilly, as what little heat there was in the Fortress was always directed to living quarters and offices that were in use.

She had no reason to reject his familial affection. She never had before, had always accepted him as uncle, as part of her family, just as she accepted his sons.

"I know…but there are things to do. My father's work…"

"Is being looked after during his absence," Thomas assured her with a friendly and polite tilt of his head. He was never anything but polite to her, sociable and cordial, but there was something in his eyes, in the scent of him, she did not trust.

Today her nose wrinkled at that smell again, a scent both familiar and new at the same time, something she could almost touch now that she had never contemplated before.

Was that why? How could she never have noticed?

Had Roland known? Was this the covering that, once the corner had lifted, shed light upon the Marrock secret and exposed it to the Channons for the first time?

How, she wondered, would she ever prove it?

"Oh." She tried to sound disappointed without expressing knowing resentment toward Lowell's aide. Taking over the Marrock duties was precisely what father and daughter suspected of Quentin. There might be no visible smugness in his behavior now that he had begun to latch onto what he had longed for from the start, but Jia knew it was there. Scratch the surface deep enough, and the man's ambition would come oozing out. "Well, I appreciate that, Mr. Quentin, but I am perfectly capable of assuming his duties. I assure you I will settle into them as quickly as I am able."

"We understand, precious…do not fret over it. Take all of the time you need. His desk will be waiting for you when you're ready, or," Lowell added contritely, "or for Roland when he returns."

"He will, I promise. I'm surprised he did not notify you of his journey." Roland had always left such notices in writing, barring emergencies, but he obviously had not left any notice this time and it felt, to Jia, that all of them understood why. "I do have some things to attend to, however…correspondences he asked me to make before he left…I should take care of them without delay."

Jonni smiled and slipped an arm around her shoulders. "Of course you should," he said earnestly as if expecting his father or Quentin to discourage her. Jia had served as her father's correspondent, secretary, and schedule organizer for several years; if she had been given tasks to perform, Lowell and his aide would not necessarily know of it. Quentin might have usurped Marrock's day to day responsibilities, but he could not know what tasks had slipped from father to daughter before the man's absence.

Wanting a private word with Jonni required getting him away from others, and so Jia looked at him with her warmest smile and said, "There is one thing I need assistance with, Jonni, if you are available?"

The smile did the trick and made Jonni brighten more than seeing her had done, eliciting a look of disapproval from Lowell and one of revulsion from Donn. While Lowell had discouraged his son's courting of the Marrock heiress, his outward dissatisfaction had never been visible. Perhaps it now bore the added weight of Jonni's refusal to accept the arranged marriage. More likely, Jia thought as Jonni grinned and replied, "I can help you," was that Lowell knew the truth and was disgusted by the notion of mixing Channon blood with anything less than a pure gene pool.

Given Lowell's dislike of anthro, Jia did not imagine she would be welcome in the Fortress much longer. With Roland's absence, the remaining Laedan could fabricate any excuse to keep her out and she imagined he would do so as soon as it became politically expedient. She would do what needed doing, gather what she had come for, and be gone from this place soon enough. She had already learned what was necessary this day, or enough of it to satisfy her curiosity and offer the mage further points of reference for his search.

And by now, the Pack would be looking for her.

"Join us for lunch," Lowell offered magnanimously. "You should before you go."

A last meal? Jia bit the inside of her cheek but still managed to smile. "I would like that, Lowell, thank you."

The Laedan's smile was sincerer this time before he continued down the hall flanked by Quentin and Donn, the younger Channon never having said a word.

That, and the glance he threw back over his shoulder at her, Jia found to be more than a little unnerving.

"You got my message then?" Jonni asked the moment the door of Roland's office was closed, taking care to keep his voice from carrying in case anyone passed in the corridor or his father or brother happened to return without notice. "I'm glad you're safe."

Without mincing words, Jia went to the desk and began opening drawers, rummaging through them and removing items into a pile on the flat top. "How did you know?"

"That you...? Oh..." About the raid. It was obvious how he knew she was safe; she was standing before him with no visible sign of injury. Watching her, wondering what she was looking for, he stayed where he was, hands fidgeting at his sides. "I came upon them planning..."

"Donn and Thomas?"

He noted the glance she gave him but did not gauge it to be a measuring of his honesty. "Yes."

"And your father?"

"My...no...he wasn't there...Thomas was seeking Donn's permission, I think...and from what I heard, they did not want Father to know what they were doing."

Permission Thomas would not have needed, Jia knew, if the Laedan was behind the raid. Or perhaps seeking Donn's agreement had been part of some ruse between Lowell and his aide to hide the Laedan's involvement. Whatever his failings, however, whatever his faults, Lowell loved his sons, doted on them, and wanted them to succeed. He would help them, not hinder them. Jia could not imagine him setting one of them up in such a way.

She had less difficulty believing it of Quentin.

"And you?"

Blinking in surprise that she would question his loyalty, that she might think him capable of such duplicity, he stared with hurt in his eyes. "Why would I...?"

"Outrage...retaliation...because I cannot marry you..."

His face colored with something she interpreted as offense. It was enough to tell her the truth. Jonni had never been as good of an actor as Donn or their father. "That doesn't matter," he spluttered. "I'm not as petty as that. I might be a Channon...but I would never do that to you...not to..." Another drawer closed, the grating sound cutting short his sentence, so he swallowed the incomplete words and instead muttered, "I've never been the one lying."

Hands freezing mid-shuffle, Jia stared at him, hearing the accusation in his tone without his stating her offense outright. "I have never lied to you."

"You withheld the truth...it's the same thing."

"No." She shook her head and continued her task. She did not know when she might be able to return to this room, when her father would return to it, and there were personal effects she did not want to leave for the Laedan or his right hand to either discard or put to their own uses. "It isn't."

"Then tell me the truth now. Is Roland...are you...and Addi..." He choked on the words he wanted, afraid of the confirmation of his fears and the rumors that fueled them. He cleared his throat, tipped his chin in an effort to add confidence to his question, and ground out the words as carefully as he could. "Are the Marrocks Cana?"

Having heard that question coming, Jia did not flinch or twitch or even look at Jonni when the words were said aloud and instead began to rummage through the cabinets on the wall. Wine bottles clanked as she slid them aside, reaching for the safe behind them, but she left the bottles. Let Lowell and Quentin have those. She wanted the coins, the artifacts, and the books hidden behind. Her father had drilled into her a sense of caution when speaking within this room, as if the chance that someone might be listening to them was a real threat. She could not be certain that there were none of the rumored listening devices installed here, that Lowell had not had some means of hearing his co-Laedan's conversations even when they were private ones between family members, and so she chose not to answer Jonni's question. He would take her silence in the way he preferred. There was no need to expose herself further.

What he thought about the safe, her ability to open it, her removal of items from it, was a risk she needed to take.

Instead of answering him, she countered, "Are you HOPE?"

Jonni choked and grunted, "I've never hidden that from you…"

"But you never told me either. If withholding information is the same as lying, then you've been lying to me." There was no bitterness to the statement, no accusation, only the comparison between two similar secrets.

"I know how you feel about HOPE…and my father made all of us join when we were just children…" Jonni sighed and looked toward the window with its overview of the grey, churning sea. If she was Cana, it was by less of a choice then Jonni had been given in joining that powerful society, and if he had been afraid to tell her out of deference to her feelings about HOPE, it was even more logical that she would be reluctant to share the truth with him, for if she was Cana, revealing oneself to a member of HOPE was akin to suicide.

Surely she knew he did not support the teachings, did not study the Corpus any longer nor attend the invocations, and that he would never sanction the hunt and extermination of other people. Anthro or not, mutani or not, they were all part of humanity to him.

But if he had never said it aloud, however, to his family or to her, and he had never actively done anything to show support for either group out of fear of his father, how could she know? She, at least, had expressed pro-anthro leanings as far back as Jonni could remember, and Roland had done his best, within the confines of the powers of his office, to argue for the rights of those who were different. Without a doubt, if she took up her father's post, Jia would do the same.

Perhaps, he realized for the first time, he should strive harder to show his father he was capable of leadership. Perhaps it was time to let the dream of a medipractice go and show his support here in the halls of power for those who were persecuted. If he did not, the duties of co-Laedan were likely to fall onto Donn's shoulders, and there was no way that Donn Channon and Jia Marrock would govern the borough together as equals.

"Is there anything I can do?" He felt useless watching her without helping, now that the conversation had unexpectedly come to an end.

Jia shook her head, again without looking at him. They had been friends for so long, but now that her father's absence, and the truth of her lineage, lingered between them, the awkwardness was almost tangible. Perhaps he could accept her, but the rest of the family would not. Openly admitting anything was not an option. It felt, as she opened another cabinet, that their years of friendship ended here...or perhaps had ended when she refused to marry him. They were unlikely to ever rekindle the level of trust and affection shared before his insistence on marriage had sprung up between them.

He had ruined everything.

"No...I just want some of my father's things..." The majority of items piled on the desk were personal trinkets, mementos given to Roland by his children, a small painted portrait of the family from the days before her mother had died and another of Roland's father in the twilight of his years in office, paperweights and pens and the like which had been left to him when the position had passed from father to son. There were some documents as well, stuffed into a folder wrapped in waxed canvas, but from where he stood, Jonni could not tell what they were. Some had children's drawings and pictures on them, some were written in the more formal flow of an adult hand, possibly letters between Roland and Jia, between Roland and his late wife and his father, or correspondence from friends and supporters that had some sentimental or political value.

The possibility that some might be important state documents was a fleetingly troubling one, but as he could think of no reason why she would want such things, Jonni chose to believe they were personal documents rather than political ones.

If Roland was merely absent rather than missing, why was she taking his things? To keep them out of Quentin's hands, or something else?

It was impossible to guess.

"You're not coming back, are you?"

Jia shrugged. Her life was in flux, with no way of knowing what the next hour would hold. She could not gaze into the future to guess if she would return to the Fortress or not.

"You can go back to your..." she started.

"You should not be here alone."

Scowling, she bit her lip. She supposed he was right; now that it was known she was alive, whether the result of the hunt had come to light yet or not, Donn and Quentin were going to seek some other means of disposing of her…if it was her death they wanted.

Maybe her death would mean the rest of the Pack would be safe. The rest, perhaps, except for Addi and his family, for any other Marrocks would provide the same threat Donn and Quentin perceived her to be.

"I am almost finished." She had two cabinets left to look through, and a filing drawer that she hoped contained details of her father's efforts during his tenure. She had not yet found his personal journals, and she was beginning to worry that Quentin, Lowell, or someone else had confiscated them.

"I'll wait…escort you out…"

"There's no need. I'm keeping you from your duties, but if you could make sure I've got a clear path out, I'd appreciate it."

She wanted privacy. She wanted to be rid of him. Jonni regretted that, regretted the walls now rising between them, but it was impossible to take back what had been said and done. There was only what he could do now, and that included making certain she left the Fortress unharmed.

"I'll do my best," he promised. He wanted to embrace her as friends, bid her farewell as they had done hundreds of times before, but as that no longer felt appropriate, he refrained. "And whatever lies ahead…I swear…I will do everything I can to protect you and your…family." He would not say pack, but he hoped she understood that it was implied, a gesture to prove that he bore her no hatred for the hand that genetics may have dealt them both.

She did not watch him depart, although she did murmur, "Thank you," before the closing door separated them. It was easier to breathe, the air less tense and heavy once he was gone, a fact she regretted as she continued her search. Everything she found, everything that held personal value or might prove to be of use, was stuffed into the satchel she had brought, an item kept hidden in one of the many secret stashes of clothes and supplies the Pack kept around the borough. Clothing was discarded during a change, other personal effects as well, and so it served the Pack to have access to things they could wear should a change to human form be required somewhere far from the den.

Such places also served as ideal hiding places for messages, treasures, and sometimes stashes of food and water. She wondered, as the last cabinet was closed and the satchel securely buckled, if one such stash might contain her father's journals and maybe even the map and ledger Roland had referred to on the day of his disappearance. It was worth investigating, but she would not have time to do so today. It would be a long trek back across the borough to the Wilds, made longer, she imagined, by the need to avoid the eyes she could feel following her as she closed the door to her father's office for what might be the final time. She could not see or smell anyone, but she could feel them there, trailing her return to the staircase, lingering on her as she descended and forced herself not to look around her for the source.

She was nearly to the bottom, noting that Nik was no longer sprawled on the bench where she had left him and that his paraphernalia was gone as well, when the wailing warning of a siren blasted through the Fortress, unable to echo as it filled every room, corridor, and crevice with enough force to rattle the windows. So much for her welcome in the Fortress. Beyond the dirty windows lining the front of the building, armed shadows began to swarm, and the echo of boots on the tile floor began to converge upon her location. Maybe Jonni had betrayed her, thinking her a thief as well as a monster. Maybe one of the others, Lowell, Donn, or Thomas, had sent spies to monitor her movements in order to alert the soldiers of her leaving. There were passages less known, ways to flee with little chance of seizure, but she did not know if she could get to any of them in time to evade capture. Jerking in surprise when a hand closed around hers, she heard a familiar voice demand, "Come with me!" before her gaze settled on Nik's pasty face.

Jia trusted him. He, more than either of his brothers, knew routes in and out of the Fortress, paths used to avoid curfews and rules in order to feed the hunger in his blood. She followed as he ran to the rear of the vast room, directly to a paneled wall that should have presented no way out, and there he quickly pried a corner to pop one panel loose. It opened to reveal a dark, musty passage, where little air flowed and where the dust had been undisturbed for some time.

"Follow it down to the sea…if the tide's out, you'll be fine…"

"If it's not?" she whispered, already scrambling inside as the sounds of approaching chaos drew nearer.

"Swim." Nik grinned and shoved the panel back into place, catching her foot painfully as he did so, but there was no time to be angry over the accidental injury. She heard a heavy thud against the panel, the sliding of a body as it sank to the floor, and she held her breath as she waited, expecting that someone had noted Nik's actions, knocked him out, and would soon pull the panel open to expose her. But the running feet continued, crossing this way and that, and she imagined now that Nik had sunk against the panel with the appearance of having passed out in an all too familiar drugged stupor. Such a sight was so common that not one of the guards would give Nik a second look, and no one would suspect that his position masked the escape route of their quarry.

Trusting that the sound of boots and the wailing alarm would mask sounds within the tunnel, she crawled hastily in the only direction it ran until the concrete path dropped beneath her, creating a long slide on its dust-slickened surface. There were matching grooves in the floor as if some manner of tracks had once run here, but for what purpose she could not imagine. Unable to see, she had no warning of the wooden door that sealed the bottom entrance until she crashed into it with a loud oomph of pain. The wood buckled but did not give way, but that buckling did create a sliver of light between the door panels. Beyond she could hear the eternal rumble of the sea; it was close, but the slapping of waves did not seem to be hitting anything nearby so she guessed, as her fingers felt for hinges, latches, any way of opening the doors, that the tide was low enough that she would not drop into the water when the doors opened.

She found what felt to be a latch, stiff as if rusted from exposure to water and the salt of the sea, and braced herself against each side of the passage to prevent falling. From the satchel she carried, she withdrew her father's stone and metal letter opener, an ideal tool to pry the tongue of metal from the groove in which it rested. The opener dropped from her hand when the metal tongue swung free; the rusty hinges held the door panels in place but the pressure of her boot heel against it forced it to drop open and released the offering of the letter opener into the shallow creeping waves beneath her. Jia tried to catch it but could not, and the effort dislodged her from her wedged position and allowed her to fall as well.

The tide was low, but beginning to shift. Her boots kept her feet dry but each successive wave threatened to leave her cold and wet. Nearly ten feet above, the open panel was set into an overhang propped up with stone and steel beams that had been replaced at least once since the Undoing. The sea had dug a trench into what had once been a section of the runway and now had freedom to lap at the Fortress walls. There were nearly twenty feet from her position back to the building's façade, but if she climbed up the side either to the left or to the right, she could run, hidden by the overhang, and make it clear of the Fortress. No one was likely to seek her here. Focusing on their search within, they should not suspect she was already on the outside. But if she was going to make it home and avoid the search that was likely to extend soon into the streets around the Fortress, she was going to have to run as the wolf would run. It was the only way she could outrun so many men on foot and horse.

Chapter 10

Sal Mareno was an average woman, average in appearance, average in intelligence, average in her attitudes toward the world. She lived in an average single room flat surrounded by others in their single rooms, raised a small share of chickens and vegetables on her balcony, and carried on an average life.

She was also an average Protector, doing her job with no press for promotion or to make a name for herself. She never sought to make her life anything more than what it was. Despite the low profile of her existence, however, she was not afraid of doing that job, despite its many hazards, and her stoic dedication and unwavering calm approach to the world made her the ideal partner. Perhaps not for those on the force who wanted to impress the chiefs, or the Laedan, with exploits and bravery, and perhaps not for those who preferred to cut corners, to work lazily, or who preferred to take advantage of their position and use it for their own gains. But for a private, unassuming man like Mage Segara, Sal's averageness was a perfect fit. He rarely asked for things he would not attempt or do himself, and he never demanded anything more than respect and trust from those he worked with. In the years they had served the Protectorate, they had worked together more than any two people in their squad. They had never failed to solve a case, which gave Sal the unexpected distinction of being the only Protector in their office with a perfect case record. It was the sole area in which she was above average, but she attributed that success to the mage and remained content in her average place in the world.

For the official record, Vance did not count as an officer. Tracker Mages, with their uncanny skill at finding the unfindable, tracing the untraceable, recovering the lost and the guilty, were in a class of their own. Comparing an officer's success to those of a mage made too many Protectors feel inadequate and resentful.

But not Sal.

Vance did not care to be compared to anyone. He preferred being his own man. He preferred being left alone.

When he presented her with the choice of addresses that morning upon his arrival at the Protectorate, the job had seemed simple enough. A medishipment had been stolen while in transport from one warehouse to another, from a location of storage to one of distribution. Learning what had been loaded on that transport was vital, as was taking stock of the delivery location, for if the goods in dispute could be accounted for at either end of the system, then the theft was a fabrication, a ruse that Vance would need to get to the bottom of. It was assumed, without Sal asking, that a mediplies warehouse was managed by the Laedans, for they had always controlled as much of the borough's medical and fuel supplies as they could access, the source of power they wielded over LaGuardia. No one had ever questioned their right to that control, at least not publically, for in the early days of the Undoing, the world had been chaos as people fought over what limited supplies there were. Someone with the power to control the distribution of needed resources, who guaranteed fairer access to everyone rather than just to those who could bully it out of the hands of the needy, helped to keep the peace. The Marrocks and Channons had offered peace to all, their problem solving and people handling skills proving to be what the borough needed to survive and rebuild, and a people hungry for peace and stability had been eager to accept that control.

Distribution had always appeared fair. If it was otherwise, none of the common people knew it.

A theft of this magnitude, of supplies stolen from the Laedans that were intended to benefit everyone, if it indeed had occurred, was stealing from the entire borough. It could not be tolerated and was one of the few crimes still punishable by death. If execution was on the table, it was vital the truth be known so that the innocent was not punished in the place of the guilty.

The choice of addresses was Sal's and she opted for the warehouse of origination. The Laedans were known to keep detailed accounts of the supplies on hand, and so learning what had been shipped would be an easy way to spend a few hours of her morning. With a decent head for figures, her duty was to compare the inventory logs to the manifests to make sure the numbers balanced.

Vance had further to travel to reach the other warehouse, a dodgier area to travel into amongst a segment of the population who were less educated, wilder in disposition. The distribution warehouse might be under the nebulous control of the Laedans, but it was staffed by those who might not, Sal knew, be as prone to keeping accurate records. Those agents were accountable to the Laedans for fair distribution, to see to it that every medifac in their orbit received an equitable portion of mediplies, food, and other equipment according to the size of the population they served, and most of the time, the records balanced. But it often took hours or days to make sense of the creative way in which the barely literate kept record of their transactions. For a mage like Vance, making sense of those records would be a less complicated task than it would have been for Sal or anyone else. Giving him a crack at that location was the logical choice, and Sal had no desire to take it from him. Both would do what they were good at, combine their findings, and the mage would then have a clearer picture of the crime he was investigating.

In duty uniform from the moment she dressed in the morning until the end of her shift each evening, Sal crossed the borough, unafraid, unassuming, greeting familiar faces, assisting an elderly man through the maze of a rubbish-littered street, retrieving a ball wedged into a wall of falling debris for a gaggle of children, pausing to tie her hanker around a dog's bleeding flank and offering a voucher for treatment to the decrepit, mournful woman carrying the wounded animal. All were everyday, average duties for the Protector. She had time. No matter how long it took her to examine the mediplies warehouse's ledgers, she was likely to return to the Protectorate long before Vance did, and there was always room, in her average heart, for small acts of kindness that would make people's lives better and endear her to them.

People who trusted Protectors were people prone to treating them with respect and to be helpful. Respect equaled safety. Safety preserved lives.

As she rounded the final corner, with the warehouse in sight, protected behind the spiked wire fencing meant to keep the contents safe from unsavory, unscrupulous scavs, Sal counted half a dozen armed men provided and trained by the Laedans and hand-selected to be unimpeachable and loyal to their orders. No wagons today, no deliveries to be made, thus the doors of the windowless warehouse remained shut against the cold. Where there had been windows, there were now planks of thin wood, rusted metal sheeting, or cracking plastic, all of which made it impossible to see what or who was inside. It might be empty. It might be crammed with people. The building was shabby, bearing faded graffiti scars, but with resources better spent on what the building contained, upkeep of the structure was, as was often the case in the borough, less of a concern.

Why fret about upkeep when there were so many other empty buildings to move into if the need arose? That would not always be the case; eventually upkeep would become a more pressing concern, but for now, the Laedans, and many others, were content to take advantage of the abundance of vacant structures.

With the insignia on her breast pocket identifying her as a Protector, Sal stopped at the gate with a friendly smile for the two men posted there who barely looked at her. Presenting the sealed writ which gave her permission to enter, she said, "Protector Mareno. I am here at legal request to inspect your accounts…"

The last word was barely past her lips when the uncommon crack of gunfire cut the air and brought with it a slicing pain that lanced through her upper chest and knocked Sal off her feet. The men at the gate barely reacted, did no more than look at her, and made no effort to assist the woman as her blood spread beneath her upon the cold, damp earth, feeding her life to the insects and moss which cemented the cracks of LaGuardia's crumbling infrastructure.

❧*❦

Irritated by failure, Lowell slammed the door on his way into the family room where his wife diligently worked on a floral bouquet for the table, something she did for him every few days since the day he commented that having fresh flowers in a room made him feel alive, connected to the outside world, the multitude of vibrant colors soothing in rooms awash with white, gray, and pale dusty blue.

But no flowers would soothe him today, not when his anger stemmed from too many sources, sources close to him. The hunt they had heard last evening, spurred by his youngest son, yielded no results, not even a name or trace of whatever pack the soldiers had been pursuing. The waste of resources, too many good men dead or failing to return, was an expense the borough could not easily shoulder, not, Lowell knew, if his plans were to come to fruition. Then accusations of theft against Jia, unsubstantiated as they had yet to be proven, resulted in nearly thirty minutes of screeching sirens and no trace of the woman anywhere in the Fortress. Perhaps she was still hiding, eluding the soldiers who continued to seek her in a complex she was intimately familiar with, or perhaps she had left before the alarm went off, but at least the air horns had grown still, allowing Lowell to hear his own thoughts again. Stock was being taken of every file, every object, within Roland's office, but as acting co-Laedan in her father's stead, unofficial as the position was, and as Roland's daughter, Jia had a right to her father's personal property; and if she was working on her father's behalf, she even had legitimate access to his papers.

The accusations made were flimsy, and wrong, but now that they had been levied against a member of a ruling family, by law Lowell had to investigate. In the secret corners of his soul, he hoped the accusations proved true, as it would provide him with a valid excuse to be rid of her before she got too close…as her father had done. But the level-headed politician in him knew that keeping her employed here, keeping her close enough to watch, was a far wiser course.

Now she was beyond his reach, scared away most likely, gone where he could never monitor her actions. A dangerous position to be in, unless someone could produce her body…dead or alive.

From the liquor cabinet, a bottle of berry wine was produced, an expensive vintage but one that would hopefully still his nerves and clear the blaring from his head. He noticed, with the pouring of the glass, the way Yiva turned away from him, noticed as he paced that she kept the same side of her face and body always toward him. He was not suspicious, but the behavior was odd enough to be irritating, like a piece of meat wedged between his teeth. He said her name when he stopped to put the glass, now empty from its third filling, on the cabinet shelf, but though he noted hesitancy in her movement, she did not speak or look at him, and seemed not to have heard him.

Seizing her shoulders, he yanked her about to face him, and though she tried to hide the darkening bruises, he saw enough to warrant grasping her chin and snapping her head sideways.

Yiva froze, lowered her gaze, and said, "It is nothing…I fell…"

"Into someone's hand?" Lowell had left his share of handprints on flesh, blows he had given his sons in their youth meant to toughen them into manhood, marks left intentionally upon staff members who displeased him so that others would see and know the shame of disappointing Lowell Channon. He also knew fear, recognized it in his wife's trembling lips, in the tension of her shoulders, in the way her body prepared to fight or flee. "Who did this?" he demanded. He waited barely long enough for a reply before barking again, "Who?"

"I insulted him; I deserved…it is nothing, I swear. I'm okay."

Her babbling was proof that she was not okay. "Who, Yiv…answer me!"

Unable to look him in the eye, believing he would see through her as he did everyone else, her gaze shifted to the side, then down, and her eyes closed. "Chief…" she stuttered, the man's title the first thing that came to mind…other than the truth…and sticking in her throat as she said it.

Lowell stared with incredulous anger. "Ernest? Ernest did this?"

It seemed unlikely. Walter Ernest had always been a man slow to anger, and never, in the years Lowell had known him, had he witnessed the man hitting a woman, or anyone else, or heard of any instances of the same. Nor had he ever known Yiva to utter an insulting word to anyone except her husband when they use to fight in their younger days. She was the perfect diplomat's wife. It was a significant part of the reason Lowell had married her.

But he thought back to that morning, to the Chief's weary mood, the faintness of stale alcohol upon him, the frustration with which he seemed to do his duty. He had been that way more and more of late, with something dark, perhaps, festering beneath the surface. If something Yiva had said or done prompted the man to strike her with enough force to blacken her eye, Lowell was going to see to it that Ernest paid dearly for such a crime, chief or not.

"I'll take care of it…"

Yiva shook her head fiercely. "No…it isn't important…"

"It is…"

"Please, Low…let it go…don't…"

Lowell's gaze narrowed further, suspecting for the first time that his wife, his ever honest, dutiful, humble wife, was lying to him. About what was the question.

When his head nodded in agreement, Yiva's stance relaxed enough to allow a small smile to blossom. "Thank you, Lowell. Would you like…shall I draw a bath? Bring you a meal perhaps…?"

"No…I only came in for a drink. I will see you this evening…dinner on the balcony." She had given him enough of a distraction to subdue his previous anger, although it had been replaced with one of a different sort.

"Yes," she bubbled, hurrying off now with the discarded flower stems and the blade she had used to trim them.

Lowell watched her, determination blending with the fury in his eyes. Let her think the matter dropped. Someone harming his wife was not a slight the Laedan would easily forget, or forgive. Unlike his wife, Lowell would lie to anyone to get what he wanted. Now he wanted the truth.

❧*❧

Following the fresh scent of water and damp, wild earth, step after step more difficult as he struggled to lead Vanya to a safe haven, Kato fought not to give in to the blood loss last night's injury had cost him. He had not thought it a significant injury, had thought the flow staunched by the pressure of his hand before he finally gave in to sleep, but the wound reopened during the night and continued to ooze throughout the day. He kept his sister from seeing the blood by positioning her on his right side, but as he stumbled again, weakened by the stabbing pain, he knew he was not going to be capable of protecting her sufficiently much longer. If he bled to death, he would not be able to protect her at all, but he had no mediplies with which to stitch the gash closed, no alcohol to clean it or deaden the pain, and no way, he realized, of hiding it indefinitely. Not when she wrapped her arm around him to keep him upright, not when she deliberately slowed her pace to accommodate his. For all of the difficulties she faced in life, Vanya was not stupid. She would notice, and she would be afraid.

He barely discerned the moment they stepped clear of the city's jagged-toothed jaws and into the forest growth of a long overgrown park. And he did not detect the presence of others, watchful, wary eyes following their agonizing step-by-step progress, until his legs gave way and brought him to his knees with a painful jolt. The shock of it elicited a yelp that turned Vanya in time to see him crumble to the earth, exposing the bloody swath of fabric for the first time.

"Kato!" she cried, oblivious to the others as well as she thrust her stuffed bear into her brother's arms and tried to use the flat of her hands to stop the seepage. She did not know where the blood was coming from, how it had happened or when, and it did not occur to her to get a better view by lifting the fabric. She only understood that bleeding equaled dying and that dying meant she would be alone. As simple as her mind could be, being alone was a reality she understood, and in moments of particular clarity, one she feared.

"Kato…wake up! Stop bleeding! Make it stop!"

It was the woman's frightened-girl voice that drew the observers from the foliage, the older, more muscled of the two from upwind and the younger woman from downwind, a woman who stared warily at the other as if to determine what threat he might be not just to her but also to the injured man and the woman crying over him, frantically trying to push blood back into his body. Deuce cocked his head, sniffed the air, and then took the risk that the darker skinned woman across from him was hesitant to take. He knew Trill to be a good woman, kindhearted and helpful, but last night's hunt and the precariousness of their current situation made her justifiably wary.

She did not know their scents as Deuce did. He knew this man, knew enough to feel that his condition warranted Pack resources.

But Deuce's size and the wildness about him frightened the already panicked young woman and kept him from being able to help, whereas she seemed less frightened by Trill's slow and easy approach. Trill noted this as well and took initiative, her gentle hand eventually covering the other woman's and drawing her attention away from the blood.

"Help him," Vanya whimpered. "I need him."

Trill pealed the cloth back to gauge the seriousness of the injury. Skin sliced through, exposing muscle but not deep enough to threaten the organs, a clean wound, recent but not immediate, fresh, likely obtained within the past twelve hours. If properly tended, stitched, bandaged and given time to heal, it would not have become the vulnerability it was now. She deduced that he had been traveling with this injury for some time, fleeing the danger that had caused this, perhaps, seeking safety…leaving a trail that would be too easy for even a novice hunter to follow.

"I will," she promised the other woman, human, child-like, but not, as far as Trill could tell, mutani. If she was going to help him, she would need supplies, bandages and alcohol to clean the wound, and she had none of those things with her. There was another better suited to the task of treating the injured man, and it would likely take her calming influence to keep the other woman still while medicare was given.

She looked at the Omega Cana beseechingly. "Bring Addi…I will stay with them."

Deuce scowled. Leaving them unprotected went against his instincts. The likelihood the Marrock boy, or any in the Pack, would heed him without immediate defensiveness or attack, was slim. But this frightened woman-child would not remain calm if Trill tried to leave her; she would likely devolve into a state of panic that Deuce was not equipped to manage. It had been a long time since he had offered comfort to anyone. Providing it to a stranger was beyond him. Bringing help, however, was not…so long as Addison agreed.

And an order from another within the Flushing Pack was something he had no choice but to obey, no matter the cost.

The Pack was camped nearly seven hundred yards from where the stranger had fallen, protected by the forest and Pack sentries. The pair might have been allowed to pass without incident so long as they had come no closer to where the wagon and the children were guarded. It took Deuce less than two minutes of dodging between trees, leaping over fallen logs, and a pair of rivulets, to reach the encampment. As expected, his abrupt eruption into the heart of camp brought every adult to face him, some armed, many with angry, frightened countenances, but Deuce chose to ignore the threats. They did not know him. They knew only rumor and legends based on the fears and prejudices of others, not the man himself. Let them fear and distrust him if they must. He was intent on being the better man.

"Addison…Trill needs you…bring your medibag…"

The surprise of all at hearing the Omega speak, when none had ever considered that he could, lasted only long enough for Addi to act. The mention of his wife's name moved him, thinking her injured and in need of aid. If Deuce had left her injured and at the mercy of some malicious force, there would be repercussions. Her brother Xan and Pain Jusic burst into a run in the direction from which Deuce had come. The Omega growled to himself at their impetuous folly that was going to complicate the situation, but he waited for Addi to grab his supply pack and follow.

By the time the doctor and Omega reached Trill's location, the female outsider was wailing in fear, startled by the men who burst into the clearing, her voice shrilly carrying back toward the camp and announcing their location to anyone, predator or pursuer, who might be in this corner of the Wilds. Pain lifted his hand to strike and silence her, and though both Trill and Addi cried, "No!" the hand fell…and came short of its target when the Omega took the risk of plowing hard against the other Cana, knocking him to the ground. Pain threw the bulky man off, able to do so only because Deuce did not resist or fight him, and when Pain rose, snarling to his feet, the Omega dutifully retreated to the edge of the clearing.

There would be a fight later, punishment meted out by the other Cana to the impudent Omega, but for the moment, Xan's growl of "Enough," pushed the fight into the background.

"Who…?" Pain snapped, attention directed to the injured man whom Addi was examining. Trill wrapped her arms around the flailing woman and held her tight, a mothering embrace she used to soothe frightened children in the Foundling Center and within the Pack. Though she was no longer screaming, Vanya still struggled to get to her brother's side, particularly when the unconscious man jerked awake at the sting of alcohol burning the gash on his side.

"It doesn't matter," grunted Addi, one hand pressing upon the injured man's chest to keep him from rising. It was an unnecessary gesture; the pain of the burn was enough to wake him but also, as weak as he was, enough to drop him back into unconsciousness. The clear fluid washed away enough blood for Addi to better see the damage beneath the midmorning shadows of the forest, enough to give him a clear indication of what was needed to make the bleeding stop and save the man's life.

"It does matter! He could be a scout…"

"He's not…"

Narrowed eyes leveled upon Deuce, Pain spat, "No one asked you, Omega."

Deuce dropped his gaze and did not speak again.

As Addi brought a needle and thread from his pack and began to stitch, Vanya yelped, certain that such a pricking of the skin was harming Kato more than helping.

"Shut her up…"

Trill glared at Pain. "He's her brother." Pain had no siblings, but Trill knew what she would do, how she would feel, if her brother, her husband, her children were similarly injured and she was unable to help them. "We should bring them back with us."

"Send them away. None of our business."

But Pain's bitter views went unheeded. The past that had brought him into the Flushing Pack was an unknown to most, only Maz, and Roland, as Pack leader, had ever learned the secrets that brought the young wolf into their Pack. Whatever history he shouldered, it left a cloud lingering above him, and it made him ideally suited for duties that required violence and the meting out of suffering. It made him an excellent hunter, an excellent lookout, and an excellent protector of the Pack, but it also frequently left him on the outside of Pack decisions, frequently the lone dissenting voice in plans that might put the Pack at risk, whether it was a necessary risk or not.

His stance now was no surprise.

A sound, Deuce clearing his throat, made Addi look up from the wound he had just sewn shut. What was on the Omega's mind, he could not tell, but Deuce clearly felt differently than Pain, felt that this man and his sister were worth the risk they were taking in treating him here in the open…the risk they would have to take in bringing him back to the camp. Until the stranger awoke, until he could move freely on his own and Addi was confident there was no more risk of infection, they could not leave the pair alone and defenseless in the Wilds. The woman would never survive.

"We'll let Jia decide," Addi said as he gestured for Xan to help lift the unconscious man. Between the two of them, they could carry him to safety, so long as Trill kept the other woman from interfering.

"Jia is not…" started Pain. His protest was cut short by Addi's searing gaze and his gesture for someone to pick up the fallen packs.

Not prone to obeying Addi's demand, seeing him a lesser successor to Roland's leadership just as he did Jia, Pain tossed his head with a snort and stalked back in the direction of camp.

Although he scowled and swore silently where no one would ever hear him, Addi too did not feel himself to be suitable alpha material, and thus felt he had little right to demand anything from Pain. He was relieved that Deuce picked up the strangers' fallen belongings and shifted them in his arms so that he could carry all of them with ease for the short distance necessary. Only the stuffed bear was removed from his grasp, the young woman now clutching it to her chest as she stumbled along as close to her brother as she could get, accepting Trill's arm about her shoulders as both comfort in her worry and support over the uneven terrain.

Damn it, Jia, Addi thought with concern. Where are you?

❦Scratch the Sky❦

Chapter 11

She had left the Laedan's pursuers behind long ago, her knowledge of these streets more intimate than most after so many childhood nights spent with her father and mother running through them, hunting, learning what it meant to be Cana, how to work with the wolf instead of allowing those more primal instincts to control her. Unlike the blood wolf in nature, Cana packs were forced by their humanity to share territory, to cross them for work and trade, and it was to their advantage to know every detail of streets and structures and the areas other packs called home.

For those reasons, it was rare that a state-sanctioned hunt of Cana was successful. Invariably when it was, it was due to luck on the hunter's part, to carelessness, to vigilant surveillance, or to betrayal. Which of those had led to her father's capture, Jia mused as she crossed the street that delineated the southeastern border of LaGuardia into the few block stretch of no man's land designated as a safe zone between LaGuardia and Kennedy. It was the only place she knew of where no weapons fire was permitted or tolerated, a guaranteed route of passage between boroughs that neither owned, maintained by both and, some said, by HOPE. It was the easiest route east, one that took her south of what had been her home and around the crossroad of carnage her pack had left behind last night. If the Laedan's troops had tracked their missing fellows to where they had fallen, they might still be there, retrieving their dead, looking for clues as to where their prey had escaped to.

Jia would not lead anyone there or to the Pack. An indirect route into the Wilds would take longer, but it was safer for those she loved.

There were border guards here, but a single female with few visible weapons was given passage without question. Carrying a weapon was almost required, the only means to ensure one's safety, so few sentries thought twice about allowing travelers to carry. And someone daring enough, for whatever reason, to travel east into untamed territory, would be foolish not to carry some form of protection. The knife on Jia's hip, little more than a sharpened length of steel bartered for as she weaved her way across the borough, would be enough protection for anyone trained to use it. If she was not trained and was making this journey anyhow…well, what was it to the sentries if she was willing to risk her life in the Wilds?

It was crossing the border to the east that made her both warier and more at ease. Noon was upon her, though the sun, as usual, was little more than a bright glow behind the sheath of gray clouds, and she was confident she had lost any Fortress guards who might have followed her, confident that she had picked up no other tails. But these were unfamiliar streets now, inhabited by unfamiliar people and, she scented on the wind, other anthro, any of whom might take offense at her movement through their territory. She could feel the wary gazes as she passed. Though there appeared to be no 'normal' life here, no merchants bartering scavenged goods for other things, no families trading foods they had grown for ones they had not or had run short of, people trading animals, milk or eggs for items they required for survival, no visible trace of industry, there were people. People hidden behind barred doors and shuttered windows, people peering from behind window coverings or around partially open doors or decaying walls, watching her pass, gauging the level of threat she might be. By the time they judged her to be nothing more than a traveler without interest in them, she had already moved on.

The further she traveled beyond the cluster of border residents, beyond what was likely a trading place for goods that passed between boroughs, the fewer sets of staring eyes she drew until the streets felt more deserted than inhabited. With that desertion came a woman's cries, the shouts of children, another woman barking orders, all voices carrying enough panic to draw unwanted attention. The jumble was undecipherable at first, the voices tangled as they rebounded from one collapsing wall to another, but as Jia's slow pace brought her nearer the point of origin, demands to stay still, not to move, not to fall began to sift out of the muddled words.

It was none of her concern. Another's child, the safety of strangers, was someone else's priority. But what she detected on the cold wind were Cana. Females, adults…and pups. Perhaps not her own, but if she could help them, maybe they, in turn, could help her. The diplomacy of aiding another pack in need, of helping other Cana, meant help for her pack later. At least, that was what her mother had taught her from the earliest days of her childhood. Helping others had been a lesson Addi had taken to heart, had spurred his journey on the path of medicine, and while Jia was no doctor, she did understand diplomacy. There were different ways to help and this, Jia knew, was hers.

She scaled a collapsed wall, cautiously listening to the sounds beyond it, until, perching upon the top, she could see a boy, maybe eight or ten, who had crawled out on a jagged extension of girder that balanced precariously on the other end with fallen concrete to ballast it. There were two other boys, older, bearing obvious kinship, who looked to be trying to add additional weight to the beam, like a giant, deadly teeter-totter, a woman who joined them, her blond hair hanging wet and limp about her face, and a second woman with hair a similar shade to the boys who tried to stretch herself flat against the iron surface, her hand out, pleading with the boy to take it. A third woman, darker of skin with raven-black hair, held her ankles to keep her from plunging the fifteen or twenty feet to the rocky ground.

It was not that far of a drop. For a human child, deadly to be sure, but for a Cana old enough to shift, an easy jump to make. The adults were Cana, Jia was certain, so the odds of genetics meant that the boys would be as well. The boy appeared old enough to have experienced a few changes by now, accidental, impulsive, perhaps, but changes all the same. To Jia, making a recommendation to change, to jump, was the natural thing to do. But if the adults were not encouraging him to do so, perhaps he could not, or there was some reason they did not want him to. Jia had no right to encourage disobedience.

But it was obvious he was not going to reach for the outstretched hand, just as it was obvious he was not afraid of his precarious perch. If the boys and woman on the other end moved, however, took their combined weight from the beam's other end, both woman and child would likely fall, and the woman reaching for him was no more inclined to get off the beam than the boy was.

The women saw Jia first, then the boys on the steadier end of the girder saw her, as Jia dropped to the ground, shed her pack and jacket, and stood directly beneath the adventurous child.

"Hello," she said in as friendly a tone as she could. Her small size and youthful features would, she hoped, be enough to bridge any barriers between them. "I'm Jia...what's your name?"

The woman lying on the beam froze, eyes wide and fearful as the boy's attention shifted to the stranger on the ground. He smiled at seeing her, any wariness warranted by the approach of a stranger of no concern to him as he replied, "Eddie."

Jia had the feeling that he was overly-protected and sheltered, kept from interacting with anyone outside of his family, and that he was desperate to make new friends.

"Well, Eddie...don't you think you should come down from there? It isn't..."

"I won't fall." There was confidence in his voice as he shifted to crouch on hands and bare feet, not foolhardiness or childish inexperience, as if he knew something the adults did not. He had a good sense of balance, that much was obvious.

Jia continued to smile, hoping to diffuse the tension that spiked in the other women at his bold assertion. "I can see that...but it isn't fair to worry your mother, is it? Put her in danger of falling? Is that a responsible thing to do?"

Eddie scowled, the notion of responsibility sticking in his head as he glanced at the woman reaching for him. Jia could feel the war in him, a boy wanting to be respected, trusted, seen as something more than a child, not only by the adults but by the other boys as well. A boy pushing toward becoming a man and, she guessed, battling with the beast he carried inside.

"They won't accept me…" he muttered.

"Then show them you can do the right thing…the wise thing. Show them who you are, Eddie…not what you think they want you to be." They were, perhaps, dangerous words, interfering in how another raised their child. But they were words similar to those she had spoken to every pup in her Pack, words her father had passed on to her, words that had encouraged Addi to follow his dreams despite Roland's desires. Respect begot respect, honesty and determination too. Whatever Eddie faced that made him fear rejection had to be confronted, and a mother willing to risk her life for his safety was not likely to reject him for it.

"Come down, Eddie," his mother called. "We will talk…we will sort this…"

"Nothing to sort, Ma. I can't change it; you can't change it."

"Then talk to me, Eddie…I will listen…" Jia offered, "I will help if I can…come down from there and talk to me. It can't be so bad…"

His skepticism lasted a few more moments until he found something in her face, her voice, or some other aspect of her, to be worth trusting. His balance unfaltering, Eddie wiggled out of his ill-fitted clothes, letting them drop to the ground at Jia's feet, despite his mother's protests and admonitions against exposure to the cold and to a stranger. What could have been a display of defiance proved to be something more; his small body shuddered, arched and twisted, shedding the vestiges of humanity for something other. Something graceful and feline.

It explained the peculiarity of his scent, and his mother's crestfallen expression of horror illuminated the situation further. A mother afraid for her child's life.

It was a rare circumstance, but the genetics of anthrozooidism were still in flux and not easily explained. Between individuals of the same subspecies, there was a chance that children would carry the traits of their parents and a chance that they might carry none at all…to be outwardly 'normal' with no anthro tendencies. It was why normals with seemingly unencumbered genetics could give birth to an anthro child, a situation that resulted in more than one divorce and the rejection of the child. The humanity within them allowed for interbreeding between anthro sub-species, though most stuck to their own kind; children resulting from such a union could be normal, could resemble one parent or the other, or, rarer still, a strange hybrid of both anthro blood-lines. Such hybrids rarely lived, but the other children, whether resembling mother or father, frequently did. It appeared, as the young Fela leaped from his perch onto the ground beside Jia, his skin covered with dark tawny fur mottled with the lighter and darker spots of camouflage frequently seen in Fela cubs, that Eddie was either a foundling or else the result of a pairing between Cana and Fela. If he was a hybrid, it was not noticeable.

The Fela in his blood was unmistakable, and something, it appeared, that his mother was uncomfortable with. Now that the boy was safely off the girder, she began a hasty crawl backward to where the other boys were whistling in support of their brother's antics.

They would be joined soon enough, a conflict Jia did not look forward to, but as promised, she squatted down in front of the seated Fela so that they were at eye level, her smile bringing the boy back to himself with the swiftness of a well-practiced adult.

"Well done," Jia said. "You've been changing for some time…"

Eddie's relief at being accepted, finding no reproach in the stranger, was warming to see. "A year now…but Ma doesn't want me to…thinks it is dangerous."

"Changing is always dangerous." The words were true, not merely spoken for the benefit of those who were running to join them. They stayed his mother's impulse to grab her son and yank him away from this stranger. "Normals do not approve."

"I don't do it where they can see," he protested, disappointed that his ally seemed less of an ally now.

"Good...smart. But...you've seen cats, haven't you, Eddie?"

"Of course." Cats had thrived since the Undoing, unaltered pets producing litter after litter of kittens until they were nearly as abundant as birds and squirrels through the borough streets. The overabundance made them a food source for those living a hand to mouth existence; the likelihood that Eddie had never encountered one was slim.

"And you know you're different from them?" Though furred, with catlike features and claws and some having some sort of a tail at the base of their spine, Fela, like other anthro, were bipedal, maintaining a human shape overall. An anthro, in its animal-like form, might be disguisable as a human, but without a disguise, there was no mistaking them for either normals or animals. What they were was obvious. "Anyone seeing you will know you're Fela..."

"But I'm stronger...faster..."

"One day, maybe," Jia agreed with a grin. "But strong and fast isn't always enough. If you rush into growing up, you might never get to be stronger and faster...do you understand?"

He crossed his arms petulantly over his chest but nodded, a bright enough boy to understand that he was no man yet, no matter how strong and mature he felt. "You're not afraid of me?"

"Why should I be?" She smirked at the look he threw her and asked, "Because you're not Cana?"

"Because I don't belong."

"Oh, Eddie." His mother rushed forward then and enveloped him in her arms. "Of course you belong! I never meant to..."

"If anyone doesn't belong," grunted one of the other boys, "it's me."

"You all belong...you're all my boys," the woman said earnestly, holding out one arm to him. Though he pouted as if he did not believe her, the boy accepted the hug while the eldest kept himself apart, his expression uncertain as he scanned around them, watchful for a danger that was not there. "None of that matters...but we all need to be careful..."

"We always need to be careful," Jia agreed, rising to her feet, satisfied that her duty to the child was complete.

The black-haired woman, her arm around the blonde, looked Jia over skeptically. "You took a risk with us…"

Retrieving her coat and pulling it around her shoulders, Jia replied with a shrug. "It was worth it." The boy was safe.

"Are you alone? This isn't a good place…"

Perhaps the question was asked in curiosity, perhaps there was some other motive. When Jia replied, "I'm returning to my Pack," it was with enough darkness in her tone to let the other women know that others were expecting her, others that would seek her out if she did not return…others who might offer protection if the women and boys needed it. "You?"

"They're gone…" the blonde murmured sadly. "All of them."

"Gone?"

Drawing her sons to their feet as she stood, the third woman said, "HOPE." Any explanation needed was wrapped into that one word.

"They're here?"

"South…in the borough…or they were two weeks ago. You're not going there? It isn't safe for us," said the dark-skinned woman.

"Going north." Jia studied the group with a quick appraising gaze. The three were lucky, no doubt, to have escaped whatever hunt had resulted in the eradication of their pack, but they were also, she wagered, strong and resourceful to have survived with three children for two weeks in this forsaken place. They were dirty and thin from a scarcity of food and water, and likely had few belongings to call their own, but they appeared otherwise healthy, and in a pack that lacked females, they would be a welcome addition…if they were willing to take the risk of trusting her. "Do you want to join me?"

The three women looked at one another, sharing an unspoken dialogue that was punctuated by the eager gaze of two of the three boys and indifference by the other.

"Are there other kids?" Eddie asked. "Any like me?"

"None like you," Jia said with sympathetic regret, "but there are children. We're…" She shrugged. If she wanted the trust of the she-wolves, she needed to be honest with them. "We're between homes at the moment; our alpha, my father, is missing, but we're a big enough Pack to protect ourselves...and you too...and we have food and shelter for now. You'll be safe with us, safer than out here..."

"We couldn't repay you...you've already done enough." Eddie's mother looked at her Fela son with appreciative relief.

"There's nothing to repay; the offer isn't about owing me. Safety in numbers...for all of us. You're welcome if you want to come."

There was another exchange of glances between the women before the mother offered an accepting hand. "Candace...my sister, Brie...Helena...and my sons Petr, Neel, and Eddie."

"Jia." It felt good to have names for the faces. They might have heard her introduction to Eddie before, but she felt that introducing herself to the women as well was the polite thing to do. "They're expecting me...we should go..."

"Get the bags." Candace instructed her sons, "And Eddie...put your clothes on." The mother Cana seemed to be their functioning alpha, the voice the others listened to as the boys scattered back into the building except for Eddie who dutifully obeyed the mandate to dress against the cold. When Petr returned, it was with some of the packs, a pair of shoes and a raggedy coat he threw in his youngest brother's direction, and by the time Eddie was fully dressed, the rest of the bundles had been brought out. It looked to be no more than bedding wrapped around whatever food and clothes they had scavenged on their flight north. As Jia led them through the streets toward the Wilds, Helena took up a protective rear position, and Jia was already gauging in her head what clothing the Pack might be able to spare...and how she was going to sell the addition of outsiders to her already unsettled pack.

❧*❦

"None, sir...for a month or more...there hasn't been anything scheduled either..."

Relieved to have discovered no hidden supplies at the destination warehouse, Vance was, however, troubled by the claims made by these people, claims repeated by everyone in command, anyone who had access to the store, that he interviewed. Most of these medifacs could barely function as it was, if no mediplies had been sent, none scheduled or reported to be so, on the night the wagon load was claimed to have gone missing, it would explain their meager stores. It might also explain why someone might want to rob any transport they stumbled across. Still, none of the possibilities presented, as to what had actually happened to the shipment, were favorable ones, save for the off chance that the shipment was to have been an unscheduled delivery to make up for the previous lack. The possibility that there had been no delivery at all, that Laedan Channon meant either to preoccupy the mage with frivolity to distract him from something else, or meant to cause trouble for Addison Marrock, burned like bile in the back of Vance's throat, an irritation he craved a good strong drink to wash clean. He imagined that was the story Channon would tell if this discrepancy was presented to him, that it had indeed been an unscheduled delivery, but Vance imagined with equal certainty that story would be a lie.

Why did people lie to him? Didn't they realize, he mused bitterly as he climbed the steps of the Protectorate headquarters, that sooner or later the mage would have the truth, no matter their cooperation or lack of it?

He felt the heavy gazes of his fellow Protectors as he entered the central office, curious, accusatory, more persistent glances than usual, but usual all the same, and though a few of them he deigned to return with vacant eyes that made the others look away, he chose mostly to ignore them.

A door latch clicked. Old, tired hinges creaked. Normal sounds in an office where people moved about performing their day's duties.

"Segara...my office."

The icy prickle that connected the Chief's weary words with the persistent observation of his fellow Protectors made Vance rub the back of his neck, a casual-seeming gesture but one meant to soothe the raw nerves that lifted the tiny hairs and drew beads of sweat from beneath the surface of his skin. He nodded at Ernest, hesitating on route to his desk, opting for keeping his long coat on for the meeting instead of hanging it over the back of his chair, a fabric shield that would serve little protection if a reprimand was in order.

What else could it be? While that somnolent tone dragged behind Ernest's voice more and more of late, it was one that Vance had equated with bad news over the years, and so it was a short leap between the tone and the unsanctioned business he had undertaken for Laedan Channon.

"Shut the door."

Vance fought against the scowl that tugged at the corners of his mouth and eyes, that tried to furrow his brow, as he closed the heavy door as requested. Definitely a reprimand. When he turned to face the desk, it was with his shoulders back, his hands at his side, as formal a stance as he could manage with eyes focused unwaveringly ahead of him, not on the Chief's face but at a point just to the side and behind him.

It was a stance Ernest recognized, but he did not have the strength to correct Vance's misconceptions. Vance was a man used to accepting...or at least...expecting...reprimand and punishment, an emotional remnant of a childhood caught between a weak but doting father, a drunkard stepfather, and a hard-working mother too lost in providing for her boys to actually provide for them. Ernest did not know all the details, had never asked, but he had learned enough over drinks shared on nights when his personal demons sought out the company of someone else's...and the mage had solemnly obliged. Segara was the closest thing the Chief had to a friend, though a true friendship was something their positions of employment kept stunted and malformed.

Maybe now that Ernest was set to retire, that would change.

"Sal's dead." He saw no point in softening the news. Better to lay it out between them and let the chips fall where they would.

Vance's hands curled into white-knuckled fists, the only visible reaction other than a twitch at the corner of his right eye. "How?"

No unnecessary words, no outbursts of emotion. Just as Ernest expected. He started to sink into the overused metal chair, adjusted his weight to compensate for the wobble, but after leaning his elbows on his desk, he grunted and rose again. He did not feel like looking up at the mage; it made him feel uncomfortably vulnerable. "I was hoping you could tell me."

Any thoughts going on behind the pools of murky brown were not discernable, depriving Ernest of any clues he hoped to find there. It was expected, however. A Tracker Mage was only as good as their ability to keep their thoughts to themselves. They had to keep their thoughts and emotions hidden, or else everything they picked up from everyone around them would make social interactions awkward and impossible.

"Has she been processed?"

"She's on ice."

Keeping a corpse in cold storage presented the risk of a grubber loose in the Protectorate, as the cold only slowed the deterioration process instead of stopping it completely. Yet Ernest had demanded the risk taken. There had been time enough to wait for the mage's return; the sooner Vance inspected her, however, the better Ernest would feel. Soon, normal processing and disposal would have to commence. Vance needed a still intact body to learn everything he could about the crime that had taken her life.

It did not matter where her body had been found; even the Protectors brought her in recognized a dump when they saw one. A mage was their best hope of learning the truth of her death, able to see clues in the smallest details, able to see and hear beyond the curtains where no normal individual could penetrate. And this particular dump, this particular loss to the Protectorate, was going to be one that Mage Segara would want to tend to personally.

Segara was loyal to the department, to the borough; they could all say that much about him. And he would be especially loyal to the only partner he ever chose on his own.

"I'll see her."

Whatever Vance already knew, if he knew anything, was not going to be shared until he had more facts, until he saw the woman himself. Ernest nodded, opened the office door, and followed the mage to the stairwell that led to the basement, or up to the second-floor tier of offices and judicial chambers. Anything above the second level was inaccessible, and often the basement flooded despite continuing efforts to shore it against frequent squalls, but today, in spite of recent rain, the ill-lit passages between prison cells, forensics storage, and the morgue, were mostly dry. Dry, but cold, and the morgue was colder still. Two of the bodies he had found the day before, the man mutilated by some large anthro, now headless to prevent the rise of infection, and the unfortunate mutani child who would never have survived to adulthood regardless of any care given, lay side by side on a rusted metal table on one side of the room, their torsos sewn closed from whatever part of the study the on-duty forepath had been undertaking. On the opposite wall, in a lidded, insulated cask meant to contain the dead before processing, Sal appeared asleep, pensive and uneasy but asleep all the same…except for the round puncture of red at the level of her heart, stained with the red of her life, made with the precision of a marksman.

Made with a weapon that barely existed and was rarely utilized any longer. That single clue told Vance more than the set of her mouth, the spread of crystalized crimson across the front of her uniform, or the discomfort of the man at his side. Ernest wanted his assessment, wanted his report, though likely less desperately than Vance wanted the truth.

He could not look into the milky haze of her eyes, as they were locked behind lids held stiffly closed by the cold in which she was stored. Looking there would be more expedient, but the attendants of the dead rarely thought to open the eyes, or to keep them open, for the mage's work. Few were comfortable looking into the eyes of the dead. For Vance, it was part of the job, part of the way his talents worked, as well as an act of respect he felt the dead deserved.

There was mud on her clothes, suggesting she had fallen in the street, and the stench of rotten vegetable matter spoke of her body being deposited in a mulch heap; it clung to her long after he thought it should have. Not a box, for the smell permeated her hair and clothing too deeply instead of merely lingering on the surface like a splash of perfumed water. She had lain in that place long enough for the scent to settle, but not long enough for it to soak through her uniform, an hour or two at most, and she had lain on ice for nearly twice that judging by the depth of freeze on her skin. Her hair and the creases in her icy stiff uniform indicated exposure to rain, no covering of a mulch box would allow that, and the caked in mud and bits of tomato and some form of greenery frozen into her hair, as well as the spread of blood down the left side of her breast were all clues that she had fallen on her back and then been dumped and left upon her side. They were all external clues that Vance expected the forepath had already made note of and may have already given the Chief. It was the invisible details that were expected of him, evidence both men wanted and dreaded at the same time.

One hand covered her clasped ones, the cold removing the usual soft callous feel of her work-hardened skin. The other pressed lightly on her forehead, and Vance closed his eyes and senses to external stimuli in favor of the senses within. Flashes of sight and sound, muted by the shades of death as they fought to take hold, showed him polished leather boots that squeaked with each step, tailored gray trousers whose stiffness could be heard as leg brushed against leg. Indifferent hands…cold…so cold…

"She was alive when they moved her, but dead before dumped judging by the rate of blood loss such a shot would have caused." He did not turn the body over to examine her back. That would show him more of her blood than he wanted to see. Seeing Sal like this was difficult enough. Lifted shortly after the shot, though already dying, shot from a distance, the echoes of that thunder lingering on the periphery that marked a closed gate.

A gate whose archway Vance recognized with another surge of bile in his throat.

"She never made it there…"

"Where? Where did this happen? Who would…?"

"Sniper." Vance withdrew his hands, tucked them into his armpits to warm them, and avoided Ernest's first two questions. "She was on an errand for me..."

"What sort of errand?"

Vance shook his head, not inclined to share that detail as it would lead to further questions, but Ernest would not be put off. "Channon's asked me to watch you," he said in a low voice, the secret he had been asked to keep refusing to be silenced. He trusted Vance's work. He was not going to hide such a detail that might hinder the mage's efforts. "Whatever it is he asked you to do...do you think it has something to do with this?"

The mage did not resist the scowl this time, but as he was not looking at his Chief, he hoped it was not noticed. He had no idea if this was the first time the Chief was asked by the Laedan to monitor his work, but it was the first time Ernest had told him about it. Either Channon did not trust him to do his job...or he was expecting that the mage would do it too well and wanted to be forewarned should Vance learn something the Laedan did not want to be known.

"She was supposed to take an inventory...that's all, and..." Vance snorted, "she did not make it there." What he did not admit to was that she had reached her destination but had been kept from entering and completing her assignment by the sniper's bullet. Having faced the gate and warehouse when struck, the bullet having entered straight on, entering the front and exiting her back, it was obvious to Vance that the shot had come from the warehouse.

What was not obvious was the motive, but the most logical one would have been to prevent her from doing her duty, from seeing whatever was, or was not, inside.

He was going to need to get in there himself, learn the truth on his own. A difficult feat and one he did not relish undertaking. He had no desire to end up on ice next to, or in the place of, Sal.

"Did anyone else know where she was headed?"

"I..." Vance had made sure that they spoke in private, intending to keep the investigation out of Ernest's hearing, but the building they stood in offered little privacy, and he could not guess who Sal might have spoken to on the way out of the Protectorate. She was not a gossip, not one to speak unnecessarily, but that did not rule out that this time was an exception. If she had mentioned her destination to anyone, it meant that someone in the office was a security leak, a threat to other Protectors, a scandal Ernest could not afford so near to retirement.

"I don't believe so...not that I am aware of..." Vance shrugged before adding, "It is possible, I guess." The possibility of internal corruption within the Protectorate was numbing, but investigating even a hint of it would keep Ernest busy, keep him from involving himself too deeply in Vance's investigation. It was a distraction both men wanted for that same reason, an excuse to offer the Laedan when the man asked for news about the mage's work. It was not, however, the sort of distraction that Ernest wanted as his retirement loomed. "I'll investigate where she was found...do the inventory myself...see if I can find where the shooting occurred..."

"You'll let me know as soon as you learn anything."

It was a command, not a question, so Vance nodded his head, even though he had no intention of giving the Chief all of the details. He did not need clumsy Protectors mucking up his crime scenes or his investigation, and he knew that, in spite of the question, Ernest did not honestly want the details. He just wanted the matter done before it ruined him, and was trusting Vance to do exactly that.

Chapter 12

T he group of women and children traveled in silence for some
time, wary that the previous ruckus of getting Eddie to safety had
attracted unwanted attention. But as the minutes passed and no
threat presented itself, the women began to open up to one another, the
three strangers recounting a tale that sounded hauntingly familiar. The
hunt, the capture, the systematic extermination, it was feared, of any
Cana pack who strayed too near the far reaches of HOPE's deadly
fingers. Such hunts had increased throughout the boroughs and even,
it seemed, occasionally into the Wilds, but HOPE's agenda, as always,
was unclear to those being hunted. It was the other rumors Helena
spoke of, tales of harvest, of experiments, of a drug so deadly in its
addiction that it made Jia frown pensively as they neared the perimeter
of her Pack's encampment. These were things whispered about for
more than a year, tales that wove from pack to pack, when paths
crossed or a hunt ended in the disappearance of yet more Cana. They
were rumors Roland had been unable to confirm, even with his
political pull; if they held truth and he had known, surely he would
have warned the Pack. Candace spoke of one amongst her pack who
returned to them with wild accounts of unspeakable horrors mere days
before the rest of her pack was lost. The three women believed those
stories and rumor to hold dark truths as to the root cause of the
increased hunts.

If it were so, perhaps Lowell Channon had nothing to do with Roland's disappearance. The possibility that both Roland and Liam were suffering torment at the hands of madmen made it more imperative that Jia find and rescue them.

Midstep, Jia paused to sniff the air, the tang of blood fresh here, blood recently spilled though not, she realized with another sniff, the familiar blood smell of Cana. Not Pack. She crouched, fingers to the noticeable stains on the trampled grass and fallen leaves at her feet and brought them to her nose. There was something familiar there, a memory that refused to form a picture. The trail led into the clearing ahead, the fresh remnants of Pack presence, particularly her brother, remained where he had passed through the foliage. Every scent, that of the injured included, led toward the wagon, and with no trace of a threat lingering in the air, she motioned for her guests to follow her slow but sure steps into the heart of the camp.

Heads lifted, wary eyes and warier growls greeting them, none warier and more displeased than Pain's. The man was swiftly on his feet, circling with a caginess that brought a growl from Jia's in response. Pain was inspecting them, inspecting her, with the attentiveness of an alpha, and his audacity at assuming the role that was rightfully hers made Jia snarl, spin to face him when he dared draw close enough to make the women and boys crowd against her, and when he snarled back, she charged him. Her unexpected attack, his confidence in assuming she would never dare assault a much larger opponent, ended with Pain stumbling backward, tripping over the pile of firewood gathered for the night, and staring up at her with narrowed, indignant black eyes.

"How dare you bring strangers…" Pain began as he scrambled to his feet and wiped damp leaves and earth from his trousers.

"How dare you!" Jia challenged, the scent of two strangers close though she had not yet seen them. Pain's dominant personality would surely not allow anyone else to be brought into camp, non-Cana, if he objected to the she-wolves and pups around her. Deuce paced the fringes of the camp, out of easy eyesight but near enough to involve himself in a fight should he decide to do so. The Pack, as always, knew he was there, but as always, most chose to pay him no heed and did not see him as a threat so long as he stayed away.

At the sound of his sister's voice, Addi emerged from the makeshift tent erected between the wagon and the side of the dilapidated outbuilding they had camped beside, wiping his hands on the front of his bloodstained apron.

"I'm afraid I didn't give him much choice," the doctor said with a lopsided welcoming grin. He knew how preposterous it was for him to have overruled Pain in any matter related to Pack security, even if he was Roland Marrock's son. If not for the support of his wife, Xan, and Deuce, Pain would never have given in to Addi's demands to bring a wounded stranger to their camp for treatment.

Jia accepted her brother's relieved embrace but did not take her eyes off of Pain. "Thank the stars you're safe," Addi grunted. He would not question her about the wheres and whys of her absence in front of the Pack. By their father's choice, Jia was Pack leader, whether she had yet to be officially initiated or not, and it was not Addi's place to publically challenge her choices. Only Liam might have gotten away with such a challenge, Liam being the closest thing to her equal that Jia accepted.

Pain, however, did not share Addi's sensibilities. "You abandoned us," he hissed.

"Never." She had expected some within the Pack to feel that way about her choice to be absent at such a crucial time, but there were things that needed to be done. "We are safe here…"

"We won't be safe," Xan muttered bitterly, "until we have a sensible Alpha…until Roland is…"

"Roland is not coming back." Uncle put down the blade he had been sharpening and came to stand between Xan and Pain. "It is time we admit that, accept it, and take a new alpha…"

"We have an alpha…a Caller…"

Trill's claim made some of those, pups and adults who gathered around the fire, shift uneasily. Trill had always had a knack for exposing things that others could not see, some innate instinct that would have made her an ideal alpha female if not for Addi's disinclination to assume pack leadership. Some thought she possessed a trace of mage power. More than once she had served Roland as the Pack's leading female voice after the death of his wife, at times when a second voice was required, an opinionated voice in a position that Roland could not allow his daughter to take. Pack dynamics meant that a child always deferred to its parent, unless the parent was weak and infirm, and though Roland valued Jia's input, she could never have a position of power within the Pack so long as he led them. Trill, however, as her brother's wife, was unencumbered by the distinction of shared blood, and her particular sixth sense made her one of Roland's most valued advisors.

"I am not..." Jia began, refusing that legendary distinction. Nearly every pack had one, that individual with the charisma and ability to draw other Cana into the pack. Theba had been such a one, her presence proving to be the lure that brought other Cana into Roland's orbit in order to grow the Flushing Pack into what had once been the largest pack in LaGuardia. Since her death, the numbers had fallen, accident, disease, and capture having thinned the Pack to what it was now. For whatever reason, be it fortune or chance or charisma, Jia had been the one to draw new blood into the Pack, assuming, each of them knew, the three women and the boys were to stay. That intent had not been spoken, but the adults knew that was what the strangers' presence meant. An alpha rarely brought unattached Cana to the pack for any other reason.

The Flushing Pack needed a Caller if they were to survive, needed fertile adults with which to grow the Pack.

They also, undeniably, needed a leader. With Roland's absence and an obvious division forming within their ranks, someone had to formally claim the title. If Jia was not ready to take up the responsibility, failed to claim it, Pain was more than ready to do so.

"You are nothing...an accident of parentage..."

"Pain..." Maz's face twisted into an aggrieved expression as the man dearest to his heart took a long foreseen stance against the one Roland intended to take his place. The Alpha's intention aside, it was up to Jia to stand up for herself, take her place, to choose to lead, something she had thus far refused in the hopes that Roland would return to them quickly. Maz had faith in her ability, but if it meant a showdown between her and Pain, he would find his loyalties torn and tested. He hoped the ache in his voice would be enough to encourage Pain to abandon his threat.

"I am my father's daughter…"

Whatever argument Jia intended to make, whatever precursor to confrontation or diffuser of it she might have presented, it was interrupted by the rustling of heavy canvas and a weak, groaning cough from behind Addi. Heads turned. Jia shifted her gaze.

And stared.

Thick dark waves flopped limply around a slightly too long face, the skin of his cheeks and high forehead pale in comparison to the bronze of his arms and well-defined muscles of his torso, flushed with pain and exhaustion caused by whatever injury was hidden beneath Addison's expert wrapping. He clung to the canvas as he slouched sideways against the crumbling building, his knuckles white in their grip, while the fingers of his other hand, long and finely shaped, clutched at the bandaging, an effort to hold the fabric in place perhaps, or else an effort meant to subdue the pain that surged and ebbed in his heavy-lidded steel grey eyes. His was an exotic face, with scars and the fine lines of weariness that suggested a burden of responsibility too heavy and carried too long for a man little older than Jia. It was a common enough look, worn by those orphaned and lost amidst the refuse the Undoing had wrought, but one which, on his face, unexpectedly tore Jia's heart with remorse. A handsome face, less so because of its structure then because of the scars left on flesh and soul and reflected in those eyes.

A face Jia thought she should know but could not remember…until a woman, perhaps older, perhaps younger, appeared at his side, sliding beneath his arm to keep him on his feet. It was not her face that Jia recognized, it was her smell, youthful and innocent, and the small voice that whispered, "Kato?" in a frightened tone that forced his identity upon her.

The Fela who had saved her life…whom Jia had saved in return.

If he recognized her, however, through the haze and disorientation of fever and pain, it did not show on his face. "Did I interrupt…?" he murmured. He knew he had, the tension between warring voices had suggested a brewing storm, and as long as he was too hampered by injuries to walk away on his own, he did not want to find himself in the middle of these peoples' war. Drawing their attention and focus onto himself diffused the situation long enough to avert a fight that could have proven deadly for him and his sister.

"You shouldn't be on your feet," Addi scolded, secretly as thankful for the interruption as the rest of the Pack was. Regardless of which potential alpha the members sided with, the impending battle for supremacy was not one any of them looked forward to. A pack that could not agree on an alpha often suffered fracturing, or at the very least the loss of valuable pack members, as the loser, if they lived, rarely remained within the pack they were denied. The strangers seeing their Pack at its weakest could not be a good thing.

Addi reached his patient as the man's knees buckled, and caught him when the woman at his side failed in her efforts to keep the injured man upright. His stumble made Jia's heart seize, cutting off the flow of air into her lungs, but she held her ground and did not move. She did not want to reveal either his breeding, if the others did not know, or the fact that she recognized him. So long as those details remained hidden, the stranger would be safe. At least, as safe as a Fela could be in the midst of a Cana pack. Jia glanced at Eddie to see if the young man recognized anything about the injured stranger, but he, like his mother, was more intent on Jia and Pain and what would inevitably come to pass.

"Inside with you." Addi looked back at his sister, summoning her to join him in the tent, but she shook her head. She did not trust the safety of the she-wolves and pups in Pain's presence.

"Their pack has been taken," she said as evenly as her hammering heart would allow as soon as Addi and the distracting stranger were out of sight. "They need shelter…protection…and I give that to them if they wish to join us."

"You have no right…" Pain began again.

Maz leveled a look strained with sorrow at the dissenter and sighed. "She has every right...and she is right to bring them here." Cana pups without packs were particularly vulnerable, and the Flushing Pack needed numbers. Even if two of those pups were not Cana but were of a different bloodline, they needed safety if they were to reach adulthood. Maz bowed his head to the women and added, "You are welcome here." With his head down still, he looked at each adult around the fire, expecting agreement, challenge, or in the matter of needed new blood, at least the support of Jia's decision.

No dissension came. The others in the pack agreed in their acceptance of the women and pups.

"Good," Jia muttered, grateful for Maz's support, grateful that the majority of the Pack had backed down from the previous rush of negativity and were willing to shelter the newcomers.

But Maz was not finished speaking. "Pain is right too," he said softly, his seniority in the Pack affording him the right to speak. "We deserve the truth, Jia...we deserve to know what was so pressing that it took you secretly away when we are at our weakest..."

"You are not weak...none of you. The Pack is strong." While she wholeheartedly believed those words, she also understood what Maz was asking. Sighing, she tossed the pack she carried at his feet, the partial answer to his inquest contained within. "I wanted to be sure they know where we are...if they come looking for us."

The stress on the word they, though subtle, was enough to separate 'they' the hunters from 'they' the pack members lost. It was a selfless thing to do, necessary if their missing Alpha was to have an inkling where to track them to after the scent of their trail was washed away by wind and rain. Whether it was brave or foolish was a matter of perception, but she had made it back to the Pack without incident and so faulting her for reaching out to her father and best friend was a weak standing point for dissent as far as Maz and some of the others were concerned. They were all worried about the missing men, they were all afraid...they all wanted them back.

Squatting, Maz opened the pack and removed items from within, items that lifted the calm that began to settle upon his shoulders and replaced it with a rush of anxiety.

"You have been to the Fortress?"

The mention of that place was enough to strike panic and Jia hastened to soothe the collective fears. "I had to know the truth…we need to know who is hunting us…and why…?"

Pain spat, "It doesn't matter why…"

"It does if Lowell is behind this…behind Father's disappearance and the hunt and…"

"Those were not Channon forces," Xan began.

"They were HOPE," continued Ilba.

"They were acting under orders from Quentin and Donnovan and I want to know why. I think we need to know…"

That was a detail the Pack had not previously known. Some were frightened, some relieved to know their foes, and some did not care who was behind their recent spate of ill fortune so long as they found safe shelter once again. "Extermination is excuse enough."

Jia growled though she knew Uncle had a point. The extermination of all anthro would be cause enough for such a hunt. But she was certain there was more behind the loss of Roland and Liam than exterminating hunts. To her, particularly because the hunts had been instigated, arranged and conducted by Quentin and Donnovan, these hunts were personal. "Lowell is planning something. Father knew it…and I believe…"

"There has never been proof of that," snorted Pain.

"Lack of tangible proof does not make it less true. The map…the ledger…are real…"

There had never been any documents that they had seen, but the Pack trusted, for the most part, that Roland would never have claimed their existence if they were not real. Lifting his head as he shoved Roland's personal effects into Jia's pack, Maz asked, "You found them? You have seen them?"

Unable to say the word, to admit failure verbally, Jia shook her head. "But I believe," she started defensively, "that Lowell considers

Father a threat. Father saw those documents, knew enough to convince him they're real, enough to make him a target."

"The Channons and Marrocks have been allies for generations. Why has that changed?" asked Ilba.

"And Liam?" Zen muttered bitterly. "Was he a target too?"

Trill curled her hand around the woman's arm. "Liam's a victim just like we…"

"We will find him," Jia promised, choosing not to speak of experimentation or a drug said to be produced from Cana blood, or any other unsubstantiated rumor that would only serve to frighten instead of reassure. She needed to believe her words herself. The alternative was too painful to contemplate.

"What we need," the blonde woman said with equal bitterness, "is a den…safety for the pups." The catch in the situation was that, no matter which path Jia chose, the security of the Pack over Liam and Roland's lives, or their rescue over the safety of the weakest in the Pack, she was going to disappoint someone, perhaps Zen most of all as the one to point out the dilemma the Pack faced."

"I know of a place…"

"Where?"

Jia did not respond to Ilba's question. How could she admit that she was following the recommendation of the Pack's Omega? Her ability, her suitability to lead, would certainly be called into question then, despite an Alpha's right to utilize whatever resources were available…including the Omega if necessary. "It isn't far. Once we are established there, we will find Liam and my father."

"They'll be dead by then," Zen snorted.

"Would you rather we go into battle with pups in tow?" growled Jia, her patience with being challenged gradually reaching a breaking point. "Candace, Brie, Helena and the boys stay…and as soon as our guest is on his feet, we go east…"

"No Fela is welcome here."

Eddie scooted closer to his mother as the women and his older brothers encircled him. Jia's eyes shifted from brown to amber as the instinct to shift clawed to the surface, seeking to respond to the rival who pushed her at every turn. For the moment, at least, seeing the change in Jia's eyes, Pain backed down as she barked, "I decide who is welcome and who is not." It was the first time a clear threat and challenge had surfaced within her, the clearest indication that she would fight for her birthright that any in the Pack had seen, enough to give some confidence and enough to cause Pain to have second thoughts about whatever course of action he was contemplating.

"We need all of the strength we can get. They stay."

Jia threw a glance at Maz, signifying her trust in his position as second to her alpha, the position he had held for Roland, and then, surprisingly, a glance toward the camouflaged Omega they knew to be present though none had cared enough to look for or acknowledge him. It was a bold move, choosing Deuce to aid in protecting the newcomers, a stone thrown that would create ripples throughout the Pack but Jia's right as justly appointed Alpha.

By night's end, the Pack understood without speaking as she stalked into the tent where her brother and the Fela stranger waited, the Flushing Pack would have its rightful Alpha. Deuce's fate too hung in the balance, for her choice meant that, should Jia lose, Pain would surely kill the outcast Cana.

Or both men would die in the attempt.

≈*≈

He might be a tracker-mage, an expert at retrieving information that few others could find, but making his way past guards into a locked facility was at the low end of Vance's particular set of skills. From his vantage point in an empty neighboring building, a precarious hiding place that had required picking his way over the remains of collapsed walls and murky pools of poisoned rainwater to reach, he could see where Sal had fallen. There was no trace of her there now, of course, there at the feet of the two stoic guards stationed before the warehouse gates. Sal's blood had been washed away by rain, by the boots and tools of men, leaving no visible traces behind that anything had happened there. But the imagery that lingered within her head, barely perceptible electric sparks that formed the basis of vision, of life, of humanity, was imagery Vance had harvested and retained as if they were his own memories, and from them he could conjecture where she had lain, the angle of her eyes in those last moments of consciousness. In the stone of the walls around him, the fragmented echoes of the gunshot remained, along with the flash of heat and light lingering at the gunshot's point of origin. A thin gap that existed between rusted metal sheets that served as window coverings at the front of the warehouse. There was no light there now, only a narrow swath of darkness that he could not see behind from where he stood.

If anyone was there, another sniper, a lookout, a worried worker, they could not be seen, and none of Vance's senses detected anyone there. Deeper within the warehouse there was movement, a distant shuffling as goods were moved from one location to another. Nothing in that collection of sounds gave an indication of what was being moved, and without seeing the ledgers or speaking to the employees, it was impossible to learn what Vance most needed to know. But the honest direct approach through the front door came with the risk of death, as Sal's loss had proven, and Vance did not have what it would take to muscle his way inside. He could, he knew, get past the gate guards, but it was the people within, too many and too far away to easily manipulate, that posed a problem. He had to hope, he mused as the side door of the structure slid open with an echoing rumble of worn wheels in cracked grooves, that those inside would leave while the night offered enough cover to get in and out again safely.

Four wagons, loaded high with hemplastic crates, groaned as they were pulled out of the building by stocky grey oxen, animals of such mass and size that few could afford to house and feed them. Despite the beasts' strength, the weight of their burden proved a struggle, but none of the dark attired figures with them showed concern or care for that. Binding straps were checked and tightened, the loads secured from falling, before the wagons, one by one, crawled through now open front gates.

Vance scowled, looking back and forth between the closing warehouse doors and the wagons that made their way onto the ill-

illuminated borough streets. Those who came out with the wagons, who adjusted the cargo and closed the door, followed their wares, seemingly the answer to the mage's unvoiced prayer. Even the two sentries at the main entry, after closing and locking the rusted gates they had been charged with guarding, marched behind the wagons with weapons at the ready in case of an unexpected ambush.

The warehouse, it seemed, was being abandoned.

It left Vance with the opportunity to enter unhindered, and though there would be no records left to study he assumed, there were other details a mage as experienced as himself could learn. But did he accept that opportunity or follow the cargo?

There was no reason to believe the relocation was suspicious or covert. The movement of bulk cargo across the borough most frequently occurred at night, when the best streets were less congested. Goods were often relocated when a facility was deemed no longer structurally safe, and if Laedan Channon believed this facility was at risk because of the previous theft, moving his stores was a wise precaution.

On the other hand, a Protector had been killed to protect whatever had been stored here. Moving the goods to avoid unnecessary questions was a prudent precaution of a different sort, and suggested that someone assumed Sal's death would be traced back to this place, and eventually back to the Laedan.

The empty storeroom would wait. What he could learn there would linger in the air, the walls, the floor, the fixtures, until he was able to return. The wagons, their creaking wheels, plodding hooves on fractured stone, the wheeze of beasts as they dragged their burden slowly behind, would be easy to follow. Vance might not learn what those loads contained, but he would discover their destination and in doing so, hopefully learn why Sal was killed to protect it.

≈*≈

"You ordered a Protector killed? In my district?"

Jonni's fists clenched as he glared at his father, fighting the war within as outrage, offense, and disbelief struggled for prominence. He had known since his youngest memories, the lengths to which Lowell was capable of going to control the borough, lengths that only Roland had been able to influence, that only Roland had been willing to try to temper. With the co-Laedan's absence, there was no one to make that effort, and Jonni realized yet again, with Quentin urging him on, temperance was no longer part of the equation when it came to governing LaGuardia.

"Don't be absurd. I ordered no such thing," Lowell grunted dismissively.

"Your warehouse…your hires…your orders."

The Channon brothers served as mayors of LaGuardia's three districts, managing the day to day duties of finance and peace-keeping, levy collection, maintenance, duties that Jonni resisted and that he often left to be carried out by the overeager Donnovan. But the true power in LaGuardia was held in the hands of the Laedans, and now entirely in the hands of Lowell. Even in the days when he and Roland stood side by side in the governing duties, however, Roland had been the idea man, the innovator, the problem solver, while Lowell had been the voice, the face, the power. Nothing happened within the district government that Lowell did not know about, did not oversee, did not control. Warehouse facilities, soldier training camps, the manufacture of hemp fuel and other hemp products, while scattered throughout each district, was ultimately controlled by the Laedans and not one of the mayors was allowed to interfere. Jonni suspected that not even Donn knew what was housed in the warehouses maintained in his district. Nik sure as hell did not. Nik cared even less for the trappings of government than Jonni did and likewise left the majority of the responsibility, save for public appearances and parties, to Donn.

"Are you suggesting I knew a Protector would come?" Lowell poured himself a drink and leaned back to prop his feet on the ornamental table before him. Light laughter came from the corridor and his attention strayed there, his eyes meeting those of his son's wife and following her smile as she continued past. The exchange lasted mere moments, not long enough for either Donn or Jonni to notice, but Jonni did not miss the peculiar lightening of his father's expression. By that time, however, Lowell was again staring at his son and any connection between his brief change in demeanor and the woman who passed was erased.

"I'm suggesting you left standing orders to protect whatever was in that warehouse…"

"Of course there were…"

"…at all costs…"

"How else do we keep them from stealing every ounce of the supplies we manage and distribute?"

"The Protectorate is not the enemy." Jonni crossed his arms with a sneer. "Perhaps it is time we cease managing peoples' lives and allow them to learn to manage their own."

"Allow society to descend back into chaos? Hasn't history taught you anything, boy?" It was Lowell's turn to sneer, an expression which grew more set as the words sank beyond his son's hearing into the core of his mind. In the first days of the Undoing, civilization had been chaos and anarchy, the survivors fighting over what remained of the old world as they struggled to build a life in the new one. The founders of the Marrock and Channon dynasties had ended that chaos, forged a world in which access to the precious remaining commodities was monitored to allow access to everyone.

While the lion's share of those commodities served the interests of men like Lowell Channon.

"By letting the Protectors do their jobs…the jobs we gave them authority to do. If we butcher them, allow their slaughter and look the other way, that makes us agents of the anarchy we're supposed to shield the borough against."

The fine creases at the corners of Lowell's mouth and eyes twitched, tightened, and stretched, as father and son stared at one another. Lowell's breathing was easy, his position calm and contained, while Jonni's shoulders were tense, his breath coming fast and shallow, as the efforts to control his rage devoured him. Whatever faults and failings his eldest son possessed, passion and conviction and the Channon propensity to temper were not among them. If only Lowell had done a better job of channeling that conviction into the office of Laedan, Jonni could have become the most powerful Laedan LaGuardia had ever known, the sort of man capable of uniting the two boroughs and ruling them both.

That, alas, would never come to fruition.

"I will see to it that the guilty party is found and punished accordingly. Will that appease your sensibilities, Jon?"

It would not, Jonni thought as he could not believe punishment would be meted out in a just and expedient fashion. But it was a start, and the only acquiescence his father was likely to give.

"I want to see proof that it is done," he snarled before stalking out of his father's study. He paused in the doorway and without looking back added, "And I demand to know what was in that warehouse. What is in all of them."

Lowell's silence as Jonni left the room proved that the Laedan would never give in to such a demand. Not even to his eldest son.

If Jonni wanted the truth, he would have to find it another way.

☙*☙

It had taken a long time, and a belly full of good food, before Vanya trusted Jia enough to fall asleep at her brother's side. Or maybe sleep had come on the tail of terror's exhaustion, fear for their safety and Kato's life having dogged the woman on travel-worn heels until she could fight it no longer. Vanya was, to the eye, an adult, but her understanding of the world and the way she interacted with it was that of a child, and Jia understood, as she watched the pair sleep, why the Fela was so determined to protect her. Had that been less than twenty-four hours ago?

So much had happened since the street fight that it felt as if a week had passed.

It felt as if Liam and Roland had been gone much longer.

"No change?" Addi entered the tent and put his hand on Jia's shoulder, visually assessing the patient's condition in the pale light cast by the lantern he carried. The bandaging showed less blood than the last wrapping had, meaning, he hoped, that the bleeding had finally stopped and that his sutures held the wound closed enough to allow proper healing. So long as the stranger did not overstrain himself, he should be healed enough to be on his way in a little more than a week's time.

For Jia's sake, Addi hoped the stranger chose to go. The Pack did not need further complications. Nor did Jia.

"They sleep...as you should be doing," she scolded gently, pressing her cheek against her brother's hand.

"I was...but not well." The night was absent of rain, and mild enough that most of the Pack had curled up near the fire, finding warmth enough within blankets and the shared body warmth of fellow packmates. There was room within the canvas structure that all could have slept inside, save for those chosen for the night's watch, but wariness of the wounded Fela and the Cana's preference for sleeping beneath the stars left the tent to the privacy of his patient, the man's sister, and Jia, who had chosen to guard the pair while they slept. "I would sleep better if I was here...near them..."

"Near me, you mean," Jia teased.

His mouth quirked into a smile but he did not voice a reply. "You should rest...you have been awake too long.

It was true; two days and two nights, and now weariness was beginning to tear her down. Over their evening meal it had been decided that, so long as they could move the injured man come morning, the Pack would press east, seeking whatever haven Jia meant them to find. She would need her sleep before then, however brief it might be, but she was agitated by thoughts of Liam and her father and unable to find a peaceful place inside herself to rest. Sitting at Kato's side, watching his pensive expression, proved less soothing than she had thought it would. Sensing her discomfiture, Addi kissed the top of her head and sat cross-legged beside her.

"Get some air, some water, then return. I'll give you something to help you sleep if you need it."

The first impulse to protest and decline was abandoned in favor of the choice to take her brother's advice. As much as she wanted to speak to their guest, question his arrival, demand answers from him, she knew words would not come easily and he was unlikely to awake before morning. Sleep would be the best thing for her.

Above her, as Jia emerged into the night, the cloud cover seemed a thinner veil than usual, leaving the scatter of brightest stars barely visible to the eye. Only at night, when the air was coolest and the earth unheated by the rays of the sun, did the clouds sometimes thin to allow a glimpse of the sky. Blue beyond the clouds was something most only dreamed of seeing, whereas the black of night came and went in irregular surges. It led to speculation amongst the uneducated that blue sky was a myth. Here in the expanse of the Flushing Wilds, with a skyline made of trees instead of crumbling, manmade towers of stone and glass and metal, Jia could almost believe that someday her longing for a sky of blue would be fulfilled. She turned sideways at the edge of the clearing in which they camped, the fire and the Pack behind her, and stared upward with her head thrown back to the sky.

What was out there beyond the clouds? Was it possible that humanity, what remained of it, would ever actually know?

A low snarl from the thick overgrowth before her was the only warning Jia received but it was enough that, when Pain, in true Cana form, sprang at her, she landed on her back mid-change, clothing ripping and falling away as the muscles of her body reshaped into the creature she was meant to be. That instinctual shift was enough to disallow her attacker's jaws from closing around her throat, snapping her neck, and allowed her enough strength to fling him off with the thrust of lean rear legs. His fangs raked along the base of her neck and shoulder, producing a yelp of pain that roused the rest of the Pack from slumber.

It was not a proper challenge. Underhanded, unannounced, his attack was not that of a legitimate Alpha contender, and the wrongness of it made Jia more determined to put down his bid for Alpha with finality. Theft of the pack from the rightful Marrock heir could never be allowed.

The larger wolf circled the smaller one, his lunges and swipes met each time by her clearheaded parry. He looked for an opening, a weakness, expecting that exhaustion would hinder her enough to allow for a quick and easy dispatch of her tentative hold on Pack leadership. Confident of his strengths, of the likelihood of success, ignoring the other shifted Cana gathering around them and whether they had witnessed the illegitimate way in which he had made this challenge, Pain howled his fury and when he believed he had a shot at her vulnerable belly, his fangs clapped shut, grazing her skin but coming free with only a mouthful of fur and fabric instead of the flesh he intended. The paw that swiped at her face ended up trapped between her jaws, the unanticipated pain drawing a squawk, and though he tried to yank away, she rolled with him, their bodies tumbling as a dark ball of fur across the cold earth. Leaves and dirt sprayed in all directions as feet tried to dig in, an effort to stop their momentum, but their roll only stopped when their tangled bodies collided with the base of a wide tree.

All Cana pups learned to wrestle and fight in their true form; it was as much a part of their education as was the hunt and the scholarly pursuits that Roland demanded his Pack's young undertake. But Jia had never had to enter a true fight with another Cana, not in this form, not in her normal form, a disadvantage against the older, more proficient, more violent Pain. Her inexperience was used against her as he time and again bettered her, pinning her to the ground, striking for the kill. But her smaller size and youth made her more agile, and each time she wiggled free, learning with each attempt he made the moves he favored, the patterns in his choices that left an opening with each effort made to kill her. Jia twisted, body doubled in two, forcing him to rear up on his back legs. Arching her neck to the side as his claws raked along her back, she bit deep into the soft flesh low over his genitals.

The agony of the bite shot through Pain so that he dropped back, expecting that she would fall away with the seat of his masculinity in her jaws. But she did not release him, not until he was flat on his back, four limbs flailing to dislodge her but fearing as he did so that she would rip away what he dared not lose. That fear, and the uncertainty that her bite had not already done its worst, forced him to still. The moment he did so, she twisted and leaped again so that her jaws tightened around his throat and her scarred front limbs pinned his to the ground.

He could have resumed the fight. He could have attempted to throw her aside. But her grip on his throat meant the risk of severing arteries and tendons there, maiming him further, perhaps killing him. He might be the elder, the stronger, but Jia had the cunning, the audacity, to better him, taught, no doubt, by Roland's expertise. She had proven that her Cana was as capable of leading the Pack as her normal was of guiding them in the world of man. Pain whined, the sound a gurgle that he feared meant she had already punctured his throat, and forced the change so that the man who had challenged her lay beneath the wolf that had won.

The Pack collectively held their breath, watching, judging, waiting for a decision to be made for the challenger's fate. It was within the Alpha's right to kill the offender, particularly since the fight had been entered into without the proper, legitimate challenge, to discourage further attempts from other pack members in the future. Some packs operated that way, ruled by whichever alpha proved strong enough to put down opposition, unconcerned by the loss of life. Never, since the day of its creation, had the Flushing Pack, had the Marrock alpha, killed another within the pack to maintain leadership. There had been fights, sometimes long and bloody, sometimes brief and free of lasting damage, but the alpha Marrock always allowed the opposition to live because the Pack, until now, intellectually accepted Marrock leadership. Pain had proven to be the exception, and although he was submitting, there was no guarantee that his capitulation would last.

Whether to kill him or not, Jia knew the man could not remain within the Flushing Pack. If he had challenged her properly, perhaps she would have allowed him to stay. She could not condone his disobedience to Pack rules. From the swirl of anger, perhaps even hatred, in his black eyes, she knew that Pain knew it too. Though the obvious choice meant a devastating blow to the Pack, it was the only one she could make.

She would not kill a man simply for disagreeing with her…not even for trying to kill her…if it meant breaking Marrock and Flushing traditions.

Feet planted beneath her, she reclaimed her normal form, her naked skin smeared with wet earth and leaves and the crimson of life shed in combat. Straddling his torso, she stared at Pain, the pact made between them without a word being uttered, and when she stepped away without offering a hand up, her back turned to him as she faced the Pack, her decision on Pain's fate spoke for itself.

Behind her, clutching the bite marks low on his belly, slow pulses of blood seeping out between his fingers to trickle through the black curls and drip from the tip of his flaccid penis, Pain struggled to his feet with excruciating discomfort. He did not attack again.

Jia looked at each member of her Pack, in turn, men and women she had known her whole life, pups she had known all of theirs, newcomers huddled nervously together and her brother pushing to the fore, medibag in hand to treat injuries on winner and loser alike, if they allowed. She judged what she saw in each person's eyes, what she smelled in their auras, and knew the outcome of this night before ever speaking the words that must be said.

"The Flushing Pack is a Marrock Pack. I assume Father's mantle as Alpha with the knowledge and hope that he will again move amongst us and lead us. To kill those I have loved…that I continue to love…would be to dishonor what it means to be a Marrock. But I will not," she emphasized the word and again met each person's gaze, "tolerate dissension or illegitimate challenges to my authority any more than my father did. I expel this wolf from our Pack, under the threat of death should he return to lay challenge again. Any of you who think his action has merit…who intend to…"

She chose not to speak the words, to frighten the children with what lay ahead for the Pack. Their lives were in upheaval enough. "We leave at daybreak. If you stay…you are mine."

If any left, Fates protect them on their newly embarked life. It was the most, in her exhausted, weakened condition, that she could do. The fate of the Flushing Pack was out of her hands for the night.

Chapter 13

"**D**on't open your eyes."

Liam turned his head toward the voice, hissed and strained and sounding far away as if reaching into his brain through too many layers of fabric. As he clawed nearer to full consciousness, the itch on his dry, taut skin, like a thousand ants scurrying toward his eyes, toward his brain, grew impossible to ignore, but the effort to scratch was thwarted by the thickly woven cords that bound his arms at his sides. A frustrated sound rose in his throat, but as the temptation to study his surroundings came again, the whisper returned.

"Don't open your eyes."

He knew that voice. He did not know where he was, how he had come to be here, but damn it, he knew that voice. He almost said it aloud, naming the individual in what had to be a nightmare, but being afraid that the result would somehow prove disastrous for them both, Liam bit his cheek and gave nothing more than a rumbling, irritated groan.

"Here…drink…"

Cool metal pressed to his parched lips, instigating a reflexive opening that welcomed a gush of cool water over his tongue and into his throat. What dribbled along his chin and down his neck temporarily eased the insect-like itch.

He wanted to ask questions, but a finger followed the touch of the cup to his mouth and he swallowed his queries with another sip. Beyond his closed lids, he realized that wherever he was, it was lit by artificial light, not the usual muted light of the sun but bright in a way that convinced him he was somewhere the sun did not reach. His last conscious memory was of night. A fight in a dead end alley. Jia screaming his name as he was bludgeoned into unconsciousness.

How long ago had that been?

"Is he awake?"

The unfamiliar female voice followed the click, creak, and pop of a door opening and closing.

"No...I thought he was...but..." The man made a point of swabbing droplets from Liam's chin and neck to show he had not consumed drunk any water yet.

The woman grunted, the sound of hard, light heels clacking on tile as she approached. "He will be soon enough." Her fingers pressed to Liam's throat and wrist, checking his pulse and then she ruffled the blond hair on the side of his head to examine the bloody lump barely hidden there. It took effort for Liam not to react in pain to the probing touch. "Animals," she grunted again. "Prep that one there...and do it right this time."

The other man muttered his acceptance of duty and Liam, confident that the woman moving away was no longer looking at him, shuddered. Was she calling them animals, or was she referring to those who had beaten him? Perhaps she meant both.

The echoes of her words drown out the ring of 'animals' within his ears. Prep someone for what? He was heartened to find his Alpha alive, for that was the only man he could attribute that voice to, but what in the name of fates was Roland Marrock caught up in?

"Good morning, Dr. Torrance."

The smile shared between them as the elegant, dark-skinned woman emerged from the holding area adjoining her lab gave every appearance of professional courtesy, hers cool but cordial, his neutral and slightly patronizing. Her staff, if they chose to glance at her, would see nothing unusual between the doctor and Laedan Hallister. Nor was it unusual for the man to be here as he wandered between the rows of tables in the lab and stared callously at the dozens of individuals strapped to identical vertical steel slabs which, when lowered onto the wheeled frames lined against one wall turned them into easily transportable gurneys. The stock rotated frequently, as the efforts to extract what was needed inevitably led to their premature demise, the one flaw in the process that both he and Doctor Gayle Torrance hoped to work out before they ran out of stock to milk.

There was no danger of that in the near future. Of all anthrozooids, Cana were the most common, and so long as they continued to be born, the lab would have a healthy, steady supply with which to work. If official HOPE policy did not change, however, if extermination of non-Normals continued to be the organization's foremost priority, that surplus would not last.

Elder Lord, however, was a man of vision, a man prone to making the most productive use of the resources at hand. Now that a use for Cana more lucrative then slave labor had been concocted, a use that meant wealth and power for those who controlled the outcome, Hallister was confident that it was only a matter of a few more meetings, of offered proof of benefit, before the Elder turned HOPE away from eradication and enslavement toward maintenance and harvest.

"Everything is as scheduled, Laedan, I assure you." Dr. Torrance sounded more annoyed at his intrusion in her lab then she felt, but there were appearances to be kept.

A scowl partially eclipsed his smile as one man moved within the storage chamber, a man who could not see him through the polarized glass which separated them. "Is it wise to give him…"

"It makes him think he can stay their fate…ease their suffering with kindness…guarantees his cooperation," she explained without looking up from the clipboard upon which she wrote.

"He should not be here. Does he know where he is?"

"How could he? He can't see us…hear us…or smell us…and he and I have never met before."

That reassurance did little to soothe Hallister's sensibilities. It should not matter; the man was Cana, from a family of Cana, a ruse carried on for too many decades that in Hallister's view was a threat to the people the man had helped govern. But Hallister respected Marrock's mind, his capabilities, and if the man had remained at the Fortress in his long-held governing position, Channon would be much easier to manipulate and control. Subtle exchanges between himself and Lowell, between himself and Elder Lord, suggested something foul was afoot; finding out what was the only reason Hallister had accepted the marriage alliance between his daughter and one of the Channon heirs. Someone needed to learn the truth; he had confidence Oasis would succeed.

She had her mother's persuasiveness, after all.

But not for the first time in recent days did he wonder if releasing Marrock back into the streets of LaGuardia would be for the best. Doing it without raising the ire of Elder Lord and the other leaders of HOPE would be a sticky risk, but might be worth taking.

"Keep it that way; he mustn't know…ever."

"Of course." Dr. Torrance lay her clipboard on the edge of the nearest desk. "Shall I give a full report over lunch, Laedan?"

Again, nothing unusual in the question, as they were known to meet once each week to discuss the details of the project at length, but the question brought a spark into Hallister's eyes and an upturn to the corners of his mouth that no one else could see.

"Yes." By the time he turned from the window, his expression was as banal as it had been when he had entered the laboratory. "I will expect you at half-day."

"I will be there."

The promise undercutting her words birthed a lusty grin on Hallister's face by the time the lab door shut between them.

᠗*᠗

Draping over his back, fingers tracing his hairline above and behind his ear in a way she had quickly learned he enjoyed, Oasis rubbed her cheek against the side of Donn's neck, her head angled in such a way that she could not easily view the spread out documents on the desk before him. With her gaze to the side, however, she could see what he read, and because of the tilt of her face, Donn made no effort to close the files or hide his work. She could not see it, he believed, and the purr vibrating against his skin distracted him enough from his concern for privacy that he chose not to worry.

"You work too hard, husband...come back to bed..." Returning to their bed, submitting to his sadistic preferences, was not what she wanted, but in the throes of his passion, she might be able to learn something important, and temptation was the only tool she had, for now, with which to manipulate him.

"Something doesn't add up," he muttered, attempting half-heartedly to ignore her and focus on the registries in the ledgers he studied. He should not have them, had taken a dangerous risk to get them, but it had been deemed a necessary one, for he believed that making sense of the rambled scrawlings his father had tried so diligently to protect would give him the leverage he needed to further his plans. "He wouldn't dare..."

But Lowell would dare. In that, father and son were much alike.

"It's early...whatever it is...it will wait..."

Two words caught Donn's eye as she began to nibble at his ear, causing him to growl and shove her away with a backhanded blow to the side of her neck as he surged to his feet. "Leave me alone!" he snapped, the progress she had made to woo him evaporating in that instant. Oasis fell, his rising momentum knocking her down more than the blow had done, and she stared with surprise and dismay.

But she had caught those words too, Lowell's writing not her husband's, and though Donn had slammed the book closed before storming away from it, she made note to investigate those words herself. She had heard them before...but what if the rumors were true? Was this the secret her father had sent her here to find?

Had Lowell Channon found the location of, and the route to, the mythical Fort Hamilton?

⮞*⮜

He did not care that the hour was early. Duties the day before had kept him imprisoned in his offices and he had not wanted to risk tipping his hand to Chief Ernest by summoning him to the Fortress twice in one day. It was better if Lowell went to him, and safer if he traveled the borough streets disguised beneath the cover of early morning fog. He brought no sentries, as he feared no one, and did not want the hindrance, nor the possibility of rumor, to follow him by bringing anyone else. It had not occurred to him that the Chief might not hold such hours until he flung open the Protectorate's main doors and faced the Chief's dark office. Protectors on duty, or those departing as the night shift gave way to the day, lurched to attention, trying not to stare, when the Laedan threw open the Chief's door and slammed it again after charging into the room. The glow of the main office lights provided him enough to see by, and he was riled enough not to bother finding the room switch as he paced back and forth, waiting for answers he believed the Chief had.

It was the thumping of heavy boots that voiced the violation of his workspace as soon as Ernest arrived, and he frowned at the sight of Laedan Channon pacing before his desk in the unlit room. Not recalling a scheduled meeting or any expected report he had failed to make by the previous day's end, he opened the door as coolly as he could only to be grabbed by the lapels of his jacket and pushed into the cabinet, the office door banging shut behind them.

"What did you do to Yiva?"

"What did I…?"

Lowell would have noted how honestly confused the Chief was if he had been less angry in the first eruptive moment. "I will have your hands for what you…"

"What did I do?" Ernest repeated, managing to yank free, refusing to look into the main office to find sympathy or assistance from his Protectors. Most carried a powerful dose of respect or fear or both for Laedan Channon, and Ernest imagined that, if it came down to accusations, no matter how fabricated, most would side with the Laedan rather than risk life or career.

Where the hell was Vance when he needed an ally?"

"Nothing she could have done warrants a blow like that!" At least, the thought flitted through the shadows of Lowell's mind, nothing could have warranted it from anyone other than her husband.

"I don't hit women," Ernest growled, pulling a bottle of amber ale from his drawer and pouring its contents into a short glass. Damn the early hour. He needed a drink already. "I saw it too…the handprint. She wouldn't tell me who…but I could guess…"

Lowell snorted and though he swiped across the desk, Ernest was beyond his reach. "Me?" he snarled, surprised at the man's audacity. "Why would I…?"

"Why do you hit anyone?"

The Laedan's face flushed dark crimson in fury. His temper was well known, his presence here, the violent nature of his initial attack to the moment of his swing across the desk spoke of his propensity to solve emotional affronts with his fists. And though it had never been revealed publically, to his knowledge, there were instances of him striking women, most prior to his marriage. Doubting that the Chief knew of those long ago private occurrences, it was Lowell's opinion that the man had no right to accuse him. "She is my wife!"

Maybe that was meant to excuse him if he had hit her. Maybe it meant that he would never strike the woman who had birthed his sons. Ernest did not care what he meant, but he did want to get to the bottom of the matter.

"If you didn't, and I didn't, someone else obviously did. I can't make her file a complaint report, but if you don't protect her, I will."

"You will?" Lowell sneered. Ernest would not be the first man to lust after his wife, and at this stage of their marriage, their sons grown and his eyes wandering over younger, more luxuriant pastures, he did not care if she took lovers…so long as she remained his wife and maintained all of the public appearances expected of her station. Lowell was a practical enough man to perceive a valuable hold over the Chief if Yiva did choose him for a tryst, but he would never stand for a man abusing his wife.

Ernest shrugged. "It is my job," he mumbled into the glass before emptying it a second time. "Someone has to…she deserves that much." He did not care if his unspoken charges offended Lowell, nor did he care that the Laedan might choose to retaliate…and might not even believe his innocence. He only cared about Yiva's safety and he fretted now about the danger she might be in should Lowell call her out on a lie.

Maybe I should have lied for her…taken the blame, he thought bitterly. Maybe by not doing so, he had exposed her to further harm.

But if not Lowell, then the man, her husband, needed to find the violent individual responsible for this, the hands of someone within his own house.

"Watch your back."

It was the only warning Lowell gave before escaping into the cold morning. Ernest hoped he had done enough to prompt an investigation that might save her life. It was, for now, the most he could do.

෨*෪

Exhaustion and injury forced Jia into the wagon when the Pack began the journey eastward again, although she did not remember how she had gotten there. As groggy as she had been, she did not clearly remember anything after the fight with Pain, and thus assumed her brother must have placed her in the wagon, along with Kato, Vanya, the youngest pups and their Pack livestock. As clarity began to return, bringing with it the discomfort of bites, scratches, abrasions, and bruises she had collected during the last two days, she used each of her senses to determine who remained with the Pack now that Pain had, she knew, followed her command and gone his own way.

There were few surprises. Xan and Zen, as husband and wife, along with Ilba, had all chosen Pain over the Pack. Uncle had as well, leading Jia to worry over what path Liam would take when she brought him home. Would he choose their friendship over his sister and Uncle?

Did they have so little faith in his being alive, in her willingness and determination to bring him back, that they would force him into such a choice when that day came? Had she failed in her friendship with Zen in ways she was unaware of or was Zen's loyalty to her husband the deciding factor?

Was Jia so unlike her father that others dared not trust her leadership?

While not a shock, it was painful to realize that Maz, too, had been forced to make the difficult choice between a lover and the Pack's rightful alpha. But he was here, leading the wagon east, shoulders square, head held high without knowing exactly where their intended destination was, following the lead of the Omega who traveled consistently ahead of them. So long as Deuce was ahead, it was reasonable to assume he knew where they were going, even if it was peculiar for him to know the Alpha's intentions when others did not. Maz was quiet, his handsome features both frowning and neutral at the same time. Now and then he glanced behind at the older children who remained near the wagon while the other adults, nearly all female now, fewer in number now than before, protected them from the sides and rear of the caravan. The three new women did not entirely make up for the loss of the five, but at least their presence helped soften the loss. Jia hoped Trill was right, that she proved to be not only the Alpha like her father but the Caller her mother had been, or else she feared the Pack's continued existence would be short-lived.

Whatever Pain thought of her ability to lead and protect the Pack, however, all of the pups remained. None who had left had living children of their own, and as a smaller, newly created pack also without a home, the five had made the wise choice not to put any of the pups at risk by taking them. With the majority under the care of Addi and Trill, stolen pups would have meant war, and the ties between the adults, strained by the break though they might be, would likely discourage that result.

Her silent musings were intruded upon by the grey eyes that stared at her as she shifted her weight and drew herself into a sitting position. Her movement also drew Addi's attention, but he only nodded and smiled, relieved to see his sister awake; his attention returning to the older children and he resumed the story he was telling. Further ahead in the wagon, in a niche created to protect them, the youngest children were clustered around Vanya as she shared one sing-song chant after another, teaching letters, numbers, and the names of animals with each one. Vanya seemed more comfortable then she had last night, no longer clinging to her brother but instead finding a place to fit into the Pack; it made Jia smile a little to see it and brought her attention back to the grey eyes that had temporarily shifted away from her face to look at his sister as well.

"She's never been around children," he said, his voice low though no longer as laden with pain as it had been the night before. "It is good to see her happy." She was older than him by four years, but from the time he was old enough, it had been his duty to look after her, not the other way around.

"She is a natural with them."

He shrugged and looked up at Jia, admiring her bruised yet beautiful features in the light of early morning, confident that his sister was safe. "She would be; she's a child herself in most ways."

Blushing under his scrutiny, embarrassed that she might have somehow implied offense, she murmured, "I did not mean…"

"I know." Kato felt the need to defend his sister with the truth but now realized his tone had been more defensive then it needed to be. But the color to her cheeks added to her striking round features and encouraged him to shift to his uninjured side to face her fully. He winced, the movement stretching the stitches and scowled as he noted the sun's position behind the clouds. "Why are we going east?" East was where he had come from. He had no desire to return to that life, though he knew his condition left him at the mercy of the Cana who tended him for now.

If not for Vanya, who giggled at something one of the children said, but clung more tightly to the yellow bear as another child reached for it, Kato would have been tempted to roll out of the wagon and go his way, fend for himself, even if he was injured. The proximity of the woman at his side, however, dissuaded him from trying; she would surely stop him.

He was tempted to test her, to see if she would try.

Jia watched the childish woman again, defending her favored toy from the others as any child would do. Traveling alone with her, for however long he had been doing so, must have been a challenged for the Fela, for she clearly did not share his feline characteristics. Wondering if Vanya had been born into her innocent state or if some ailment or accident in childhood had caused such naiveté, Jia chose not to ask. Such private prying would be rude, and so she decided to give the strangers the same respect she hoped they would afford her.

"Northeast," she replied to his question. "It isn't safe for us in the borough now. We need to find somewhere that the Laedan isn't likely to come looking."

"Laedan?" Kato had never heard the term, and he hoped his asking did not reflect a low level of education. As his mother had been unable to devote her time to intense teaching when the effort to survive came first, he was left with only the basic skills, and where he was from, such things as Laedans did not exist.

"Actually co-Laedan…leaders of LaGuardia borough…the other is missing."

That revelation revealed her pain and he nodded sympathetically. Whoever the co-Laedan was, she had been close enough to find the loss painful, just as losing his mother was still painful to Kato.

"The others?" He gestured to those walking around them. He did not yet know faces, beyond the doctor who had tended him and now the woman riding beside him, but there were others he could recall hazily through last night's fog, faces no longer here. He had not yet heard names either; if they had been spoken, his mind had not been clear enough to retain them.

Jia bristled, wondering if the Fela would perceive the Pack, perceive her, to be weak enough to overthrow. Not that he was in any condition to make the effort, and he would have to be a fool to think that he could take on an entire Cana pack alone even in peak condition. More likely, she decided, forcing herself to relax, he was assessing how much of a threat the pack might be to him and his sister, an understandable precaution.

"No one will trouble you. You are safe with us while you recover." Her gaze traveled along the edge of the blanket that draped around his shoulders, over his bare torso to the fresh bandaging there. As though self-conscious, he covered the bandage again with one hand and pulled the blanket close over his chest, although his expression, both bemused and slightly cocky, did not express the same insecurity. Knowing nothing about his history, it seemed reasonable to assume that he was accustomed to being the center of female attention. "How did you find me?"

"What makes you think I was looking for you?"

It was her turn to flush. "I...I don't...I mean...after that night..."

"You helped protect my sister...me...and I helped you." He took pride in reminding her that he had done his share of life-saving that night. For a man largely alone, isolated by mother and sister, helping another, a stranger, was an accomplishment he felt good about, despite the resulting injury. "And then we went our ways. I was following the scent of water...trees...grass..." Now he scowled to realize that the wagon had left that haven of nature behind to once again creak and groan through the devastated manmade passages. He had been so distracted by the woman's face that he had not noticed before. "I wasn't following you."

Although, he decided, inhaling the perfume of her embarrassment, fortune had been in his favor by crossing their paths again, this time in forms other than Cana and Fela. Fates had not randomly twisted their paths to cross for nothing; it was no coincidence, he believed, that this woman had twice been brought to him...or he to her...but what did it mean? Anyone else finding him and Vanya, when he was weak and unable to defend them, might have taken the opportunity to take their belongings and leave them for dead...or worse...instead of using precious rare supplies to tend his injuries and nurse him back to health. She had twice been instrumental in saving his life and Vanya's.

Perhaps, he thought with a shadowed scowl of annoyance, he was meant to be forever in her debt.

"Well, you're lucky we found you," she muttered to salve over the awkward sting, her words unknowingly mirroring his thoughts. "I thought…when we met the other night…she was your child…"

Kato arched one brow and cocked his head in a very feline fashion that sparked warmth low in her belly and soothed away the remaining discomfort. "Sometimes it feels that way," he agreed. "After our mother…I'm all she has. She would not survive without me." Nor I without her, he admitted to himself. As isolated as they had been growing up, without his sister to care for, Kato would have been entirely alone. Sometimes the burden of her felt too great to carry, but without Vanya, he could not imagine another reason to get up every day and press on. He needed his sister as much as she needed him. "The doctor…you are siblings?" Their closeness was obvious, the similarities in their scents more so, but each member of the Pack, save for the newcomers, carried the scents of the others, their usual sleeping proximity and a lifetime of living together leaving a similar combination of scents on each of them.

"Addi…we…that is not any of your concern." She huffed as if the question was an imposition, a reaction that made little sense even to her. She was proud of her brother, proud to call him that. But she would be safer, she suddenly felt, if she pretended that Addi was something else to her, something that would put her off-limits to the grey-eyed Fela whose penetrating gaze barely left her face. He was not the sort of complication she needed.

Seeming disappointed by her reaction, he muttered something beneath his breath that she could not hear. It was her turn to cock her head in curiosity, but he did not elaborate nor seem inclined to say anymore as he abruptly closed his eyes as if to sleep again.

He had not even asked her name.

Jia scowled. They would stop for midday meal soon, judging by the position of the sun behind the pale clouds. It would do her good to get out of the wagon and walk…and get her away from this intriguing, irritating man.

ঝ*ঙ

It came as no surprise to discover that the contents of the old warehouse, whatever had been left behind when the wagons had hauled the majority of goods away, had been torched and turned into a thick layer of black soot and ash that covered the walls, the floors, the ceiling of the building's interior. Any window coverings or furnishings made of wood, empty hemplastic containers and the documents they had held, had been consumed but the metal walls had contained the blaze and kept it from spreading unchecked into the borough streets. There was no accident in this fire, no loss of life, no significant loss of property, but no accident either. Vance felt reasonably certain, as he turned to study his footprints across the sooty floor, that the fire had been set with the intent to conceal the nature of what had been stored here.

The secret behind why Sal had been executed.

He had followed the wagons to a different structure eight lengthy blocks away. The slow speed of the oxen with their burden, and the rutty, cracked roads, meant the journey took too long. Then there had been the unloading and hauling of the hempcrates from the wagon into what had once likely been a shopping center, leaving Vance few hours of darkness in which to finish his reconnaissance of the first building…leaving plenty of time for someone to destroy whatever remained behind.

With smoke still lingering in the air and glowing embers clinging to life amidst the ash and soot, it had not long ago burned itself out. And while the stench of burnt hemplastic and the chemical accelerant used to ignite the fire masked the scents of whoever had been here, and the echoing growl of the extinguished flames drowned out the voices, Vance stopped in the center of the room, head tipped, eyes closed. Like a ripe onion, the distractions were peeled away, the effort stinging his eyes, burning his lungs, until only the core remained, sweet and pure but pungent in its clarity.

He could hear crates shifting, being opened, rifled through, closed and sealed. Now and then there came a sliding sound, a click, metallic and unfamiliar enough that he could not immediately identify what he was hearing. But each shed layer of distraction brought him closer to the truth, closer to recognition.

Loud voices and running footsteps from the street broke his concentration just before he could grasp onto the truth. Protectors, he instantly deduced, recognizing a few of the voices, a few of the names shouted to one another. When the nearest running set of boots came to an abrupt halt and the barked command of "Stop there!" was joined by a sound so similar to what his vision had come near to revealing, Vance's eyes flew open to stare into the barrel of one of the Protectorate's only firearms. Pubby's handgun. The realization filled him with a cold, tight pit of terrorizing impossibility.

"Oh...it's you..." Pubby lowered his weapon but did not holster it. "What happened here?"

"What does it look like?" snarked Vance, the hands clasped behind his head now dropping to his side.

"We had a report of a fire...of an intruder..."

"Fire was out when I got here." Given how long it had burned, he was a little surprised that it had taken the Protectorate so long to arrive. Then again, the building was surrounded by other warehouses, uninhabited by any except vagrants and animals, so only a passerby would have noticed a fire burning within a contained structure, the glow of it through the covered windows and the smoke that curled out through any available orifices. It would have taken time to reach the Protectorate, to file a report, to arrange for this many Protectors to attend the scene. If these men and women, the majority of on-duty daytime officers it appeared, had come in response to an intruder call, they had come at a run...and none of them looked winded enough for that.

"Did you see anyone...anything?"

Vance shook his head. The things he had seen, the precursor to the fire and then what his mage senses allowed him to deduce, were not details he intended to share with anyone until he learned more.

Pubby frowned and wiped his gloved fingers over a nearby metal support pole that ran from floor to ceiling. The pole was likely still hot to the touch, but the leather glove protected his skin. He held his fingers to his nose, as he looked around the room instead of at Vance. "Isn't this one of the Laedan's warehouses?"

"Was." The locations of the Laedans warehouses were a guarded secret, but the Protectorate always knew. How else were they supposed to protect the contents? Pubby recognizing the location was hardly suspicious.

"Heads are going to drop…" Not to mention, the Protector thought as he slid his gun back into the carrier on his hip, that people were going to suffer the loss of whatever goods had been stored here. Pubby did not know what those goods might have been, any more than anyone else did. Vance doubted even Ernest knew. No one except the Laedan's own people, a very select few, would have known, and Vance knew that not even those paid to relocate the crates were likely to have known what they hauled.

Vance could not claim to know what had been housed here, but he knew enough. "We should let the Chief report this one." Vance doing so would put him at the scene before anyone else, put him at risk of knowing too much. Better to follow protocol and let the Laedan decide what to do. Normally the recovery of goods stolen or lost would fall into the mage's hands, but not this time. This time, he wagered, the apparent loss would go uninvestigated at the Laedan's behest. It would throw further suspicion on the theft Channon had asked him to investigate, but that could not be helped.

And if what Vance now believed was true, finding that stolen shipment was now on the bottom of his list of things to do.

Chapter 14

Without being under the control of the boroughs, what had once been roads in the Eastern Wilds had long ago become overgrown paths between vine-covered edifices. Some showed signs of recurrent foot traffic and the ruts made by the wheels of carts and wagons, making those the choice of passages taken as the Pack pushed to the northeast. Scavs had undoubtedly been here, as the hulks of abandoned vehicles were stripped bare of usable materials and some of the fallen building debris had been taken for other purposes since the passable streets showed little of it. And though there were people here, clusters within secure buildings, individuals combing the streets and abandoned structures for food and goods, unseen children heard laughing and screaming as they amused themselves with games, they were fewer in number, more distant from their neighbors, less trusting of strangers struggling with their wagon. The path's condition slowed their progress, but as twilight settled behind them, they watched a sprawl of buildings that seemed out of place amidst the city's decay.

Someone had gone to lengths to maintain the façade of one large building, suggesting that others might have taken refuge here as well, although no lights were visible from the street and they passed no one as they approached. It was enough for the Pack to tighten their ranks, and Jia, now walking in the lead with Maz, was more watchful, noting that Deuce had slowed his pace and no longer raced ahead and then back as he scouted their route for danger. Watchful and protective, she was gaining more respect for the Omega and his devotion and wondered more often what the matter of contention had been between Deuce and her father. She listened, tempted to take Cana form to enhance her senses when she heard nothing beyond the wind, the evening insects, and the call of birds settling into their roosts to wait out the darkness. Above the crumbling arched doorway, a word visibly etched into stone, a word kept clean of dirt and ivy despite the overgrowth allowed to spread around it.

Science.

Her heart soared. Was this the place her father had often spoken of, the place he had visited as a boy with his own father, the secret place he occasionally disappeared to in the east for days at a time, only to return with books and treasures and hope in his eyes?

The place he had promised to take her and yet never had?

From his place unseen in the foliage ahead, Deuce's encouraging yip spurred the Pack forward. The others who had noticed that the Omega appeared to be leading and not just scouting, looked at one another with wary skepticism, but none questioned Jia's choice to continue deeper into unfamiliar territory, north now into a tangle of shrubs and trees and thick tall grass.

"Look."

The first word Kato had spoken to the group, the first word to anyone other than his sister after his brief conversation with Jia earlier, turned heads to the east. Through the dense foliage, a green tarnished statue of a man, headless now, listed to one side embraced by the gurgle of bubbling water. Aerated water meant clean water, at least fresher than any they had found today, and with their flasks now empty, or nearly so, the temptation to take their fill was too great to ignore. Not daring to leave the wagon behind, even if the area did appear to be vacant, they had to backtrack to the edge of the grove, follow an easier trail to the east, until they reached the first conspicuous sign of inhabitation they had witnessed here.

A partially cleared building façade was one thing. A fountain, maintained to continue operating, to keep the water circulating so it did not stagnate, the pool clean of most leaves and debris, meant that someone cared enough about this location to keep the water usable.

"We shouldn't stay here," murmured Candace, keeping her boys close as she looked around them with frightened eyes. Trill, Maz, and Addi, however, were already taking sentry positions as others filled their water supplies, reducing the likelihood that anyone was going to approach without notice.

"We're safe." Kato crouched on the edge of the fountain, scooping water with his hands to drink before filling his and Vanya's hemplastic flasks. Vanya splashed and giggled and tried to climb over the fountain's rim to get into the water. One scolding glance from her brother, however, had her plopping down on the ground, back to the fountain, arms crossed, a pout on her innocent features as she glowered back at him. Beyond her, Eddie stared at the man with the untamed dark curls, smiling sheepishly when their gazes met. Though he did not see it, Kato could feel another set of eyes staring at him behind his back. The same young set of eyes he had felt off and on throughout the day, when he had been awake enough to pay attention to his surroundings.

It was reasonable that he, the stranger among them, the Fela among Cana, would draw stares but that did not make him feel at ease, despite his proclamation of safety. Only a quick exchange of glances with Jia, the obvious Pack leader, gave him the peace of mind to consider staying as his strength returned.

"I'd feel better with a roof over our heads," Trill admitted, filling her goat bladder with water as Jia took her place on watch.

Alpha and Omega shared a glance and Jia nodded. "We're almost there," she said as Deuce too consumed his fill of water and then waited at the northern edge of the path that led past the fountain and disappeared between two large buildings.

"Almost where? Where are we?" Brie ran a handful of water through her hair, plastering it away from her dusty face. Traces of tears lingered on her cheeks, disappearing as she splashed water over them next, but Jia had heard no sound from her all day and wondered when the woman had been weeping and if it was for her lost pack that she mourned.

"A campus…a college…" Jia replied, grateful that no one had bristled at Kato's remark. They might not have addressed or acknowledged it, but the lack of animosity and outright distrust between the Fela and the Pack was a relief.

"Queens?" Addi asked, a hint of awe in his voice. He knew that place by repute through their father's tales, but he did not recall mention of a fountain. Maybe it had not been functioning when Roland had been here last. Maybe he had never come to this part of the campus.

Nodding, Jia said, "I think so." If it was, then it meant that, despite their long, indirect route to get here, the Flushing Wilds were not too far to the west, and Zone M not too far to the north. That fortuitous location ought to protect them from the Channons, from Quentin, and even from HOPE. If any one of these buildings, as large as they were, was unoccupied, or barely occupied, and was still intact, it would make an ideal den.

Deuce appeared to have the same idea as she noted his anxious, excited shuffling in the near darkness of his hiding place.

Thunder rumbled in the distance, somewhere to the east over the sea. Cold and tired, none of them wanted to be caught in the rain.

"Come on…let's find shelter."

Not much further, another fifteen minutes of dragging the wagon over the lesser used trail between buildings, brought them to a clock tower, intact but no longer functioning, the hands on the great round face forever stuck in a formation few could read. There were watches still, decorative items passed through families, but without a means to power them or people with the knowledge to repair them, most no longer gave the time, and the ability to read them was now dwindling knowledge. The purpose of the tower, however, was not lost, and Jia and Addi exchanged excited glances.

Roland had spoken of a tower, a place of broken glass windows he had covered over with anything he could find. A place of books.

"This is it."

Jia knew it without any signal from Deuce. He must have followed Roland here at some time; she found it difficult to believe her father would trust the Omega enough to welcome his company on any of his excursions east but Deuce stalking him, following Roland's scent, that made sense. The building of brick and stone was vast, tall enough, sprawled enough to house a much larger Pack. Big enough for them all…and safe provided it was unoccupied.

"Addi…Trill…let's make sure no one is home…"

"I can…"

Jia gave Kato a sharp look that made him shrink back and bow his head in what would have been an instinctive act of submission to an alpha if he had been Cana, if he had been a member of the Pack. The tense set of his shoulders, however, spoke of annoyance at being refused. But she was right. He was healing, in no condition to hunt or fight anyone who might be hiding here. What he also knew, what the softening of Jia's features and the look in her eyes, suggested in reaction to his annoyance, was that the Pack, the pups, and Vanya, would need protection should anyone come upon the wagon from the outside, and she was trusting him, Maz, and the three new Cana women to be that protection.

Trusting a stranger with the safety of the children was no small matter. She had little reason to trust him.

And yet, it seemed, she did.

The trio disappeared through the front door, scattering to search each level, each room, for signs of inhabitation, relying on Cana senses to tell them what normal senses could not. The air within was thick with the smell of musty pages, a familiar smell that had clung to Roland every time he returned to the Pack with another satchel of books. Books now loaded in the wagon outside, books now returning home. Disturbed patterns in the dust wove between shelves, patterns that, with her nose pressed to the floor, carried a faint, lingering trace of her father. It had only been weeks ago, not long before his disappearance, that Roland had been here last, and with no rain or wind to wash the scent away, it would remain for many more weeks.

Not having anticipated the scent, the memories brought with it stirred the heartache in her soul. The she-wolf sat on her haunches unexpectedly, tipped back her head, and gave voice to a mournful cry. Not a sound of warning, not a sound of danger, but a sound that every member of the Pack understood. One by one, each voice joined hers, less animal in tone but equally haunting, as children huddled closer to the adults, wide-eyed but just as vocal. Vanya scooted across the wagon's bed to wrap her frightened arms around Kato who smoothed her hair and stared at the doors, struggling against the impulse to follow that originating voice and protect Jia from whatever had hurt her.

Inside, Addi followed his sister's voice until he sat beside her, his muzzle pressed to hers, their voices intertwined. He could smell it too, the traces driving home their father's absence in a way that nothing had before. An exchange of glances with his wife, the last to arrive at that haunted spot, sent the other woman back to the Pack, her expression long but also relieved and determined.

"It is safe," she said softly with a touch to each member of the Pack. "Roland has been here."

Those who could carried packs, trunks, potted plants and animals into the building, a solemn procession filing back and forth to empty the wagon of their belongings. The wagon would not fit through the double doors without removing the center post that divided the entryway, which meant they would have to leave it in the open, a dangerous announcement of their presence, but one that could not be helped tonight. Vanya went inside as well, her arms full of more than she had ever carried during their journey from home, but Kato remained with the wagon, handing things down to others if he could do so without straining the stitches, his senses rubbed raw to alertness now that the Cana cry had drawn attention to their presence. Drawn the attention of one other, to be specific, a strong presence of a sort the Fela had never encountered before. Not Fela...not Cana...but not Normal either. Mutani, he presumed; their variety of scents was diverse and in his limited experience, if someone did not fit into either of the groups he was familiar with, it left only the mutani fringe. The unfamiliarity of the scent made it difficult to determine the threat level, but being the only one with the wagon when the scent arrived, and wounded, Kato decided to shed the blanket and his torn jeans in favor of the black Fela form. The change pulled at the stitches and loosened the bandages to draw blood once more. The pain made him growl and wince, but it was pain he was determined to ignore.

Against what might be a stronger opponent, the Fela form was the only hope he had of defending those within and the wagon upon which he perched. Unarmed as a Normal, he would stand no chance in a fight against such a threat.

But whoever was there, watching, remained hidden and chose not to approach. Kato paced, agitated and watchful, listening to those inside arranging a makeshift camp for the night around the warmth of lanterns and an oil stove. Vanya's laughter was easy, relaxed, as if she had been with these people all of her life, as if she did not notice her brother's absence, and despite the stab of self-pity and the realization that he might no longer be so needed now that there were others to protect her, he was also relieved that she remained indoors. Her love of his Fela form, without knowing it was him, might endanger them both if she came looking for him.

It was not Vanya who came onto the steps, however, nearly an hour after the unloading of the wagon was complete. The grief she had held at bay over her father's absence finally spent, Jia had joined the Pack in the round, open atrium, Addi at her side with his arm around her shoulders, her head high without regret. The Pack was protected, safe beneath Deuce's watchful eye where he crouched on a balcony two levels up, uncompromised by the unexpected outpouring of sorrow. When one in a pack mourned, they all mourned, sometimes to the detriment of their security, but not this time. If any threat existed in the library's vicinity, it had not taken advantage of the Pack's moment of weakness.

But Jia did notice, as Addi joined his wife and the children and began the grooming ritual that tied a Cana family together, that Kato was not among them. Nuzzles, sniffs and licks, fingers combing through hair and touching skin in search of injury, making sure that each member was fit, unharmed, happy and whole. It was attention that Vanya wiggled her way into the middle of, attention which Addi and Trill had no reservations about offering though she was no pup nor Cana by blood. Candace, Brie, and Helena similarly shared that affection amongst themselves and with the boys. Only the middle son, Neel, a Normal in the midst of his family unit, showed an embarrassing distaste for it, particularly when he caught the gentle eyes of Reif watching him and his brothers. It was her acceptance of such attention from her aunt and uncle and the persistence of his mother, that made Neel relent and accept what he could not avoid.

And yet where, Jia wondered as she dressed again, was Kato?

Refusing to admit she was worried about his absence, excusing her concern as being for Vanya's sake, she stepped outside into the cold wind as a crackle of lightning opened up the encroaching storm clouds to release their burden of rain. She could smell it, the tang of burnt air, though rain was not yet upon them. She closed the door to keep the warmth of their haven in and the cold of the night out and turned slowly on the steps to face the presence hunkered nearby in the shadows.

"Kato."

It made no sense that she should be so familiar with his aura and scent already, so comfortable in his company that she felt no hesitation in crouching to his level and holding forth her hand. When he growled, it was a sound not directed at her but a warning of something she had sensed upon coming outside and had not yet focused on.

"Come here."

The hunched black form snarled, hesitated, and then gave in to her summons only because it suited him to do so. There was no compulsion, no need to be near her, he told himself, only the belief that the two of them side by side would stand better against any opponent than either of them would alone. They had fought well together before. If it came to another fight, he was certain they would do the same again.

"You're bleeding."

It was not pain caused by her fingertips on sensitive flesh that caused him to jerk away, but rather the unbidden, unexpected purr that began in his chest, a sound he covered with a low growl and an intent stare across the street into the bushes. He was relieved when his efforts diverted her attention away from him.

Unaware of the purr, assuming she had hurt him, the distraction and focus on whatever was watching them kept her from a needless apology or unwanted scolding about an unnecessary shift in his condition. Unlike Kato, however, Jia recognized the elements in that invading scent that she had not crossed paths with in a long time.

"We know you are there, Ursa...we will not be frightened off so easily." There was no immediate response, only a spike of tension in the other's very masculine aura and a withdrawal further into the shadows. He had to have known his presence was no secret, so Jia guessed that it was being called Ursa that frightened him into retreat. "Nor do we mean you harm...we only want shelter."

Then the shadow and its presence were gone. Jia frowned and pursued only far enough to poke for clues in the cluster of bushes where the Ursa had hidden. As expected, there was nothing there except the smell of the bear. Kato followed only as far as the wagon, where he took advantage of her turned back to shift to Normal and pull his trousers back on. His mother had taught him modesty by always making certain to dress herself and Vanya behind closed doors or sending him to his room to dress. The necessities of keeping his Fela form from Vanya made such private changes important and he assumed that everyone else shared the same modesty.

"Ursa?" he asked when he was properly clothed again, grimacing with shift induced pain for the second time. "They are real?"

"Of course." She glanced over her shoulder, catching the discomfort in his movement as he cupped his hand over his side, and came back to him.

"I've never encountered one," he growled defensively, as if he needed to excuse his lack of knowledge. It was not defensive enough, however, to deter her from pulling the loose bandages off to examine the injury in the pale glow that emanated from within the library. She could smell blood but there was little of it on the bandages or on his skin.

"They're even rarer than Fela…and more solitary. At least," she added with a shrug, "that's what Father told us. I met one once, a woman…an herbalist. She did work for the Laedans…for Father and Lowell…for the people…and provided the clinics with herbs for treatment. Addi knew her better than I did…we might have been the only people to know about her." After dabbing at the wound with the cleanest part of the bandage, she murmured, "Being anthro in the Fortress was a risk."

"But your father raised you there?" It was what he surmised from the talk he had overheard.

She shrugged again. "It was the only life we knew…but it taught us caution." That the risk might have cost Roland his life and pulled the cloud of threat down over the Pack was a too obvious conclusion. "Someone had to fight for the rights of our kind…from the inside."

Fighting for rights, a world of politics and intrigue, were things unfamiliar to Kato. Coming from a world far outside the boroughs, he knew family and he knew survival, he knew the value of honesty and respect and strength in a fight. And he knew the threat of HOPE's uniformed forces, although that was a threat he knew only as rumor and myth since he had never seen those uniforms himself. It was the threat of HOPE and the occasional cruelty of others…as well as his mother's own awkwardness around him as his Fela nature blossomed…that had taught him that the world was not kind to those who were different, and it was that knowledge that helped him understand why some might choose to protect others like himself, even at the risk to their own lives.

"Did you?" Jia met his gaze with an unvoiced question in her eyes and he asked, "Fight from the inside?"

Jia tugged him toward the door, thinking about his question. "In my own way," she murmured. But, she thought with a sigh as she opened the door, she had not fought hard enough.

Chapter 15

Jonni looked at the severed, blue-grey hand in the metal box he was certain his father had left, the note with it falling from his fingers as he quickly covered his mouth to hold back the impulse to vomit. "It is done," was all that it read, his father's handwriting, to show that the Laedan had a direct hand in this deed, or had at least overseen and approved of it, in response to his son's demands. Jonni tried to force his eyes closed but they refused to obey, and even after he let the lid drop shut, the image within clung to his memory like heavily oiled water dripping down a window, slippery, persistent, and unwanted. His father knew his eldest son's stomach was weaker than his brothers', knew that he abhorred violence for the sake of violence, and sent him this in direct contradiction to that...and because Jonni had dared to demand something from him.

Yet the item in the box proved nothing except that somewhere some unfortunate bastard had lost a hand. It might not have come from a guilty man. Jonni's knowledge of medicine, as incomplete as it was, suggested that this hand was not fresh enough to have been recently removed, the splatters of blood appearing more painted on than the result of the act of cutting it away, thus not likely the hand of whoever had killed, or ordered killed, the Protector in Jonni's district. Even if it did belong to that individual, a man judging by the size and thickness of the fingers, was the loss of his hand an equal punishment for the murder of a Protector? Maybe the man had also been executed for his misdeed, the hand removed and sent as proof that punishment had been meted out, but experience told Jonni that it was just as likely that the murderer lived. He might never kill again, but if the act had come at the behest of Laedan Channon, sparing his life would serve as a thank you for his duty.

Or the Laedan's gratitude had come in the form of a silencing execution.

Hardly appeased, believing still that his father was duplicitous in the Protector's death, Jonni cranked open the window and heaved the hand, still encased in its box, into the rolling high tide below. What became of it now, where it might wash up on a beach, who might find it, what its fate might be, Jonni did not consider or care.

He cared only for the proof of what his father had been storing in that warehouse that had been worth a hand, a life, a soul to protect.

≈*≈

"Drink?"

Vance looked up from his barstool where he brooded over his nearly empty glass, surprised to see the Chief there but not surprised that the man would seek him out as company in intoxication. Neither of them frequented the dive in which they found themselves, except for the occasional company gathering that was sometimes held here due to its proximity to the Protectorate. Neither was the sort of man to seek company or solace from a room full of people, most too inebriated, or in the throes of whatever substance they were enjoying, to care about anyone else. Drinking for both Vance and the Chief was an act of solitude, a means to forget, an escape best done in the privacy of their own dingy apartments.

But Vance had desperately not wanted to be alone tonight, not until he was well on his way to oblivion, and Ernest, the flask in his desk drawer now empty, had not wanted to wait until he got home for another drink.

That they both happened to choose this place on the same night was either coincidence or providence.

Determining which would require more mental effort than either was prepared to make.

Looking into his glass again, swishing the dregs of thick dark amber around the bottom, Vance nodded in response to the offer and slid the glass across the counter for the tender to refill as he poured a glass of the same for Ernest. The older man settled on an unsteady stool and cupped his hands around the drink when it arrived, staring hard at it for several quiet moments. Vance took a swallow, the ale no longer burning his throat or belly after the two glasses he had already consumed, and kept his eyes anywhere except on his chief.

Ernest eventually downed his liquid comfort in a long series of swallows and then asked the tender for a refill with a gesture. As he waited, he murmured, "Learn anything?"

Vance shrugged. "Nothing you want to know." The details he had learned were things Earnest would have to report to the Laedan if he knew them, so sparing the man those tidbits meant secrets the Chief would not have to keep. Until he had a better idea of what he was dealing with, Vance felt more secure in keeping his knowledge to himself. "What I will say is…tell the others…watch for guns."

"Guns…" Ernest scowled and downed his second glass in a quick gulp. Firearms were such a rare thing that the Protectors were ill-equipped with defenses against them. Deaths like Sal's were rare, no more than once or twice a year, and often accidental, at the hands of someone who did not know what they had. To suggest there could be an increase on a noticeable scale was grim news. "You sure?"

He did not know why he asked; the mage's forewarnings were nearly always accurate. Vance shrugged again, this time brief eye contact with his boss being all of the confirmation Ernest required. He scowled and downed a third drink. He had intended to make his drinking last, now he felt woozy and sick to his stomach, though how much of that was due to the alcohol and how much related to the news he could not guess. Swaying, he got to his feet; he white-knuckled the lip of the counter and waited for the nausea to pass.

"Need a hand home?" Vance was little better off, but by some trick or genetic disposition, the mage held his liquor better than most. It was time for him to be going as well, lest he find some alley or doorstep to serve as a bed for the night. Though they lived in opposite directions, making the offer was the polite thing to do.

Ernest shook his head. "No…just…" This time when his gaze met Vance's, he held it steady. "If you hear anything…see anything…about who's beating Yiva Channon…"

It was Vance's turn to scowl. The obvious candidate for such brutality was the woman's husband, but if it was a new development, then perhaps there was someone else. Or perhaps Lowell had been the one to report it. Vance had no details beyond the Chief's request, and knew he was in no condition tonight to absorb any information if the other man offered.

"If I hear anything," he agreed as they staggered together into the street. The fog was rolling in thick tonight, carrying the heavy scent of sea salt and storm with it. Though neither spoke their thoughts as they nodded and parted ways, both men wondered if they would ever find their drunken ways home.

❧*❧

Her hand felt small beneath his, their fingers entwined on the desk as he leaned beside her to examine what she was writing. Quentin had no doubt that his room, as with most offices within the Fortress, was under audio surveillance though he had yet to find proof of it; Laedan Channon was just paranoid enough to make such precautions necessary, particularly since the suspicions about Marrock that had been planted in his head had, at least on appearance, come to fruition. He seemed to trust Quentin as much as he trusted anyone, but Lowell was a man adept at keeping up appearances and frequently kept a close eye on even his own sons. Of course they, like Quentin, had found ways to get around those possible surveillance methods, and they, he imagined, at least had the privacy of their bedrooms. Quentin wished he believed he had the same, but he was unwilling to take that chance.

So long as he kept his business unseen and kept what might be heard as innocuous as possible, the Laedan should never have cause to suspect him.

So be it, he mused, kissing the side of the woman's neck, absorbing her scent that he had missed for longer than he could admit to. He had known her since childhood, a young man brought up in the shadow of Kennedy's Fortress, trained to be a diplomat, a soldier, by the very best Kennedy had to offer. As an orphan, however, there had been little chance of advancement and despite his early months of service to Hallister's regime, he had not stood out in any way that would make him memorable to the Laedan. Only to his daughter, the girl he had left brokenhearted when he chose to leave Kennedy borough in favor of LaGuardia.

There had been no chance for advancement beneath Hallister, only the probability of his affair with Oasis being discovered. A man of ambition, the plan had been to establish himself in the employ of Channon and Marrock, make himself indispensable, and when his prospects looked promising, he would request Oasis' hand.

He should have anticipated Geary's plan for Oasis. He should have acted sooner, saved her from a loveless union to a sadistic boy. Things were what they were, however, fortune working a tandem path for them, but it had, at least, brought them to each other again.

After years of silence, with the way he had left, he had not been certain she would want to pick up their relationship where they left off, even if she had once offered to aid his career in any way she could. The flush of her skin as his lips and breath brushed against her neck, however, was answer enough.

He read the words again. He believed the fort to be real, knew Channon had been seeking details and information about its location for longer than Quentin had known him. He knew Marrock had gotten his hands on some of that information, details Lowell had shared with no one else, not even Quentin. And now it appeared that Donn knew about his father's hunt for the fort as well and believed the stories true enough to be worth investigation. It meant that at least four people had similar visions of what the future of Queens could be and might be willing to pursue that vision.

Which of them had the resources and willpower to find and claim that vision was the only question that needed to be answered.

Oasis turned, the round curves of her body beneath the saffron and gold gown she wore moving temptingly against him. He smiled and bent low to be rewarded with a compliant, welcoming kiss.

"Thank you," he murmured into her mouth, confident that no observation equipment would hear him.

The tightening of her arms about his neck was the most reassuring response he could ask for.

࿊*࿊

Unable to fight the need to know where he was, unable to feign unconsciousness any longer, Liam peered out from behind sleep crusted lids at the dim metallic glow, understanding as he did so that the lights were but one of the sources of the constant whir and hum he heard. It was a relief to be assured that the sound was not coming from within his skull. The relief was short-lived, however, when the slight turn of his head left and right, the only movement his neck was allowed, revealed his place in a long row of similarly strapped, vertical bodies, some male, some female, some with eyes closed, others staring blankly across the room. He could not tell how many were living, how many were dead, but he could hear breathing below the mechanical and electrical drone, could feel the pulse of their collectively beating hearts.

Or maybe that was his own heart, his own breath, labored and colored with horror as he deduced there were others behind him, others in front of him, that he was not alone in this nightmare. Maybe fifty in all, though some of the binding contraptions seemed empty, suspended two to three feet apart by cables, pulleys, and metal bars that held them rigid, whereas the occupied units swayed slightly, propelled by the smallest movements of the captives.

Perhaps they were trying to escape. Perhaps they moved, swayed, merely to give themselves the sensation of living.

It was easy, in this suspended place with little light and stagnant sound, to believe this was a dream, no existence at all. But the ache of muscles, the burn of cuts and bruises sustained in the battle that had resulted in his being here, were fresh enough to remind Liam of the world outside, the world he needed to get back to, the Pack that had surely given him up for dead.

Well, not Jia, he thought with the satisfaction of trusting her friendship. She had not given up on her father; she would not give up on Liam either. Finding him in this place, when he did not know where he was or how long he had been here, would be nearly impossible, however. It might be better for all concerned if he gave in to the inevitable, believed himself to be lost, to pray that she never found him here and put her life at risk to rescue him.

He must have uttered a sound, a sigh, although he did not hear it, did not feel it. The appearance of a gaunt but familiar face before him, the thin hand on his shoulder, jarred him from his fog and he stared at the man in disbelief.

"Fight, Liam. Fight and live." He pressed water once more to the younger man's lips and Liam gratefully accepted the offer. "To give up is death."

"We feared you might be…"

"Not yet I'm not," Roland chuckled darkly and provided more water. "They need us alive as long as possible…"

"They? Who?"

"I don't know." The cup was lowered and replaced with a damp cloth that swabbed the sweat from Liam's brow. "You've got a fever…that ought to spare you for a day or two…so long as you don't get worse…or they don't deem you contagious."

"What happens then…if they deem me…?"

Roland shook his head, answer enough for Liam to understand that death awaited if he did not fight off whatever infection his wounds were generating. A shift in form would help, often healed injuries and illnesses more quickly, but Roland squeezed his shoulder and shook his head as if reading his thoughts.

"Don't shift. It's what they want…our blood…"

"Cana blood?" it explained the pungent strength of Cana scent in the crowded room, but there were others as well, others who were not Cana but were not Normals either.

"Anthro blood…mostly Cana. They draw from a few of us every day…and this may not be the only facility. I don't know where the others are…and I'm not sure why…but I have my suspicions…" The cool rag was dropped into the cart Roland had been pushing and Liam scowled to realize he had not noticed that sound earlier.

"It's the…drug…isn't it?" That rumor had persisted for months without proof of its reality. What did not need proof, however, was that many Normals clung to the belief that the bodily fluids, bones, hair, and organs of anthro could enhance their senses, their abilities, their health, their libido. Of course, the benefits were believed to come with the risk of side-effects, most notably one becoming anthro by exposure. HOPE perpetuated the myths, adding them to the bounty often placed on anthro' heads, encouraging their murder or capture. It was believed that HOPE was the originator for such lore, and the key to the rumored experimentation. Although no one Liam had ever known had proof, few taken by HOPE lived or escaped to tell the tale and of those said to have escaped, none were willing to speak of the horrors they endured.

"HOPE?"

Roland sighed. "Maybe." He did not believe that was who had captured him, but the likelihood of having been transferred to a HOPE facility was high. Who else would have the medical capabilities to extract, store, and process blood? No one in LaGuardia, to Roland's knowledge; he knew more about the workings of the borough than almost anyone else.

More, he often believed, then Lowell.

"Jia? Addi?"

"Were fine…good…strong…looking for you. There was another hunt…but they got away safely." Without proof to the contrary, Liam chose to believe it was true. None of the others were here, else Roland would have said so, which meant the Pack was either dead or safe. Faith that they lived and had fled to safety was a preferable alternative to believing they had died.

Nodding, Roland accepted those words to mean that his daughter had taken leadership of the Pack as intended, and the Pack, in good hands, was safe. He did not believe they would ever be found here since he did not know where 'here' was, but he had not given up hope of finding a way out. He intended to rescue all of those here, but he knew he would be lucky if he could rescue just this one and himself.

"Why aren't you…?" Liam's eyes flicked down toward the leather strap cinched across his chest.

"They want to ensure my cooperation…"

Liam nodded once, although it did not make sense to him. They could just as easily have left Roland strapped to a pallet and bled him the way they were bleeding everyone else. Maybe they knew who he was, felt him to be a valued commodity worth more than the blood in his veins. Liam knew Roland would fight against mistreatment of these poor souls as he had fought for the rights of others on the outside all of his life. Anyone who knew who he was could have guaranteed him the right to offer kindness to the patients in exchange for his cooperation. Roland, no matter how much he hated these conditions, would have agreed to anything if it meant making the last days of life better for the condemned.

They were condemned. Liam knew it, even if Roland did not say it. The wait time between withdrawing blood from each individual was not enough and would inevitably lead to the weakening and death of the donor. And though the naked victims were connected to tubes meant to provide sustenance and encourage the rapid production of more blood, the lack of decent meals, exercise, bodily hygiene, and hope meant that they would waste, wither, and succumb to death within a matter of weeks. Months at the most. Liam did not want to know how long he had to live. Provided he was not left in the same vegetative state as the others, he would watch for the opportunity to escape too, learn everything he could about this place, and take that information back to the Pack.

Somehow, he and Roland would bring this place down.

He had no idea how. But the only other choice was death, and that was not a choice Liam was willing to settle for.

"They'll examine you in the morning. Don't speak…don't let them know you know me. Keep what you see and hear to yourself…and never give up, Liam. I'll get you out of here. I promise you that."

Liam did not ask how but he chose to believe his Alpha would keep him alive, help him escape, or they would die together.

Chapter 16

U nable to sleep, restless from pain and frustration, Kato prowled the building, moving silently from room to room, floor to floor astounded by the sheer number of gradually decaying books and the smell of must and damp that permeated so much of the structure. Surprisingly, many of the windows were intact, and though the smooth surfaces of shelves, books, and the molding along the edges of the floor were layered in dust, just as the ground floor had been, he had a feeling that others had been here, that this place was appreciated for its contents by those who knew of it. Not all would treasure the pages contained here, as most could no longer read the words, but of those Kato had met as a child, those he crossed paths with on his journey west, most would have protected those books without ever knowing what they said. How often had he found a traveler, a discarded pack, a dead man's trove, with at least one book in its possession?

Books were history. Books were knowledge. Books were the future.

Kato could not read them, not well enough to appreciate those things, but he understood as he rubbed his fingers over the ancient spines, that books represented a world, a time, lost to mankind, that they contained the accumulation of everything up to the day the world had ceased to advance.

If Jia and her people could read these, as he had already deduced, what better place to take refuge at least until the spring and warmer weather accommodated easier travel?

Though the Cana standing watch throughout the night eyed him cautiously when his searches brought him full circle to the smoky campfire on the ground level, none of them followed and none tried to keep him at the fire. Even when he went into the pre-dawn air to stand in the light rain and fog that wrapped their shelter and hid it from view from all but those passing nearest to it, they left him alone. It hid him from sight, although any Cana who chose to follow would not need their eyes to do so. They would rely on other senses to seek threats in the fog, to find him, in the same way Kato used his as he circled the building, clinging to the shadows, wanting to be certain that those within were safe, were keeping Vanya safe.

He should not care about any of them except Vanya. But her security relied on the Pack's strength, and thus, for the time being, until he was healthy enough to protect her himself and travel, they remained with the Cana, and the Cana had to remain safe.

A few more days. Nothing more.

His inattentive thoughts tangled with the threads of survival and brief image flashes of the Cana alpha garnered through their short acquaintance made him pay less attention than he should have been. The shifting wind that came from his upwind side and the thickening of the fog as daylight began to claw into the sky, hid the smaller, wiry figure until they stood face to face at the front corner of the library furthest from the door. One moment Kato was alone, the next he had a knife pressed against his throat and one arm twisted and held behind his back. A sniff of the air, now that they were so close together, revealed that this was the same one who had watched the library the previous evening, the Ursa of unknown threat level.

Kato had seen pictures of bears, but he could not imagine this obviously shorter, sinewy fellow transforming into anything akin to the size of a bear.

"Fela…why are you here?" the stranger hissed against his ear, voice muffled by the grey cloth covering his mouth and nose. Only his eyes were visible, as even his head was covered, the grey of his attire having made him more difficult to spot as it blended so well with the churning fog.

"Why are you here?" Kato challenged back, unafraid to fight with this smaller man despite his injury and the knife at his throat. The ache in his side, however, reminded him that he was not invincible and kept him from trying to subdue or overpower the man just yet, but if it came to a fight, at least in normal form, he felt confident he could win.

A rumble in the other man's chest, something Kato judged to be a warning growl, made him shrug and answer the question. "They found me...are tending my wounds..." The stranger gave another disgruntled sound, his demeanor suggesting he was weighing his options. Finally, he grunted again and nodded.

"Take me to them."

Either equally confident of his strengths or stupid, Kato thought with another shrug and stumble forward, the knife pressed against his back while the Ursa kept hold of his arm. If not for the injury, he could pull free, but he suspected the Ursa was not above throwing that knife should Kato bolt, and so he kept his back to the man and moved as instructed. The Ursa had no accomplices, was alone as far as Kato could tell, and it seemed unlikely he would be able to do any substantial harm to the Pack once they entered the building. It did not ease his nerves; if the Ursa thought threatening his life would manipulate the Cana, he would soon learn to the contrary. Scowling with that realization, Kato hesitated before pushing the door open and stepping cautiously across the threshold, drawing the attention of those already awake and rousing those who were not.

Despite a few sharp glares of accusation aimed at him, Kato kept his shoulders squared as the Ursa entered and stood beside him, still gripping and twisting his arm. They were met by the Cana adults rising to their feet, Jia among them, the one to step forward with worry and anger in her eyes. She recognized the Ursa's scent from the night before, and though she had expected his return, she had not expected it so soon. Nor had she expected he would threaten one of her companions when he did so, at least not alone. Ursa, according to her father, rarely acted unless they felt threatened. If this man felt threatened by the Pack's presence, it was her duty to assure him they meant no harm, her responsibility to negotiate their right to be here. It was what her father had trained her to do by exposing her to the inner workings of the Fortress.

Wondering if there were others, aware of the knife pressed against Kato's back inches away from his bandages, Jia kept her approach calm and slow until she stood just beyond the Ursa's reach. She held Kato's gaze long enough to bid him be still, to trust her, and focused on the man of Asian descent who had crashed their refuge.

"We mean no harm," she said, choosing diplomacy rather than defensiveness or threats.

"Why are you here?"

Jia began to pace a slow arc from left to right, studying the Ursa's stance and voice. Though she could see no more of his features than the area around his eyes, stretching from temple to temple, something in those eyes, in his voice, said she should know this man, though it was unlikely they could have met. She thought she would have remembered him if she had. She would have remembered crossing paths with an Ursa before. "We need shelter…my father spoke of this place being a…"

"You're a Marrock."

Addi, already alert like the other adults, lurched to his feet in surprise and joined his sister. "QiangXu…?" It was the voice, raspy and thick from smoke and chemical exposure more than the man's mostly covered face, that sparked recognition.

The smaller man, his brown eyes squinted as if to see Addison more clearly, and the doctor, with his hand outstretched, studied each other for several moments before the Ursa released Kato and shoved the knife back into the sheath at his hip. Kato sidestepped away and unconsciously retreated to a secure position at Jia's side, keeping her between him and the Ursa, slightly behind her in deference to her status and near enough to be protective should the Ursa turn on her.

Before accepting the offer with a cordialness that erased the tension from the air, the Ursa unwrapped the coverings that hid his face to reveal chiseled features on a face pocked with scars.

"Addison. Where is Roland? I did not see him with you…"

"Doctor Feng…we thought you were dead," Addi remarked, clutching the other man's hand. "It has been ten years…"

It was the man's surname that brought back vague memories of the chemist's presence within the Fortress, a man who had, as Jia recalled, been hired to find a chemical solution to Nik's ever-increasing addiction problem, as well as to supply other services as the Laedans' required. The chemist maintained his lab elsewhere, worked primarily out of his home, but for a time he had come to the Fortress two or three times a week to work with Nik. Jia knew of him, had seen him occasionally from a distance, and could only recall a handful of times she, in her father's company, had come into contact with the chemist. She had been a child then, perhaps twelve years old the last time their paths crossed, and for whatever reason, she had never identified him as Ursa. Addi, however, as part of his meditraining, had spent hours following the chemist around, asking questions, and had even been sent to his home to work in the man's lab occasionally. It was little surprise, therefore, that Addi was the one to recognize him, and the one to be recognized in return. Jia imagined that the skinny tomboy of a creature she had been, all elbows and knees, had been unremarkable enough to escape the Ursa's notice, just as he had escaped hers.

She remembered when he stopped coming to the Fortress, however, rumors involving his son's health that had surprised many for none, except perhaps Addi and Roland, had known Feng had a child or a wife. Nik had sulked with abstract fury for weeks after his leaving, falling into a depression and a binge of substance misuse, in response to the perceived rejection that he had never crawled out of. He never accepted another's efforts to heal him of his addictions, though his parents had tried other chemists and 'specialists' in the years since, until at last their efforts ceased and Nik was left to wallow in his chemical fog. From the day the chemist left the Fortress for the last time, Roland had refused to talk about him. Jia had never known why, but she wondered now, as she stood face to face with the man, if her father had known his secret and was protecting the Ursa from Lowell by not speaking of him.

"It was no longer safe in LaGuardia." QiangXu did not need to elaborate. If there had been suspicion regarding his nature, or perhaps his son's, fleeing would have been his only choice.

The Flushing Pack knew that from experience.

"Jia…" His gloved hand was extended to her as he determined who she must be. "Your father…why is he not with you?"

"He has been…taken…" Not killed, she refused to believe that, but captivity for a Cana was just as bad, for should the urge to shift overtake him, he would be at the mercy of his captors, at risk of exposure, at risk of proving the truth of who and what he was.

She motioned QiangXu toward the fire, welcoming him into the company of the Pack, trusting their safety to his presence. QiangXu, with a tilt of his head, accepted the hospitality and followed the siblings into the circle. Rubbing his throat where the knife had been, glad Vanya had not awakened to witness the threat to his life, Kato followed, tensed to spring should the Ursa prove to be a threat despite his seeming familiarity and friendship. Jia and her brother might know him, might trust and welcome the Ursa as they had done Kato, but the Fela was not ready to offer those same luxuries. He could not yet admit to fully trusting the Pack, not even Jia.

He would rather trust the Omega who crouched behind a rail on the level above them and watched the stranger with equal unease, than trust the man who had just held a blade to his throat.

"By HOPE or…?"

Jia felt something in the words unspoken, a question and confirmation of her fears all in one, and though QiangXu had not been in LaGuardia for the past decade, she realized her father had kept in contact with him. It might have been Roland who suggested the abandoned campus in the wilds as a hideaway. Perhaps the two had explored this library and surrounding area together. Perhaps the Ursa and Pack Alpha met here often during the man's years of self-exile, and if that was the case, Jia mused, how much might the Ursa know of events in the borough?

"We don't know," she admitted after a glance at each member of the Pack gathered around the fire. "From things Father said, I believe the Channons...Quentin...that Lowell..."

"Did he find them? The journal? The ledger? Do you have them?"

It was surprising that this man, a stranger to most of the Pack, might be aware of the items their Alpha had risked his life for. "We don't...I think he found them...or at least he saw them...but if he had them..." She shrugged. "He did not tell us where they might be. I'm not sure if that is why..." She had been less skeptical about the existence of secret documents than others in the Pack, documents whose contents Roland had never discussed, but not only did the Ursa know about them, he believed in their existence. "Lowell...the Channons...they know about us...the Pack..."

"And thus you are here." The Marrocks had been skirting detection since the second generation after the Undoing, when the anthrozooidic mutations began to emerge in the human population. As far as anyone knew, the Marrocks were one of the oldest Cana bloodlines in the boroughs, in Queens, perhaps in the world. They had been fortunate not to have been discovered by the Channons, or others, sooner. They had been fortunate to avoid extermination as long as they had. "Were you followed?"

"Only as far as the neutral sector. We..."

"Slaughtered the bastards...with Kato's help," Addi chuckled, acknowledging to the Ursa that the Fela had value and was not merely some stray they had picked up along their journey. Not normally a violent man, not a fighter like his sister, the doctor was, however, protective of his family, his Pack, and whoever the hunters had been, they had taken one of his friends, possibly his father, and threatened all of their lives. They deserved to die.

Kato stared at Addi with surprise and suspicion, but as Vanya was awake now, sitting amidst the other children, he did not attempt to raise a question or draw attention to himself.

QiangXu nodded. Whatever the world had been before the Undoing, survival was now the paramount priority. Killing those who hunted them was as acceptable as breathing.

"It is safe here. There are others…mutani…a small Pack on the eastern edge of campus…" The Ursa's gaze traveled up toward Deuce, acknowledging his presence when he had no need to do so, a gesture Jia noted and intended to question later. "They have no cause to trouble you…and I will see that they do not. We watch out for each other here."

"I would like to meet them." Establishing a truce or an alliance with the other Pack would be in everyone's' best interest, and creating a working relationship with the mutani would help keep all of them safe.

"You will. The Pack came after the last time Roland…" Again he eyed Deuce with a largely blank expression. "But he knew the others." His lips dropped in a frown. "You believe the Laedan's men took Roland?"

Addi reached for his sister's hand when her expression darkened. Others around the fire, Trill readying breakfast for the children, the three newest pack members who kept the children entertained, Maz who poked at the fire to keep it burning while water boiled in an iron pot for tea, paused what they were doing to listen more closely to the conversation.

"They did not wear HOPE uniforms…nor those of the Laedan guard. They wore dark grey and black…covered top to foot with gloves, boots and dark sights. I do know…" She hesitated, shrugged, and continued. "The hunt that drove us here…that cost us another of our pack…was launched by Donnovan and Quentin. Lowell may have sanctioned it…or may not have known about it…but I do not believe he ordered it. As for my father…perhaps it was the same…"

"It would not surprise me. Roland never did trust Quentin…or Donnovan…" The Ursa shook his head grimly. Donnovan had been a devious, untrustworthy, sadistic child when he had known him. He had heard much about the young man over the years; that Donn had not grown out of that behavior was not a surprise.

"It is still likely they ended up in HOPE's hands," muttered Maz. Heads around the fire bobbed in agreement.

"Or he is being held for interrogation by the Channons," Jia snorted. It was the possibility she hoped for, for rescuing her father and Liam from a holding room in the Fortress that she had not had the chance to look for, or from another location in the borough, would be significantly easier than rescuing them from HOPE. It was only a matter of finding them, and for that, she needed the Mage. For the first time in a day, Mage Segara crossed her thoughts and made her shift uneasily in her cross-legged position. She felt Kato's eyes rake over her, an uncomfortable, questioning bit of attention that she decided to ignore by focusing on QiangXu as he spoke again.

"There is another possibility." QiangXu scratched absently at his thigh before continuing. "There are facilities…secret ones where A-plas is synthesized…"

"A-plas?" asked Addi, frowning at the unfamiliar term.

"It goes by many names on the street…I've lost track of them now. Plasma is taken from anthro blood…usually Cana…freeze-dried for storage…then added to sterile alcohol for injection, combined with any smokable substance or mixed in alcohol for drinking. It's more potent in its natural form, but harder to store and transport…more expensive."

The three newest adults in the Pack looked at one another with the same alarm and distress that the others displayed. "Then it is true…the rumors of a street drug…?" whispered Candace. Brie gave a hitching sob and buried her face against Helena's shoulder.

QiangXu nodded. "The discovery arose from genetic studies meant to determine why anthro are not afflicted with the grubber virus." His discomfort was obvious, as if he was being forced to reveal a painful secret. "Once the mind-altering effects of our plasma on Normals was discovered, it was, I suppose, inevitable that the information would be twisted and used for gain…that other sources of plasma for study and use would be sought…willing sources or not. We tried to keep the research out of HOPE's hands…"

"This isn't your fault," chided Addi, his hand on the Ursa's shoulder. Whatever part QiangXu had played in the initial research, the doctor knew from their past acquaintance that he would never turn against his kind to profit from their suffering, nor would he have used his research for anything other than the betterment of all people.

Jia was less concerned with blame or fault than with what else the chemist knew. "Who else is involved? Do you know who…?"

"The discovery is more than a decade old. By now, the number of those with the knowledge might have doubled…tripled…but without the facility to draw, store, and process blood…" QiangXu shook his head. "It requires the proper equipment…a reliable energy source to run generators, freezing equipment, cold storage…"

"And to house donors or dispose of bodies," Helena spat.

The Ursa coughed awkwardly. "If the rumors are true…the supply has been too steady…even with the continuing capture of anthro…for the extermination of donors to be a regular thing."

"Unless they can now synthesize…"

"If they can do that," Addi cut Maz off, "they have no need for fresh sources…save for further experimentation."

"Do you know anywhere in LaGuardia that could facilitate such harvesting?" Clinging to the possibility that meant the highest probability of Liam and Roland's survival, Jia's question was hopeful. There could not be many such places, and if she could identify where they were, it was information that could be given to the Mage…or that she could investigate herself in the hopes of finding the two missing men.

"I knew of such labs years ago…now…" Again QiangXu shook his head. "Given the addictive nature of the substance, I would think such facilities must relocate often to avoid the Protectors…"

"Or else they are already under the Laedan's protection," offered Trill. The worrisome implications that the Channons could run such facilities without Roland's knowledge, or that Roland had known and done nothing to stop it, brought tight, cold balls of disgust into each member of the Pack.

Defensively, Jia growled. "He did not know." She knew what they were thinking...and she knew her father. Roland had spoken of the rumored drug as just that, a rumor. Nothing he had done or said, allowed Jia to believe he could have been complicit in the trade of anthro blood.

If he had discovered such an operation under his partner's control, however, it could be yet another excuse for Lowell to remove him from political office.

The itch to seek out the Mage grew stronger.

"If the labs are run by HOPE, they could be anywhere, even outside of the borough." There was a large territory to the southeast, adjacent to Kennedy borough, over which HOPE held sway, territory used as training and recruitment grounds, as a source to finance their activities in the surrounding lands, a place where no Laedan's law could hamper them, where they ruled and thrived unchecked. Entering that territory, crossing it, searching it, would be a suicide mission for any anthro foolish enough to attempt it.

If that was where Roland and Liam had been taken, Jia knew she was going to have to attempt it, or else give up and accept the inevitable loss of them both.

Outside, the world was beginning to brighten with the arrival of dawn, and QiangXu, as if he had somewhere to be, rose to his feet with cumbersome grace, his movements suggesting pain though there were no visible injuries and he appeared younger than the age Jia knew he had to be. "I need to get back," he said, "if I am to reach the others in time to keep the peace."

"Will you join us for the evening meal?" Addi offered, cordial and eager to speak with his mentor further. QiangXu's presence here made this relocation less discomforting then it might be otherwise.

"I shall try." My routines do not always permit...but," he smiled, "I shall try." He glanced at each person, eyes lingering on the two non-anthro in the group, on the two out of place Fela, and lastly up to the Omega to whom he nodded his head once before turning toward the door. "It is a pleasure to have you all here...you are welcome."

"And it is fortunate to find a friend of Father's here," Jia said as she trailed him to the door, ignoring Kato's harsh stare. Whatever the Fela's issues were, she had no inclination to allow him to interfere with the building of trust between the Pack and their new neighbors. She would corner him and confront him later.

Taking Alpha initiative in hopes that he could give her further answers about her father, when they paused at the door with his hand on the latch she asked in a low voice, "The ledger and journal…what do you know of them?"

QiangXu stepped outside and inhaled deeply of the early dawn air, both to clear his lungs of smoke and to test the wind for danger. "He did not tell you?"

"He mentioned their existence. I know they contain some secret that puts the borough, perhaps all of Queens, in danger…but he never spoke of their contents. I never saw them. Lowell confirmed the loss of state documents, but nothing specific…at least not to anyone outside of the Fortress. Maybe only Quentin knows. Maybe if I knew their contents, knew why they're important, I might be able to find where Father must have hidden them."

"If he had them," the Ursa cautioned. "I knew he was seeking them…but I do not know if he ever obtained them."

Jia tilted her face toward the sun, listening to him as well as to the sounds of the morning around them. There was the faint clink of metal cookware joined by the thin aroma of frying eggs, both of which reminded her of the breakfast of which she had not yet partaken. "What secrets do they contain?" she whispered. "Do you know? What was worth killing…or dying…for?"

Voice equally low, QiangXu murmured, "If Roland was right, a counting of a great stash of military ordnance lost at the Undoing and the location of the cache…a place called Fort Hamilton."

The name of the place held no meaning to her, but she understood military ordnance, understood what the possession of such a cache might mean to anyone who sought the ultimate, sole control of an area…be it LaGuardia, Queens, or some measure of territory larger still. How long had Roland speculated that Lowell would prefer to rule as sole Laedan of LaGuardia? Hadn't she seen with her own eyes the tell-tale hints of a man always seeking more control of his world than his co-governing position allowed?

And if Lowell's seeking such a prize was instead on HOPE's behalf, what more could the organization do with such power that they were not doing already?

Jia shuddered beneath the shadow of that secret. It was no wonder her father had been willing to die to obtain those documents while keeping their secrets out of his children's hands. It was also little wonder that Lowell would go to great lengths to keep that knowledge away from the man who had been his best friend. The one man who could thwart his plans.

"We'll find it," she swore. "We'll find him...and Liam...bring them home...and if he hid them anywhere...we will find that ledger and map as well."

"If Roland took that secret down with him, perhaps it is best to let it stay buried." So long as the Laedan lacked those important documents, his ability to proceed would be hindered. "But I will help you if I can."

It was the least he could do for his friend...the least he could do for these new allies...the least he could do for the people of Queens he had been forced to leave behind.

☙Scratch the Sky❧

Chapter 17

Viva adjusted her skirt with mechanical, numb movements, listening to the familiar sounds of the man behind her, soft sounds that belied the violence of moments before. The scratching of his fingers on skin through the coarse curls at his groin, the grunted labored breathing, the rustle of stiff fabric being secured into place as he returned his appearance to what it had been when he barged into the family room where she had been reading alone. She imagined she could hear his lips moving, his tongue sliding over the smirk that so often frightened her into compliance. Soft sounds, but there was nothing soft about her youngest son, not a single thing she could find loveable any longer. Any love she had ever felt for him had evaporated the day he had grown strong enough to overpower her and rob her of dignity and peace of mind.

Any affection she showed him in public was now pretense only. At any other time, her feelings ranged from apathy to coldness, to anger and loathing or, most often, fear and despair. At this moment she felt sick and bitter, but showing it would result in a raining of fists and open-handed slaps. With Lowell already suspicious, she dared not risk such an assault again, but why, she wondered, had it taken her husband so long to notice evidence that had been there sporadically for years?

That question brought a flush of angry indignation to her cheeks, but as she kept her back to her son and her head down while she tidied her hair and wiped her face of sweat and tears, Donnovan was not likely to notice.

It seemed she had become invisible to most of the men in her life. When, she wondered forlornly, had that happened?

Even the sounds of running boots in the corridor did not turn her. The curt knock on the door was left to her son to address, which he did with an ill-suited air of self-importance.

"Come to the infirmary at once…" the young woman, one of innumerable staff who came and went from the Fortress and Channon employ, said in a breathless command. "Nikolaj is…"

☙*❧

"Oh…I did not mean to…"

Lowell glanced up from the document he studied and felt his heart begin to thunder in his chest. Oasis, silhouetted in the doorway by the golden lamplight behind her, appeared ethereal in the off-white gown she wore, the cut of it draping from the neck to present one bare shoulder. Her contrite expression tugged at his soul so that he motioned her into his office, any annoyance he felt instantly evaporating. He was rewarded with a smile both radiant and, he believed, deeply personal. He returned to the document he was creating, the annual speech he gave in the Fortress courtyard that, to him, seemed doubly important this year in light of the changes the borough was facing with the loss of his co-Laedan, but when Oasis closed the previously propped open door and began a slow circle of the room, studying books on shelves and art on the walls, her fingers tracing lazy patterns on the surfaces she passed, he realized that the only things he could concentrate on now was her proximity, the near-silent sound of her bare feet upon the woven floor mats, the graceful movements of her body that he imagined he could feel, see and hear even when she moved out of his line of sight.

He always found beautiful women to be a distraction, but never one so much as his son's new bride.

The sound of her steps barely gave the opportunity to announce her approach before one hand rested on his shoulder and then caressed a path from there to the back of his neck, a feathery touch that followed the outline of his hair and made his nerves prickle with unexpected anticipation. Unable to focus on the words that jumbled and congealed into an incoherent mess before his eyes, he set the quill stylus down with a forced effort to keep his hand steady and squeezed his eyes closed as he tried to control his breathing and the thundering of his heart.

"I didn't come to interrupt," she murmured, her low voice husky and sweet, sounding as if it was uttered against his ear though he felt none of the breath that should have accompanied it.

"Your company is most welcome…" Interruption or not, he was happy she was here without the distraction of either Donnovan or Yiva to intrude. He began to ask, "What have you come to…?" as he swiveled the chair around to face her, only to find in doing so that she was straddled across his lap, her tight thighs and firm backside resting on his legs, the allure of her sex inches, and layers of cloth, away from his own. His question ended in a groan, his gaze captivated by her sultry one, but then he blinked and she was gone, standing now far enough away that they could only touch if they extended their arms toward one another.

He wondered if he had imagined that moment between them.

"What is Fort Hamilton?"

He began to scowl, words of anger and accusation rising with the downturn of his lips, but everything about the woman, the innocence of her expression and her tone kept him from lashing out. Seeing the rise of fury, Oasis stepped back in regret, dropping her gaze in a fashion that should have appeared apologetic but which Lowell found so alluring that the tightening of his groin was surely noticeable if she was to look there.

Fortunately, she did not.

"I'm sorry…I saw…and thought you the best person to ask…"

"Saw what? Who? Where?"

His tone was demanding, her response innocent and contrite. "In a book...that Donnovan has. He was reading it...closed it hastily when I approached as if to hide it. I didn't get to read more, but those words jumped out at me. I asked him, but he would not say...said I should not ask..."

Lowell's frown deepened as he rose from the chair to pace the narrow room. It was possible that Donnovan had overheard a conversation between Lowell and Roland in the days before Marrock's disappearance, enough to peak his interest and drive him to seek information about the historical site. Curiosity was natural, and generally good, so long as it did not lead to interference in the Laedan's plans. And Donn was a bright boy, able to make quick connections between details where most others might not. The likelihood that he had chosen to investigate such a reference, that he might understand without asking why his father might be interested in such a place, was equally high.

Knowing his son's level of ambition, however, Donn was not likely to be content with understanding. He was going to want in on the action, whatever Lowell's course of action was, so the Laedan needed to prepare for that inevitability.

He would also need to make certain that no one else, not his other sons nor Quentin, knew his plans. Not until he was ready to put them into action. Not until he was certain that no one would be able to undercut his endeavors and ruin the future he foresaw for Queens.

"Don't you fret over that," he said, catching Oasis' hand to kiss her knuckles. "It is said there were once many such places...where soldiers housed and trained...but they were lost during the Undoing. A part of history, nothing more. But...if you ever come across a reference to it in your readings, would you show me?"

"Oh yes, yes...I will do that, Lowell." Oasis gave the appearance of both disappointment and eagerness to please him and did not press the issue further or ask why he wanted to know of references to the fort in other sources. She gave no indication of understanding the nuances of what the existence of such a place might offer to the person who controlled it. By the subtle shift of light in her eyes, it seemed she thought it a fairytale story discussed by men, nothing more. Her expression only changed when Lowell's lips moved lingeringly up the back of her hand to the inside of her wrist when he turned her hand over. There was an invitation there, but an invitation cut short by the shrieking of his name from far down the corridor.

Lowell moved so quickly to release her and turn his chair back toward the desk that by the time the door flew open, nothing appeared amiss. Not even Oasis' expression as she leaned on the window sill and peered out at the sea below, seemed suspicious.

"Lowell!" Yiva screeched again.

ᔡ*ᔥ

It was a club like any other his brother was known to frequent, dark save for the random splashes of colored light that erupted on the ceiling, the walls, the floor, in time to pulses of music that seemed to throb from the very walls around them. If it even was music, Jonni thought with annoyance as he turned up the high collar of his long coat to protect himself from the fetid stench of alcohol, greasy food, and unwashed bodies that permeated such dives. He had never understood the appeal of such a throng of writhing bodies, most either heavily under the influence of alcohol or other questionable substances or else working diligently toward succumbing to the oblivion such pursuits offered. There were five such dives within easy distance of the Fortress, and Nik was intimately familiar with each of them, sometimes spending his day staggering between all five in his quest for his substance of choice that day. Although their parents seemed to have given up on their middle son's recovery, his brothers, at least, did their best to look out for him, keeping him clean when they could, rescuing him from himself when they could not, doing what they could to keep their brother ahead of the Protectors and out of the hands of the forepaths, their freeze units, and the furnaces or lye vats of the dead.

This was not the first time Nik had failed to return to the Fortress for the night. Sometimes he took up with questionable friends in flops or abandoned apartments and slept among them, their pale, sickly bodies entwined in the heap where their addictions fell them. Other times he slept off his highs, or the interim lows, in the dive he had last visited, slumped over on a sticky leather booth bench, slouched beneath a table strewn with empty cups, bottles and drug paraphernalia, or collapsed on the filthy floor where no one else had bothered to pick him up from. Such sights broke Jonni's heart again and again, and dragging him home from such degrading conditions and episodes was often the only time Jonni and Donn could cooperate. How many times had Jia and Addi and Liam helped bring Nik home from a binger?

He elbowed his way through a sea of dancers, scanning those at the tables and benches along the perimeter, hoping to spot Nik amongst them. Damn, he wished Jia was here to help him.

Damn, how he missed her.

The flashing lights synced into blackness, robbing him of vision so that he froze midstep and held his breath, a reflex he did not understand but which brought with it a surge of panic as if there was danger to be had in that darkness, something hunting him he could neither see nor sense nor hear over the momentarily deafening silent beat without the bass and percussion-driven music. When each came back, a flare of blue and red accompanied by a pounding staccato of a deep drum pulse, Jonni saw the backlit outline of Nik on a corner stool, a band tightened around his bicep, the metal spike sunk deep into tissue bruised by repeated abuse. He watched in horrified fascination the familiar sight of Nik's eyes rolling back into his head and his hand dropping away, leaving the needle in place as his head lolled to one side. There were others seated on either side of him, the cluttered table surrounded by his 'friends', each of whom was already enmeshed in their own psychedelic journey for the evening.

None of them reacted when Jonni pushed them aside, dumping their limp bodies onto the floor so that he could reach his brother's side. Jonni doubted any of them would question how they came to be on the floor, and none of those dancing or drinking at the bar paid him any mind. So long as he did not start a fight, rape or kill anyone, no one would care what he was doing here. And of those who worked here, serving drinks and keeping the peace, Jonni's face was as recognizable as the brother he came to collect. They were Channon boys. No one hassled the Laedan's sons.

"Come on, Niki...time to get home." It was early still, mid-afternoon creeping away from them although within the dive it was impossible to note the hour, but as Nik had not been home the previous night, the hour was late enough.

"One more juice..." Nik slurred, the syllables sounding like a single word as his cracked lips slipped against one another, barely parting to speak. With the obvious symptoms of dehydration visible to Jonni, he pulled the needle free, stuffed it absently into his pocket, and scanned the table for anything resembling the juice his brother requested. Not seeing anything, he slid an arm beneath Nik's and pulled him to his feet, supporting his weight as he dragged the sluggish, corpse-like body toward the door.

"Juice..."

"Think he's had enough," the tender snorted as they passed the bar, his voice heavy with the derision his face did not express. Sometimes tenders used just as their clients did, sometimes they were baggers themselves. And sometimes, as with this fellow, they looked down on the very people, habits, and lifestyles that lined their pockets with credits and kept their businesses open.

If Jonni had not had his hands full, he would have punched the tender in his smug, round, sweaty face.

Hoping the outside air would sober Nik enough that he could walk on his own, Jonni paused to adjust his brother's weight. Nik groaned, his labored breathing coming faster, his body beginning to shudder and shiver more than Jonni thought it should in this weather. With Nik showing no signs of being able to walk on, Jonni took his full weight, lifting him off his feet, and hurried toward the Fortress gates. He pushed past enough people who stopped, who swore, who shouted insults or offered to help, that Jonni lost count of them.

One hundred yards, no more, but despite his slight, addiction-induced weight, Nik was awkward to carry, and Jonni was glad he had not had to transport him from the most distant of his brother's favorite dives. He was even more grateful because, as he reached the gates now opened by the guards attending it, Nik began to convulse, making carrying him impossible for a single man. This was not the first seizure Jonni had nursed his brother through, but the blood at the corner of his mouth, his nose, his ears, was something new. Jonni yanked his belt from around his waist and forced the material into his brother's mouth to keep him from biting his own tongue, and shouted to the guards, "Help me get him to the infirmary!"

Jonni was no doctor. He had read every text that Addi could provide him, however, and had discussed practice and procedure, symptoms and treatments, ailments and disease and deformities with the medical student during many late nights. But as the pursuit of a medicareer was against his father's wishes, Jonni lacked any practical experience required to effectively help Nik, and the infirmary staff, even though they knew more about his interest and knowledge than his father did, they could not permit him to assist in treatment except in cases of dire emergency. An odose, in Jonni's view, was emergency enough, and he helped rip away Nik's shirt, held him down as a variety of antitoxins were dripped into his bloodstream from sterilized glass bottles through long tubes and more needles. In the gaslight that warmed the room, Nik's true sickly condition was more obvious. Strapping him to the infirmary bed, keeping him there for however many hours or days it would take to stabilize his condition, was the only hope Nik had of surviving.

As before, however, there was no surety that sobriety would stick. Something in Nik refused to live without foreign chemicals in his blood.

Or maybe he did not want to live at all.

"I want to see my son!"

There was no protocol that Lowell Channon would obey when it came to the welfare of his family. Though his features twisted with alarm, as he elbowed into the room and barely refrained from dragging the medics away so he could be near the bed, expressing concern, even fear for Nik's well-being, to Jonni it was a sham. Their mother, at least, had the decency to remain on the other side of the glass window, wringing her hands, standing stiff and frightened with Donn at her side. Jonni blamed both of their parents for Nik's life of addiction but it was a belief for which there was no concrete proof.

Pushed to the fringes where he could not help by the swarm of medics and his bullying father, Jonni slid from the room. His mother would not look at him but he exchanged a glance with his nearly dispassionate brother over her head and swallowed his annoyance.

"What was it this time?" Donn might appear uncaring, might sound flippant, but Jonni knew him to be fiercely protective of his twin. But the only reply Jonni could give was a shrug. Nik exposed himself to every substance available, sometimes took two or more at a time. It was impossible, without an analysis of his blood and urine, to say what he had taken or how much. Jonni shoved his hands into his coat pockets with frustration; his fist curling around the syringe there, and he wondered, as another joined their window vigil, if there was someone he should give that to. If giving it to anyone could make a difference.

Chief Ernest, without ceremony or word, fit himself between Yiva and Donnovan, causing an immediate relaxing of the woman's body which Jonni thought he was the only one to notice but did not find it unusual. The Chief had been a family acquaintance, perhaps even friend, for as many years as Jonni could remember, and as a man of authority, it was reasonable she would find comfort in someone who might, through some miracle of his position, be able to save her son. The four stood quietly, unable to hear what was happening on the other side of the glass, only able to watch as efforts to purge Nik's body of what it had been fed resulted in retching into a hemplastic pail, blood drawn by needles in an effort to drain that source as well. Dirty cloths were dropped to the floor after being used to clean his face, his chest, and the skin nearest his ears. The seconds dragged into minutes until Yiva, unable to watch any longer, fled the sight of what was surely her son dying. Donn watched her go, appeared at first to weigh the possibility of going after her, but then marched down the corridor in the other direction, his steps not one of flight but of purpose.

Jonni imagined Donn was going somewhere to pick a fight. It was something he often did when angry. Jonni felt pity for whomever the victim would be this time…unless that victim turned out to be a bagger or Thom Quentin. Today, Jonni had no sympathy for such men. He never did when Nik overdosed. And Quentin had never done anything to warrant his sympathy either.

He was left at the window with Chief Ernest, one refusing to leave out of concern for his brother, the other out of an interest not yet spoken or expressed. Jonni side-eyed him, curious as to his purpose, but did not speak until the medics' work appeared to be done and Lowell emerged from the infirmary, red-faced with anger but, for the moment, colored over with relief.

"Is that the sort of shart you allow on the streets?" Lowell spat, gesturing to the young man behind the window. The medics now appeared to be making Nik comfortable, one trying to force water into his throat while others covered him with blankets for warmth and cleaned up the room. Nik was breathing on his own and was no longer thrashing in his bonds. It appeared the worst was over.

"You know there are no laws against…" It had been long-standing public policy, since the day the Marrocks and the Channons initiated rule in the borough, that such substance consumption was permitted so long as the user committed no crime while under the influence. There were better uses of manpower and borough resources than to make an effort to monitor the creation, the provision, and the use of recreational substances. There were enough of those things to be found in nature to make such monitoring impractical, and in truth, very few cared what others did any longer, so long as it did not interfere with their lives. Nik was old enough to make his choices and had broken no laws to satisfy his addictions.

The Chief was only here because he had been in the vicinity when a disturbance was reported, the disturbance caused by Jonni forcing his way through the streets in his haste to get Nik home. He came because of the disturbance; he came to check on Nik's welfare.

He came to see that Yiva was well.

"There should be!" It was, Jonni knew, an empty threat from his father, a declaration made often but never acted upon. A population wallowing in addiction was a population easily satisfied, easily controlled. He would never admit that out loud, but Jonni knew his father's way of thinking. It was only that his son was one of those who had yielded to that wallowing that made Lowell care about recreational elements at all. "I want to know what he took, who gave it to him, where he got it…and I want them shut down immediately!"

It was a demand for private revenge, not for the execution of any law; all the Chief could do was nod and suggest compliance. If the pattern followed its usual course, Lowell would forget his demand in a matter of days. If Ernest made an effort to find the bagger that put the supply into Nik's hands, fine him on a public nuisance charge or brought him before the Laedan for a sound berating, the matter would thereafter be dropped until Nik's next odose.

Only when the day came that an odose claimed the young man's life would any law likely be effected. Ernest hoped that day would wait until well after he retired.

Lowell did not wait for a reply, did not speak to Jonni, not even to thank him for bringing Nik home and facilitating the prompt care that might have saved Nik's life. But that was nothing new to Jonni, and so he stared at his brother's still form, debating if he should go into the room now. Most of the medics had scattered; none of them would stop him if he chose to sit at Nik's bedside. He was one of only two Channons likely to do so until Nik opened his eyes.

"He's lucky you were there."

"One of these days, I won't be," Jonni muttered. "They did this to him…and they act so damned shocked and devastated every time he…" He shook his head once, not knowing how much personal Channon family history the Chief knew and not feeling like going into the details. "How will you find the bagger?"

Ernest shrugged. "There are ways…" There were always those who would share information with the Protectors for a favor or two, and baggers tended to be a jealous lot, protective over their clientele to the point of willingly snitching out anyone who put goods into their clients' hands. Someone in that dive would know who the baggers were for every substance sold inside its walls, and someone would know what Nik had bought for consumption that night. Whether Nik would know and be able to tell them would only be discovered when the young man woke up.

If he woke up.

After a scowl and an internal debate that lasted the duration of nearly a dozen slow rise and fall motions of Nik's chest, Jonni pulled his fist from his pocket and offered the syringe in his open palm. The needle was dirty, the glass vial cracked, but it still contained a measure of murky yellow fluid that Jonni had not noticed before.

He was lucky he had not accidentally injected himself.

"Would this help?" he asked, voice low. "I don't know what he took before I…he'd been missing since some time yesterday…gone overnight. But this was in his arm when I found him"

Ernest held the syringe up to the light to study its contents.

"What is it?"

The Chief shrugged. "Can't say without tests…could be piss for all I know." He had heard of people injecting all manners of odd shart so very little surprised him anymore. "I'll find out though…and if this is what nearly killed him…"

He smirked spitefully. This syringe, a material witness in his hand, might be all he needed to satisfy his own need for knowledge as well as to find the responsible bagger for the Laedan. All he needed was Mage Segara.

He wrapped the syringe in his kerchief and put it in his breast pocket where it was least likely to get damaged or lost. "Thank you for this…I'm sure it will help."

"You'll let me know what you find?" He had been frightened enough of losing Nik this time that he too was contemplating violence. Maybe he should have gone with Donn to pick a fight with a bagger.

"It may take a day or two…but I will. You take care of your brother, okay? Keep him off the shart…"

"If I can," Jonni finished the sentence, but both knew that the only way to get Nik clean was to lock him up or let the shart kill him. Nothing else would do.

≈Scratch the Sky≈

Chapter 18

"**D**o not make me regret this."

The woman's voice held warning, but it was a warning Roland had expected from the moment he considered the idea. Undoing the straps that kept Liam in the vertical stasis chamber, having already removed the feeding tubes that kept the younger man sedated and compliant, Roland was surprised to be granted the request. He claimed no intimate knowledge of the thin blond, but he was able to claim having seen the young man at work in one of the many medifacs scattered throughout LaGuardia, a claim not fully a lie since Liam had, on occasion, lent hands to Addison's purpose at the clinic in which he worked. With the stasis pods full, another collection of anthro having arrived during the night to fill the remainder with blood donors, one man too many, Roland had argued that it made little sense to allow any of the others to die just to make room for one extra. He asserted that he would be hard-pressed to care for them, as the pods had never been full while he had been under their service, so why not allow him the extra body, this man who he knew to have some medical experience, to aid in his lab duties? Their keeper had left to again contemplate his request, during which time Roland took the initiative and disconnected the IVs that had been sustaining Liam, hopeful of the outcome.

In the end, the doctor's return coming sooner than Roland expected, it took agreeing to share his sleeping cot and meal rations with his assistant, as she claimed there was no extra bed nor extra food to spare for another mouth, and the promise that it would be Roland's responsibility to see that the newcomer knew his duties and followed every rule and protocol laid out by the facility staff. One failure on Liam's part and both men would learn how expendable to the lab's efforts they were. While their captors preferred a self-perpetuating source of blood, there was no shortage of anthro on the outside. Their deaths would be an inconvenience, nothing more.

Half dragging, half carrying the conscious but weak young man across the room, Roland propped him up on one of the lab stools and thrust a hemplastic cup of liquid into his hands as the doctor went out. "Drink this," Roland instructed, watching the door close, wanting to be sure she was gone and they were alone before he said too much. He knew that the mirrored wall allowed others to see in though he could not see out, but he did not know how much anyone outside could hear. With the dinner hour past, he knew the lab staff was gone, the doors of the warehouse and lab locked with a keycard sequence to prevent his escape thus requiring no guards to monitor the chamber full of comatose subjects.

Liam glanced at the cup warily, his arm heavy as he lifted it to his lips. "It will give you strength," Roland encouraged. Liam nodded once and drank as instructed, finding the cup to be filled with a cold, bittersweet tea of unfamiliar mix.

"What am I…?"

"You're going to help me…and soon as you can, I have a plan."

"A plan?" His whisper mirrored Roland's, but he could not sense anyone beyond the lab door, and none of those in stasis around them could respond even if they could hear what was being said.

Roland shook his head. He was not ready to share yet, not until he was certain of the course and confident in Liam's condition. "You're going to watch…learn…help…until I can get you out." Seeing Liam's almost protest, he shook his head and clamped his hand over his mouth. "No…you rest…the cot is over there." He thumbed in the direction of an alcove darker than the rest of the room. "I have one more to install...and morning will come early...a lot of work to be done. I will tell you more then. Can you make it?"

"I...think so..." His legs felt rubbery, unsteady, but by leaning on the perimeter wall and taking slow steps, Liam believed he could make it. Was that, he wondered, where Roland slept? But he did not ask. The effort to walk winded him, stole his breath, making further dialog impossible. By the time he collapsed on the cot, he could barely keep his eyes open. He was awake long enough to witness Roland cinching the straps on the pod that had previously held him over some new unlucky bastard. Liam shuddered and closed his eyes and was asleep almost at once.

It was just as well. Dawn would bring back the lab techs, but the opportunity Roland wanted would present itself. He had been formulating the plan since his arrival, but the sense of obligation he felt toward the other helpless anthro, and the lack of opportunity, had kept him from acting. Now Liam was here, Pack...family...the son of the woman he had been captured trying to save. He owed it to her...to Liam...to get the young man out of this place. Once out, they could find their way back to their family, find a way to expose this place and free every one of these poor souls.

He just had to be patient...for Liam's sake.

⁊*⁊

The small pack QiangXu referred to consisted of an older brother and sister, her mate, and a younger male, barely older than a pup himself, who had found shelter in a building on the eastern-most side of the campus complex near where a herd of wild goats grazed amidst the scrubby orchard of apple trees. Both provided the four with sustainable sources of nourishment, if managed wisely, and by trading what they harvested with the mutani, who had established a sizable plot of grain, hemp, and potatoes, and the Ursa who had the equipment necessary to brew alcohol from the foodstuffs of others and who had enough chickens to provide all of the eggs they could want, the complex of small populations had an adequate community capable of sustaining themselves.

But the smaller pack was, they admitted freely, not otherwise comfortable with the prospects of their own survival. There was no skill among them that enabled them to provide themselves additional clothing or tools, and what goods could be scavenged from the campus perimeter had long ago been claimed. Orliss Urban, a Cana of mixed heritage, was a tall, bald man of considerable bulk, a mountain of a fellow with an infectious smile capable of hauling great weight, which made him the scav of the pack, the one to roam further and further away in an effort to provide much-needed commodities. His broad torso bore the evidence of those adventures, the scars of fights and accidental injuries crisscrossing his skin like a historical roadmap of his life. His wife, Ayla, was a stately woman, perhaps a little older than Orliss, but the prime of her beauty had passed and the pups they had raised together had either died or had, in the case of a single daughter, left the pack to create a pack and family of her own. Ayla's brother Ele, rough in appearance from an early life spent in constant conflict, nose askew and jaw offset and face pocked with scars, maimed by the loss of one hand to a battle injury and infection, was older still, but sharp of mind and capable enough to act as the pack's moral core. He was also still capable of harvesting apples, milking the goats, and gathering wood for the pack's nightly fire when the need arose. He had been a force to be reckoned with in his youth, and it was pure stubbornness and tenacity that kept him from giving into the crippling loss. He might have lost a hand, but he was not going to lose his life without a fight.

That left the wild, barely controllable, scrawny dark-skinned pup Wist, young enough to be foolhardy, old enough to believe he knew more than his elders, and yet grudgingly knowing that, should he stray from the protection of his pack, he would be picked off by another, stronger pack or else fall victim to those HOPE soldiers who had claimed the rest of their pack. Wist was the first to recognize the potential of joining forces with the larger Flushing Pack, or perhaps, Jia realized as the four slipped into the darkness for the security of their own fire and shelter, Wist's seeming eagerness to shift his allegiance to her and the Flushing Pack was due more to his desire to spread his wings than it was any confidence that she could provide a more secure, existence.

But the others, too, were considering their options, an alliance between the packs seemed likely, if not a merging of the two, and it appeared, to Addi at least, that Trill's proclamation of Jia being a Caller as well as an Alpha might be an accurate one.

The logistic of merging, however, would be a topic for debate on another night. After a day spent arranging their crop pots where they would get the best light and be easily tended, rearranging shelves so that the chickens, rabbits, and goats had decent warmth but would not harm the books, and settling into the security of the library, the Pack gathered again, sharing the warmth of the evening fire and the company of those with whom they were familiar and comfortable. Kato and Vanya, after doing their share of the work necessary to settle the Pack, were treated as welcome additions to the family, particularly by young Eddie...who for the first time in his life had found the company of another Fela...and Reif who, despite her obligation to look after the younger children that day, spent most of her time watching Kato every time he passed through her field of vision. Kind and accommodating to both, exhibiting an affinity for the young that came from a lifetime of tending the needs of his sister, Kato reminded Jia more and more of the men she admired most...her father, her brother, and Liam...and it was disconcerting to consider that perhaps it would be in the Pack's best interest to initiate the Fela and his sister as members.

Despite his helpfulness, however, she had no reason to believe Kato wanted to stay any longer than it took to heal his wound. There was something in his eyes, a wanderlust, the look of a man seeking something he had not yet found, that would surely draw him away. His work today had not torn his stitches, and the bandaging Addi had changed twice over the course of the day had been clean of blood or infection. Another day or two and Kato would be healthy enough to continue on his way without the Pack's care. Just because Vanya was happy to have other children to gather around her and to frolic with did not mean Kato would feel inclined to remain.

He escorted her and Addi to the small village of mutani at the north edge of the campus, either out of restlessness or an imagined need to protect the woman who was generously sheltering him and his sister. They found nearly two dozen of the outcasts, men, women, and children with a variety of genetically altered features, struggling through their differences to create life where there had been only despair and death before. Having never traveled to the Zone, this was the largest group of mutani Jia had seen, the largest Kato had seen, and, also, the friendliest. The majority of the group was hunched in their fields when Jia found them, preparing the earth for spring planting, while others threshed and milled their grain and hemp stock or sealed some of the precious seeds into glazed pots for use during the lean winter months. With QiangXu accompanying them, introducing them as they sought the mutani leader, the strangers were welcomed with waves or handshakes before the mutani fell into their work again. As the chemist had said, the mutani were far from stand-offish, desired nothing but tranquility free of the constricting Zone where so many of their kind were forced to eke out an existence.

The friendliness of their new neighbors eased Jia's concerns about the security of the Pack in this unfamiliar territory. The Pack needed to be safe, needed to be protected, if she was to foray back into LaGuardia to seek contact with the Mage. She did not doubt the capabilities of her Pack, had no reason to think they would be followed and hunted here, but there was Pain and the others to consider, and the possibility they could turn up and decide to poach her Pack, make off with the pups, kill or lure away the adults, was a concern she had to bear in mind as she cleared her throat and looked at those around her.

The eyes of the others turned; though she felt a rush of nerves coil and burn beneath her skin, it was not enough to keep her from speaking. "I need to go back."

Addi studied her with a raised brow. "Back where?" he asked, voicing the question the others were thinking, expecting the answer she was destined to give without her having to say it.

"We're not going to find Father or Liam here. If QiangXu is correct...if they were taken for their blood...then they may still be alive. We have to find..."

"How? We have no way of knowing where...?" started Trill.

"We don't know we can trust him," Maz interposed. "Not to discount that you knew him, Addi...but ten years? Even if Roland was meeting him here, we don't know his purpose, his intent."

Jia shook her head. "Father trusted him...that is enough...and he knows about the journal and ledger that..."

"That we don't even know if they're real." Reif rolled her eyes. Nearly old enough to graduate into the Pack as an adult, she had begun to show more interest in the grownup matters involved in keeping the Pack safe, particularly since Kato's arrival but a few days ago. The fact that Petr Arden sat with his mother, listening with the intent maturity of a Cana boy who understood leadership, and the cocky young Cana Wist who had reappeared at their fire as the Pack gathered for the evening meal, also listening though with less visible interest, seemed a further draw for her. With Kato's attendance, rarely being far from his sister and, it seemed, interest in the working of Pack dynamics, Jia suspected her young cousin was as interested in the unattached males as she was in Pack politics.

"They exist." Addi was as certain of that fact as he was of QiangXu's trustworthiness. "Father would never have risked his life if it was a fairy myth..."

"He believed they contained something important...and I believe we owe it to him, to ourselves, to uncover the secrets the Channons seem determined to protect...the secrets that drove us from our home, our rightful place." For the first time since the Undoing, no Marrock sat at the Channons' side. That alone, Jia felt, was worth rectifying, even if she was not certain she wanted the job.

"You're not going back to the Fortress."

Deuce's voice, still unfamiliar to most in the Pack, sounded from the shadows at the edge of the fire's circle. Children scurried toward the protection of the nearest adult and even Addi involuntarily shifted away from him. The pack always kept stock of his proximity, but they never expected him to come close, or to interrupt the Alpha's business. If Jia had been her father, a single snarling growl would send the Omega scurrying into the shadows, reminding him of his place, of his being tolerated but never accepted. But since being forced into her father's place, Deuce had proven himself loyal to Jia, and to the Pack, and that loyalty was something she needed and would find some way to reward.

"You're right...I'm not." Going anywhere near the Fortress, anywhere that one of the Channons might see her, would be a foolhardy risk. Expecting a backlash now, she swallowed and said, "I've employed a Mage."

Kato snorted. "Mages are not real." His mother had believed in them, had warned him to stay clear of the mythical mages, men and women said to be able to track and find anyone or anything they sought, who were threats to anthro because they could tell an anthro's identity without witnessing a shift. Mages were dangerous, she said, and yet Jia believed they were real, and claimed to be consorting with one.

Kato did not believe they existed, as he had never encountered one, but what if they were? What had Jia done? Perhaps she felt there were no other options, but now he was torn between his own disbelief and the wariness that she would take such a risk with her life and the Pack's safety.

"They are...he is...and he is looking for Father for..."

"You should've discussed this with us." But Addi understood why she had not. Pain, Xan, and Uncle would have protested the involvement of a Mage, might have blamed such an individual for their troubles, with or without proof. And it would have put Jia's leadership on a more precarious footing than it had been at the time of her fight with Pain. "It's the one who came asking about the mediplies shipment, isn't it?"

She nodded, relieved he remembered, that he had met the Mage and could offer an opinion on the man. "He knows about Father and about Liam. He believes there is a connection between the hunts and a stolen medishipment he has been charged to locate. If anyone can find them…well…at least he can point me in a direction. If there's a chance those supplies were diverted to a blood harvesting facility, it is a place to start. He might not know about the blood drug…"

"Everyone knows about that," Wist sneered before flashing Reif a smile that hinted he was proud of proving he was wiser and smarter than the other adults.

The girl smiled back and lowered her gaze.

Helena glowered at the young man's rudeness; he might be sharing their food and company, but he was not part of the Pack and had no say in the matters at hand. It was not her place to say so, however, and for the moment, at least, she refrained from chastising him. "Addicts maybe…for the rest of us, it's been a rumor until…"

"Protectors are employed to know," Trill sighed. "He must have at least heard the same rumors…"

"Rumors aren't the same as product…and unless a bagger or user creates a public menace, there would be no reason for them to concern themselves with yet another new street drug," Addi offered.

"Unless the Laedan is behind its creation…either by sanctioning the abduction of his citizens or by ignoring what he…"

Addi squeezed his wife's hand and she fell silent. He did not think she believed what she said, as she frequently voiced unpopular notions merely to be certain that the others in a discussion considered all of the angles, but from what they knew of Laedan Channon, who may have ordered the capture or death of Roland, and of the son who had sanctioned the most recent hunt, the possibility held more truth than Addi, at least, had considered.

"They're tied to HOPE…I don't think they count us as citizens," Maz snorted bitterly over the rim of his cup.

Heads bobbed around the fire, even those who did not know the Channons believing that ties to HOPE automatically meant full acceptance of their doctrine.

That belief was enough for Jia to gauge her opening. "A few days…not much more…long enough to find Mage Segara, give him what we have learned…find out what he has learned in return. I'll avoid the Channons and…"

The Fela squirmed where he sat, and without thinking, opened his mouth. "You should not go alone. I'll…"

"You're healing," scowled Addi.

"I'm fine."

Addi cut him off again with a shake of his head and Kato, feeling as if his voice was being discounted because he was Fela, not Cana, crossed his arms with a bitter frown. The doctor spoke again. "It should be me. We need mediplies…" In the borough, he had steady access to such things as part of the medisystem. What little the Pack had on hand had been depleted, used to patch up their Fela guest and Jia and Pain after their fight. Addi did not regret his choice to offer care to any of them, but he was realistic about their need for more supplies.

"There must be abandoned hospitals…"

"I know where," Wist interrupted Trill with a proud exclamation.

Stubbornly, Addi continued, "They need to know where I am…they rely on me…"

Trill's grip tightened on Addi's hand. "We rely on you too," she murmured, though she understood how he felt. The Foundling Center…all of those children…they relied on her as well and were undoubtedly asking questions now that she had failed to appear for several days in a row.

"Addi's right," Jia sighed. "The medics deserve to know the truth…and it's our best chance of picking up supplies. A straight run across the Flushing…a day and a half…two days top…should get us what we need…and get us news…get word to the Foundling Center too. If it is just the two of us…"

"I'd feel better if we brought the others in."

Jia held Maz's gaze and nodded once. There was little reason to doubt the Pack's safety, no reason to believe the adults under Maz's leadership as Second Alpha, could not protect themselves unless something unusual happened. But the benefits of coaxing the Queens College Pack into a mutual protection treaty were sound. "I'll meet with them tonight if they are willing."

"I'll take you," Wist volunteered, at last having some way to make himself useful to the larger pack. Though she did not feel the escort was necessary, going with his invitation might be beneficial and might convince the others that she was not seeking trouble.

"If they agree…Addi and I will go back tomorrow…and make it back by week's end with supplies and any news…"

"And honey?" bubbled Reif. There were few known sources within the borough, the precious commodity was often used as a treat, an incentive to coerce good behavior out of younger children, and until they found a source nearby…if there was one…an additional supply would be highly valued.

"And honey," Jia promised, brushing off the seat of her pants as she got to her feet. The Pack had voiced their opinions about her proposed trip, the objections and concerns made known, but none were likely to hold her back from a course of action she felt best. The retrieval of the Primary Alpha and Liam were too important. There would be words shared between Addi and Trill in private, and it appeared the Fela had his own words to share since he had been prevented from participation in the discussion, but the rest would consider the matter settled. As she picked up her heaviest jacket to ward off the night's chill, she caught Kato's eye and willed him to join her for the short walk across campus while saying, "Wist…go on ahead and tell them I am coming."

The young Cana leaped up and sprinted through the door into the darkness. Kato kissed his sister's temple, murmuring something into her ear that made the young woman nod with enthusiasm, and then he trailed the Alpha Cana through that same door. Rain was falling, cold and heavy, and he wrapped his bare arms around himself with a glance into the sky.

"You could get your…"

"I don't need it," Kato snapped, his annoyance at being discounted bleeding into his voice. His shivering suggested otherwise, however, and Jia could not help but smirk.

"You want mine?"

For a second, the Fela weighed the thought of having her coat against his skin, her scent wrapped around him in an intimate way he had never considered with another, but the thought was a fleeting one, dragged away by the possibility that she was belittling him with her offer, considering him weak. "I don't need it," he repeated, voice surly as he marched in the direction where Wist had disappeared.

Her coat would not fit him anyhow.

Jia shrugged and walked beside him, regretting the teasing he apparently had not understood, but not about to apologize for it. Instead, she changed the subject to the one she had intended when this summons had been made.

"You are welcome to remain with the Pack while I am away…if that is your wish. I promise no harm will come to you or Vanya." She paused, her step hesitating and her head cocked as if she was listening for something, but then she continued and Kato, who had also hesitated at her words, fell into step again.

"We're not Cana."

"No…you're not…but what should that matter?"

"I doubt they will appreciate…"

"They will do as I bid them. You saved my life…"

"And you saved mine," he reminded her.

"And so we are even…but Vanya seems happy…and there is something to be said for safety in numbers…"

"And for solitude."

"It can't have been easy…caring for her on your own…to hunt and scavenge and survive…"

"We survived well enough." Though his tone was still surly, he reluctantly admitted she was right. He had not hunted or scavenged since the Pack found them and took them under their protection, but doing those things had been difficult as he and Vanya made their way west, when his worry for her safety and welfare precluded him wandering far from her. If not for the Pack, his injury might have killed him, and he dreaded the thought of what might have become of Vanya then. Regardless of his disquiet and the lingering tendrils of distrust, he admitted that Vanya, with playmates for the first time in her life, was the happiest he had ever seen her, and that she was safer in the Pack's care then she may have been alone with him.

"Admirably," Jia agreed. "I only meant that protecting her alone must have been difficult. Where were you headed?"

"West."

"Anywhere in particular?" She had met nomads before, individuals and families always on the move in search of something, someplace, elusive. But even that first night they had met, amidst the fight for life that had thrown the Cana into his path, or him into theirs, Jia had sensed that he was on a mission.

Kato opened his mouth, closed it again, and shrugged. West was all he had known, all he had intended. West in search of somewhere safe for Vanya. West had brought them to the Flushing Pack, and in this place, he and Vanya were, as far as he could tell, safer than they had been in their mother's orbit. Here there were many eyes to watch her when Kato could not, others to make her laugh, fulfill her needs, and, he hoped, teach her in ways he could not.

Wasn't that west enough?

Sighing thoughtfully, she continued, "I've heard of the vast land to the west...the nation that had been before the Undoing...but I don't believe I'll ever see it." Her world was the Pack, LaGuardia borough, and now the Wilds of the east. The need to find her friend and father and to prevent whatever catastrophe Roland believed was on the horizon was as much adventure as she could shoulder. "Will you go there? When you are well enough to travel?"

"Maybe." His tone suggested the wistfulness of the wanderlust she detected in him and a detachment from people and places that had become his world since his mother's death. But the tug within bid him in an entirely different direction, a direction that included the woman at his side.

She did her best to hide her disappointment. What did it matter if he stayed or went? She did not know him...and he was Fela. How could their differences ever work to their advantage? "Well, as I said, you are welcome here until you are ready to continue your journey. Vanya too. Stay as long as you want; we like having you here."

"We?"

It was not the word he heard, though he repeated it as a question seeking affirmation of her intent. Jia did not reply or clarify, however, for a shadow emerged from the mist. Wist was there to beckon them into the building which sprung up through the fog as if from the ground, dark with no visible trace of light, well hidden by the foliage and nighttime fog. Kato allowed her to enter first but remained near, protecting her back, sniffing the air for any trace of threat. She was competent and capable, else she would not be the voice of her Pack, and unlike Kato, she was not injured badly, but it did not suspend his need to protect her. It was the way his mother had raised him, and whether Jia appreciated or accepted it, it was who Kato was. The small pack consisted of strangers, and although Jia might be willing to trust them, Kato was not ready to do so.

They climbed a flight of cement stairs, the cracks in their surface filled with some darker substance that kept them from crumbling beneath their own weight. The metal rails on one side were secured with the same black material and straps of metal, with shanks sunk into the cement to keep them upright. The attention showed concern for their shelter, and Jia was not surprised to find that the room where the other three were gathered was clean, dry and lit by a fire that belched smoke into the sky through a makeshift metal pipe, the room and the smoking pipe hiding the light from the outside world and thus protecting those in the room from the layer of soot that such fires were prone to leave and keeping them less visible to passersby.

It was an addition her Pack would certainly have to consider in order to preserve the contents of the library.

"Alpha Marrock." Orliss, squatting before the fire, poking at it with a metal rod with a wooden handle, rose to greet his guests.

"I hope I am not intruding."

Ayla rose too, with a smile and outstretched hand. "Of course not. You are welcome here. Wist says you have a proposition?"

Cautiously, not wanting to damage their fragile budding relationship, Jia took a breath before speaking. She suspected what Wist's proposition entailed, but it was a step she was not ready to take.

The Queen's Campus Pack, as Trill had dubbed them, seemed genuine and trustworthy, and Jia had invited the three women and their children into the Flushing Pack on less initiative, but the women had been vulnerable, in search of the protection a group could offer. The Campus Pack contained no pups and Orliss was a natural Alpha already in a position of leadership she did not think he would be eager to relinquish. After the recent confrontation with Pain that left bruises and injuries still healing, Jia was not interested in another fight for domination.

"I have pack business that will take me west for a few days...no more than three or four I suspect...I hope..." she began. "I come seeking alliance...in protection of the pups should the need arise..."

"They will be safe here, I assure you."

Jia bowed her head toward Ele in respect. "If I doubted that, I would not leave them. We have brought no enemies and we are strong...but the territory is unfamiliar and providing for the pack will leave the pups more vulnerable than I am comfortable with."

"Is he going with you?" The older Cana's eyes scanned Kato from head to toe with a suspicious, cool gaze."

"I..."

"I am." It was not the first time that Kato had heard such a tone from a Cana, that tone of superiority and mistrust that was all too common between anthro sub-species, despite their common struggles and origins. If his remaining with the Pack during Jia's absence meant a lack of cooperation and mutual protection from these four, he would travel with her, regardless of his physical condition.

Her surprise curbed so that it would not be visible to the others, Jia nodded her agreement, as if the matter had been previously settled. "My brother as well. We'll be bringing back mediplies, assuming we can get them, which you will be welcome to share as repayment for your aid."

Orliss cut off Ele's next words before they could be spoken. "We do not need payment...but sharing between our packs will make us all stronger. You travel at daybreak?"

"As early as we can manage." Leaving under the cover of darkness meant an earlier crossing of the Wilds, and an earlier arrival across the borough border. "We want to be gone only as long as necessary."

"Three days is not so long. We will protect the pups." Again Ayla smiled and though Jia knew Orliss to be the backbone of their pack, it seemed that his wife had assumed the position of the pack voice and that Orliss was comfortable with that. The two knew each other well enough to be of one mind on most important matters. Whatever Ele's position was, it was secondary to the wishes of his brother-in-law, and he was strong enough in his place not to want a confrontation.

"All of them?" Kato pushed with a wary growl in his throat. There were two Normals in the group, and one other Fela, and he wanted assurance that each of them, but especially his sister, would be safe from any prejudicial views Ele and the others might harbor.

Orliss offered his hand, the gesture intended to prove he supported his sister's stance, and replied. "All of them. On my life."

Kato looked to Jia without moving to accept the offered handshake, seeking clues, verbal or otherwise, that she believed the other Cana's promise. A slight nod of her head, the relaxing of muscles around the corners of her mouth and eyes, the lessening of tightness in her shoulders, were enough for Kato to accept the risk. "On your life," he repeated, grasping the offered hand tightly. He might be accepting a position of trust, but he would reserve the right to retaliate if anything happened to Vanya.

From Orliss' air, it was a stipulation he willingly accepted.

⤧*⤦

"You're in late."

Vance heard no accusation in the words, and if he was guilty about his absence that day, he did not show it. Between the alcohol and the nightmarish images that kept forcing their way into his brain, it had been all he could do to get any sleep after parting company with the Chief the night before. He had tossed restlessly, snatching a few minutes' repose between the dreams, and when he had eventually given up on sleep, he spent what energy he had won resisting the temptation to get blindingly drunk again.

The drinking had to stop, he told himself. He was never going to be of any use to anyone if he gave in to the bottle the way his father, stepfather, and mother had done. And obviously, the drink did nothing to silence the mage within him, unless the dreams were a product of imagination instead of the snatches of reality he believed them to be. They had been too tenuous to hold onto upon waking, however, leaving only a feeling of dread in their wake when he finally gave up on sleep.

Ernest caught a glimpse of the shadow of torment in the man's eyes and decided not to press the matter. He did not understand what made a Mage work, how Segara must feel every moment of every day with external stimuli pressing into his head in addition to the everyday sights, sounds, and smells that most people had to cope with. He was sure, however, that it had to be hell to endure, and he was thankful he had not been given that burden to bear.

"Channon kid odosed again...thought you should know."

Groaning, not clear why the Chief thought he should know this, Vance filled his cup with steaming tea from the office kettle and asked, "He okay?"

Ernest shrugged. His mug, while steaming, contained something stronger than tea, and he nursed it with loving desperation between cupped hands. "He was stable when I left the Fortress...but who knows. Laedan wants someone to hang for it..."

"Literally or figuratively?"

"Maybe both." Again he shrugged and shrouded his pause with a long sip before speaking again. "You busy?"

Though Vance shook his head no, he suspected he was about to be. Truth was, a diversion might be just what he needed, as he had no leads to follow for the missing cargo Channon expected an update on, nor was he any closer to learning the location or fates of the two missing Cana men. His plan had been to come to the Protectorate and scan the written reports of all missing Cana to see if he could determine a pattern that did not lead back to HOPE at every turn, but as he already expected that HOPE would be the answer found at the end of the investigation, he would be thankful for anything that kept him from what felt likely to be a fruitless time-waster.

He trudged behind Ernest into the man's office, both ignored by the nightshift officers, feeling the strength of the tea slowly invigorating his brain and his limbs. Office tea rarely tasted as good as what he brewed at home, but it packed more of a punch. Vance sank into the chair Ernest offered, leaned forward to set the mug on the desk, and watched the Chief open the hanker that lay at the center of an area on the desk devoid of clutter, as if its presence had banished everything around it.

"This was in the kid's arm…" Vance could see the pale yellow liquid in the vial when Ernest held it to the light. It could have been any number of substances, but the sheen of it brought back memories from the haze of his forgotten nightmares and made him frown as Ernest continued. "He was in the Billows…the baggers that frequent there are being rounded up for questioning, to find out what it is, where it came from, who gave it to him…"

But baggers, Vance knew, were prone to lying. Not because what they did was illegal: only when someone died from a too toxic product or from an intentional poisoning was there likely to be punishment. No, they lied to protect the secrets of their sources, the proprietary product they sold, as if each had their own brands of the same shart. Truth was, many baggers distributed from the same supply sources, and even the users knew that, but there was some sort of professional pride in a bagger believing he or she was the only source of some special ticket to states of altered consciousness.

And often a bagger knew as little about what they sold as the users did. If the name was catchy, the effect sufficiently numbing, exhilarating, or psychedelic, and the product brought the bagger influence and other commodities they could horde, trade, or use, that was all that mattered.

The contents of the vial might not even be the catalyst of the odose. From the condition of the bent needle, the cracking across the glass tube, it could have been some previous substance or a combination of the previous with the new.

Or maybe Nik Channon had ingested too many pills and alcohol in addition to whatever this was.

None of those possibilities would be a surprise.

There was no point in asking questions. If Ernest had answers, he would not present this needle now. Or he could be seeking confirmation for what he already knew. There was no point in blocking the details of it while inspecting it visually. His eyes would not tell Vance as much as he would learn from holding it in his hand. Too scattered still from a difficult twenty-four hours, Vance stretched his hand across the desk and braced himself for the flood of impressions such an object was likely to bring.

Nothing prepared him, however, for the hammer shock of dizziness that slammed into him and threw him backward out of the chair with his hand clenched around the vial in a vice-like grip. Nik Channon, the familiar smell of Channon blood mixed with the reek of stale alcohol and the days' old mustiness of hemp smoke burned his nasal cavity, blocking anything else there might have been to smell except for something sizzling faintly beneath it, a coppery smell both bitter and sweet. Vance tried to focus his vision on any one image, but the violent whirring that caught him in its arms refused to allow anything to congeal into recognizable forms. A hand…scarred with decorative ink around the fingers and wrist…a clear bag of fine yellow dust. The mechanical buzz and click that seemed to spin in time to the dizzying force. A pulsing crimson propelled through a narrow conduit, the force behind it bearing the thumping regularity of a struggling heartbeat that ended in a weak howl of despair and the rancid decay of surrender and death.

Unable to free himself from the sense of out of control spinning, unable to uncouple the sense of death dragging his senses with it, the spasms of his body caused his hand to clutch tighter until metal and glass ripped his flesh. The liquid within, now free of its constraints, spilled across his hand, mingled with his blood, and seeped into the open wounds to burn its way through his bloodstream. This time when his body convulsed it was the last; he went rigid, pupils dilated and fixed on a point on the ceiling that held no significance to the Chief as he knelt at the Mage's side to revive him.

"Don't you dare," he snarled. It took force to pry the now twisted, broken vessel that had been evidence from Vance's hand, and the effort to clean the wounds with the alcohol-laden tea caused no reaction in the man when it should have made him wince and swear with the burning. Vance was breathing, shallow and rapid but breathing, and his slack jaw moved from side to side as if to form words, but they were the only signs of life he exhibited. Not knowing if his condition was an after-effect of vision or some violent response to what the man might have seen, or if it was the result of the possibly toxic substance the syringe contained, Ernest had no idea how to help.

All he could do was seat himself at Vance's side, watch over him, and hope for the best…and wonder what sort of shart poison he had on his hands.

Chapter 19

"**W**e'll travel faster if we shift."

Jia could not argue with her brother's statement once the three were out of sight of the library that the Pack, for now, called home. The return trip, assuming they procured the mediplies Addi intended to bring back, would require normal movement, since trying to maneuver a cart of any kind or a multitude of heavy packages, might mean sticking to paths and roads. It would require slower travel, and if the weather turned foul, as the black billows above suggested, their return could be significantly delayed. In the pre-dawn darkness and the cover of those clouds, Cana could run free, fleet and unmolested, through the wilds and the shadows of the borough until they reached their destination.

Cana…and Fela.

Would Kato want to run with them? Could his cat keep pace with the wolves? As she began to strip, she decided there was only one way to find out.

The choice to shift explained the decision not to carry provisions, Kato thought, keeping his focus there rather than on the delicate sheen of her skin. Perhaps Addi was a healer by nature, reluctant to use violence, but Kato knew how he would feel, what he would do, if he caught anyone looking at Vanya the way he was valiantly resisting looking at Jia. If he had considered for one moment that he would be expected to run with them, a Fela in the company of Cana, he might have reconsidered joining this outing.

Reconsidered…but he knew his decision would have been the same. The opportunity for that glimpse of her bare back, brief as it was, was worth every bit of discomfort. And the feel of her gaze on him as he undressed with his back to her sent another, stronger, tingle across his nerve endings, cementing his certainty about joining this short trip west. They would be unable to speak with one another until their destination was reached, but given the shortness of breath he expected after days of inactivity and the healing injury on his side…as well as the certainty that he had no words for what he wanted to express, that was, he believed, for the best.

She watched the exposed skin of his back, unmarred by the scars of combat or accident, ripple and erupt with the short black patina of Fela fur, the color, the image, she remembered from their initial meeting. His scent changed as well, more feline, less human, and whereas her brother wrinkled his nose, Jia felt drawn to move closer, to know the scent more intimately, to burn it into her memory. She told herself it was Alpha instinct, so that like everyone else within her Pack, she would know his scent and never lose track of him. There was more to it than that, and though she realized, as she forced herself to turn away rather than draw closer as he turned around, that she had not properly laid claim to the Pack as an Alpha should, any such claim, which had to be her first priority on her return, would have to include the glossy, well-muscled Fela at her side.

If, that was, he would allow and accept it.

At her other side, Addi yipped and bounced like a pup eager to run. Another hour and dawn would be upon them, whether the clouds parted to reveal that or not, and time was wasting. They needed to run if they were to cross the Wilds before daybreak.

Run she did.

She had been told the Flushing Wilds had once been a park, a place of recreation where city dwellers could find refuge in a natural haven surrounded by the concrete, stone, metal, glass, and plastic of the 'modern' world. That world was in tatters now, what had once been modern steadily devoured by the nature they had tried to contain in such special places as Flushing. Now nature had overgrown its confines, spreading into every street, every building, in an effort to reclaim everything that mankind did not struggle to protect. In the heart of Flushing, the lake drew all manner of beasts, making the stretch of nature less a place of recreation and more a truly wild place that lived up to its name. Herds of deer and goats, small clusters of horses, wolves, pumas, coyotes, and bobcats all dwelt in a balance unmarred by man, and even the occasional foray of those with anthro blood who came for the hunt could not unsettle that balance. It was here, in the wild, Cana, Fela, and Ursa were accepted as natural parts of the world order. Here they were not hunted. Here they belonged.

Through the zigzag maze of tombstones and mausoleums of a once sacred burial ground, beneath the crumbling ruins of an ancient roadway, the trio left civilization behind for a time until they reached the lake's edge. A swim through the icy water would take too long, hamper their movement as the cold bound their limbs, and so they ran along the shore to the north, growing nearer the border of the Zone and its armed guards meant to keep those within from escaping as if they were some sort of prisoners rather than people afflicted with the oddities radiation and other man-made and natural poisons had thrust upon their genetics. The possibilities that some of those guards might forage the northern reaches of the Wild for meat or for sport meant increased vigilance, but at this hour of the day there were no Normals to be found, and the three rounded the lake to run south again without incident.

This was the stretch of Wilds the Marrocks knew, the western side of the Wilds where pups learned to hunt, to shift at will, to be comfortable with the duality of what nature had created them to be. The game trails were fresh and familiar, crisscrossing the forest as the threads of life wove between the lake and the protection of dense thickets. Kato smelled it too, a different hunt-scent then he was used to, though the game was no wilder here than the herds that roamed the suburban streets where he had grown up. He attributed the difference to the sweetness of damp leaves, damp earth, the smell of the air as it skimmed the surface of the water, the cleansing scent of heavy rain which began to fall not long after they entered the Wilds, and the heavier scent of exertion from the Cana female running at his side. It was her scent more than any other that made his nerves tingle, his heart hammer…made him feel unexpectedly alive.

Jia remained alert to danger, as did her brother, but both were more comfortable in this place than they had been in the library, running as if pulled or propelled by an unseen force until both she and Addi drew up short amidst thinning trees as the distant smell of oil smoke, too strong to be washed from the air by the torrential rain, reached their nostrils. Oil smoke meant civilization, and though the sky was still devoid of light, it was the shroud of the storm clouds that produced that artificial perception, not the lingering fingers of night. They skirted the edges of the city for several minutes, traveling south, catching glimpses of tall ruins through the overgrowth, listening to the sounds of a waking world, until, satisfied with her location, Jia led them from the Wilds into an empty street cluttered with abandoned rusts stripped of tires and usable materials. The road was nearly impassible, the metal skeletons dragged here to serve as a shield between civilization and the Wilds. Holes in the pavement had grown over the decades and were filling again to become black puddles, the rain producing cascading waterfalls from broken windows as it accumulated inside of listing buildings with cracked and caved in rooftops.

It was behind one of these weirs that Jia ducked, ignoring the splashes of cold water on her fur as she traversed the pitfalls of collapsed walls and led them deeper into one of the buildings. Only the faint lingering scent of past inhabitation remained, the scent of other Cana having been here too, although here and there Kato noted a stronger scent, the urine marker of territorial claiming left by one Cana or another. It would have been enough to keep the most unsuspecting Normal out, as they, on a primal level, would have detected and understood the markers even if their noses could not detect the scent. Kato only passed, ignoring the markers, because he believed Jia and Addy would vouch for him should another take offense at a Fela entering this ordinary, yet seemingly special, place.

A place in which, in a room full of nooks seemingly haphazardly created by the fall of debris and the collapse of inner walls, Jia resumed her normal shape, her body now seeming small and frail in comparison to the larger, more muscularly defined Cana. She pulled aside several large chunks of stone, aided by her brother, and eventually drew out a hemplastic box tied closed with coarse fabric straps, while Addi returned to the room's entrance to stand watch. From the box, she removed a bundle of clothing wrapped with a waxy tarp and offered the first shirt she found to Kato.

When he did not immediately shift, did not move to take the offered bit of deep blue fabric, Jia shrugged and tossed it to her brother. "Suit yourself. It isn't safe to move about like that now that the world's awake." She stared up and down the lean Fela, eager for his change and feeling a pang of regret that he had to abandon the feline form.

"Running about nude isn't advisable either," Addi's voice, his chuckle, indicated his change of form as well, though Kato had not seen it happen. The medic grinned when Kato snatched the second offered item of clothing from Jia's outstretched hand and withdrew to a separate corner of the room behind a protective shield of a fallen wall to shift and dress.

Kato wondered, as he drew the long, faded red, button shirt around him, his back to the others, if Jia was watching him. He did not look back to find out.

"Makes more sense to split here," Addi went on, the rustle of fabric continuing as he dressed. "I'll get what I can, talk to the Foundling Center, and meet you back here?" The question in his voice begged only to be told what hour to meet, but Jia's response was vague as she quickly dressed.

"We'll have to find Segara…and that could take time. And if he has found any detail of use…"

Addi grunted, not satisfied to be excluded from a potentially more dangerous excursion deeper into the borough. "Mid-afternoon…and if you're not here, I'll go to the Bunker and wait."

From the woman's nod, a gesture Kato barely caught as he turned to accept the trousers and well-scuffed boots scooted across the cold dusty floor in his direction, he guessed that the Bunker was a place known to the pair, although the word meant nothing to him, an undefined term that conjured no imagery within his mind.

"How long…?" he began.

Addi's first reply was a scowl. "As long as I dare." That suggested a risk factor in the 'Bunker' that meant he and Jia would need to be there, regardless of the completeness of their day's mission. The sudden tension in the woman's jaw and shoulders spoke of feeling rushed, or perhaps a surge of worry for her brother's safety, but none of those things were matters Kato could address. He had come out of a sense of duty…to protect her…and now he felt certain, when her eyes swept over him, lingered, and then turned to the boot she was lacing up, that she was going to assign him to protect her brother and the mediplies instead.

Kato steeled himself for the imagined rejection, scrambled to think of a reason to refuse such a request, but instead, she murmured, "We'll be there."

We.

Kato's breath of relief was louder than intended and he abruptly pretended to focus on the buttons of the thigh-long rain slicker he had been offered so that he did not have to see the looks on the Canas' faces.

Dressed now, clothing ill-fitting but functional, Kato followed the siblings through a different maze of tunnels that took them out of the building on the western side where it emptied into a population center just beginning to come to life. Even at this early hour, there were more people coming in and out of buildings than Kato had ever seen in one street, enough to make him shuffle nervously closer to Jia, perhaps to protect her, perhaps to protect himself.

She did not seem to mind.

"Watch yourself," Addi murmured with a squeeze to his sister's hand before turning north, alone, to attend his mission.

Jia glanced at the windows above them, her gaze traveling along the rooftops toward the north until her brother disappeared, a slightly uneasy expression creased around her eyes and mouth, before starting west with a tilt of her head that beckoned Kato to follow. The hood of her jacket was pulled up as both protection against the rain and as a disguise. Kato had no such protection, but no one here would recognize him…and he did not mind the rain. Their efforts to move quickly from one sheltered doorway to the next was barely successful in keeping the rain off, and by the time they traveled to the end of the first block, Kato's dark curls clung to his skull.

The compulsion to ruffle his hair and shake the droplets from it was difficult to ignore once they scurried down a set of iron steps into a long, dank tunnel. "Sorry," Jia mumbled, giving in to the temptation and raking the fingers of both hands through his curls. "Father wasn't big on headwear."

These were her father's clothes. Kato looked down at the damp trousers that clung tightly to his legs and the muddy boots that had thus far kept his feet dry with a new sense of appreciation, ignoring the tremors in his body created by the touch of her fingers in his hair. The legs of the pants were too short, the sleeves of the shirt and jacket as well, and the fabric across his chest was snug enough to be mildly uncomfortable, but those were facts that now gave him a sense of the man, one of the two they were hoping to find alive.

"I don't mind the rain," he murmured

"I thought cats hated to get wet."

Kato began to protest that he was not a cat any more than she was a dog, but the sparkle in her eyes revealed she was teasing and he quickly forced a chuckle into the vacuum his annoyance created. "Not all of them. My mother said that tigers love to swim." He did not know how she had known that, did not know if it was true, but he believed it all the same.

"Do you?" She moved into the stairwell, into thicker blackness, following a path she knew by heart without the advantage of her eyes. "Swim that is?"

"We lived near the sea…she thought it was important we know how. She used to take us there frequently when we were younger…before…" His voice trailed away with a melancholy note.

"Before?"

Whatever he had begun to say, he decided to leave unsaid and Jia chose not to pursue an answer.

"Where does this tunnel go?"

They reached the bottom of the stairs, emerging into a cavern dotted with small fires around which people clustered in little groups, lost-looking souls with vacant eyes in grimy faces that watched the pair as they moved but made no effort to detain or obstruct them.

"There are tunnels beneath much of the boroughs, old transportation tunnels, waste tunnels." She leaped down into a wide space with metal rails disappearing to the left and right further into the dark and waited for him. "Many are collapsed now…filling with water…but the Unders clear the way when they can. It makes for quicker travel if you know your way."

"Unders?" He glanced back at those huddled around the fires.

"Some say they've been down here since the Undoing…that they were trapped or hid here…that they never come above ground." She smiled, a look he could not see from his position. "Obviously they do…to scavenge burnables, clothes…food…but they move at night, in the shadows, and then return down here. Some people leave them gifts at the tunnel openings, to gain their favor. I think some hide down here…criminals, the ill…mutani…even some anthro. Father traded with them…food and medicare for things they scavenged. They don't bother us and we don't bother them. They're peaceful, mostly, and usually hide when top-siders come down."

"They don't seem to say much."

Jia nodded. The firelight was far behind them, and Kato was watching the placement of his own feet in case there were hazards on the ground and so he did not see the gesture. "I don't believe I've ever heard them speak."

Anthro blood allowed them to see well enough to traverse the hazards in the passage, fallen debris, foul-smelling pools of collected rainwater, the occasional corpses of small animals, cats and dogs and rats. She remembered there were rooms for the dead here as well, and if one was not cautious, there were grubbers trapped in this underworld, unable to find their way to the surface…or who had fallen here from above and thus were caught amidst the decay until their bodies decomposed too much to be functional. Grubbers were the biggest hazard in places like this, next to losing one's way, but fortunately, they were incapable of stealth and moved too slowly and clumsily to be a threat to anyone who was paying attention. Jia could hear them moaning in side passages and behind barred doors, leaden feet shuffling about, their bony fingers clawing at whatever surface they were nearest to, as they searched for anything they could devour. Kato heard them as well and moved closer to her, his level of alert assuring her that, should she fail to notice a threat, he would be there to do so and confront it with her.

His devotion reminded her of Liam, of the way he had always been by her side since their earliest childhood days, and the memories made her heart ache. They had never been separated for more than a day or two, and always with the knowledge that they would be reunited soon. Now he had been gone too long and each passing hour was one closer to the certainty that she would never see him, or her father, again. The painful realization caused her to quicken her pace, leading Kato on a snaking path until the tunnel opened into another platformed area with a large cluster of Unders gathered around another fire, this one lit inside of a metal barrel. The sudden appearance of strangers from the mostly unused tunnel made the entire congregation face them, some stooping to pick up the handcrafted weaponry that lay at their feet.

"I thought you said they're peaceful…"

"Stay close; don't look at them. Once they see we're not a threat…"

But as they climbed onto the platform and headed toward the stairs which would take them back to the outside world, it was almost impossible not to look at the men and women who stood in the way and their approach, slow and cautious as it was, drew the Unders into a tightly clustered group that inched closer to the pair. Kato repositioned himself, insinuating his larger body between the Unders and Jia, choosing to face the threat with a glint of gold in his eyes and a body posture that proved he would fight them all if they continued to threaten the woman with him.

It was not until Jia had climbed the first two steps, with Kato backing up the stairs behind her, that the Unders ceased their advance. They continued to watch, however, until Kato could no longer see them, but he dared not let his guard down until he and Jia were out of hearing distance of the snuffling, coughing horde and the ascent up the final flight of stairs was begun. He moved sideways, eyes and ears attuned to what they left below, his hand gripping the rusted metal railing, his footsteps following the lighter ones of the woman in front of him. Her hand upon his shoulder drew him around to face a sight that momentarily left him breathless.

The walls were taller than any man could see over, the height of at least four men one atop the other. Piecemealed from stone, concrete, brick, and hunks of dark metal, he guessed it was a wall constructed after the Undoing. In the distance, the complex of buildings within seemed taller still, and a domed, octagonal pinnacle towered over it, its sides made of scavenged glass plates which allowed the men and women moving within to see everything inside the compound and, to some degree, beyond it. Without visual aid, Kato did not believe those within could see the pair that emerged into the dimly lit morning, and from that distance between them, if they could be seen, they were little more than a duo of insignificant mismatched dots. He imagined people in a place like this would be watching for threats, not random passersby.

He and Jia were certainly no threat. They were unarmed and on a mission of their own. She was watchful, looking for something he could not see, but she did not speak, only scowled and eventually nodded, satisfied, perhaps, or disappointed.

"The Fortress," she murmured, grabbing his hand and steering him left into the city and away from the walls. The rain had turned into a fine mist, but the hood of her jacket remained raised to allow her to hide.

He nodded, only partially comprehending what she meant. He had heard mention of this place in discussions amongst the Pack, in the exchange with QiangXu. It was the place where the one called Laedan resided, where Jia had spent time growing up, where men led the lives of others, where the ones responsible for the hunt, and possibly the abduction or death of kin, lived in protection from those they maligned. She had said nothing of coming here, but perhaps she had not wanted to concern her brother. If she was considering entering the Fortress, Kato was prepared to support her, but he was relieved that their path kept the Fortress to their right for a handful of streets, past a drinking establishment crawling with men and women in uniform and those who were not.

Someone had died, Jia assumed. It was the only occasion she could think of that would attract so many Protectors into a single place at the same time…although the hour seemed too early for drinking. She lingered in the street, peering inside long enough to be certain the man she sought was not here, and when she was satisfied, she turned onto a southerly street to leave the Fortress behind.

Of course, the mage would not be there. He had been given a directive by the Laedan. He had taken on the duty of finding her father, finding Liam. They were missions enough for one man. As the hour was barely past daybreak, he might not even be awake yet.

There was no Protectorate near where he had spent his boyhood years, but Kato recognized the uniforms as belonging to people of importance, people who carried a certain scent about them that made the tiny hairs on his arms, the back of his neck, up and down his legs and across his chest stand up as if in preparation for an attack. The overpowering weight of alcohol and a variety of unfamiliar chemicals made Kato's nose wrinkle and his eyes narrow, but Jia neither noticed nor cared. Her relative calm was sufficient to keep him at her side and when she chose to leave that cluster of people behind, Kato went too.

The tension of travel below ground with the Unders, the watchfulness of passing the Fortress, the temporary spike of adrenalin caused by the chaos in the dive, all bled away as the pair casually covered the remaining distance, past structures that, at least at the street level, were maintained to be livable. If he kept his eyes straight ahead, avoided looking toward the sky, there was little evidence of the borough's, the world's, decay. Only the green that sprouted between cracks in the streets, the moss and ivy that covered long abandoned hulks, the faded colors of ancient signs, hinted at the story of the place. Looking upward, however, gave evidence of the crumbling skyline, the places where materials had been stripped away to fulfill a new purpose somewhere else. Children played in the streets here, something none dared do without an adult present in the region he had called home. Neighbors stood on their steps, or on the buckling, twisting remains of the sidewalks, conversing about the trivial matters of the day or gossiping about the host of Protectors that had passed earlier, sipping steaming tea, all seemingly oblivious to the gray mist that shimmered in the backlight of window lanterns and porch lamps lit as an invitation to others.

There was a sense of welcome here, noticeable in the tilted heads and smiles as they passed, that was unfamiliar to Kato. Without knowing the passersby were Cana and Fela, there was no reason to shun them, no reason to mistrust them. The naiveté of safety in a world far from safe made Kato's skin prickle with an unease that Jia did not appear to share. She was watchful but not fearful, familiar with this world, these streets, if not specifically with these people. It was a reminder of how worldly she was, carrying experience it would take him a lifetime to gain.

He envied her.

Another staircase of dark gray stone led up to a set of double doors with writing stenciled upon the hemplastic that had replaced the long ago broken windows. The letters he knew, the words he did not, but he hid that lack of knowledge with a hand that shielded his eyes against the bright light tube that shone down above the doorframe. Jia pulled the well-loosened door open and glanced at Kato with a nervous expression.

"We're here."

Kato blinked, confused as he passed with her into a room full of women and men in uniforms…the same uniforms they had seen on that other group not long before. He had known the man they were seeking was a mage, a Tracker, but as he was still skeptical of their reality, he had not considered where they might find such a man. He had not imagined that finding a mage would thrust him into a room of people who felt like a threat. Kato realized it then, that uniforms reminded him of HOPE, of people who came and took anthro away in the dead of night, or the quiet of day, any time one was identified for extraction or eradication. Those were the only uniforms he had ever seen, uniforms from a distance, whom his mother had gone to great lengths to warn him about and protect him from. The people she claimed had taken his father away not long after he was born. He had no way to know if her tale was true, but he had no reason to doubt her either, and her efforts to instill caution had been successful. He had avoided all uniforms before today. Jaw clenched and lips tightening to hid the eruption of fangs, he turned his eyes to the floor in case they too might give his nature away.

With a casualness he did not share, Jia approached the nearest desk where a uniformed woman was filling in a regulation form. "Excuse me," she asked, her eyes taking in the form, the words being written on it in the few seconds it took the Protector to finish what she was writing and look up. "I'm looking for Protector Segara."

She did not use the word mage. It was unlikely that his nature was a secret from the others he worked with, as it was likely why he was part of the Protectorate in the first place, but it was not necessary for anyone to know what she knew about him. Witness or client or friend…or something else, Jia could be anyone, anything, just another walk-in looking for a Protector who had crossed her life at some point. The Protector eyed her with no more than a curious but bored glance that could have, Jia knew, assessed a number of traits despite its brevity, and then pointed at the closed door at the side of the room, centered in a line of windows. The man pacing the room behind the door, one hand tugging through his hair, his mouth moving as if in speech though no voices were heard, was a familiar face to anyone who had spent significant time in the Fortress, for the Chief's advisory status to both Laedans was a given fact.

Jia nodded to the woman who had already returned to her forms and paid no further attention to the pair as Jia and Kato approached the barred door. The Chief looked up at the knock on the glass, recognized the woman behind it though he was not sure from where, and beckoned her to enter. It was not until the door opened that her name and identity came to him and he swallowed an uneasy pang.

The nervous shifting of his gaze drew Jia's attention to the man lying unresponsive on the long settee on one side of the room and she dashed to him without a thought. "What happened?" She ignored Kato's abrupt defensive posture and the way his wary yellow eyes darted between the unconscious man and the one whose pacing reminded him of a caged beast seeking freedom. Caged beasts were prone to attack those who got too close. Kato was not going to let that happen and focusing on Ernest meant less attention paid to the one receiving Jia's care.

"He was reading something for me." It was the only explanation Ernest had. "Welcome to the Protectorate, Ms. Marrock…is there something I can do for you?" He waved her companion into the room and gestured for him to close the door, making note of both the man's hostility, which he chose to monitor but not react to for the time being, and the fact that she seemed to know his mage.

"The Protector was looking for something for me…" she began, turning Vance's unbandaged hand over to feel his wrist for a pulse, making certain he was alive.

Hunch proven, instinct correct, Ernest nodded. "Your father." Grimly he added, "I am sorry to hear about his disappearance."

"He didn't…" she began, about to protest that he was only off on a scav mission east, as she maintained with the Channons. But she imagined Segara had deemed it necessary to tell his Chief what he was working on, was perhaps even duty-bound to report work matters that drew him away from the Protectorate, just as she imagined it was a requirement of the Chief's position to know what his people were doing. There was no point in denying a truth the Chief already knew; it would not be productive or fair.

"He had some leads he was going to look into…he was going to let me know what he learned," she said instead, turning her aborted statement into one referring to the mage instead of her father.

"Did it have anything to do with the d-three hunt?" When she looked at him with a suspicious scowl, Ernest shrugged and grabbed his jacket from the metal tree near the door. "I heard there was an unauthorized one…" Not like hunts were ever authorized in his book, but he did know that the Laedans, and even the Protectorate, sometimes sanctioned hunts in order to bring a perpetrator to justice. Not this sort of hunt, however. Not the hunt of anthro by those seeking to capture or destroy them.

"I don't…" Before she spoke the final word of the sentence, the hand beneath hers spasmed, tightened around her fingers, and the mage jolted up from the settee in an eruption of panic and confusion that brought Ernest and Kato to Jia's sides, one with the intent to protect her from a possible threat, the other out of concern for his mage.

"Welcome back." Ernest pressed Vance against the back of the settee with his hand flat across the other man's chest, an act meant to soothe him but which, for a moment, elicited further panic in the mage's eyes.

"I…what…where…?" The questions were meant for his chief, but his gaze was transfixed by the hand clutching his. He did not need to see her face to know who she was. Her touch told him enough. That dazed moment lasted only long enough for him to register the presence of another in the room; once he did, his eyes left their joined hands to study the unfamiliar individual's face. Not her brother, not Cana, as he would have expected. Fela. Vance knew that without touching him, without any visible clues beyond the man's hostile aura.

When he lifted his eyes, she released his hand, but the warmth of her touch remained.

Ernest cleared his throat. "My office…that reading threw you…" Literally, he thought, with a glance at the now righted guest chair at his desk where Vance had been sitting before. "Miss Marrock just arrived to speak with you. Are you alright? Do you need anything…a medic…a drink…?"

"I'm fine." His head felt as if it were splitting in two, his mouth tasted foul, and every fiber in his body hurt, but he would live.

"Well…then…I will leave you to your discussion…was just going for a tea…and Segara…don't forget…" Whatever evidence Vance had obtained in that reading, the Chief could wait to get it for just a little longer.

"No…wait…" Her proximity was adding to the dizziness in his head, so he scooted sideways and leaned forward with his elbows on his knees, putting distance between her and Ernest. It put him closer to the Fela, but that, at least, was not contributing to his discomfort. After noting the wrapping around his palm, the sight bringing back memories of the reading to which the Chief referred, he adjusted the bandage and planted his face in his hands, careful to rub his stinging eyes with his good hand to keep the yellow stain on the other from getting into his eyes. It took several moments to clear his head, arrange his thoughts, to make sense of the echoes left by her touch and the residual sensory impressions that lingered from the contaminated syringe and the drug it contained.

When he lifted his head, meeting first Jia's gaze and then Ernest's, he murmured, "Blood, anthro blood, more specifically plasma." He rubbed his eyes again, pushing against the symptoms of the substance still lingering in his veins and the crimson-tinged yellow haze that kept his sight from focusing. "Dried…the powder mixed with…" He shook his head again, that bit of knowledge unclear despite his efforts to untangle the thread for proof. His eyes lingered on Jia again after sliding over the wild-haired man's face, wondering what the two of them knew about such things. They obviously knew. That knowledge had been present in the press of her hand against his.

"Where did he get it?" Ernest demanded, aware of the exchanged glances between Jia and the stranger but choosing not to question them now. His duty was to find someone for the Laedan to use as an example, someone to blame for Nik's near-death experience. As repulsive as the thought was of injecting someone else's blood, dried into a powder or not, without it being a life-saving necessity, it gave the Chief a place to start.

Though Vance shrugged as if he did not know, he murmured, "Brac…"

The Chief knew that name. Brac was the biggest name in this district, the most dominant source of mind-altering substances on the street. The man…at least it was believed Brac was a man…had the largest score of baggers beneath his control. Brac did not deal with trivial substances, leaving alcohol and mari procurement in the hands of petty providers. No, Brac's distributors pursued more exotic substances, extracts from rare plants, lab-synthesized chemicals, experimental combinations of naturally occurring ingredients that should not, in themselves, be dangerous or addicting, but were when combined with something else.

Brac would not have been the originator of this new drug. The technology necessary to process blood would be limited. Ernest could not think of any such place in all of Queens where this could be done, but his lack of knowledge did not mean that such places did not exist. A medifac perhaps, where blood was prepared for the most severe surgeries…and the sudden exchange of looks between him and Segara suggested to the Chief that the mage had jumped to the same conclusion.

Could a drug-producing medifac be involved in the theft of the Laedan's mediplies?

"Find Asan…he'll know."

Ernest nodded and hurried from the room, letting the door bang shut behind him. Asan was one of the more active baggers in d1. He moved between dives, supplying clients with their heart's desires, typically remaining beneath the Protectorate's radar while always being known to them. A bald man covered from head to toe with body ink, it had been his hand Vance had seen depositing the tiny bag of yellow powder into Nik Channon's pale, shaky one. It was common knowledge in the Protectorate that Asan bagged for Brac. They might not be able to find Brac for questioning…no one ever found Brac…but tapping Asan for details might provide clues as to where this particular product came from.

That was a facet, however, that Vance already knew. Or suspected he knew. The howl echoing in his head was Cana, he was sure of that, someone tortured and bled, possibly dead, in the pursuit of pure plasma. Something in that echo, in the memory of spinning, perhaps aided by the substance in his body acting like a magnetizing lure to his mage blood, was pulling him toward the southeastern corner of District 3. If he followed it, it might give him answers.

Or it would lead him to his death.

"What did you find?"

Vance grabbed both of Jia's hands tightly, his eyes wide. "I don't know where they are," he said apologetically, "but I know where they might be…where they could be…if you want me to…"

"Take us there."

He scowled, eyes returning to the other man in the room, having not expected that he might be included in this quest. Perhaps he had some stake in the matter, someone also taken, and that was why Cana and Fela were working together. That had to be it. So far the Fela had not spoken, however, perhaps out of deference to Jia, or perhaps because he could not. That, Vance decided with admitted selfishness, would be a blessing. The taller man's grating presence would be less so if he kept his mouth shut.

"I cannot be certain of your…"

Expecting to be excluded in some misguided effort to protect her, Jia squeezed his hands back, a grip as strong as it was sure. "If my father…if Liam…are there…wherever this drug is being created…I have to bring them home."

"I don't know that they are there," Vance tried to protest again, "only that…I think I can find the facility where this one dose was made. Who might be there…where it is precisely…I cannot say…"

"Then you lied."

Fela and mage glowered at one another, Vance's expression revealing his annoyance and disappointment that the other man could speak and taking exception at not being trusted, though he knew trust between anthro and mages was a rare thing.

"That's not how this works," he groused, straightening his shirt to casually brush her touch from his hands. "I can follow what I saw, what I sense, but where that will take me, I cannot be certain…"

"Yet you expect us to…"

Vance growled. "I expect to go alone, to do some reconnaissance, let you know what I…"

"And I expect to be there to rescue my father…you knew I would." She heard the offer in his tone, whether intentional or not; if he intended to go alone, he would have found some better way of addressing the matter and would not have allowed her to be in the room when he revealed some of what he knew to the Chief. His objection to her company, she suspected, had less to do with her safety then it did with Kato.

"If it is anthro blood they are after…Cana blood…"

"I will keep her safe," Kato snarled. "Tell us where…"

Jia grunted and made an effort not to roll her eyes. "I can protect myself. I don't need either of you for that. But you know the way," she said with a pointed stare at Vance, her eyes demanding that if he did not know the way, he should speak up now so as not to keep her hopes high, "and have the authority that we do not. We don't know what we'll run into when we get there, how many might be guarding the facility. We'll need the additional ears…eyes…hands…" If the facility Vance intended to investigate held other anthro prisoners, whether her packmates or strangers, they would need help to rescue them. And, she realized with a fleeting thought to Addi, having a medic around would come in useful as well.

"We'll meet up with Addi and then follow you anywhere."

Kato's growl suggested that his following anyone other than Jia might be too much to ask, but he moved to stand by her side again, choosing a protective stance although she did not see the mage as a threat. Vance's narrowed gaze and pursed lips reflected annoyance, but he was the first to shake his head in reply to the demand.

"You'll wait here while I change up." He was supposed to report to the Laedan today, but this seemed more important, especially if it helped to locate the supposedly missing delivery of mediplies that Vance was beginning to doubt existed. If he could connect the blood trade to the missing supplies...be they medicals or weapons...and if his efforts offered up the head of someone responsible for both Nik's odose and the theft as well, even connect it to Marrock's disappearance, it ought to stand Vance in good stead with the Chief and, possibly, with the Channons. If, however, all of those connections led back to the Laedan in an unsavory way, it was better that Vance made those connections before taking his suspicions to his employer. Too many scattered pieces did not fit into the picture the Laedan had painted and the mage wanted the truth.

His clothes felt sticky, his skin crawled with the effect of the drug still in his blood, and getting a shower and a change of clothes before trekking across the borough would at least allow him to feel more normal. It was tempting to look for a drink in the hopes of dispelling that crawling sensation, but he could not be sure of the effect of mixing alcohol with that substance. Not after the reaction that Nik Channon had reportedly experienced.

And he expected he was going to need that uncomfortable crawling bug sensation in his veins if he was to find his way to wherever their eventual destination would be.

"We will wait," Jia replied, cutting off whatever likely off-colored remark Kato seemed prepared to make.

Chapter 20

D awn did come too soon, as Roland promised, and while Liam felt strong enough to follow the other man about on his early morning duties, his limbs felt heavy and slow, his mind sluggish, and every blinking light or twinge of sound bombarded his brain like a swarm of tiny knives. It was a weakness Roland assured him would pass after stressing that they needed to pretend, for the sake of their captors, that they did not know one another, needed to prove that Liam was competent enough to carry out the tasks asked of him. The consequences of suspicious behavior, or any failures to complete their duties correctly that could not be explained due to equipment malfunction or the assignment of other duties, would be unpleasant and potentially fatal. Changing IV bags, cleaning the nude, comatose bodies and the stasis chambers of waste, wiping down every surface in the room and the lab, and, when the hour came, taking the day's donors from stasis to the lab where they were prepped for blood-letting.

The doctor normally oversaw that duty herself, was one of only three people to take the filled bags away, once extraction was complete, to whatever end they were destined for. That day it was one of the others, a stocky woman with a long gray braid coiled high on her head, a woman who refused to look at Roland or Liam as she worked with an anxious tremor. To Roland, that tremor, always present when she was alone with him, suggested fear and anxiety in his presence. She would not be the first person to fear anthro; Roland saw it too often, just as he had seen any number of anthro use that fear to their advantage for either self-preservation or intimidation.

The tray of instruments she moved between patients, a collection of scalpels, clean needles and tubing, swabs and bandages had to be picked up, cleaned or discarded when it slipped from her quaking hands and clattered to the floor, meaning time wasted, but soon enough the donors were returned to stasis and Roland and Liam were again secured behind a locked door with the sleeping shells for company. The woman failed to notice the absence of the keycard she had dropped when the tray fell, and left the lab without it, and Roland, quick to seize the offered advantage, tucked the key away where it would not likely be found, even if security came and searched the warehouse.

No one checked the sleepers closely unless they were being bled.

Only when they were alone, returning to the task of cleaning the sleepers as needed, did Liam dare to speak. He spent the morning in silence, listening to Roland's directions, watching closely, examining everything, but conserving his strength and questions for a time when the lab staff was not milling about checking vital readings on their stock and assessing the thoroughness with which Roland performed his duties. Liam sank wearily onto the stool he had rested on the night before, picking up half of the sandwich they had been provided for lunch, watching Roland continue to work. He groaned, set the sandwich down, and rose to follow again.

"You know her." He had watched the way Roland reacted to one of the doctors who held their futures in her hands, noting the tiny tells that only one Cana keenly familiar with another would detect.

"Not really…but she's been here before…"

"But she knows you?"

"At least by name," Roland grunted with a shrug. "I've seen her…at a distance…before coming here. I know her name. We were never introduced…and I don't believe she knows I know who she is."

He continued working in silence for many minutes, expecting Liam to voice the question hanging in the air between them. When he did not, either out of weariness or respect for his Alpha's personal business, Roland sighed and said. "She works for Hallister."

"Kennedy?" It seemed a stretch, an unbelievable possibility, that they could have been captured in LaGuardia by men they each assumed were HOPE, to then be transported to the rival borough. Taken to the bowels of one of HOPE's many strongholds, perhaps, but Kennedy hardly sounded like the place for this prison.

"Kennedy," Roland said with a nod, not looking up as he added, "But not for long."

Liam's chance to seek clarification was waylaid by the arrival of the lab tech returning for the second donors of the day. Liam and Roland exchanged a look before complying. This was not yet over.

☙*☙

Addison paced the width of the building his father had dubbed The Bunker, a partially collapsed structure that once held level upon level of parked automobiles, was now filled with nothing more than carcasses stripped bare of usable materials and left to rot. The collapse of weight from above allowed some of nature's elements in, allowed wind to whistle through thin cracks and rainwater to dribble through the gaps and accumulate in puddles here and there across the building's ground floor. There was a level below his feet as well, where nature had not yet gained a firm toehold, a level with access to the subterranean train tunnels. The Bunker afforded enough protection from the outside world to have been kept by the Flushing Pack as an emergency shelter. The Pack could have come here when the hunt had driven them from their home, except that their hunters had blocked the escape routes, forcing them to take more extreme action. There were stores hidden here, cans of food scavenged from around the city and bagged grains, dried fruits and vegetables and meat, enough to have lasted the Pack several weeks had it been necessary to hide here, and Addi had already stuffed as much as he could into the medikits he collected from the infirmary.

It was risky going there, confronting those he had worked beside for the last several years, people who, by necessity, he had been forced to hide his true self from. The hunt that expelled the Flushing Pack from the outskirts of LaGuardia had begun with the hunters having to pass the clinic's doors and gossip about hunts inevitably spread like a firestorm. The following absence of Addi and Trill would have forced an equation in the minds of those the couple had worked with that could only have a single outcome.

Addison Marrock, or someone he was close to, was anthro.

Unlike so many others, however, his fellow medics, men and women who had to deal with ailing individuals of all sorts, harbored few prejudices and showed no rejection or hatred when he crept into the clinic through a side door reserved for the staff and made it quickly to his office. The hasty clatter as he cleared his shelves and drawers of medical paraphernalia and texts he had stashed there brought first one coworker, then another, until every one of the six who worked there was gathered around him.

They did not ask for details, either of the hunt or where he had been and why; and if they had determined his status as Cana, they did not say it out loud. Instead, they asked what he needed, how they could help, and after taking from their own supplies what they felt they could realistically spare, had sent messengers to the nearest clinics as well to fill in the deficiencies in his collection of goods. The three backpacks he accumulated, two stuffed to bursting and a third under one-third full, would, Addi hoped, hold the Pack until it was possible to return for more. If they were lucky, if he, the Pack, and the clinic were lucky, they would soon return to the borough, make their home amongst the familiar once more, and never again have to be concerned with what, to Addi's way of thinking, was a theft of goods from others who might need these supplies just as much as his family did.

After everything he had given to the clinic, to the community, however, not one of his coworkers begrudged him the supplies that would be scarce in the eastern Wilds. It was as if Addi had gone on a mission, nothing more, to help the less fortunate. That he happened to take his entire extended family with him was beside the point.

Here in the Bunker, a quick reshuffling of supplies enabled him to pack additional food into the backpacks, and clothes were bundled within a natty blanket to create a fourth pack tied with lengths of hemp cord that had been included in the collection stored here. With Jia and Kato's help, they would be able to build a few more bundles and bring home all of what was stored in the Bunker in order to replenish the Pack's supplies. Then they would scavenge their new territory, seek out anything they could use from the surrounding streets and buildings, but the odds were that, even in the Wilds, those streets had already been picked clean. Until they established trading routines with those living around them, until their livestock and potted herbs and vegetables were ready for the next harvest, the Pack would have to rely on their wits and the strengths of their Alpha.

He paced from one narrow gap of a window on that ground level to another, the windows there to allow light and ventilation no longer holding glass to keep out the cold and wet. The Pack had scent marked the Bunker to protect it from other anthro, other Cana, but there was never a guarantee that others would respect that marking. Nor would that subtle scent keep grubbers from entering, if any detected Addi's body heat and scent, and though he took every precaution to avoid being seen, it was not implausible that someone had spotted him, or could hear him moving about despite his efforts to be quiet. It was also possible that someone, one of his fellow medics or anyone who had seen him at the clinic, had alerted HOPE...or whoever wanted his Pack removed from the borough...of his return. That could mean he had been followed, and so it seemed prudent to watch from every window on that ground level he could reach for any indication of danger, as well as for Jia's arrival.

There was no way of knowing what hour that would be. Addi knew where the central Protectorate office was, but would she find the mage there or have to seek him elsewhere? Once she found him, the nature of her business, seeking answers to their father's whereabouts and what connection, if any, the existence of this blood drug might have to his abduction, might be completed by the answering of a few questions or might require more effort and time. Addi could afford to wait in the Bunker until dark unless someone discovered him here. The cover of night would afford him camouflage to begin the journey back to rejoin the Pack, but he was uneasy about leaving his sister behind. She had the Fela to fight beside her, if a fight was required, but even that might not be enough. How easily the Pack had been out-maneuvered by those hunters. How easily Jia too might encounter such a threat. Darkness was hours away, however, and though his head told him to rest, to conserve energy for the journey home, his nerves refused to allow it. He would not be able to rest until he knew his sister was safe.

He leaned his chin on the cold cement sill, eyes scanning those who passed his field of vision, people going about their lives without notice of being secretly observed. Carts rolled past pulled by men or animals, heavy boots of Protectors sloshed through the puddles left by the rain, and later, a pair of Laedan guards followed, a sight that struck unexpected fear in Addi's heart. The Bunker was almost as far south in LaGuardia as one could get, less than a city block from the border into unclaimed, thus far neutral, territory, territory contested by both LaGuardia and Kennedy, by Channon, Marrock and Hallister, territory raided by both but filled with untamed collections of lawless folk who fought the rule of anyone. Citizens passed freely across the borders, unhindered and mostly unnoticed, but those who lived this close to the border knew there were eyes there, watchful and vicious, looking for the crossing of a Protector, a Guard, anyone looking for trouble or conquest.

Protectors in this cluster of streets were no more common than anywhere else in LaGuardia. Laedan Guards, however, this far from the Fortress, meant trouble. Shrinking from the window far enough to be hidden in shadow but near enough to see the pair as they passed, Addi assumed their presence here was connected to the recent hunt, that they, on the Laedan's behest, were seeking the remnants of the Flushing Pack. He no longer felt safe in this hideout, but he knew he was safer than his sister would be should she step into the sector without suspicion and thus directly into danger.

How could he get a message to her when he did not know where she was?

And again he had the feeling that someone was watching him, a feeling that had followed since he and Jia separated. Whoever it was, they remained on the outskirts of his perceptions, always upwind where he could not get a good scenting, always hidden from his sight. Whoever it was seemed to mean no harm, and, he believed, had been following them for much of their journey west. Deuce then? It was no secret now that the Omega had become increasingly protective of Jia since Roland's disappearance and her ascension to acting pack alpha, and it was logical that he would follow her into danger without her command instead of staying behind to protect the Pack. There was a reason he was Omega after all, even though Addi, like the rest of the pack, did not know that reason. His refusal to be obedient might be reason enough. If Deuce had followed them, however, it seemed more likely that he would have followed Jia into LaGuardia instead of choosing to remain to look after Addi.

Thus the tail was likely someone else. Without knowing friend or foe, Addi had been reluctant to seek out the medifac, to transport the packs of supplies across town alone when he could be too easily ambushed, to come to the Bunker and take shelter where the individual might corner him. It made Addi wary, kept him pacing on alert, expecting to be attacked. But after more than an hour of pacing, whoever was there came no closer, only continued to watch from somewhere far enough away that they remained mostly hidden.

It was a scent, a noise from below, a muffled echo reverberating up the cluttered cement staircase that made Addi scramble to attention, eyeing the dark grey hulk in which he had hidden his supplies in case necessity forced him out of this room before Jia rejoined him. The sound had no connection to whoever might be following him; that presence had not moved from its position outside of the Bunker. If someone else had found him here, accidentally or intentionally, it was better he appeared to be alone, unarmed, and unencumbered, just a man seeking refuge from the rain. He wished he had brought some sort of weapon, even a knife or club, but his tendency to think in nonviolent terms was precisely the reason he would never be pack Alpha, regardless of his father's wishes. His gift was healing, caring…not fighting or leading…not even a persuasive way with words, and so from the narrow gap between cars where he tried to hide, he trembled, listening, eyes darting to and fro for some better place to ensconce himself.

Too late, however, for the six hastily scrambling figures, Unders in drab, dank clothes with hollow, sunken eyes and pale skin that made them look more like grubbers than anything human, were already close enough to scent him. It was the only way they could find him, since he imagined even the relatively dim light of morning was brighter than what the Unders were used to. Generations below ground had adapted their eyes to darkness, generations in must and mold and mildew had changed the way their sense of smell worked. If they were here now, they were either hunting, drawn by Addi's relentless pacing…

Or, the medic realized with a seizing surge of panic, they had been driven upward by something…or someone. His nose wrinkled, a rising stench of decay beginning to permeate the ground level, rolling through the wind on the shuffling sound of a mass of dragging feet.

Grubbers.

Alone or in pairs or small groups, grubbers were not something for an adult to fear, as they were easy to outrun and just as easy to put down. He imagined the Unders had long ago learned how to deal with the infected dead, and a half dozen Unders surely had the strength of numbers to protect themselves. But though he could not see them, this was no small group of grubbers, but rather a horde forced from Below by, he guessed from the stench filling the Bunker, rising water levels in the tunnels. It happened sometimes, that a hard enough, long enough rainfall and a shifting in the rubble, directed the flow of accumulated water to flood the tunnels and lower levels, making places normally dry, or nearly so, uninhabitable. And it happened just as often that solitary grubbers would stumble across others to form an ever-growing mass. Sometimes people drove or lured grubbers into an area, trapping them, removing the threat without having to resort to killing the unfortunate souls. When their containment failed and the grubber horde found its way into the world, it was always in the direction of the nearest food source.

Grubbers could not drown, but nor could they swim, and though they normally could not manage stairs…sometimes they were successful in climbing over one another to make it to higher ground. This time, it appeared, was one of those times.

Addi guessed that this group of Unders had the misfortune of being singled out as a meal, that a backup of water and sewage had contributed to the horde's creation and the migration of the Unders to the surface guided the course of their movement. Unable to outrun so many in a confined space, unable to fight them, Addi hastily climbed through the open door of the nearest car and drew it closed behind him as he cowered on the floorboards behind the front seats. The thud and click of the closing, latching door were heard throughout the level and Addi held his breath as he realized that some of the grubbers would turn in the direction of the sound. Soon, those few were bumping against the car's frame, seeking the source of the noise, the commotion they made enough to draw others to join them.

A howl, Cana in creation, a familiar voice that Addi had only half believed could be there, drew the focus of both Unders and grubbers alike, and likely the attention of men and women in the streets and surrounding buildings. The sound was near enough to send the Unders scattering as they reached the city street, and the lone scent that accompanied it was enough to draw the attention of most of the grubbers. Human or not, they neither cared nor felt a threat in that primal sound. They cared only for the proximity and ease with which they might feed, and so many turned and shuffled after their new prey into the light of day, where, undaunted, they split into smaller groups to wander aimlessly after any living thing that existed there.

Not all of them took the bait, however, preferring to remain in the Bunker to bump and claw at the vehicle in which Addi hid. He did not think they could smell him behind the boarded windows of the car to know he was there. More than likely they were kept here by the lure of the creaks and groans the rocking metal shell made because of their clamoring to get into it. He did not know how long they could continue their snarling, grunting efforts to reach him. The howl was gone, the sense of the Omega's presence too distant to know his whereabouts. To Addi's best guess, he was alone, and for the moment, he was marginally safe. If Jia did manage to get past the Protectors and Guards to approach the Bunker unscathed, she was likely to be confronted by the grubber herd...and Addi was helpless, at the moment, to aid her.

Chapter 21

"It's time."

Liam rolled over, half asleep, vaguely aware that the weight of the other man's body was no longer beside him on the narrow cot they were forced to share, and that there was a hand clasping his shoulder, shaking him awake. The alcove was dimly lit, but as the lighting there and in the stasis room never changed, he had no idea how much time had passed.

"Morning already?" he groused, rolling to face Roland, noticing the unusual stiffness in his limbs, the remnants, it felt, of too much physical exertion. Nothing he had done the day before explained the feeling, except that it had been a period of mild activity after days held vertical and motionless in the stasis pod.

"Not morning." Roland shook his head and shifted his eyes to a grated panel on the wall that now hung loosely by a single screw. The tunnel beyond, about six feet off the floor, was wide enough, barely, for a man to fit into, and from the cool air blowing out of it, was likely a ventilation shaft. Liam scowled, wondering why he had not noticed the grate before. "Come."

Liam struggled to stand, groaned, and sank back onto the cot with a shake of his head. "You go."

"Liam…"

The instinct to obey his Alpha was barely overridden by the other instinct in his gut, the instinct that told him this would never work. "I'll slow you down…I'm not strong enough."

"You are." Roland realized he was rushing the younger man's recovery, but events had come together to make this night the ideal time to put his plan into action.

"I'm not." He held up his hands so Roland could see the tremors. The injuries he had sustained in the previous hunt, now turned to dark bruises beneath the faded jumpsuit he had been given to wear, and the residual drug-induced weakness, would never let him keep up. "Besides…someone has to be here…for them…" His gaze traveled across the suspended bodies filling the room. "You spared me…taught me what to do, how to help them…for a reason. You're strong enough…you can bring back help."

He scowled, but Roland reluctantly accepted that Liam was right. Though he intended to get them both out alive in order to bring help back for the men and women trapped here, the fates had not given Liam enough time to heal before drawing the other necessary factors into alignment. When the repair tech came into the chamber the day before, an unfamiliar man with shifty eyes and a heavy blanket of cologne wrapped around him, intending to replace the grungy cloth air filter in the duct with a clean one, it had been the first time Roland had considered that passage to be usable. The new filter had torn from corner to corner, a peculiar tear to Roland, who watched the process without being obvious about it. With the new filter now useless, the tech replaced the grate and took both the old and new one away. On the way out, his screwdriver fell from his pocket, the sound of it lost in the clatter of the opening door, a fortuitous moment for Roland, who hid the tool in the hollow metal leg of his cot. Liam had not noticed any of it. The technician had not returned to finish the filter replacement, and a little experimentation showed that he had not tightened the screws of the grate very well. The tool's absence, and that of the key card Roland had obtained, would be noted soon enough. But this night, while the lab staff slept and no guards stood watch at the door, with the screwdriver to remove the grate and the keycard to pass through any doors and gates he encountered…he hoped…was the best chance of escape.

His…but not Liam's.

"You're stronger…faster," the younger Cana reiterated, this time with a familiar smirk meant to atone for the sacrifice he was making and any poor taste in humor he offered, "for now. Find the Pack; make sure they're safe…far away from here." On the outside, under peak health, Liam had been the fleetest member of the Flushing Pack. Here, now, he could barely function without growing winded and weary.

"They might kill you for…"

"They won't." Liam was adept at feigning ignorance, as he and Jia and Addi had often done as pups. As a scav, he was able to talk his way out of any number of precarious predicaments. If anyone could survive here, now that he was no longer strapped into one of the pods, sedated and bled, with a job he could show he was made to do, he was confident he could survive.

Even if he did not, Roland's survival meant much more to the Pack…and to LaGuardia.

It was the right choice to make.

Tying a loose twist of cloth, into which he secured both screwdriver and key, loosely about his neck, Roland shrugged out of his clothing with a shake of his head. "I'm not going to abandon you. Jia and Zen will never forgive me. We will come back for you…all of you…as quickly as we can."

"Pack comes first, Alpha. Don't risk all of them for me." The thought of his sister's grief, and Jia's, increased the trembling throughout his body and he quickly looked away from the older man, refusing to show further weakness. Roland would know, however, would smell the scent of sadness and fear, would hear the change in his breathing, in the louder pounding of his occasionally seizing heart. He could not hide those things. "Tell her…"

Roland took Liam's hand and the two clasped tightly, Liam's request left unfinished. Roland understood the message, knew who it was intended for, and would see that it was delivered…as soon as he was away from here. "I will be back," he promised again. He chose to trust Liam's belief in his survival, chose to believe Doctor Torrance would keep Liam alive to care for the donors instead of killing him for punishment for Roland's escape, and he had to trust that he could make it through the ducts and to the outside alive and unnoticed. Any hesitation, any doubt, would doom them both.

Once Roland was free, Jia would demand a rescue attempt. His daughter would never stand for abandoning another member of the Pack…particularly Liam.

"One more thing…" Roland hated to do it. But Liam's choice to remain behind, as right as it was, left the younger Cana exposed, and Roland would not leave him in danger. He would not risk Torrance believing her newest assistant was somehow complicit in Roland's actions. He swung hard, his balled fist catching Liam on the side of the head with enough strength to knock him off his feet but not hard enough to kill him. His head struck the floor with jarring force, leaving him breathing but unresponsive. Squatting, Roland checked his pulse, his breathing, checked for blood at the back of Liam's head, and once satisfied that the man was unconscious but otherwise unharmed, he used the key card to open both lab doors, which would, he hoped, lead to a manhunt throughout the complex rather than in the passage he would use. He then hoisted himself into the duct, pulled the grate loosely into place behind him, and glanced through the slots at the man on the floor beside the bed. "Sorry," he murmured, hoping Liam would understand the purpose of that blow. Roland would make up for it later, by doing his utmost to get Liam out of this place alive.

On hands and knees, on the cold metal floor of the duct, with the breeze blowing against his face, Roland began to crawl, following the strongest current of air.

≈*≈

Though reluctant to enter the Fortress again, feeling more and more since his visit the day before that being within those high walls and big windowed corridors and rooms was a trap best avoided, Chief Ernest strode behind his escort, his hands at his side in an effort to keep his posture relaxed and casual. He could have found his way to any room directed to, but his escort claimed to be uncertain where the Laedan was and therefore chose to lead the way until they found him rather than allow the Chief to wander aimlessly about the Fortress. Ernest was not surprised to find the Laedan standing at the infirmary window, looking at the unmoving body of his son. Lowell glanced at the arrivals and nodded, the look dismissing the attendant and welcoming the Chief at the same time before turning his attention back to Nik.

"No change?" For the moment, at least, their confrontation over Yiva was set aside in favor of the incident at hand.

"The medics say he is out of danger, but what do they know? He hasn't opened his eyes…he looks dead." The man's tone was bitter, resentful, his hands behind his back clenching and unclenching as he spoke. "Tell me you found something."

Inhaling once, letting the air whistle softly through his teeth as he exhaled, Ernest grunted. "We got his bagger in custody…we know what he took. We haven't been able to backtrace the source, but Protector Segara believes there is a connection between the drug, the source, and the stolen shipment you assigned him to find."

Ernest did not know any more about Vance's assignment than that, only that there was a stolen shipment of goods that Lowell wanted to be found. From Lowell's frown and the bunching of lines at the corners of his eyes, Ernest wondered what that connection might be. It seemed obvious that whatever it was, it was something that troubled the Laedan and that, for the moment at least, Lowell carried a fleeting sense that he might have poisoned his own son.

Wisely, Ernest kept his suspicions to himself, but he did make mental note of the shifts in the Laedan's expression and demeanor so that he could share them with Vance later.

"He was supposed to be here today…not you."

Ignoring the gravelly annoyance, Ernest shrugged. "He's following some new leads, asked me to let you know that he thinks he is on to something."

The grunt that was his response sounded to Ernest like the Laedan would rather Vance be here now than following a trail to an end that Lowell was not going to like.

"You said you know what he took?" The direction of the conversation steered away from the mage and his pursuit of the truth back to Nik's suffering.

"Relatively new…been cropping up for a few months across LaGuardia," Ernest answered, relieved with the change of subject. He knew nothing else about Vance's business, but he did believe that informing the Laedan that Jia Marrock was now involved would be a conversation that would not end well. "Powerful shart…made from anthro blood…the plasma to be exact…"

"Anthro?" Again there was that note, as if the answer did not come as a surprise to the Laedan, only a surprise that his son was caught in a much broader web of details Ernest knew nothing about.

"A sophisticated process…there can't be many places to make it…or many with the knowledge to produce it. We'll find them, shut them down if we can. You want me to have the bagger…?"

"No," Lowell sighed with conflicted defeat. "No need to bring him here. Do what you think best with him."

Suspicious now, wondering if the incarcerated bagger knew the Laedan, had ties that could be traced backward and bind the two men together in an unfortunate manner, Ernest nodded. "Very well. I thought you should know we have him, since you instructed…"

"I know what I instructed, but now I don't care. I just want Nik back." Whatever his son had consumed, he surely could not remain in this coma-state forever.

Flattened against the wall, Donnovan balled his fists, much the same as his father had done, and clenched his jaw to keep the outburst burning in his throat from erupting into the space between himself and the other two men around the corner out of his line of sight. Unlike Chief Ernest, he could not see his father's face to read the unspoken nuances, but also unlike the Chief, Donn did not need facial expressions to hear the things his father was not saying. Things that clawed within Donn's belly and sent him back down the corridor from whence he had come, his intent to visit his twin alone temporarily averted. Growling and muttering to himself, he elbowed past others in the corridor, violently pushing aside any who got in his way. As if feeling the radiating heat of his ire, those individuals grew fewer as he barreled down the stairs into the lobby, swept aside to give him an unobstructed path.

The elderly man stepping across the entrance threshold, lowering the hood of his dark blue cloak and wiping the rain from his face, was unaware of the storm brewing inside the Fortress. His head lifted, the words, "Good even, Mas Donnovan..." spoken in greeting.

The gap between the men closed before the words were out of his mouth, Donn grabbing him by the lapels of his cloak and shoving him back against the mullion. The glass in the doors shuttered and creaked, and the older man gestured with one hand for his armed attendants to stand down as Donn cried, "You did this to him!"

Francis Lord used both hands, his grip on Donn's wrist firm but light, to push Donn's hands away from their hold on him. "Why don't we discuss this in private after I meet with your..." he suggested with amicable calmness. Whatever the young Channon was upset about, Francis was astute enough to know that it would be best not discussed in public. By the time his business was complete with the Laedan, Donn would likely have calmed enough to make rational dialogue possible and might give Francis an inkling of the cause of his upset.

"Fa is busy," Donn spat, unaware of any scheduled meeting between the older men when he felt he should always know when HOPE's prelate was due in the Fortress. That the prelate had not told him he was coming, that his father had hidden such detail from him, further soured his mood. "You will answer me now...or you will leave this hall at once."

Such words, a command without giving one, brought the Fortress security agents scattered about the lobby to attention, each one's focus now on the HOPE representative more than it had been moments before. The Prelate's own guard drew into tighter formation around him, weapons at the ready, but Francis remained nonplussed.

"Of course," he said with a genial smile and respectful bow. One day this Channon would sit in his father's place, would be the Laedan HOPE would have to cooperate with, the Laedan his father, and Francis, were grooming him to be. Treating him respectfully, attending his concerns, was a wise choice, and so he added, "Is there someplace private we can talk?"

Donn snorted and marched down another side corridor, expecting the prelate to follow. Fortress security officers stepped aside and trailed at a distance as the prelate and his escort followed Donn. Ducking into a conference room, one he knew would be empty at this hour, Donn waited for Francis to close the door, leaving all of the guards and attendants in the corridor. None of them were happy with that arrangement since the son's temper was well known, but they had orders to give the men privacy, orders that would be obeyed so long as no sounds of distress or violence came from within that private room.

"I want you to get that shart off the streets now!"

"What 'shart' are you referring to?" Francis asked, seating himself at the head of the meeting table when Donn refused to sit for a cordial conversation. The tactical move of placing himself as the head was, for the moment, not recognized as Donn's temper raged.

"The blood drug! The one that nearly killed my brother!"

Francis scowled, and with his elbows on the arms of the chair, he steepled his fingers beneath his chin and stared at Donn without a hint of regret, remorse, or acknowledgment of the claims.

"Yes, our chemists have developed..." he began innocently.

"You do more than develop..."

"Do you believe we would want to poison our own kind? Contaminate them with the blood of the unclean? Risk infecting them?" Sounding appropriately disgusted by the thought, Francis inspected his fingernails as if already bored of the conversation.

"No games. We both know that making benefit of the vermin is better than slaughter. Experimental subjects...manual labor...but a drug that can kill Nik?" Donn spat. "That has got to cease!"

"HOPE does not manufacture..."

"But you know who does!"

"I can find out," Francis challenged, admitting to or denying nothing. "If it is any of our members..." He shrugged before staring into the young man's face. Donn understood too much of HOPE's secret ways, which might turn out to be a benefit to the organization...or a problem. "Made of anthro blood you say? How peculiar." He shuddered with revulsion. "If anyone of ours is poisoning our people...none of this will be available to your brother again. That is my promise to you." It was a promise he could not keep, and they both knew it, but it was a good-faith promise meant to maintain goodwill between HOPE and the Channons, and they both knew that too. If the product was working its way into the communities around the Fortress from sources other than HOPE, then even the organization's reach might not be able to stem the tide.

At least now Francis had an inkling of what the Laedan might want to see him about. And Donn did as well.

"The Marrocks?"

"No longer a problem, I assure you. They have been eradicated from LaGuardia, as you requested."

"Good." There was already the proven promise that Roland had been removed from his position of power and influence, and Addison had not been seen since the hunt at the clinic where he served. After her narrow escape from the Fortress, Jia had not been seen within the borough either, and it was presumed that she had either died in her attempted escape or fled LaGuardia's reaches. There was no proof to support claims of her death, of course, but Donn knew her to be a smart girl, one too smart to return and risk capture or death. Or at least too smart to be caught. So long as she gave the Fortress and the Channons a wide berth and did not demand her father's seat, Donn was confident that the Marrocks would no longer present a problem.

Why demand that position if she, like her father, was Cana as suspected? Too many would be placed at risk if she did so.

No, she would not go that far.

And what could she realistically know that might endanger the Channon's growing choke-grip on power in LaGuardia?

The subject dropped into the position of an uneasy truce. Francis got to his feet, his smile sliding into something feral and lude. "Will we be expecting Channon children soon?" he asked.

"Of course," Donn replied with flippant certainty. He was only just married, and he knew the difficulties of conception which had existed since the Undoing, but he was confident of his chances. Oasis was young and healthy, and the Channons were known for their genetic predisposition to large families. There was no doubt in Donn's mind that his marriage would be equally fruitful, but secretly he was not yet ready for fatherhood. A child would secure his place as the next Laedan, but it was also a responsibility that would tie him down in ways he did not want to be tied.

"Good. I will be happy to hear it. Now, where can I find your father? He will not be pleased that I am late."

"The infirmary…at least that is where he was." Donn could not know if Lowell was still there, and frankly, he did not care. He needed to find Quentin, to feel out what he might know of the existence of this blood drug, what it truly was, where it came from, and how it had come to nearly rob him of his twin. Prelate Francis could fend for himself.

≈*≈

Within the sanctuary of ducts that he hoped would take him to freedom, Roland closed his eyes, rolled his neck from side to side, and welcomed the shift of skin he had not allowed since his capture. He had witnessed his jailers trying to force the change on others, presumably, he imagined, to test the differences in a Cana's blood, seeking the ideal potency for whatever purpose they had planned. It appeared they were seeking the same element within the smattering of Ursa and Fela brought here, as the staff endeavored to force shifts in them as well. It demonstrated their lack of understanding of anthro, however, for in Roland's experience, it was a rare individual, a very immature one or one in tremendous pain or stress, who could not control their body's impulses. Fortunately, the lead doctor and her technicians had never put his belief to the test. They let him be, so long as he cooperated with their demands, but after so many days of captivity, he burned with the itch to run in the night, to don wolf senses and hunt.

Not only did the shift feel good, it also made crawling through the vents less cumbersome and made following the scents of rain, of city air, of damp earth and concrete, a simpler thing.

He scurried left down one passage, and then right again, sometimes rising with the angle of the vents, other times dropping, waiting for the wail of an alarm behind him, in front of him, around him. Occasionally the night watchmen were known to enter the warehouse for a brief look around; if such were the case tonight, Liam would be found unconscious on the floor with the grate haphazardly closed nearby and the lab doors left open. With no sign of Roland, the attempted escape would be obvious, an alarm would go up, and another hunt would begin.

No one had tried to escape during his brief time here, but even though the captives were incapacitated, there had to be some contingency plan in the event of a breakout…or a break-in.

But minute after minute passed, the scents of the world growing stronger as the outside grew nearer, the sterile, medicinal smells left behind, and still no alarm was raised. He was forced to pause now and again as a vent was reached and the sounds of his scurrying seemed likely to be audible in the rooms he passed over. At this hour, however, most were settling in for the night or already asleep, and the few who were awake had duties to perform that precluded investigating sounds in the vents. Roland had seen his share of rats in the warehouse, had needed to keep them away from the comatose subjects in their stasis pods. Wherever this place was, rats in the walls and ventilation system were as common as they were in the Fortress and anywhere else Roland had ever visited.

His lips curled in amusement. Tonight, he was one very big rat.

Perhaps, he thought, moving forward again, fortune was with him. More importantly, he prayed it was with Liam, for when Roland's absence was noted, there was no guarantee what fate might befall his young packmate.

꣒*꣒

"I never did trust them," Quentin muttered over the rim of the glass of hemp ale he had poured for himself, watching Donn likewise drink. At this hour, he should have been in bed with his new bride, but Quentin was well aware that Donn's hours, his time spent with his wife, were nothing normal…nothing like the hours Quentin would spend in her bed if given the chance. The tip of his tongue traced over his lips, savoring both the droplets of liquor there and the memory of other, sweeter pursuits he had once had the pleasure of tasting. That, he reminded himself as he lowered his glass and refilled it, was a secret he could never share. Not with her father, not with his employer, and not with her volatile new husband.

If he had his way, however, it was a secret he would one day enjoy again.

Donn slid his glass across the table for more ale, expecting Quentin to pour it. "I thought you were…" he began with a scowl.

"Were what?" He looked at the glass with a disapproving glance but refilled it as expected. He could guess at Donn's meaning, but he was not going to volunteer words that might hint at his knowing Donnovan better than he wanted to be known.

Shoulders lifting in a shrug, Donn grunted. "A member," he finally replied. There were a number of other words he could have chosen, but member was the most innocuous he could think of.

"I am…as, I believe, are you." Quentin leaned back and tugged his thin robe across his chest to shield himself from the cold. The room was just warm enough, but there was a chill that had nothing to do with temperature and he fought against it with the casual gesture. "Any sane man or woman would be; they're mankind's only hope for restoring civilization." The well-practiced party line rolled easily off his tongue as if he had said it hundreds of times before.

"There is no one? In my father's employ? No one who could do this…make this…atrocity?"

Quentin shrugged. "One of the chemists? One of the biologists? I'm no scientist; I don't know what it would take to extract blood and process it into some usable form. Those I'm aware of…perhaps they could…but why would they risk your father's wrath and waste LaGuardia's resources on such frivolous endeavors?"

"Maybe it was a by-product of other research." Research on anthro was ongoing as attempts to find a cure, attempts to keep a fetus from developing anthrozooidic traits, attempts to understand the variances between anthro and normal, or attempts to find ways to more quickly eradicate that segment of the population without harming anyone else, were sanctioned by HOPE in the name of racial cleansing. Lowell supported such research, as did Donn, and so, perhaps unknowingly, had sanctioned the research that led to the creation of what seemed to be a highly addictive, powerful, drug. That he might have somehow supported something that led to his twin's brush with death made Donn's blood burn.

"Such things often are," Quentin agreed. "The best inventions frequently come by accident."

Suspicious, wondering if Quentin thought this drug was one of those 'best inventions', Donn emptied his glass. "Dunno about that…" But it was easier to believe the creation of this drug was an accident than to think it was an intentional creation, though Donn would never call it a good thing. Believing in the accidentalness of the situation took some of the sting out of Nik's close call.

He was going to have a word with his twin as soon as the other awoke in the hopes that Nik knew more about the substances he had imbibed that night than merely their addictive qualities.

"Well, they've found the bagger…Chief Ernest and his Protectors…so perhaps we will know more soon." With some of his explosive ire scorched away by the burn of alcohol and no obvious satisfaction gained by confronting his father's closest advisor, Donnovan left his glass on the table between them, stood, and yanked open the door. Maybe he should have opted for coming into the room swinging. It might have given him more answers than he had gotten. "If I get my hands on the person behind this…get my hands on the bagger's neck…"

He did not need to finish. With the door thudding closed between them, Quentin guessed at the rest and stared at the younger man with a thoughtful expression.

ふ*ぐ

The exterior grate was rusted in place, a worrisome discovery that frustrated the steel-grey Cana as he pushed, hoping to find some easy way of opening it. The bolts that held the grate to the wooden frame they were inset into were on the outside of the duct to allow for cleaning, with no consideration given to the possibility of needing to open it from the inside. With no tool to budge the bolts, the only obvious possibility was to go back, but that was not an option. Roland paused, considering his alternatives, sniffing the air and peering through the louvered slats to judge his location and the threats that might be nearby.

The compound, whatever it had once been, contained, as far as he could see, only the single level building he was in and two dual-level towers to his left and right marking the corners of a tall fence topped with sharp-tipped wire. Three metal container units, the sort he knew had once been delivered on large trucks, waited side by side, near enough to the fence that he could use them to vault over it, if he could get past the six individuals taking boxes from one container to transfer into another. They were the only people Roland could sense, workmen in dark grey jumpsuits similar to what he was given to wear every day he had been here, covered, in response to the rain, with black coats and high boots that protected them from mud and water. The temperature was warmer than normal for this time of year, and the rainfall was light, but the six worked quickly, one marking tally as the others shifted contents back and forth.

Inventory, Roland concluded, but of what sort he could not tell. If none carried projectile weapons, which he believed to be true as he could see none upon them, and none carried hidden charge sticks, he could fight off the six with ease under peak conditions. But he was not at his peak, malnourishment having sapped his strength, and so he watched and waited, letting minutes tick past until the six filed away from the now-closed containers, each with a box of supplies in their arms, heading to his left where he presumed a door waited to welcome them back into the warmth of the complex.

He could not see the edge of the building left or right from his angle of sight through the grating, so it was difficult to judge precisely how big the facility was. Were there other rooms of stored anthro? Other labs for other experiments? Other fates awaiting the men and women behind him that he was unable to imagine?

Too late to retract his intention. It was either escape or give up. Either risk his efforts being heard or go back to Liam. A deep breath held, tufted ears flattened against his head after another moment's careful listening to the unfamiliar landscape beyond the duct, beyond the building, beyond the fences meant to protect whatever work was being done here...

...wherever he was...

...and his choice was made. Hearing nothing unusual or suspicious, he charged, head turned to the side, thick muscular Cana shoulder dropped low to bear the brunt of the impact with the metal grate. The metal itself, thin, rusted, and worn with age, buckled beneath the blow, but it was the wood around the grate that splintered and gave way so that the entire assembly erupted outward and fell with a clatter that was thankfully muted by the mud into which it landed. The sound of his body slamming into the grate, however, could be heard by the guards in both distant towers; men's voices cried out, shouting commands, as the hairy half-beast burst out of the duct and landed on its feet.

Twelve bounding steps, his strides longer than any man could make, ended in a leap that turned into a roll on the roof of the nearest metal container. Several cracks cut the air, accompanied by the newly birthed wail of an alarm, some searing the air behind him, above him, until one pierced the air before him with an acidic smell he had never encountered before. It cut through his flight and turned his final leap over the fence into a stumbling jump. Something bit into his shoulder, embedding there like a fist of burrowing fire beetles, but he could not stop. The position of the moon behind the clouds indicated he was facing north, and ahead of him, across a flat expanse devoid of structures, were the dark hulks of the abandoned city, empty shadows that could, he hoped, provide somewhere to hide so that he might assess the damage. Behind him, however, the sounds of boots running in mud, the baying of tracking dogs, the shouts of men, drove him on, forcing him to run in spite of the pain, through unfamiliar streets with the chance to seek shelter.

This was not LaGuardia. This was not any place he knew. Wherever he was, he believed that if he ran north long enough, he would find freedom…or else collapse and die in the pursuit of it.

In the window, the room dark, the tall shape obscure and indistinct, watched his marksmen hit their quarry, watched the beast stumble but refuse to drop as it disappeared into the maze of city veins.

It proved Laedan Channon's suspicions, as well as his own curiosity. He had debated this course long enough and, trusting his men and their hunting dogs to do as he had bid them, felt no regrets for what he had done.

Roland Marrock was a good man. An honorable, decent man, a boon to his people as had been generations of Marrocks before him. That he was also of impure stock could not be blamed on any failing Marrock possessed. It was for that impurity that such men must die, but at least he would die on his feet, fighting for his life, not as some lab experiment that robbed him slowly of life. The man deserved an honorable death.

It was, Geary thought with his hands behind his back as he continued to listen to the wailing alarm and the baying of dogs on the scent of prey, the least he could do for the man. He admitted however that letting Marrock return to LaGuardia's Fortress to confront, and hopefully dispose, of the Channons would be an end more fitting than death by bullet and beast.

Maybe he would be lucky enough to escape and do just that. Perhaps Geary would travel to LaGuardia's Fortress to be certain.

Channon was an untrustworthy ass. Marrock, at least, had been a man of principle.

Too bad he was also a damned dog.

&Scratch the Sky&

Chapter 22

"Chart…"

Jia barely managed to grab Kato's arm to yank him back against the building in the alley that was their approach to the Bunker. There was a bitter, visual exchange, one concerned, one annoyed, until he noted a familiar scent in the air, a groaning and shuffling that forced his impulse to object to being held down into his core. Her constant control annoyed him, even though it had been his choice to follow her, but this was familiar territory for her, and this was her family at stake, not his. He had no desire to see anyone killed, not even the irritating mage with whom Jia had conversed steadily on their trek across the city.

He would have preferred to wring their destination out of the shorter man and be done with him. Between Fela and Cana senses, did they really need a Tracker…particularly one with an obvious interest in Jia?

Obvious to Kato, at least. He was not so sure either of the other two was paying attention to that detail.

It did not help Kato's attitude that the business at the Protectorate had delayed their departure, matters with the Chief and whatever other arrangements Segara felt it necessary to make dragging too long into the late morning hours. Within fifteen minutes of their departure, a pro anthro rally and the countering group of protestors they faced quickly escalated into a riot that clogged the most direct route toward wherever the mage intended to go, forcing them to take side streets cluttered with rubble and debris. There was a brief debate as to the wisdom of putting down the conflict before it erupted into something bigger and more deadly, but Jia stood firm. Surely the three of them could not control a riot. Before they could reach an agreement, several uniformed Protectors arrived to enter the fray, enough men and women to separate the combatants and eventually restore peace.

He had been uncertain, lured by the prospect of standing up for the rights of his kind in a way he had never done before, but Kato gradually concluded as he listened to the argument, that Jia was right, though it galled him to do so. Such a delay would waste more time than they had lost loitering in the Protectorate, waste more than they spent picking their way through decaying streets and collapsed buildings. Where the mage's duty might lie toward the rioters and his fellow Protectors, Addi would be waiting for his sister in the Bunker, if he had encountered no problems in his procurement of mediplies, and Jia would not make him wait any longer than necessary. Addi was Cana, but Kato had no idea if the meek man could, or would, protect himself in a fight. If it had been Vanya waiting out there alone, Kato would have stopped at nothing to return to her. He could not fault Jia for her choice.

Besides, the Pack was waiting for them too, and Jia still had a mission of her own to accomplish, one that involved the map to a blood processing facility, a map that existed only in the mage's head, in his veins. She needed the Tracker, and others needed him if the truth about Lowell Channon's plans, whatever they were, was to be uncovered and a lethal substance removed from the street. They could not risk injury or death in a brawl that was not their concern.

And judging by the grip she maintained on Kato's arm as they listened to the movements in the unseen street beyond their position, she needed him, though he was less certain, crouching to spring on any enemy, what she needed him for. Unlike Segara, Kato did not think he had a distinct purpose. But if she trusted him enough to want him here, he accepted that as reason enough to remain where someone wanted and needed him to be.

The Pack was Jia's chief concern. Her brother. Her father. Liam. Even Vanya. Kato's selfish tetchiness would result in unnecessary turmoil if she allowed it to. She looked at his arm beneath her hand, strong, sinewy, masculine. The Fela was her concern as well. She had offered him and his sister sanctuary in the Flushing Pack and would now honor that offer at all cost. The mage could do as he felt compelled, accompany her, strike out on his own, follow where duty demanded, but Jia was returning to her brother.

It was Vance's duty to her, the agreement and promise he had made to help learn her father's fate, the pledge he had made to the Laedan to find a missing shipment of mediplies that might not be medical after all, and an agreement made with the Chief to find Sal's killer and the origin of a substance that was no longer a mythological rumor but a dangerous reality, that kept the Tracker at her side despite the prickly company of the taller man. If not for duty, the lure of taking out his aggravations upon the rioters for Sal's death, the Laedan's falseness, and the attraction to a woman who sometimes looked to be little more than a vulnerable child when he stole glances at her, would have proven a strong one. Either that or he would have peeled off into the first dive he found for a drink.

That they traveled southeast in the general direction of the beacon within his head kept him moving until their abrupt stop in the decay-congested street where they were now. The howl that reverberated through the moist foggy air nearly thirty minutes before, echoed through the borough's streets and in his core, had hastened their steps, sparked a yellow glaze of panic in the Fela's eyes, and, as they ran, prompted Vance to reach for his shock stick. The howl could have belonged to anyone, some Cana other than Addi Marrock, or one of the many wild dogs and wolves that roamed the uninhabited corners of the city ruins. But Jia's resolve to reach its location of origin as quickly as possible suggested to Vance that it belonged to someone she knew.

Who else could that be but the brother she had traveled to the borough with?

"How many?" Vance knew the sound, the smell, of grubbers, the stench of sewage, putrid flesh and the cloud of rancid meat vapors that surrounded them regardless of their most recent meal or the newness of their creation. The smell was there from the moment they were 'born' and stayed with them until they ceased to function. Protectors were often called to clear out nests of the creatures that infested vacant structures and sometimes spilled into the streets or into the buildings others called home. He had not come equipped with either a blade to decapitate them nor a fire grenade to set them all on fire, however, and stopping to gather grubbers for a bonfire was no more a sensible use of time than breaking up the riot had been. The sky behind the clouds was darkening, the onset of evening looming, and unlike the anthro, the mage did not possess the ability to see well after night fall.

They should have left earlier. He was hungry, tired, and imagined he would be even more of both if he had to fight a swath through a grubber herd, with or without Jia and Kato's help.

Jia shrugged and peered around the corner of the building one more time. "They're scattered…" Most seemed to be further down the street, both to her left and to her right, but there were still some between them and the shadowy structure across the street. The Bunker. "He's in there," she whispered, pointing to the abandoned parking structure where she sensed her anxious brother to be. There was something else she sensed too, something that drew her attention to the broken windows above. Nothing to be seen, no trace of life or visible threat from her current position, but there was no mistaking the familiarity of the tickle across her skin. He had done as she wished. He was still there. They had an additional ally now, and with that help, they might make it across the street through the weaving maze of grubbers without incident.

"We can make it," she decided with a single bob of her head.

Kato grunted in agreement, but it was Vance who remarked, "Of course we can."

The men glared at one another.

"Come on."

They moved slowly, as quick movements were known to attract the attention of the dull-witted grubbers. Quicker movement might mean a quicker escape, but it would draw the grubbers toward the building they hoped to enter without notice. Sounds of grubbers already came from within, too close, Jia could tell, to wherever Addi had taken shelter. Few enough for her and the men with her to put down so long as they did not compound the problem by luring additional grubbers behind them.

The steady approach was more nerve-wracking, however, the possibility of one of the grubbers snatching at them as they passed, infecting them with a bite or a scratch if they got too close, a high one. But their measured movement, staying close behind one another, got them safely into the street and nearly across into a thicker gathering of the sluggish brutes drawn back to the Bunker by the increasing noise made within as each grubber inside converged in a cluster around one car, bumping and growling, sounds that echoed in the largely empty cement structure. The three moved closer together for protection, body to body to avoid being separated by the press of decaying flesh.

The Omega, his skin wet with rain, droplets hanging from his lashes, gauged that the odds against his Alpha's survival were growing smaller with each step she took, and dropped from an open window above to take up the rear guard position, shoving the mage forward as his feet hit the pavement, out of the reach of a grubber whose clawed, emaciated fingers were inches away from the smaller man's exposed neck. Vance stumbled as he wheeled about to face this potential threat, the shocker raised to stun in case the stranger charged him. Deuce's unexpected appearance in the barely empty space behind the trio, and the Tracker's abrupt movement, drew the focus of the surrounding grubbers, luring them in.

The grubber shoved in the opposite direction was far enough away now, slow-moving enough behind Jia, that Deuce ignored him in favor of ducking backward out of the way of the shocker. One bare foot shoved Vance again toward the retreating pair in front of him before Deuce spun, his leg catching another too close grubber mid stomach, and sent it tumbling into those nearest it. The piercing shriek of frustration as grubbers stumbled and fell, the closest thing to emotion grubber's ever showed, was short-lived; Deuce grabbed its head and ended the sound with a twisting yank that pulled head from torso with a sickening sucking sound. Kato turned at the shriek in time to catch Vance's stumbling step caused by Deuce's effort to keep him out of harm's way. He steadied Vance without losing his footing and pulled the mage the rest of the way into the building that generations of Marrocks had called The Bunker.

The Omega remained directly behind, knocking grubbers aside with elbows and forearms until he blocked the doorway, his broad body and kicking limbs protecting those behind him.

"Deuce…" Jia begged.

"See to Addison."

Torn by conflicting pulls to action, Jia looked quickly about her. The commotion Deuce was causing was pulling grubbers back from all along the street; there looked to be more than two dozen…less now that he had dispatched three bodies that began piling up outside of the door…and she did not like the odds that one scratch, one bite, could take the loyal Omega from her. To her knowledge, the grubber infection did not turn anthro, but injury and infection could kill him, and perhaps the fact that no anthro was known to have become a grubber after death was more good fortune than a blessing of genetics. She did not want Deuce to be the first to prove that theory wrong, did not want him to die.

But there were grubbers within the Bunker as well, less than she had believed, only four of them badgering and bludgeoning the car with no tires and wooden side windows, trying to reach the pungent scent of Cana distress within. Jia could not attend both, and there was nothing in the immediate vicinity with which they might block the doorway, save for an automobile door panel and a scattering of ancient, crumbling cement blocks. Even if they had to pile all of the usable ones in front of the gaping passage, the blocks would not hold against a herd indefinitely, and blocking the doorway meant no easy route of escape except down the stairs and into the sloshing of sewage sludge that filled the train tunnel deeper than she cared to travel through.

"Get him," Vance barked, seeing the only opportunistic distraction they had. The button on the side of the shocker was depressed into the locked position, igniting a popping, sparking burst of crackling light at the end of the stick. The feature allowed the stick to be used as an emergency flare, as a light source that would burn up to fifteen minutes…thirty at most…before the internal battery was depleted, leaving the shocker usable only as a club. He pushed Deuce down with one hand between the man's bare shoulder blades and heaved the shocker into the street as far from their position as he could. The hissing and sizzling the stick made as tiny sparks spat in all directions, the warmth, and the sharp stench of burning chemicals it gave off distracted many of the grubbers, and the sounds emitted by the growing cluster of decaying bodies that gathered around it drew still more until even those that had been pressed against the security gate through which cars had once entered and exited the building, were drawn away.

Pulled between the two fights still, Jia gave in to Vance's command and Kato's pull on her arm. Dividing their resources was necessary, and though he was still recovering from the injury to his side, she knew Kato was not going to allow her to enter any fight alone. He would have felt more confident surging into a fight in Fela form, or at least being more healed than he was, but those hindrances did not prevent him from yanking one grubber by the fabric of his wet, moldering sweater and heaving him against the nearest wall. Bent tongs of rebar protruded where the cement had disintegrated, and the grubber stuck there, the metal fangs tearing through his torso and holding him like a fish on a hook. Gradually the weight of his decaying flesh would mean he would slide lower, the rebar ripping muscle and skin and cracking bone, until he fell to the ground, free to hunt again if he was still able.

By then, Kato suspected they would be far away from this place and the grubber would be someone else's problem. The screeching it produced, however, a sound of frustration rather than pain, would draw those Vance and Deuce were trying to repel back to the Bunker, and so Kato scooped up a shard of glass and slit the thing's throat. It was not long enough or thick enough to permit decapitation, but it did sever what remained of the thing's vocal apparatus. Its mouth continued to move in a silent scream as it tried with outstretched arms to reach him; Kato avoided the filthy clawed points, satisfied that this particular grubber was no longer a threat.

Jia followed Kato into the fight, kicking one of the grubbers aside with enough force that it fell over a collection of discarded automotive parts and chunks of cement which tore away bits of flesh as it rolled. A grubber's decay meant the loss of agility and easy mobility, and as it struggled to rise with a second shriek, she reached for a slab of concrete. One blow to its head smashed what remained of its milky grey facial features. A second blow was enough to rupture the spine and leave the creature flailing incapacitated in the jumble where it lay.

The crash of the opening car door flung the third grubber directly into Jia with a heavy enough impact to knock her off her feet. She rolled away from the thing she had just killed, freeing herself from the one now atop her before it had the opportunity to reposition itself for an attack. Its efforts to grab her exposed arm came to an abrupt end as the crushing stomp of Kato's booted foot ripped the grubbers arm free of its body. The arm continued to twitch as though alive as the body lurched in the opposite direction. Addi scrambled from the car, kicking and thrashing his way out of the reach of the remaining grubber. While Kato drove a long length of rust-red metal through the third grubber's head with enough force to impale the thing to the pile of debris upon which it lay, Jia climbed to her feet, grabbing the handle of the car door. When Addi was clear of the vehicle, Kato shoved the last grubber toward it, enabling Jia to bash it again and again between the door and the frame of the car until the head of the creature was a pulpy mess. It was not decapitated, but its spine was severed enough to drop the grubber to the ground where it twitched several times before growing still.

There was the heavy scraping of an incapacitated vehicle being dragged across the cement floor, pushed in front of the door to produce a barrier that would keep them safe from the grubbers in the street, even those drawn back by the sound, and for the moment, at least, no others emerged from the stairwell that had given rise to the herd to begin with.

"Was afraid you weren't going to make it," Addi hissed through clenched teeth, the sound bleeding adrenalin out of his system although his tension and panting had yet to subside. He embraced his twin while eyeing the three men with her and the bodies of the grubbers they had dispatched.

"We were delayed." Though it was the truth, the mage's apologetic tone held a note of defensiveness. "Segara…"

"The Tracker…I know. We've met," Addi grunted, not surprised that the mage did not offer his hand. Physical contact might tell the Protector more than either of them wanted to know, or have known, and given the pervasive belief that mages could, and often did, locate anthro for HOPE for a healthy price, Addi was not yet prepared to fully trust the man even if his sister did.

Vance shrugged. "Yes…well…" A lot had happened between that meeting outside of the building the Pack previously called home and tonight. Use to such distrust from anthro, and aware that Addi was feeling tense and vulnerable after being trapped by the grubbers, Vance did not take offense at the doctor's demeanor. Vance's nerves too were already set on edge by both the grubber fight and having just watched Kato save Jia's life when he believed that duty should have been his. He wanted to say something, felt a number of jibes be born and die upon his lips, but the Fela had saved his life too, pulling him to safety when a fall amidst the grubbers in the street could have resulted in a swarm of them ripping him to shreds.

The other man to whom Vance owed his life, satisfied now that the grubbers would not make it past the barricade, knelt before Jia, his head bowed, the look, to Vance, of a man expecting punishment or judgment. But Jia, peeling out of her brother's embrace, put her hands on the man's solid bare shoulders and lightly squeezed, the touch enough that, as she raised her arms, he drew to his feet as if pulled by her hands.

"I should not have followed you…"

"I am grateful you did. Thank you," she murmured, feeling once more that this large, powerful, magnificent man did not deserve to be the outcast her father had made of him. Perhaps he should have remained with the Pack for their security, but since she had not given him instructions, and his position as Omega kept him outside of the Pack where he was not required to consult her before acting, she could not fault his choice. He had saved all of them. So long as an Omega did not disobey an Alpha's command and did not anger them, he was unencumbered by their demands. Deuce had already made known his dedication to her well-being. That he had chosen to protect her brother during her absence could not be overlooked.

Jia believed wholeheartedly that Deuce would have been inside the Bunker, throwing grubbers left and right to defend her brother if Addi had not found shelter in that car. The Omega would have given his life to protect someone she loved, although again she wondered why. He owed her nothing, she thought with a surge of melancholy. Maybe he was hoping to be brought back into the Pack now that her father no longer ruled. So long as Addi was protected, Deuce kept watch, biding his time for the moment when his services were needed, and she would reward him for it.

It was sad that he felt the need to apologize for those actions. His smile, in exchange for her gratitude, reinforced the need to draw him back fully into the Pack's heart.

Having looked himself over for injury and finding none, Addi turned his diagnostic focus onto the others. "Everyone alright?"

"We'll live." There were abrasions, bruises, small lacerations on what exposed skin Vance could see on each of them, torn clothing that exposed further injuries, but nothing that looked like either bites or scratches from the grubbers.

Kato shrugged, ignoring the pain in his side where his previous injury pulled and burned. Shoving his hand beneath his shirt to finger the tender, scarred flesh proved that the stitches had not torn and that, for the moment, he was not bleeding. The shift in forms earlier that morning from Fela and back again had, as expected, helped the wound knit. "You got what you were after?" he asked Addi. He knew that Jia had not, but the evening was young. There was still time to find the location of which the mage had spoken.

"Enough to last us several weeks…maybe a month or more…so long as everyone stays healthy," Addi replied with a nod, retrieving one of the packs he had stuffed. From it, he removed a bottle of distilled alcohol and a handful of cloth swabs and set to the task of cleaning wounds, starting first with his sister despite her efforts to push him away to tend someone else first. "There's food too…what I could access here…but I figured the mediplies are more important."

"They are," agreed Jia. "It's going to be a long night…we should rest and eat and give the grubs time to disperse." Now that the building was quiet, and the descending darkness brought colder temperatures with it, the grubbers movements had slowed, their attention no longer drawn toward the Bunker. Soon those within would be able to escape this place. "Where did they…?"

Addi shrugged. "You think I would have come in here if they'd infested the place? They followed some Unders out of the Below…flooded out it seems. They weren't after me." Not at first, perhaps, but grubbers did not discriminate in their pursuit of something to devour. "Still raining?"

Skin stinging where he had cleaned her wounds, Jia gently pushed his attention toward Deuce, the most heavily marked among them. In the near darkness, it was difficult to tell what was mud and what was blood, and they had no temporary light source to make the determination easier. Until the grubbers were gone, they did not want to risk a light. "Not so much." A light rain fell, a constant hiss of white noise forming the background of typical evening sounds, but the worst of the storm smelled as if it had passed.

Kato wrapped his arms around himself and squatted, limiting the exposure of body mass in order to conserve warmth. This was a condition he was accustomed to, hiding in abandoned buildings without a sufficient meal or sufficient warmth. He would have given anything for the heat of a fire, or a shift into Fela to take advantage of the warmth his fur could provide, but not while there might be dangers lurking nearby. The hunk of metal barricading the door should make him feel safe, but the open maw into the Below, despite being filled with water and sewage, might allow other dangers to reach them.

And to his knowledge, no one had checked the collapsing levels above them.

Someone should. Someone should patrol the perimeter. Someone should make sure their location was secure before they let their guards down to eat and rest. But he did not trust leaving Jia with the mage for even a few minutes, time enough to capture her affection.

He scowled at his own thoughts and wondered when affection had entered this equation. Affection was dangerous. Affection got people killed. It had cost him his father, or so his mother had claimed, and in time it had cost him his mother as well. He could not afford to let anyone other than Vanya into his heart.

But how was he going to prevent that?

Deciding that securing their refuge was a good start, putting distance between himself and the Cana alpha, Kato stood again and said, "I should…"

Vance grabbed the Fela's arm and yanked him down, the contact a risk between them, and Kato growled with narrowed amber eyes. The mage kept his shoulders square, his expression set, and released his hold only when he believed Kato would not rise again. "We stay together," he warned, mage senses warning him of Kato's intention to strike out on his own, even if it was in defense of their group. "We each take a window," he advised, shoving wrapped packages of crackers from Addi's pack into each person's hands. "We watch, we rest; we wait until the darkness stays the grubbers, then we head out.

"Watch for what?"

"Anything," Jia answered her brother, ripping open the package and shoving a cracker into her mouth. It was dry, slightly stale despite the packaging, but it was not moldy and tasted good after not having eaten since breakfast. There was the barricaded door, four small windows she could see, and a grated barricade that kept grubbers and others from swarming into the Bunker as cars had once done. Her father had secured that barricade, she had watched him, Maz, Pain, and others do that in an effort to make the Bunker a secure location to escape to. What had become of the door, the access now blocked by the corroded frame Vance and Deuce had put there, she did not know. Someone had most likely appropriated it for some other use, as was done with so much else since the Undoing. In time, the metal grate would be taken away, as well as anything else of potential use and value not already stripped from the Bunker. That would not be tonight or within the next few days, however. Tonight they should be safe.

Ignoring the Fela's agitation, not prepared to deal with that unless she was forced to do so, she asked, "Will the mediplies be secure here?" She believed they would be, but still she wanted Addi's opinion. Asking also opened a dialogue about what came next, a conversation she needed to have with her brother while they rested, a conversation she was not looking forward to.

"While we rest here? Of course?"

"For a few days."

Addi scowled. "A few days?"

With a deep breath, Jia rushed ahead. "We know where he is…he knows," she gestured toward Vance with a tilt of her head. The mage looked at her from the nearby window where he had taken watch. His expression was indiscernible in the darkness. "We know where the plasma is being processed…"

"Plasma? You mean…the anthro blood drug?" Addi's frown deepened. "What does Father have to…that is not our…"

"We have a chance to stop it, Addi, and if Father is there, Liam…"

"They won't be. Why would they?" There were several good reasons that sprang instantly to mind but Addi did not want to consider any of them possible.

But it was Vance who snorted and replied, "Because someone is going to a lot of effort to round up anthro…because their blood…your blood…is too valuable to kill you unless necessary."

"I thought you believed that Lowell…"

Grasping her brother's hands, Jia nodded urgently, "I still do."

"It would be too risky to keep a political rival alive for his blood." They were words Jia might not want to hear, and Addi did not want to speak them despite what it meant for the survivability of their father. As her expression faltered with regret, Kato growled.

"Sometimes the risks are worth it."

Those six words were a reflection of each of them at that moment as they weighed the risks that lay before them. Jia tried to smile at Kato, appreciating what he was trying to convey in a fight that was not his, but it was Vance who spoke next.

"Laedan Channon might be behind all of it…the plasma drug…the hunts…your father's abduction…the stolen…" The mage stopped short of saying the word that should have come next, instead finishing with, "supplies…"

Believing the Tracker referred to the mediplies he had been questioned about before, Addi asked, "You're saying he stole them from himself? Why would he…and why would he ask you to…?"

Vance pushed his damp hair from his face after a glance out the window, laughter alerting him to a trio of inebriated individuals staggering down the street. Inebriation sounded good right now. "I don't know. It doesn't make sense, unless he wants to throw me off the trail of the truth." The truth being perhaps, he thought bitterly, that it had not been mediplies stolen at all but had been a cache of weapons that smelled suspiciously unlike shockers and metal blades. "Claiming them stolen would be easier than telling the truth…just not as helpful."

Realizing the truth of that statement, understanding enough of politics, human nature, and the sort of savvy Channon possessed, Addi almost felt bad for the mage sent on a wild chase where, even if he uncovered the truth, he might not be able to report it if that truth ran counter to the Laedan's plans. If there was a link between missing mediplies and drug manufacturing, or anthro research, and a connection to Roland, then approaching the missing shipment from the angle of a drug inquiry, investigating one thing exposed another, it might be the only way to reconcile the truth…and expose the Channons for the conmen they were. Addi knew none of the Channons, except Jonni, as well as his sister or their father had, but what he did know often made him question how Jonni could have turned out to be a decent man.

Maybe that veneer of goodness was a hoax and Jonni was as much of a con artist as Addi believed the rest of them to be.

"You still believe Lowell had Father…?"

"Removed? Yes." Jia felt certain of that more than she did any of the other details. "If not Lowell…then Donn and Quentin…someone there knows the truth…and I believe that same person is connected with this drug trade."

"They might not be connected at all," Vance warned again. "It might only be coincidence…"

"You don't believe that."

Vance shrugged to her challenge and continued watching through the window.

Each one took a position at a vantage point to watch the night as they ate, regaining their depleted energy in the silence of the Bunker. Kato, still perturbed that the mage had dared to touch him, hold him back from his intended scouting, took the window furthest from the others and stood with his back to them, pondering again why he was here amongst people he was only marginally comfortable with. Deuce crouched atop the debris they had piled in the doorway, seemingly oblivious to the cold breeze pushing inside, while Addi stood with his sister at the wide grate where they could both see out, his hands curled around the metal to give them something to do besides fidgeting at his side.

"I should get these supplies to the Pack."

"A few days more…we might need your skills…"

"They might too."

"QiangXu says…"

"I know what he said…but you can't seriously trust the Pack's welfare to total strangers." QiangXu was no stranger, not to Addi, and the small nearby Pack was no threat to the larger Flushing Pack, but there were other threats in the world, and Addi would feel much better if he was there, with the mediplies, with his wife and children, to take care of them if necessary.

"I trust Maz and Trill."

Jia was worried about the Pack's welfare in unfamiliar territory, and she knew her brother sensed it, but she also believed that following the mage's lead would bring her to Liam and her father. She would be amiss not to try to find them, not to rescue them, if the opportunity was there.

"Our Alpha should be with the Pack."

His words, his tone, were low, barely audible, but both made Jia frown. Was that the seed of discontent between father and son that had existed for so long that Jia had been unable to identify or understand it? Had Addi believed that Roland should have been more with the Pack and less in the world, mired in politics and the extended absences made in search of things that he deemed important. Every Marrock since the Undoing had been Laedan; to expect anything else of Roland was preposterous. And thanks to secrets the Alpha had unearthed, secrets that placed his life in jeopardy, the Pack had been placed at risk and the Marrocks forced out of their long-held positions of leadership. Was it not enough for Addi that Jia would likely never take up their father's mantle as Laedan? Was it her fault that their father had been hunted, captured...possibly killed...in the name of political secrets? Did Addi expect her to turn her back on their father...on Liam...and forget what both had given so that the Flushing Pack could survive?

Or was he simply afraid?

When she did not speak, Addi sighed without looking at her. "No, of course you can't give up on them. You can't be domesticated." His hand covered hers on the grate. They were twins, yes, but Jia had always been the free spirit, the adventurer, the curious and fearless one. The one more likely to follow Roland into the world than to settle for the quiet life of raising and teaching pups. The one so much like Roland it was little wonder he had appointed her his successor, even if that meant the pack was often left to fend and protect itself. "That's not who you are."

"Someone's out there."

Everyone clustered around Kato and tried to see what he saw through the small window where he was positioned. It was difficult to get a clear view in the darkness as they jockeyed for a better line of sight, and seconds passed into minutes, dragging the feet of time with their held breaths and straining ears until the movement came again. A shadow form dragging, staggering, struggling as it pulled itself along the ivy-covered wall of a distant building. A grubber, perhaps, although it moved more like a person in agony than a cold, uncoordinated dead thing. The current of the wind blew between them, keeping the individual's scent from reaching them, or theirs from reaching it, but still the shadow paused as if feeling ill at ease, breathless and weak, before beginning what looked like a slow, painful slump to the ground, hands clawing at the vine-covered building in an effort to remain upright, barely noticing, or perhaps beyond caring, that grubbers were nearby. In the cold and dark, the grubbers were no longer a threat, likely to remain where they stood, moaning and swaying, as they waited for the warmth of day or a hot-blooded meal to pass within easy reach.

The figure made a sound, something louder than a groan of agony but not a word or any attempt at speech. A sound that could have been swallowed by the wind if the Cana and Fela had not picked it up with their above average hearing. Deuce tensed. Jia's breath caught.

"Open the door!"

She had already reached the corroded car frame and was trying to move it herself. She could have climbed over it, squeezed through the opening where the Omega was perched, but it was not getting out she was concerned about. It was getting back in.

"Jia…"

It was the first time Kato had said her name, and though the sound of it sent a tingle up her spine, one that sparked brighter as his hand covered hers, she shoved those feelings away after a brief hesitation to be examined another time.

"We move this…now!"

There was no hesitation from Deuce and only a slight one from Addi. At the window, believing one of them should continue to watch, Vance glanced back and forth between their effort to move the car frame to the figure that had now dropped to its hands and knees, its head hanging forward in a position of collapse and defeat. Though unfamiliar with anthro in their changeling forms, and despite the night settled between them, it was apparent to the mage that it was no man there, but rather a wolf in the form of a man. Perhaps Jia had seen that too and her alpha instincts were to give the Cana aid. The frame, by now, was shoved aside enough for her smaller body to squeeze out of the Bunker and into the street, despite Addi's efforts to restrain her, and Kato, refusing to allow her to face an unknown risk that might be a trap, alone, squeezed through behind her.

"Father!"

The word split the night, stirred the nearest grubbers into a disorganized shuffling. The men in the Bunker looked at one another, Addi not daring to believe what his senses, and his sister, were suggesting. Still, he scrambled to the collection of mediplies and Vance, still at the window, watched with quick wary glances up and down the street for any threat Jia's cry might have roused. Clearing the doorway enough to bring the other man inside was left to Deuce, the man's size and strength enough to finish the effort alone while in the street, Jia and Kato reached the broken form. No longer a shadow. No longer missing.

The blood scent was heavy in the air as she caught his thin body in her arms, her hand coming away red from the spread of it across his shoulder. He had been bleeding too long, running for his life on three good limbs, ignoring the injury in favor of freedom. In favor, she was sure, of reaching her, reaching Pack…reaching home. Less than a dozen blocks and he would have reached their abandoned home and then, weak with blood and apparent hunger, with the hunters likely still watching the location for the Pack's return, he surely would have died.

The miracle that had brought them both to this place on the same night would never be discounted.

His body shifted form before their eyes, the man replacing the beast, and though he tried to rise to greet her, he collapsed against her with a single, rasping word. "Jia…"

Thin though he was, his slack body was too much for her to manage alone. Kato without instruction or request, hoisted the nude man upright. He winced, the effort pulling at the stitches in his side, but Jia took Roland's other arm, draped it over her neck, and despite their disparate heights, together she and Kato brought him past the grubbers and into the Bunker, his feet leaving dragging scuffs in the mud and leaves of the street. A trail, along with the dripping blood, that any could see and follow if they chose, but maybe, she thought as they lowered Roland to the Bunker floor, the disjointed herd of grubbers in the street and the gathering of evening fog would be enough to discourage anyone who might be looking for him.

Someone was obviously hunting him. Roland would not have been running with such an injury otherwise. Deuce, concluding the same, crouched on the car frame to keep watch over the now partially cleared doorway.

The coarse chill of the Bunker's cement floor made the other man twitch and open his eyes as Addi, shocked and disbelieving, muttered, "He's lost a lot of blood."

"Can't…stay here…must…reach the…"

"Not going anywhere like this," his son scolded, already untying the loose fabric around Roland's neck as Jia clutched his limp hand between hers. The keycard dropped free and Roland reached for it with his other hand.

"Who did this? Where…?"

"Not now," Addi hissed at his sister, surprised their father was still conscious.

"We have to…" She was not insensitive to her father's state, but the fact that she feared to lose him all over again from the torn gash in his shoulder, an injury made worse by the abuse he had pushed upon himself, was too real. If there was even the slightest chance that he could tell them anything about where he had been held, who had done this to him and why, about the ledger and the journal that no one seemed able to find, she had to have those details while he drew breath. She was Alpha; it was her responsibility to know.

Just as Roland knew it was his responsibility to tell her. He winced and squeezed her hand as Addi examined the wound, both the movement and the probing sending tendrils of sharp pain from the gash to every corner of Roland's body. "Liam…" he began.

His voice faltered, a particularly sharp stab of pain robbing him of consciousness as Addi found the small metal projectile lodged in his father's shoulder. "Father!" Jia hissed, wanting to shake him awake, but Kato's hand on her arm stayed her as much as the quick glance from her brother did.

"Let him rest…nothing vital hit. I'll stitch him up but he needs to…"

Addi's words were cut short when Vance picked up the keycard without thinking about it and then dropped backward from his squatting position onto his ass beneath the onslaught of sensory input that came in that touch. The strength of the Cana's emotions this night, the tension of the escape, of injury, of flight and fear, had imprinted strongly enough on the card to leave clear images, sounds, and smells that the Tracker could read. Images that he was certain he could follow back to their point of origin, a path he believed, as he closed his eyes to clear them of the dual pictures his mind was forcing to inlay there, was the same he was already following. The sensory map was more vivid, brighter to his inner eye; it would not take questioning the injured man to get answers.

Vance believed he had all the answers they needed in his hand except for how Roland had come to be in that place to begin with.

No one else in the group seemed to notice his reaction to the card, or else were not surprised by it. The mage found both to be slightly disconcerting.

"Once he wakes I have to know…"

"Only when he wakes," Addi warned. "No one is waking him or moving him until then."

"We stay here."

No one seemed willing to disagree with the Omega.

Jia's eyes pleaded with her brother for something more definitive, more promising. What if Roland did not awaken? What would they do then? Not considering that the mage might hold the answers in his hand, how would they ever find Liam if Roland never recovered?

"He'll make it," Kato reassured her. Addi nodded, though with less confidence.

"And we'll find Liam." Jia met Vance's gaze and tried a grateful smile. She wanted to believe them, but as her father's hand grew cooler and clammier within hers, she doubted she would ever speak to her father again.

⮞Scratch the Sky⮜

Chapter 23

Far out to sea, slices of light webbed across the sky, igniting the distant clouds as the worst of the storm rolled south, away from land. Fat drops of water splatted against the wide panes of glass, but they came slower now as the worst of the storm relented and moved beyond them. Finger's interlocked with those of the man who lay beside her, their nude forms intertwined as the sheen of spent passion was slowly absorbed into the artificially warm air of this room, Oasis kept her eyes on the window, preventing underlying thoughts from being too easily read.

His focus, however, seemed to be more on the labored rise and fall of her breasts, the flushed, moist skin there, and the press of her knee between his thighs. The sporadic thrust of his groin against her knee sent shivers and tiny groans through his body, a sure indicator that soon enough he would be interested in pursuing a third joining.

She smiled wistfully at the thought. He was a far gentler, more thorough lover than his son.

She had known all along he would be.

"I remember the big storm…when I was a child…the one that flooded all of the boroughs…I hid under my bed for hours…no one could find me. I think I drove my mother to grief…I think she thought I had been lost to the sea. I wonder sometimes if that was why she died…why her heart gave out."

"I'm sure it wasn't your fault," mumbled Lowell, his heart full to bursting from having her here and listening to her tales of life in Kennedy Borough. "Such things never are. A weakness of heart cannot be…"

"That's what Da says, what the doctors said, but still, sometimes, when I watch the lightning…I wonder."

She glanced at his hooded, sleepy blue eyes. "Do you remember that great storm?"

Lowell nodded. "How could I not?"

Of course, he remembered it not through the eyes of a child but through the eyes of a leader, and a father, consoling family and subjects alike in the aftermath. He remembered Nik's fascination with watching the storm through the window, counting the lightning strikes and thunder booms, singing and howling in tandem with the wailing wind and fighting every effort to draw him to somewhere safer, where the threat of breaking glass was not imminent. He remembered Jonni's determined efforts to gather food and water and any supplies they might need if the storm worsened, actions that hinted at the sort of leader Lowell had wanted him to become but which he would never be. And he remembered Donn's wailing in terror as he hid in a closet with a pillow and blanket wrapped about his head to shut out the noise.

In that, at least, Donn and Oasis had something in common.

Mostly Lowell remembered the flooded streets, the walls that kept out the rising sea keeping the water inside as well, streets littered with the bodies of the dead who turned to grubbers, the extensive effort to gather them all, to treat the injured, to reroute the water out to sea. It had been the exposure to the suffering of so many, Lowell believed, that led to Jonni's choice towards a life of medicine, just as that disaster had affected Addison to do likewise. And it had been Lowell's decision to bring his boys into the disaster in the streets so that they could gain an appreciation for the work required of a Laedan. Lowell had turned his son to that path.

Perhaps it was time to stop blaming Jonni and accept the inevitability of a mediprofession. Being a doctor was not a bad or ignoble path. It just was not the one he wanted for his eldest son.

"There were so many casualties…I thought the water would never recede." His hand untangled from hers and his fingers slid over her belly to the secret places hidden by her bent knee.

"But it did…and the world went back to what it was." Oasis squirmed and smiled and kissed the corner of his mouth as her body reflexively arched to his touch. "It prompted my appreciation for engineering, how to make water go where we need it to go…how to keep it there…how to keep people safe."

"You know architecture and engineering?"

She laughed softly at his surprise and sat up. "There's a lot you don't know about me," she teased. She missed the warmth of him pressed to her side, but the horizon was beginning to give birth to the grey rays of day and she could not stay here any longer. Since Nik's odose, Donn had slept beside his hospital bed, leaving Oasis blissfully alone and unmolested. It had presented the perfect opportunity to corner Lowell here in his office and to take…and give…what they had both been dancing around since her coming to LaGuardia. They had no blankets, no pillows here, but the door was locked, as Lowell normally kept it when he was not here, and the desk between them provided a psychologically protective barrier in case someone was inclined to break in.

Donn would never expect to find her here. He would not return to their room until the medics came to examine Nik's condition. It gave her enough time, if she dressed and left now, to return to her bed before Donn ever noticed her absence.

And if by chance he did return to the room and find her gone, well, the Fortress was big enough, with enough corridors and rooms and secret niches, that she could be anywhere. With no adequate view from their room of this particular storm, she could claim to have been anywhere watching it and he would never know the truth.

"Lay down…"

"I have to go…you know I do." She slipped her gown over her head, allowing it to pool about her hips, exposing just enough enticement to lure his fingers back to their gentle stroking. Her legs shifted, parting in invitation as she smoothed her hair with her fingers, but once she was satisfied that she looked presentable, she reluctantly moved away from his hand and got to her feet.

Lowell scowled with frustration, but she was right. Sunrise would bring duty soon enough, and he should be dressed to meet the new day's obligations when they came.

"Breakfast?" It was a feeble attempt to keep her with him, to keep hold of the feeling of rebirth and new life that swirled inside.

Again she laughed. Her robe was tied about her waist, covering most of the areas he most wanted to touch and kiss, but she bent over him and covered his mouth with hers for a kiss full of promise.

She did not speak those promises, did not lay claim to any future day or hour or place where they might be together again. In this place, such promises would be too easily broken, too difficult to keep. They would need to be content with whatever they could get of one another.

Even, she thought with a neutral expression, her back to him as she snuck through the door and into the hall where he could no longer see her, if that meant never again.

But she was not done with Lowell Channon. In fact, she was only just beginning.

⫷*⫸

A sound roused him, though as his head jerked up from where his chin rested on his chest, the only thing he heard was the wind pushing through the ventilation shafts and the splatter of rain on the roof over his head. The faint glow of the night lighting chased complete darkness from the room, dispelled the early gloom of the storm that raged beyond the window. Not yet morning. Why was he even awake?

His chin and chest were damp from his drooling in his sleep, and he muttered something demeaning and insulting at himself as he dragged his sleeve across his face and looked at the large plate of glass into the corridor beyond. He half expected someone to be there, to have rapped on the glass to get his attention, someone who would have seen his undignified posture and state, but no one was there.

A dream then, he groaned, rubbing the back of his stiff neck to ease the pain and stretching to straighten his back and relieve the ache in his spine. Sleeping in this wooden chair was not the best for his body, his posture, and did not allow for a decent night's rest, but if his father, his brother, the doctors were not going to provide Nik with around the clock supervision, Donn sure as hell would. Jonni came off and on throughout the day, willingly staying with Nik to allow Donn to tend to business, to eat, to shower if he chose, and truthfully, Donn knew that, whatever his failings, Jonni loved Nik too and would have stayed overnight as well, if Donn did not stubbornly insist on doing it himself.

It was a damn sight better than their father was willing to do. Laedan or not, Nik deserved more from their father than five or ten minutes of being stared at through the window a few times a day. And the medistaff had many other duties to perform, both in and out of the Fortress. They were not paid to remain at Nik's side...another failing on Lowell's part.

If Donn was Laedan, he would have made damn sure one of the medics was nearby, in case Nik needed emergency attention. His vitals may have stabilized, his color normalized, enough so that the binding straps had been removed, but he had yet to open his eyes and his brothers, at least, found that worrisome.

"Water."

Donn jumped with a start at the voice he did not expect to hear, and then immediately yanked Nik into an embrace.

"You're an idiot..." Voice rough with emotion he rarely showed, never having been good at voicing love or affection in ways most people could appreciate, they were the first words that popped into Donn's head and the first ones to pass his lips. "Could have died."

Nik mumbled something unintelligible, tried to pull away and reach for the hemplastic cup that sat next to a water pitcher on the bedside medistand. Or maybe, thought Donn with a scowl, he was reaching for one of the two syringes there, one with a sedative to help Nik sleep, if necessary, and the other containing something meant to revive him if his body began to fail and he started to slip away. Donn quickly filled the cup and helped Nik sit enough to drink it, choosing to believe that after the mumbled request for water, the cup was what his brother wanted.

Three cups of water later, Donn felt relieved that his assessment was right.

"Only...wanted..." Nik's eyes began to roll back into his head. "Normal...sleep...awake now..."

His body went slack in Donn's arms, his lips drooped to one side, allowing saliva to dribble free, and though his eyes did not close, they darted from side to side as if wildly seeking something in a state of panic.

"Nik...damn you...wake up..." Donn shook his brother by the shoulders, which did little more than bring Nik's eyes into focus.

"Not sleeping..." Nik mumbled, slipping from Donn's grip like an eel from a fisherman's hands. "You know me...don't sleep..."

Though he gave a sigh of relief, Donn nodded, remembering all too well the days of their childhood when his parents struggled to determine why Nik refused to sleep like other children, like other people. There had been crying, a constant struggle against the demands of their parents to lie down and sleep. There had been doctor after doctor, chemists, even mages, come to study Nik and learn why he had such a difficult time sleeping. Nik had never suffered for that lack of sleep like others would, but Lowell and Yiva had, forcing a variety of remedies to be tried. Some had no effect at all, some resulted in horrific side-effects that left Nik sick or incapacitated for days. In time, however, the answer had been found and Nik finally slept through the night.

The result, however, was an inability to wake fully, to function, the following day. Nik trudged through his schooling like a grubber, mindless, in a haze that kept him from playing or interacting with others the way he should have. New tests, new remedies.

One to sleep, one to wake. In time each remedy failed, and new ones were sought, setting up a dependency on a cycle of substances...until by the time Nik was old enough to do so, he set out on a quest for his own answers and a never-ending reliance on pills, needles, and alcohol.

It was no wonder Nik was an addict. Thanks to their parents, he had been an addict most of his life. If…when…the shart killed him…the blame was going to fall squarely on Lowell's shoulders, and Donn was going to make sure he suffered for it.

"You can sleep now, Nik…I'm here…Jonni'll be here…he'll be happy you've…"

"Don't tell Da…he…doesn't need to know…always wants me to…sleep…"

Squeezing Nik's hand between his, wondering for the first time if Nik blamed their father as well, if he knew the root of his troubles. Maybe he had known all along. "I won't…I swear it. Sleep if you want…and when you're ready to be awake…we'll do it together."

"Do…together."

Donn was not sure what he meant for them to do together. Get Nik clean? Confront their father? Rule LaGuardia? Maybe something else or nothing at all. Maybe just sit in the quiet darkness and talk about the simpler days when the complications of adulthood did not weigh on their shoulders.

Nik's eyes closed again. His breathing, his pulse, were steady, and instead of lying rigid on his back like a man frozen in stasis, he curled onto his side, knees drawn to his chest, his fingers shoved into his mouth the way he had often slept as a child in those rare instances where sleep had come naturally to him. Anyone seeing him asleep that way would assume he was out of danger now…

…until the next odose came.

It was up to him, Donn decided, to make sure that day never came.

⮳*⮰

The teacup clattered slightly as Ernest set it back on the breakfast tray. He was never comfortable dining in the Fortress, but the Laedan most often insisted they meet over breakfast so that he had reluctantly acclimated to accepting the invitations, if not to the actual dining itself.

Today, despite the heavy rain, the summons was no different, but the Chief had no clear idea how he would answer the questions likely to be put to him. There had been small talk about the weather, questions meant to probe Yiva's condition without either man formally making inquiry, and an early invitation to the not so distant New Year celebration to which the Chief and his top Protectors were always welcome.

Eventually, the small talk fell flat and Ernest's question about Nik's welfare opened the door to the meat of the conversation that he felt Lowell was avoiding.

"I have people seeking the source...substations around the borough looking. There's a middleman...not a bagger but...someone with contacts in HOPE and..."

"You think this is HOPE's doing?" Lowell's slice of toast stopped halfway to his scowling mouth as he glowered.

The Chief shrugged, not willing to point fingers until he had all of the facts. He sat back from his empty plate, debating a request for more tea but hoping he would not have to stay in the Laedan's company long enough to actually drink it. "Someone with the means, the abilities, the knowledge; I don't know of a single source...none of those who typically supply the baggers have the know-how for this level of manufacturing. If not HOPE, then someone with access to a lab...to test subjects...to storage facilities..."

"You make it sound complicated," Lowell scoffed, automatically refilling Ernest's empty teacup. "It could be anyone..."

"To separate plasma from blood and store it..."

Ernest bit his tongue and tugged at his shirt cuffs as if adjusting the too tight fabric. He had not intended to reveal any of what he and Vance knew, and seeing Lowell's wide-eyed expression of disbelief, he knew he was going to have to backpedal the information to avoid revealing any more.

"It's a blood-based drug...mixed with alcohol...my team's working on what else is in it..."

"Someone is stealing blood?"

"Or getting it donated in exchange for something …food or credits or supplies of some sort. It takes mediknowledge, refrigeration, lab equipment…"

"There can't be many…"

Knowing what Lowell intended next, Ernest quickly interrupted, "Stay out of this, Laedan…let my team do their job. If you get Guards in the middle of this, busting down doors, making arrests on a whim…we might never get to the bottom of this. My Protectors know what they're doing. We'll find out…"

"You can't expect me to sit on my hands…"

"I expect you to let us do what we're paid to do."

Lowell grunted, pushed back his empty plate, and crossed his arms over his chest. "And Segara? He hasn't checked in?"

"He's following a lead, like I said…" the Chief answered evasively as he picked up the cup of tea and blew on it to cool it.

"What lead?"

"To be honest, he didn't say. He said he wouldn't be able to check in with me for a few days…that he'd let me know when he got back. You know how mages are…"

'You know how mages are' was an often used phrase to explain anything peculiar, inexplicable, or otherwise that a mage did, and most often, the truth was no one but a mage knew how they functioned. The belief was that mages were prone to erratic behavior, impossible to understand, and anything that could not be easily explained was chalked up to mage characteristics…including a penchant for being out of touch for weeks at a time, for sleeping, eating, or drinking too much, and for taking risks of the sort most sane men and women would not.

Lowell would not know typical mage characteristics any better than Ernest did, and despite years of occasionally employing the Tracker, the Laedan did not know Vance Segara well enough to gauge his character or his actions as anything more than professional…albeit reckless at times.

"As soon as he shows himself, tell him I want to see him. He's avoided me long enough."

"I'm sure he's not avoiding you. He's doing the job you assigned." The tea was too hot, but Ernest gulped it down and put the cup back. "You know he'll report when he has something to share."

Hoping to escape further interrogation, he stood and took his uniform jacket from the back of the chair. "May I check in on Nik while I am here? It might be helpful to know anything else the medics might have learned…to see his condition for myself."

"There's nothing they can tell you…but go."

"And Laedan…" His jacket was now in place and his raincoat pulled over it to protect him when he went outdoors, although it sounded as if the rain against the window had slowed. "Please remember, let us do our jobs. If you want to be helpful…if you want to do something, talk to your fr…contacts…in HOPE. If anyone knows something about this plasma drug, I think it would be them."

No one had friends in HOPE, only contacts. And if anyone was likely to get answers from them, or even a hint of an answer, it would be one of the Laedans. No one within HOPE was going to tell the Protectorate Chief anything.

☙*☙

The metal balcony was unsteady, the rusted bolts pulling free from the deep cement into which they had long ago been sunk, the railing loose upon the platform. There had been no need to repair it; no one came here, no one had a reason to, and deeming it unsafe, some past Laedan had locked this room to keep out the drafts and barricaded the askew sliding door onto the balcony as a further deterrent. With a rocky outcropping a few floors below, gradually being eaten away by the churning surf, any fall from this height would be fatal.

It was not the first time Yiva had been here. Once, long ago, when Lowell had courted her, when they were young and he had been keen to impress her, he had stolen the key to this room from his father's cabinet and snuck her inside, wanting to impress her with his resourcefulness, with the power of the view of the sea, and, she knew now, wanting to frighten her just enough to give him an excuse to reassure her that he would forever protect her from the dangers of this world if she married him.

It was a promise she had believed, a promise he had kept for most of the years of their marriage.

But it was a promise he could no longer keep and she was tired of fighting the world alone.

Getting access to the key had been easy. As the Laedan's wife, no one questioned her access to the cabinet, and though no one had seen her enter here, no one would question her right to be here either. No one except Lowell, if he had been paying attention.

She had not seen him since dinner the previous evening, and though he had not come to her bed, she no longer questioned where he slept or with whom. She had given him three living sons, but in this world where children were the most important resource humanity had, a man like Lowell, with the power and ability to feed them, wanted more. Yiva did not begrudge him that desire, only the broken promise of protection he had made.

Why did he not see what was happening?

He would be at work now, a meeting over breakfast or hunched behind his desk arranging a day of diplomacy and paperwork for the benefit of the borough. He was good at what he did, but under so much pressure now that Roland was missing. Once or twice Yiva had offered to assist him, to take up whatever tasks she could to ease his burden, but Lowell had only chuckled, kissed her cheek, and assured her that he had everything under control. She wanted to believe him, but she was no longer certain she believed in anything.

The biting gale pelted her with heavy drops of water, soaking through her hair and the thin fabric of her shift within moments of climbing onto the balcony. The cold metal was slippery beneath her bare feet but she wanted it that way. There would be questions, and a few might even suspect the truth, but should she lose her footing and fall, it would undoubtedly be ruled an accident, leaving only a minor stain on the Channon name which Lowell would, in time use his skill with words to gloss over and paint away until no one knew the truth.

Perhaps he would even find some poor unfortunate to blame and punish. Yiva should feel pity and sorrow for such a person, but what she did feel was barely enough to give her hesitation now. How could she feel remorse for someone else when she could not feel it for herself? Empty, dead inside, the thought of the outside matching the inside was the only driving force she knew.

"Yiva…"

Having taken the back corridors to her room, Oasis found it as she had expected, empty, unslept in, devoid of any trace of her husband. It allowed her time for a swift shower and the chance to dress, and then she snuck back down that same corridor toward a vacant room she was gradually converting into her own private sanctuary. Private for now, but in time she would need to reveal its existence to her husband.

Or perhaps she would not. He had his private places after all, even though she had already learned where they were. What he did there had yet to be discovered.

It surprised her to see this normally locked door open. It surprised her even more to spot the older woman outside on the metal frame that shuttered and clattered against the Fortress' outer wall with every gust of wind. Clothes and hair dripping, clinging to her body, Yiva might have been there for minutes or she might have been there all night. She looked cold and miserable and Oasis felt her heart go out to her. Felt a moment of guilt.

Did Yiva know what she had done? What her husband had done?

Regardless, Oasis could not leave her there. She had no interest in taking the woman's husband from her; he was the means to an end. He would need his steadfast, long-suffering wife when the day came that Oasis broke their bond, and she genuinely liked the woman and wanted to know her better.

"Don't move…I'll help you…"

She picked her way through the scatter of ceiling tile debris that littered the floor, trying to avoid any injurious steps in her own bare feet. When she reached the jarred open door, it took but a glance to know that the platform would not hold both of them. Holding onto the metal framed edge of the glass sliding door, she stretched her other arm into the rain, her hand splayed wide.

"Take my hand…come back inside…"

Yiva shook her head. Her grip on the rail, the way her entire body shook, spoke of someone not merely cold, but also terrified.

Of what, Oasis wondered. Not the storm, which was gradually subsiding, nor the churning sea which Yiva was staring at with fascinated determination. What then? Oasis looked back over her shoulder at the opened door. Not afraid of being found here; the door had been left open so that anyone passing could see her. Not Lowell since, for all of the man's failings, he appeared devoted to his wife in his own peculiar way. Was the older woman afraid of her?

"You might fall…it would kill you…"

There was a slight movement of Yiva's shoulders, a slight turn of her head, and Oasis gasped. That was what Yiva wanted? To die?

She had never been in this situation before, had never had anyone's life depend on her actions, her words. Not knowing what was wrong, what horrors or despondency the other woman faced, she could not even offer the platitudes of life getting better, of things turning out okay. Her boys loved her, yes, Lowell loved her, but did they need her? Oasis could not even answer that question as she had not been in LaGuardia long enough to learn the Channon family secrets. She could only think of one possible hook, something she would never normally resort to, a possible show of weakness that might well drive Yiva to hate her.

But hate, the potential for revenge or proving Oasis wrong, was at least a reason to live.

"I…please…don't. You're the only woman here…who might understand…who might be able to help…"

Though she did not move from the platform, Yiva turned her head enough to look into her daughter-in-law's eyes. "Help? How can I…" she sounded perplexed and uncertain, "help you?"

"I know I shouldn't…" There was no forcing the awkwardness in her voice as Oasis lowered her hand. This was not a comfortable topic of discussion. "He is my husband after all…"

"What has he done?" There was genuine panic and horror in her tone, the question dragging Yiva off of the platform and into the only slightly warmer room. "Has he hurt you?"

There was enough light from the rising sun to see the dark bruises around Yiva's throat, the sort of bruises caused by choking hands. Oasis' hand came to her own neck, an understanding blossoming within that made bile burn in her stomach. It was a sadistically favorite tool Donn employed in their joinings, the youngest Channon taking perverse pleasure in watching her struggle beneath his hands as he sought his release lower in her body. Believing herself safe, that despite the pain he inflicted he would never actually hurt her, Oasis realized just how wrong she might be.

The pain and humiliation Donn inflicted on her was frightening and unpleasant, something Oasis would avoid if she could, but it was nothing compared to what he could do. And unless these were traits learned from the father by the son, there was only one-way Yiva Channon could bear those same marks.

"He...scares me..." Oasis admitted weakly, no longer knowing what to say. She had learned quickly that her husband was a sadistic, power-driven man who would do whatever he wished to gain what he wanted. But never in the wildest corners of her imagination, would she have dreamt something like this. This was not the abuse of a parent heaped on an innocent, defenseless child.

This was the abuse of a monster on a victim who could never leave him...except by seeking her own death.

Yiva clasped Oasis' hands in her icy, shivering ones. "Don't let him scare you...or it will be worse...so much worse," she begged. "Do not refuse or fight him..." Some fear, some pain, Donn craved. Excessive amounts, however, or too much of a fight, brought with it anger, and anger brought pain and humiliation of a worse sort.

"What has he...why...?"

Shaking her head, Yiva burst into tears, for herself, for this woman trapped in a marriage she had not asked for and could not have imagined, and tears for the little boy she had lost along the way. Oasis pulled the sobbing wet woman into her arms and drew her down until they were both on their knees in the dust of the floor.

"No one else can know…never…never…know…" With her head cradled against the young woman's shoulder, her face pressed into the crook of her neck, she allowed herself to weep over her lot, their lot, for the first time. This should have been her husband offering comfort, but Lowell could never know. LaGuardia's future depended on it.

Oasis understood. The Channon name was at stake.

"This stays with us…I swear it," she whispered.

She did not know what she could do to change anything, but she would find a way. A way to protect Yiva, a way to protect herself. She did not know if it was possible to do both but she was sleeping with the woman's husband.

She owed Yiva that much.

❧Scratch the Sky❧

Chapter 24

There was no sleeping in the drafty Bunker, as Addison and Jia took turns keeping watch over their father, and Deuce, Vance and Kato kept watch over them. The three paced between windows, on alert for whoever was hunting Roland. Jia could feel their eyes on her almost as much as they were on the world outside, and the sensations left by their gazes and concerns left her nerves both soothed and irritated, the irritation contributed to by her brother's additional constant watchfulness. He knew her too well, knew that she wanted to be left alone with their father to rouse him, question him, seek answers about what had happened, where he had been, and what, if anything, he knew about Liam. Addi would not allow that. Roland would wake on his own…if he awoke at all.

The storm waxed and waned throughout the night, sometimes pounding the pavement and walls so hard that distant sounds were cut off from detection and not even the nearest grubbers could be heard, sometimes coming down as a fine misty dusting like fog pushed by the wind. The buildup of water filtered between crevices in the Bunker's upper levels to drip and pool in this ground level cavern, and the rush of it in the streets forced its way into clogged gutters that quickly led to the rise of water levels in the sewers and an overflow into damaged substructures like the basement levels of the Bunker. There was no evidence that the rising water below had crept into the ground level recently, but it was a possibility, meaning it was necessary to monitor that threat as well.

Now, beneath the stagnant smell of tainted water, came another scent, tingling faint and far off, that hinted at the rise of a new day. Each of the anthro sensed it, growing agitated, wanting to be off from this place for a destination they had already intended to reach. Vance could not sense the nearing day in the way they did, but this extended period without a drink, without a decent meal, and without a bathroom or a shower, told him that too many hours had passed since he had last been warm and comfortable. The burning in his blood from his exposure to the anthro drug had lessened, but thanks to the keycard Roland had dropped, the mage knew he could find his destination without that taint within. On and off throughout the night, he had argued with himself about the logic and feasibility of going alone. As a Protector, he had the authority to investigate wherever his leads took him. But with Sal's death still fresh in his mind and an inkling that he was wading into something bigger than any crime he had investigated before, one with the potential to swallow him and erase him from existence, he did not think alone was advisable.

Fingers on Roland's wrist, eyes closed, Addi counted to himself, judging his pulse, listening to his breathing. His father felt warmer to the touch, the bleeding had stopped, and he seemed to be resting peacefully. Deciding Roland was as stable as he was going to be without days of recuperation, Addi looked at his sister and nodded.

"I think we can move him now…get him home…"

"He'll live?"

"If he continues to rest…I don't see why he shouldn't. He's gonna be weak for a while…so much blood lost…but when he's strong enough to change, it will help."

Jia breathed a long relieved sigh and leaned back against the legs of the Fela who had stopped behind her. She took strength from Kato's presence, from the touch of his hand on her head when his fingers slid through her hair. Afraid to look at him, afraid of what she might see, she took the touch for the comfort it was meant to give. This was the best news she had heard in days, but finding Roland, rescuing him, getting him home, keeping him alive, did not negate the rest of her responsibility. Until he was strong again, until he could lead as he once had, Pack authority was still hers. There was still Liam to consider, and the creation center of this anthro blood drug to locate and thwart. Protector Segara would undoubtedly continue to seek that source and as she felt she had been the one to drag him into this, she felt obligated to help him.

She owed it to Liam if nothing else.

"You should take him home."

"Me?" Addi stared incredulously for a moment and then shook his head. "What about you?"

"I have to find Liam."

"Jia…"

"It's my fault he's…"

"Not your fault, Ji…you did everything you could that night. We get father home, get him back on his feet, then decide…"

"I'm not going to leave him out there to die…to be turned into some sort of drug for Normals' consumption," she said stubbornly.

"I'm on that," Vance's footsteps left the window and came to her side where he squatted down to examine the Cana patriarch. He was no medic, no healer-mage, but his tracker gifts did allow him to sense Roland's life force and he had to agree with Addison. Roland was considerably better than he had been the night before. He and Kato exchanged cool, slightly hostile glances, before he added, "I'm not giving up until I track this down."

"And I'm not turning my back on Liam…"

"I can't get him home by myself, Ji, and even if he wakes up, he's in no shape to walk that far…"

"Deuce and Kato can…"

Both men of whom she spoke growled their disapproval of that plan, of leaving her unguarded…of leaving her alone in the company of the Tracker.

"Fortress…"

The word was forced, strained and weak, but it was as much the word itself as the voice that spoke it which made everyone except the

Omega from his watch position look down at the injured man with degrees of surprise and alarm.

"Must...go to the..."

"Oh no," Addi growled, beginning his assessment over now that his father was awake. "You're not going anywhere near that place."

Jia had to agree with her twin this time. Clutching one of Roland's hands in hers, her heart surging with love and joy that he was with her again, she murmured, "It isn't safe for you there...someone tried to have you killed..."

Roland's hand tightened around Jia's as much as his weakness would allow. "That is why I must go back...he needs to know...to see..."

"He? Who?" Until this moment, Vance only had Jia's suspicious belief that someone intended to murder her father to go on. If there was proof, if the co-Laedan knew he had been a target, it would make the mage's job that much easier.

Roland did not reply, did not even look at the mage who was, for the moment, an unknown, unwanted commodity in this equation. Instead, he stared at his daughter, the one person he believed would understand his reason, his need, who would be willing to concede to his wishes and make it happen. They held the contact for the span of several heartbeats as Addi completed his examination, and then Jia closed her eyes with a silent, shuddering groan, something felt by the others around her rather than heard.

His belief that someone in the Fortress, Quentin, Donnovan, or Lowell himself, had orchestrated his death, was no more certain than hers. He wanted to go back, to show them that they had failed, to draw the guilty into some action that would reveal their duplicitous intentions, and, perhaps, expose the plan he believed his death had been meant to cover up. Only by proving that he lived still could he hope to draw them out. There was no choice. He had to go back.

Addi made that same assessment moments after his sister did, understanding their father nearly as well as she did without being inclined to agree with him. "You should wait until you're stronger; you're not up to walking into..."

"No…I'm not. That is why Jia is coming with me…"

Despite her surprise at his statement, Jia nodded; the danger of such a plan eliciting another pair of growls from Kato and Deuce. Roland craned his head around to make eye contact with the Omega, and though his body tensed at the man's proximity, he realized that perhaps the other man's presence here was for the best. Just as having the Fela and the Tracker here could be. What he had in mind could be accomplished with the help of each of them, and if each of those men was inclined to serve his daughter, Roland would make use of that inclination.

"It can be done…" he murmured, the effort to talk weakening him. "But I need each of you to do as I say…"

"I'm not going to like this, am I?" muttered Addi.

The scowls on each of the other men's' faces suggested they too knew they were not going to like whatever the Alpha Cana had in mind.

"Da…this is a surprise…"

It had taken longer than expected to calm Yiva's nerves and feel assured that the woman was not going to follow through on her suicide attempt. By the time Oasis convinced the woman to be strong, to stand with her against the men in the Fortress, by the time she escorted Yiva back to her room and made sure she bathed and dressed in something warmer and drier, the sun had cleared the horizon and both Lowell and Donn had come looking for her. Excusing her elusive absence on having shared breakfast with Yiva, a claim partially true as they had spent the breakfast hour together though they had not eaten, brought suspicious scowls from both men. It had been easiest to reassure Lowell of the innocence of the gesture, as she certainly had no reason to expose their tryst. Donn's misgivings, rooted as they were in reasons he would not reveal or put voice to, had been more difficult to address, but in the end, he agreed to the benefits of his wife befriending his mother. It was obvious that his suspicions were not quelled, however, a shadowy fact that bolstered her belief that whatever the situation was between mother and son, he was concerned about what the women might share with one another.

She expected the confrontational conversation to degenerate into the usual rough, almost violent, love making Donn preferred when he was feeling particularly unsettled about something, but a timely request for a meeting by Quentin interrupted her husband's intentions and allowed her to escape the bedroom in favor of anywhere else in the Fortress, preferably somewhere that would discourage unseemly behavior. Despite his often public displays of temper, Donn did care, to a degree, about how his relationship with his wife was perceived; by choosing to involve herself with any civic cause or opportunity that presented itself, it would keep his sadistic perversions behind closed doors.

Oasis understood why so many spouses of civil servants led such public lives.

The storm had ended, and though the ever-present layer of clouds still hid the sky from view, the day seemed unusually bright, leading a number of employees and guests in the Fortress to congregate in the open expanse of the lobby where the wide panes of glass allowed that unexpected brightness into the room. With a book tucked under her arm, intending to find an unclaimed bench or corner in which to enjoy that warmth and light as she read, it was there she ran into her father and his unexpected entourage of guards, retainers, and other Kennedy political officers. This gave no appearance of being a social call, but rather one of business, and yet she was disappointed, and perturbed, that no one, neither Lowell, Donn, nor her father, had seen fit to tell her he was coming.

"Sweetness…you look radiant…" Geary embraced her with all of the affection of a father to a daughter he had not seen in too long. Since the death of her mother when Oasis had been much younger, the two had been all the other had. If not for the political necessity of cementing relationships between Kennedy and LaGuardia, and that of positioning reliable eyes inside of the Channon household and LaGuardia's Fortress, Geary would have preferred his daughter to marry closer to home. But when she suggested this course of action as a means of planting someone inside, someone less suspicious and with wider access then a simple clerk or guard, the logic of the choice had been too sound to ignore. Trusting his daughter's good head for business and politics, the plan to get her here had been set into motion, and though this marriage had not been the one he intended, it was, it seemed not an entirely unpleasant one.

"I'm doing well, Da…everything here is in good order…"

Geary caught her face between his hands. "He is treating you well? You are happy? Perhaps with child?"

That the afterglow on her cheeks was likely a carryover from her night spent in Lowell's arms was a detail she would never reveal to anyone. It was better for her father to think that her husband was not the perverted monster he was rumored to be. Chuckling, forcing embarrassment into her voice that she did not feel, she replied, "It is too soon to know that, Da…you know it." As difficult as conception had become for most people since the Undoing, she would be lucky to conceive at all. This soon after her wedding day, it was unlikely that such could be true.

But the question did plant a thought within that she would have to explore and consider later.

"You did not tell me you were coming."

Finding no fault in her change of subject, Geary wrapped his arm around her shoulders and began a leisurely walk toward the stairs. "It was an impromptu decision…the cabinet raised questions that I thought should be discussed with Lowell in person, and they desired a collaborative audit with the Laedan's staff, a sharing of material as it were." He smirked. "I do not know how helpful such an audit will be, but it is best they conduct their affairs without my interference."

It was common practice for governmental agents from the boroughs to meet throughout the year, to compare population data, supply and manufacturing information, and anything else they deemed to be of relevance, so this was not an unusual event. And with the borough Laedans having entered into a new pact of alliance, such meetings between them were to be expected as well.

It was only unexpected that she had not been made aware of it.

What Geary did not reveal was an entirely different reason for coming here. The injured Cana prize had escaped Kennedy's net, a feat Geary was not disappointed about, and he had thought it prudent to follow the ex-co-Laedan into LaGuardia. The man would be a fool to return to the Fortress when the likelihood was that his 'friend' had been the one to betray him, but someone, somewhere, was bound to see Marrock, alive or dead, and when that happened, the news was going to travel like a thunderous boom to Lowell's doorstep.

Geary wanted to be here when that happened. He wanted to learn for himself just what the bone of contention, beyond Marrock's unfortunate anthro curse, was between the two.

"Do you have time for tea?" she asked hopefully, a touch of homesickness tumbling over her for the first time since her wedding. Before that day she had never been apart from her home, her father, for so long. It was good to see him again, even if he had not come for her, even if she did not need him to survive LaGuardia's ruling family. "I've heard some talk…and I want to know…"

Her voice lowered to a whisper, though by this time most of her father's escorts had peeled away to go about their own business.

"What is Fort Hamilton?"

She knew more than she admitted to. And though Lowell would not discuss it with her, nor Donn or Thomas, Oasis believed her father would. They had never kept secrets from each other before.

From Geary's wide-eyed expression of expectation, she knew, as he agreed to the prospect of tea and conversation, that he would not keep these secrets from her either.

∾*∾

Hands in his pockets, Vance watched the others peel away, no one entirely pleased with the plan or the situation at hand. The Omega, not prone to doing anything Roland asked of him, had snarled at the man who had been Pack Alpha for many years. Whatever their shared history, the mage deduced it revolved around Jia, the only one Deuce was inclined to obey. It had been her pleading that had convinced the burly man to accompany Addison back home, to see that he, the food, and the mediplies reached the Pack. Addi was right; the Pack needed those things, and no mission of Roland's, no matter how important or necessary, negated that. Despite Addi's concern for his sister and his weak, still at risk father, he would not willingly walk into the Fortress nor turn his back on the Pack. He would take the supplies to their camp and Deuce, at Jia's behest, would remain at his side…and then protect the Pack until she and Roland returned to do so themselves.

Jia and Kato, with Roland supported between them, continued their trek north. Just once, before she disappeared around a street corner, she looked back and caught the mage's eye, but he could not guess what that look was meant to convey. Vance blamed the distance between them, and his own knotted pit of worry that tangled and clenched in his belly, for the inability to know her thoughts when normally he had little difficulty with such readings.

Or maybe, he thought with a flexing of his fists to stretch and warm his fingers, he did not want to know.

It made sense to distance himself from the anthro. It was early afternoon, would be mid to late afternoon, if all went well, by the time the three reached the Fortress. Vance could imagine the fuss that would occur then, and though he and Kato shared the fear that the Channons might demand instant arrest and execution of the Marrocks, Vance, at least, was willing to concede that, after the front of concern for his co-Laedan that Lowell presented, action of that sort, particularly with Roland's current condition, would be politically damning.

Lowell was too smart for that. If he wanted to be rid of his co-ruler, he would find a savvier way to accomplish it.

And by that time, Vance would arrive at the Fortress to present his report, providing either a distraction from immediate action or putting him in a position to assist father and daughter if he could.

But whatever happened to the Cana, to Jia, Vance accepted that his duty lay to something bigger, to finding Liam and freeing him if he could and to finding and stopping the source of the blood-drug. He was a Protector after all. His responsibility did not stop with Jia and Roland, and as the only Protector to possess the knowledge of a possible manufacturing facility, a prison for untold numbers of anthro, there was no one else to do what must be done.

And as he had been engaged to uncover a stolen shipment, appearing to be involved in these potentially sticky matters between Channons and Marrocks would be detrimental to Vance's ability to continue as part of the Protectorate. He had to appear to be neutral for as long as possible.

Kato was strong. Kato was capable. And Kato was protective of Jia and concerned for her welfare. Of those things, Vance had no doubt. If trouble arose for the Marrocks while the mage was unable to help them, Kato would risk his life to defend her and get her and Roland to safety. But against the Fortress Guard, how could one Fela be enough?

Vance would feel better being there to safeguard the Cana too, but if one Fela would be overwhelmed by the strength of the Channons' forces, a Fela and Mage would fare little better.

Stay the course. It's what Ernest would say if the Chief was beside him now. Do your duty and leave the rest to fate.

Vance did not trust fate. Not this time. Not ever.

Damn, he needed a drink.

But not yet. Find Ernest…and then screw his courage into place and walk into the hornets' nest that was the LaGuardia Fortress.

࿔*࿔

Nik opened his eyes for a second time, relieved to be alone in what he realized was the Fortress infirmary. He remembered waking before, remembered the raw-rubbing presence of his twin, but he could honestly admit that he had not been certain where he was in those previous waking moments. The only clear memory, beyond his brother at his bedside, had been a suffocating in cotton sort of sensation, bound and weighted down by threads of drug haze that no longer lingered. That, and the taste of bitter copper on his tongue that no amount of water from the nearby pitcher seemed able to wash away. The more he swallowed, the worse his stomach felt, until he finally set the hemplastic cup aside, lay back, and gave up trying to be rid of the taste.

As unpleasant tastes went, it was not actually so bad. He had tasted worse after weekend binges.

He did not remember getting here, so someone had brought him home. Despite his attempts to remember anything prior to his previous semi-waking, there was nothing but a swirling multi-colored haze. Damn, that must have been good shart, he thought with a grin that only curled on one side of his face. Head turned toward the window, he tried to gauge the time but only concluded it to be day. It had been dark when he opened his eyes before, the room lit by the dim flicker of mediequipment lighting. The clouds were thick with black traces of the storm clinging to their ponderously moving billows, but the sun was behind them…somewhere.

How long had it been?

Without speaking to someone, there was no way to know, but Nik had no desire for company. He tested his arms, his legs, felt relief that they functioned, that he had not suffered a stroke or paralysis from his most recent indulgence. But he was tired. So, so tired. Fatigue was foreign to his body; he remembered that much. He hated it. Yet he was no longer certain what his body's natural state was, what it should be after so many years of chemical manipulation.

Footsteps were coming. It seemed he could feel the vibration through the floor more than hear them. He groaned, stretched out on his back and closed his eyes, hoping that whoever it was, they would pass by the infirmary and fail to notice he was awake.

One of these days it would all catch up to him. Maybe not this time, but one day. Maybe the next binge would be the last. It was not the future he wanted, but it was the only future he could foresee. The future had never existed beyond one more dance with death.

Maybe it was time for that to change.

If only he had the strength to meet that change head on and embrace it.

Jonni pressed his hand to the glass as if to touch his brother. There had been a feeling in his gut all morning that a change was due, that something unprecedented was to offer itself, and though he hoped that change would be Nik's waking, to his eyes, there was no change in Nik's condition, and he wished again he could somehow vanquish the demons that brought on so much suffering. To his knowledge, however, there had been no answers to the cause of this most recent odose, giving him no one to blame except his father.

That was blame too easy to place.

Jonni would do better than that. As soon as something better presented itself.

Chapter 25

"Open the gates! Open the gates!"

Roland did not recognize the voice shouting down from the watchtower, and it hurt too much to lift his head or to stare into the spotlight's glare that silhouetted whoever was there. It appeared, from the tilt of her head, that Jia did not recognize the voice either. He had tried to walk, tried not to be a burden on his daughter and the Fela in their company, but his fugitive run the previous evening through glass and stone littered ruins had split gashes in the soles of his bare Cana feet, and though Addison had stopped the loss of blood and Roland had slept and eaten the meager meal they provided, he was too weak to manage on his own. His feet hurt too much for shoes, so it did not matter that there were none to offer him. Too often Jia and Kato supported him or they stopped to rest in abandoned structures so Roland could catch his breath. Eventually, the decision was made for Kato to carry him the rest of the distance across the borough.

Roland was curious how this Fela had come to be in the company of his children, but asking took energy he thought best to conserve for what lay ahead.

After so many warnings for caution, he was also curious about the Mage. But Vance, like Kato, seemed friendly, trustworthy even, but that was when one needed to be on guard against someone who could read thoughts and emotions, signs and portents and the past, from a simple touch or from an item handed between them. There had been murmured hints that the Tracker was seeking both the source of the rumored blood drug...the existence of which now seemed more possible after what Roland had witnessed...some manner of shipment stolen from the Laedan, and, it seemed, Roland and Liam too.

If he was not so tired, so weak, if he was not so determined to face Lowell on his feet, Roland would have cornered the Mage demand an explanation of everything he knew...or thought he knew. He would have done his best to ensure his daughter's safety.

Instead, he was forced to trust her judgment. He believed he had taught her well, that she was strong and capable, but was she a good enough judge of character for this?

He had to believe yes.

The Fela, for whatever reason he had come to be part of this expedition, had an obvious interest in Jia. There were moments when Roland thought he saw the same interest from Vance, but then, as was typical of a mage, the Tracker's face grew blank and unreadable.

Out of sight of Fortress sentries, Roland insisted on standing on his own, on walking unaided, to present a vision of strength to those who thought him dead...or at least believed they would never see him again. Jia and Kato remained close, too close, Roland felt, to allow his deception to work, but when his focus on remaining strong was broken by the worn creak of the gates' metal hinges and a loud snapping sound that indicated the misaligned left gate panel had not yet been corrected, he stumbled, his foot catching something on the ground and one knee buckled. He was grateful Jia was close, for her grip on his arm, and the abrupt support of Kato's arm around his torso kept Roland from hitting the broken pavement and creating even more pain than the crack of one knee on the hard ground that jarred through him.

By now the gates were opened and a host of Fortress Guards and staff swarmed to offer assistance.

"Please," begged Jia, relieved to be recognized by staff who knew Roland's face, and hers, even if they had never had direct contact with either. "He needs to rest...he needs a medic..." Blood had begun to seep through the ill-fitting shirt Roland had been given to wear, meaning that the stitching had torn or else the strain of the day's movement had finally given way to seepage from the gunshot wound he had suffered.

They each looked frightful, muddy, wet, cold, bedraggled, and undoubtedly weary from the lack of sleep, and some of those around them took charge of Roland so that the weary pair could be tended as well, but both Jia and Kato remained at Roland's side.

In the chaos of shouted commands, one voice directed that they be escorted to the infirmary and that the on-call medic be summoned, while another gave order for news to be sent to the Laedan of Roland Marrock's return. The possibility of the co-Laedan's death had been kept to rumor only, all official statements reporting that the man was merely absent; whatever those assisting them believed, they were clearly excited and relieved by his arrival at the Fortress gates.

Lowell's reaction, and those of the other Channons and of Lowell's right-hand man, would be more telling, potentially more problematic, and letting Roland out of her sight filled Jia with dread. She kept her father's hand tightly in hers as the Fortress staff herded them into the building, and Kato, using his breadth of shoulder and the sometimes fierceness of his dark eyes to warn people away, walked with shuffling steps directly behind her, sometimes bumping against her as they were jostled about by their eager escorts.

And though the staff attempted to separate them at the infirmary door, seeking to tend to Jia and Kato's needs for warm, dry clothing, baths, and hearty meals, they refused to leave Roland. Nor did it seem to matter that Jia, at least, had a passing understanding of medical practice from a lifetime's exposure to her brother's study and work. The infirmary assistants, however, circled Roland, shoeing everyone out of the room to strip him of soiled clothes and treat his wounds in relative privacy.

The plate of glass hardly allowed for concealment from curious onlookers, and when Jia turned from her surveillance, feeling that watching from here was going to be the only way, if they would not allow her to be in the room with him, for her to keep her father safe, it was only then that she noticed Nik lying in the bed nearest the observation window. He looked to be asleep, the monitoring equipment beside him providing the steady beep and hum that suggested he was stable, but it took little imagination to guess that he was here because of an odose…and that it had been a serious enough incident that it kept him unconscious throughout the noisy disruption of bringing Roland in and beginning his care.

"Jia!"

"Let me through!'

Both voices brought nervous knots into her belly, but for different reasons, and her response to hearing them was enough to set Kato's nerves on edge.

"Jia! Is it true? Is Roland alive?"

Jonni reached her first and enveloped her in a bearlike embrace, the sort given by one who thought to never see the other person again. Recalling the sirens' blare and the hunt for her that had ensued after her last visit, no doubt he had believed her dead or wise enough to never risk a return to LaGuardia's Fortress. That memory made her wonder why, as she pried herself from his grasp, the Guards had not arrested her on sight.

Maybe Roland's condition, his very existence, was enough to distract them and divert any attempt to do so.

Several steps behind his son, Lowell elbowed through the crowd of staff and Guards that he sent scurrying back to their duties with nothing more than warning glances. By the time he reached the window, most of the hangers-on had moved away, leaving only a few Guards there to either protect Roland or, perhaps, see to his end.

Jia was not ready to place bets on which possibility had the best odds.

"He is…" she murmured, the answer polite and relieved but also wary as she caught the Laedan's eye.

"What happened to him? Where has he been? How did you get here?" There were a dozen or more other questions Lowell could ask, and they nearly erupted in an incomprehensible torrent. But getting most of the answers he wanted would have to wait until he could speak with Roland, and the insect-scurry of the medisistants, now joined by the medic, meant that Roland would not be accessible for discussion, for questioning, for quite some time.

"He was shot...but I don't know..."

"By a gun?" As rare as firearms were, that bit of detail alone meant that it had been no common person to have done this.

"We were scavving when we found him," Jia continued. "I tended him best I could, but he thought it best we come here for treatment..."

"Of course he would, we've got the best medics in the borough, apart from your brother, of course." There was a question in Lowell's tone, the curiosity about what had driven Roland to choose Fortress medics over his son's treatment, but asking would arouse suspicions, and as a normally careful man, Lowell did not need suspicions. "I'm glad you brought him here..."

"I argued against it after..."

"Oh...that..." Lowell shrugged and waved one hand dismissively. "We found what was reported stolen...and the thief. It was nothing...a misunderstanding."

As he watched Roland through the window, he did not see his son's skeptical scowl, nor the twitch at the corners of Jia's mouth and eyes, but she did manage to say, "I will appreciate getting him healthy enough to go home...Addi will be so happy to see him," with sufficient gratitude to make Lowell turn toward her with a smile. She was accustomed to avoiding references to 'family', as to her that meant Pack, and here in the Fortress halls, she and Addison were the only family Roland had...beyond Addi's wife and children, adopted or otherwise. Few here were even aware that Addi was married.

"Yes...of course...I'll discuss his condition with the medic now...and let you know what they say. In the meantime, Jonni will see that you two get cleaned up and..."

"Yes," Jonni started immediately, although as he put an arm around Jia, he side-eyed Kato in hopes that he could encourage the other man to stay here. He did not know who the man with the long waves of dark hair was, had never seen him with Jia before, but the protectiveness with which he moved when Jonni touched her made Jonni feel uncomfortably threatened.

Despite the wisdom of the suggestion, and the fact that she had to display trust and reliance on Roland's co-Laedan if they were to learn anything of use, she was not eager to leave her father and trust him to the care of a man she believed wanted him dead. But she believed Roland was stronger than he appeared, that his weakness was in part a ruse meant to lull the medics and lure Lowell closer. Lowell was not the sort of man to dirty his hands by taking action himself and likely, until he knew how much of a threat Roland was, he was going to keep him alive and keep a close eye on him.

It made her feel little better about leaving him, however. "I want to stay with him...I want to be sure he's safe..."

"The Guards will stay at the door until he's well...until we find out who has shot him and bring them in. You there..." Lowell snapped his fingers at one of the five guards lingering in the proximity. "Bring Chief Ernest here...I don't care if you have to drag him away from his dinner...I want to see him now."

"Yes, Laedan," the fellow bowed before running down the right side of the corridor in a haste to obey.

Believing those reassurances were satisfactory to convince her that Roland was safe, Lowell said, "Go now...take your friend with you. Jonni will see you both well cared for. I'll have dinner sent...so you can dine and rejoin your father...and by the time you're back, I'm sure the medics will be finished."

Reluctantly, Jia accepted Jonni's guiding hand steering her away from the infirmary, but not without reaching for Kato's hand and dragging him along. In no argument she made with herself was leaving the Fela unsupervised in the LaGuardia Fortress a good plan. He did not know this place, these people, and the possibility that he would interpret something as a threat and create an unprecedented amount of chaos for all of them was too high to risk.

He growled low at Jonni's familiarity with her, and Jonni looked back to stare at him without breaking his step. And when Kato returned the gentle squeeze of her hand and forced himself to dial down his protectiveness, she knew he preferred to remain with her as well. She did not feel safe within these walls and Kato knew it. He was not taking chances with her life if he could help it.

"I can hear you, you know…"

The medic was speaking to Lowell in low tones, trying to assure him that beyond cuts to his feet and hands, a variety of bruises scattered across his emaciated body, his sunken facial features that suggested a lack of food and sleep, and the single bullet wound to his shoulder, his co-Laedan was strong and likely to make a full recovery if he was allowed a few days of bed rest. The infirmary staff had bathed Roland, dressed him in a set of lightweight hospital trousers and shirt, both with ties rather than zippers or buttons for easy access, and now they had removed the instruments used for his care. Beyond Lowell, he could see Nik's still form, the young man not having moved the entire time Roland had been here, and outside the setting of the sun painted pale orange and rose colors in the western corner of the south-facing window.

Not once, he realized, had Lowell looked at his son. Nik must have been a patient here for several days to warrant that level of apathy.

"I'm just glad you're alive." Lowell dismissed the medic and stopped at Roland's bedside with a look of genuine affection on his worried face. There was something else there, darker and conflicted, that Roland was not pleased to see although he could not explain its origins without more information then he suspected his friend was willing to give.

Maybe, thought Roland with a touch of hope, Lowell had not had a part in the hunt that had ended with his capture. But Lowell did have a part in other things, a firm grasp on details that Roland intended to pry out of his hands.

"Of course I'm alive…why wouldn't I be?"

"You've been missing so long without a word, we assumed…" Lowell shrugged with an awkward expression. "Jia said you'd gone scavving in the east…that you were due back…but others said…"

Latching on to that detail, Roland managed an adequately pained chuckle as he clutched his wounded shoulder. "I'm sorry I didn't forewarn you...I'd heard rumor of an astronomy tower...I had hoped to find it...bring back a workable telescope...or at least the lenses...and anything else I could carry. Thought I'd be gone no more than a day or two...didn't expect to get trapped by a herd of grubbers...or to have to fight my way out...or to get shot and robbed of everything I'd found along the way."

They were partial truths that would hold up to scrutiny if necessary. There had been grubbers outside the Bunker. He had not had to fight his way past them, but he had needed to fight for his freedom. He had been robbed of everything upon his capture, his belongings, his clothing, his freedom, and he had been shot during his escape. Each bit of his story was true, just not in the appropriate order...or complete.

Lowell frowned. "Guns in the hands of ordinary people is a bad thing...I swear to you I'll find whoever did this and make them..."

"Guns in the hands of anyone is a bad thing," murmured Roland, his eyes closed as he grimaced and rolled his shoulder beneath his hand, using the action to mask any secrets his eyes might give away. "Thank the stars there are so few of them. As for...they're probably long gone by now. I must have hit my head when I was shot...as I don't remember anything more than waking up empty-handed in Jia's care. And thank praises she found me..."

"Yes, you are fortunate there. She never gave up on you...even when some of us did." Lowell's expression was pained, though Roland could not see it.

Roland did notice the odd note in the other man's voice, however, but only opened his eyes when he felt it safe to do so. They were dancing around the unspoken, the knowledge Roland was not supposed to have, the plans Lowell was keeping until he deemed the time was right. It was because of those plans Lowell had felt something needed to be done before. With Roland's return to LaGuardia, neither of those things, apparently, had changed.

"I hope my absence hasn't created difficulties..."

"Oh, no...no...I mean..." Lowell clenched Roland's free hand warmly, successfully burying less pleasant matters in exchange for welcoming affection. He had wanted something done with the friend that removed his influence from office, that would prevent him from interfering in Lowell's grand design for LaGuardia, but even though the man was, it was said, an anthro, Lowell had not asked for his death. Roland's death might be a necessity to move forward, but that did not mean he wanted it. "It wasn't the same...your input was missed...and there have been things that have not been done...or gone as smoothly as they should have...but we managed to..."

"We?"

"The boys and I, of course. That was...until Nik..." It was the first time his attention shifted to his son, the only moment he acknowledged him there, and it was too brief in Roland's opinion.

"Is he...will he...?"

"Well, he's alive...but he hasn't stirred yet...so he may be brain dead for all anyone will tell me. What you see is..." He shrugged, grateful he had steered Roland away from a discussion of what part Quentin had played in LaGuardia's government since Roland's absence. That was an admission Lowell did not want to make.

Roland was glad too. This was not the time nor the arena to hold that conversation. "And Jonni's a married man now?"

The dark grimace that crossed Lowell's face was tempered with a flicker almost too quick to notice. Only the brightness of it in comparison to his whole demeanor made it noticeable. "No...that boy is too stubborn for his own good..."

"Like his father," murmured Roland with a hint of amusement. He had been against the arranged marriage, had known that Jonni's refusal was not going to evaporate just because marriage was deemed to be his duty. Roland had wanted some other means of cementing a relationship with Laedan Hallister, but Lowell had insisted that intermarrying the families was the best solution. Though he had no desire to remarry, particularly someone young enough to be his child, and there was his Cana nature to consider that would have presented difficulties, Roland had offered himself as the marriage link between the boroughs. Assuming it was no serious suggestion, Lowell laughed heartily at the idea, pointed out that a marriage between contemporaries in age was much better for the boroughs, that even marrying her to Quentin would be better for LaGuardia and Kennedy, and Roland had laughed with him to cover over the discomfort of not being taken seriously.

Maybe Lowell had suspected he was Cana even then. Having had plenty of opportunity to consider things during his captivity, Roland was certain Lowell had known, or suspected, that truth by their last moments together. It was as likely that knowledge had led to Roland's incarceration as it was that Lowell had felt forced to remove his co-Laedan from office for political gain. Given the Channons' prevailing anti-anthro stance, it was actually the easiest, most logical reason to believe. Trying to believe that their friendship could have been discarded over political differences was a bitter taste choking at the back of his throat.

"Like his…" The corners of Lowell's mouth twisted to accommodate the almost birth of a grin. "Yes, well…"

"So the treaty with the Hallisters? With Kennedy?"

"Saved by Donn's choice to be the man his brother isn't."

It was Roland's turn to scowl, but he tried to hide it with a yawn partially concealed behind his hand. He knew Donnovan Channon too well, and the thought of what sort of husband that boy must be made him feel deep pity for the Hallister girl.

Interpreting the yawn as a sign of weakness and weariness, Lowell lightly squeezed Roland's good shoulder. "Oh…I'm sorry…I shouldn't be…I'm just so glad to have you back where you belong."

Lowell had never been a man good at expressing emotions beyond frustration and outrage and displeasure, but Roland recognized those warmer emotions when they were present, had learned to see them when they were young boys growing up together, and so he could see it now. He forced a weary smile and said, "It's good to see you too."

And it was good…even if it came on the shirttails of potential treason to the welfare of the citizens of LaGuardia…and betrayal between friends.

So Roland was here. Right where Geary had not expected him to run. He had not been certain the Laedan would survive the hunt or the distance he would have to run with the burden of whatever injury his guards had inflicted, but he had believed, if Roland survived, he would be wise enough not to come to the Fortress.

Not while he was weak and injured.

He paced the long, empty meeting room with its well dusted and polished wooden table, his thoughts churning. Perhaps there was some good that could come out of this…some benefit he had not anticipated. Yes, his daughter's marriage bound him to the Channons…but that did not mean he had to accept the Channons as the ultimate authority in LaGuardia.

A chance to talk to Roland Marrock, alone, was all he needed. A chance to tell him the truth…or Geary's version of it at least…a chance to turn Marrock against Channon and shift the balance of power in Queens to his favor.

It would not be an easy feat…but it was one entirely worthy of the Hallister name.

☙*☙

Kato did not like being separated from her in this hostile environment, did not like wearing someone else's clothes or being indebted to a stranger who seemed too eager to get Jia alone. It was only the reassurance she had given with her eyes, assurances that she knew these people, that she was in no danger from this man Jonni, that allowed him to step out of the room to relish his first real bath since having left his home behind with Vanya. No matter how hard he strained to hear what was being said or done in the other room, he could not, and that deficiency would keep him from enjoying the bathing any longer than required to be clean.

He did not know why she insisted that he take the opportunity first, but the trails in his imagination gave him too many ideas that failed to reassure him, failed to allow him to appreciate this luxury to its fullest.

Jia knew she was being listened to through the door that closed her off from Kato's support, but as she had nothing to hide, she began a slow circle of a room she had not visited in too long, the room she and Addi had shared when growing up until the day her brother had stopped coming to the Fortress. She had not thought of this room when she had come to comb through her father's office and, with the way she had been pursued out of the Fortress, it had never occurred to her that her clothes would still hang in the closet, alongside some of Addi's, that trinkets and keepsakes and odd bits of toys and memorabilia from her years here would still dot the shelves, the dressers, or hang on the walls.

By the way Jonni's eyes followed her as she moved, she imagined it had been his decision to leave this corner of her world untouched, in the hopes that she would return to it one day, as a shrine to the memory of the future he had hoped to build with her.

She refused to reveal how uncomfortable the thought made her.

Eventually, to break the silence when the water in the shower room stopped running and Jonni seemed content to watch rather than speak, Jia stopped at the window, where a collection of a dozen carved wooden animals lined the sill, dusty and faded but still in good condition. "How is Nik?"

It was the safest topic of discussion, and he would know from a lifetime of knowing that her concern for his brother was genuine.

"It was bad…really bad…some sort of drug made from…" He choked on the words, stumbling over the unspoken truth. Jia thought to finish the statement, but he continued hastily to cover his faltering account. "I got him home in time to save his life…and the doctors say he is breathing on his own…his heart beating…everything normal and stable…and yet he won't open his eyes. He just sleeps."

"He's done this before…" To Jia, it seemed the aftermath of every odose for Nik was sleep. She remembered him as a little boy, a few years younger than her, a child with boundless energy, always curious, who seemed never to sleep regardless of the hour of day or night. That had changed, although she did not know why; sometimes he would sleep for days, or wander about in a perpetual fog, or exist in a state of hyperactivity when no one could keep up with him. The bouts of mania had begun to level out by the time he grew to an age where he could seek his own entertainment…and his own means of self-medication. Some periods of usage kept him on an overactive high for days, a swing that would inevitably be followed by an extended period of lethargy…and an increased likelihood of odose.

"He's always pulled through." But, Jia knew, always would come to an end when Nik's body decided it had endured enough abuse. "If he's breathing on his own, he'll make it." She had to believe it. She had to cling to that hope, not just for Jonni but for herself too.

"I hope so."

The water in the other room had begun to run again. Dropping into a chair when it seemed she had no intention of doing the same, Jonni leaned his elbows on his knees and his chin on his fists. "I'm glad you found Roland…"

"He found me…or perhaps fates brought us to the same place. I'm just happy he's home." And alive went without saying, but to say it would mean admitting she had feared for his life, and after insisting he was scavving, such an admission might be suspect.

"Did he say where's he's been? Who shot him?" His father had asked the same questions, and she had tactfully refrained from giving him an answer, but Jonni hoped she would trust him more than she trusted his father…though he knew he had given her little cause of late to trust him.

"He's been too weak…too tired…to speak much. Once he's stronger, he'll tell me."

She still had not looked at him, was instead examining the carved animals one by one before stuffing them into the pack she carried which might, Jonni decided, be a good thing. If he could not see her eyes, he would not see the mistrust in them, would not have to see evidence of carefully crafted half-truths intended to answer without answering. It was easier not to see her eyes.

"And him?" He inclined his head toward the closed door, a gesture Jia did not need to see to imagine.

"We met while scavving…he'd been injured, so Addi patched him up and…"

"Addi's here too?"

"No…he took what we found home while Kato and I continued…that was when we found Father."

"Why did he help you get Roland here…why did he risk…?"

Jia's shoulders shrugged as she now turned to face him. "I asked him to. We helped him…I suppose he felt he owed it to me for the medisistance." She did not owe Jonni an explanation for whom she chose to spend time with; she would never marry Jonni no matter how much hope he continued to cling to, and she was not going live her life in an ongoing effort to avoid hurting his feelings.

"Mmm…yes…well it was fortunate for you and Roland that he was there. I can't imagine how you would have gotten him to the Fortress without assistance. I just hope…"

Sounds in the next room gave testimony to a bath complete and Jonni, not interested in sitting in the room with Kato while the image of Jia bathing danced in his head, got to his feet.

"I will check on Roland…and have your dinners brought here." He let his former statement die unaddressed. His hope for Roland and Jia's safety, two suspected Cana in a hostile house, was a hope he did not need to speak. It was reason enough for her to distrust him. And reason enough for him to regret his own mixed feelings.

☙*☙

Through the shadows they moved, remaining upwind of those who, in their normal skin were focused on reaching the heart of the Wilds before the sun set. It made a wise place for their kind to hide from the Normals, from HOPE, from whoever was hunting them. A logical, expected place…which was why there was little surprise when the pair continued on. A wise alpha never camped their pack where others might expect to find them.

Maybe this alpha was not as weak as believed.

The elder of the two was the one to watch, the one who could be a threat, for even though they were upwind, if they got even two steps too close, he would know they were there. He might be Omega, he might be outcast, and none of them knew him…but his strength as a fighter of power was legendary.

The other, the doctor, was no threat. It was tempting to take what he carried, to rob the pair, but there was dishonor in that action, and the hunters had no interest in theft or in harming those they trailed. Their leader had another agenda, one that, with luck, would give them back everything they had lost.

They just had to follow this pair to wherever they called home.

⤳*⤶

"Are you sure?"

Lowell drained the glass, having lost count now of how many that had been. It had not been enough to deposit a drunk haze on him, nor enough to abort the endless loop of his conversation with Roland that replayed in his head.

"Of course I'm sure," he grunted. "And that was no observatory he was looking for. I would have heard of one if…"

"You don't know everything," chuckled Quentin, filling the other man's glass without being asked. "Especially about the east…"

After sliding the glass toward his side of the table, Lowell hesitated to pick it up, considering Quentin's words. They were certainly true. Lowell had never scavved a day in his life, had never been beyond LaGuardia's borders. He rarely traveled beyond the streets immediately surrounding the Fortress unless duty demanded it. Roland, on the other hand, pushed east at every opportunity, and while reports sometimes came from an occasional adventurous individual who had come from the east, they were unsubstantiated rumors. If any of them were true, Roland was more likely to know than Lowell.

"Maybe…"

It was a sound of defeat and uncertainty, one that Quentin was quick to take to his advantage. "How does he know…?"

"Not hard to figure out…who else has the authority to…?"

"Where would he put them? If he was already missing when the shipment was moved…how could he have intercepted…"

"If I knew that I'd know where they are." Lowell lurched to his feet. Quentin knew his dreams for LaGuardia; had been the one to open Lowell's eyes to what had been hidden through all the years of Channon and Marrock acquaintance. Although no orders had been given, the need for something to be done had been expressed and while Lowell had not asked, he was certain that whatever had happened to Roland had been at Quentin's directive…and was meant to be fatal.

Quentin was too adept at keeping his poker face in play, and would either deny it if Lowell asked or else take the credit in hopes of reward.

The fact that the effort had failed, however, did not reflect well on him, and whether Lowell inquired or not, Quentin would find a way to make this right. Not because Lowell asked…but because Quentin could not stomach the blame of failed action.

Lowell did not want to know. He did not want, should Roland fall under the shadow of Quentin's success, to feel he had any part in whatever the man did.

And Quentin was astute enough to know that, should the co-Laedan regret or object to his action, the blame would be Quentin's. He was also sharp enough to understand that he held enough political sway to throw just enough blame on Lowell to darken the man's political future and bind him with distrust. They knew each other's faults and weaknesses, and whatever came next, either they both emerged stronger for it, unscathed…or neither of them would emerge at all.

Chapter 26

Of the dozens of times he had been here, the walls had never looked as intimidating as they did tonight. The sun had set, wherever the western edge of the world happened to be, and with the moon hidden by the eternal blanket of clouds, the shadows cast by the lit torches spaced at even intervals on the wall were like reaching claws, seeking to snatch anyone within reach and drag them inside what seemed more like a prison to Vance tonight than any sort of home or place of benevolent rule.

Of course, though he had never trusted authority, feeling vulnerable from what some twist of genetics had bestowed on him, and he had always been aware of the underlying lust for power that dictated everything the Channons...at least some of them...did, he had never been so certain that there were secrets lurking in those halls and rooms as he was tonight.

And somewhere in there, behind one of those brightly lit windows scattered across the façade of the Fortress, Jia, Roland, and Kato were deep in the swamp of those secrets, shouldering secrets of their own that could prove deadly.

After turning up his collar against the wind, Vance pulled off one glove and pressed his bare hand against the palm of the other, the hand she had clasped before they parted ways, with the hopes of even the briefest glimpse of where she was, what she was doing. But there was nothing, not even a tingling warmth remained to indicate she had touched him, and he frowned with frustration. It was a fact of being a mage: he could not summon visions just because he wanted one. And sometimes there simply was nothing to see.

His fingers caressed the leather for several moments as he watched the guards change shifts for the evening and then shoved his hand back into the empty glove before adjusting his collar one more time and stepping out of the alley. Maybe he should have told Ernest he was coming here, but the Chief had not been at the Protectorate and Vance had waited as long as he dared…as long as he felt comfortable waiting. His part was to go to the Fortress tonight, to report something to the Laedan, though he had no idea yet what he was going to say, and be there in case he was needed. That sort of stay would be far too short for his liking. How would thirty minutes, give or take, be of any benefit to the Marrocks?

Trust me, Roland had said. I have a plan.

Vance reached the gates, which were opened without him needing an introduction, and he trudged across the garden terrace toward the front doors. Whatever that plan was, he mused as he opened the door into the empty lobby, it better be a damn good one…or they were all going to be dead before they had the chance to learn the truth. It better be a damn good one that did not involve the mage cleaning up the mess and seeing this through alone.

"Where is she?"

Cold sweat broke out across the back of Addi's neck as he stared at the man who had so long been a friend, an ally…family of a sort just as the rest of those within the Flushing Pack were. It had been a hurtful surprise when Pain and others had withdrawn their support and abandoned the pack, just as hurtful, he knew, as it was for the man beside him to see the one he had called partner, return uninvited when both he and the Pack were just beginning to recover from that betrayal.

Maz had never expected to see the other man again, and though part of him wanted to believe that Pain wished to rejoin the pack for him, the tone of the other Cana's first question and the fact that he refused to look at anyone except Addi proved differently.

On Addi's other side, Deuce growled, every fiber of his body tensing for a fight he was confident he would win.

If Pain feared him, it did not show in his posture or expression, but those behind him closed ranks to find safety in one another.

"She is…" Addi began.

Pain lifted his chin and sniffed dismissively. "Not here. Your Alpha has abandoned you, leaving you weak and…"

"She has not abandoned…"

"And we are not weak." In support of Maz's assertion, the three she-wolves newly brought into the pack and the four Cana who comprised the Queen's College Pack began to gather with those who remained of the Flushing Pack. As the Pack had been in the midst of late evening trade, there were three Mutani there as well, and QiangXu stood on the fringes, the scent of the agitated Ursa as strong to Pain, Maz knew, as it was to anyone here. And while none of the three Mutani siblings, their mottled skin scaly and wet in appearance, their eyes shimmering a pale glow of blue, were above five feet in height, they were each broad of shoulder and brow and possessed long sharp eye teeth and thick claw-like nails.

Not Pack, but allies which proved the Flushing Pack was not as weak as it appeared.

All the better, Pain decided. If it was Addison he had to put down to claim the strength of this pack as his own, it would be a fight easily won. And if it was Maz…well, he would regret that battle, but he knew the Cana's fighting style, his strengths and weaknesses. He would win that fight too. Maz would never have the heart to put Pain down to end a fight. Pain would win by default.

"She is not here, has left you without guidance…"

"You think my leadership weak?" The hurt and insult in Maz's voice were strong enough to gain him a brief glance from the man he thought he knew so well. Pain had always shown support for his wisdom, in the leadership he shouldered for the Pack whenever Roland had not been with them. It had never occurred to Maz that Pain believed he could do better. And it had obviously never been Pain's intention to express those beliefs. Hurting Maz now was a necessity; but if he regretted it, Maz did not see it.

"Flushing Pack needs an Alpha who can..."

"Jia is with our father," Addi blurted, not the way he wanted to share the news, but feeling he was being forced into that decision by this impossible situation. Pain and the others must have followed him from the borough, and somehow neither Addi nor Deuce had sensed it. Their being here now was his fault, and he had to do what he could to make it right, to protect his sister's place until she returned with Roland, to sort this out. Or until Roland was strong enough to put Pain in his place.

The tall, sinewy, black-haired Cana tensed, his mouth and the corners of his eyes twitching at the mention of the alpha he had respected and who he had given up on ever returning to the Pack. It was that failure to believe that had pushed him into demanding the confrontation with Jia for the position of Alpha while she had been content to await Roland's return.

He snorted. "I see no proof," he said stubbornly.

"Then scent this." Addi rummaged in his pack and withdrew the ragged, bloodstained jumpsuit his father had been wearing when he was found and thrust it toward Pain, his action a demand to be proven wrong. "We found him...tended his injuries...and I came ahead to bring these supplies to the Pack while he recovers. They are behind us, will be along shortly..."

"When?" Pain growled. The blood could have been anyone's, but the scent of Alpha was strong, recognizable...and too fresh to have been some article of clothing retrieved from their previous home. Pain could not argue against such valid evidence of Roland's being alive, and as such, he could also not make any legitimate demands to claim the Pack as his own.

"When he is ready to travel," said the Ursa from the fringes, his voice dripping with derision. "Or would you rather he die on a death march home so you can fulfill your quest of a takeover…?"

"Shut your mouth, Bear," snarled Pain with a step in the man's direction. "You have no say in…"

Maz moved, his body blocking Pain's path. "He speaks what we all think," he added in a low voice, standing firm when Pain attempted to push him aside. "You have no claim here while…"

"And no claim against Jia…not after she won Alpha fairly against your illegitimate challenge," Trill reminded him.

"My claim is over a Pack with no obvious alpha," he shot Maz a bitter look, "a Pack available to any strong enough to assert control."

This time it was Addi who growled, a sound he did not often make, as he thrust the pack and article of clothing he carried into the nearest set of hands and closed the distance between himself and Pain. "You would kill Father for this Pack?"

"I…"

Deuce's larger, broader form appeared abruptly in the narrow space between Addi and his challenger. While Pain matched him in height, very few matched the Omega in girth and breadth, nor in the scarred fierceness of his muscled body and the red in his eyes. "Will have to kill all of us to get to him," he hissed, completing the sentence. Maybe the entire Pack would fail to rise up and protect its Alpha in favor of self-preservation, but such disrespect was rare. Deuce, however, had nothing to lose, and though Roland disliked him, protecting the Alpha, be it Roland or Jia, was Deuce's responsibility. He would either lead the others in a fight or fight alone.

Not one member of the Flushing Pack moved or spoke to show disagreement with the Omega, not one showed an inclination to rebuke him for speaking out of turn when he should not even be standing amongst them. If anything, what Pain read on their faces, in their emotions, in the way they stood their ground, was an unspoken, perhaps even unacknowledged, willingness to accept Deuce back into their midst…at least as long as he represented protection from a threat they did not want to confront. They might even be willing to accept

Deuce as Alpha if he had the courage and willingness to put an end to Pain's attempts to force his way into a position of dominance they were not comfortable giving him despite his years of being a trusted member of the Pack. But Pain's anger had gone too far, was too raw and volatile, not the stable sensibility that Roland had always exhibited. If nothing else, Deuce represented stability.

And unlike Maz, he possessed the strength, willingness, and unknown quality of combat to win a fight for dominance against this particular threat.

"When Roland returns," Pain grunted, keeping eye contact with Addi, refusing to be intimidated by the Omega, refusing to show how rattled he was by the flurry of unexpected realizations and the understanding that the Cana behind him had made those realizations too, "we will settle this."

Addi nodded once. "When Roland returns," he agreed. "In the meantime, you are not welcome here." Those Cana behind him would be, should they choose to return to the Pack, but Pain's continued shows of aggression made it unlikely he would ever be welcomed again.

☙*❧

The constant creak of the metal awning that overhung the windows of the waiting room in which he stood provided the only counter of the passage of time as Vance waited, watching the swaying arms of the barren trees threaten to snap under the assault of the wind. There was no hint of incoming rain, but the wind had grown fiercer since Vance had been escorted to this room and told to wait for the Laedan's audience. That had been long enough ago that standing in this same position caused Vance's toes to begin to grow numb and an ache to form at the base of his spine and spider throughout his lower back. He resisted the temptation to pace, not wanting to be seen as impatient when the Laedan eventually arrived, but the longer Vance stood at solitary attention, the longer he believed he was being ignored.

A form of punishment, he presumed, for having taken so long to bring any sort of report to his employer.

And he still had no idea what he was going to say, what he could say, that would not give away how much he was beginning to piece together, how much he suspected of a truth he should not know.

The Fortress was still, the sort of silence expected at this hour of the evening, but to his mage senses, it was the calm that lingered before a threat erupted, before a storm came in to drown them.

If something unfortunate had already befallen Roland, Jia, and Kato, he doubted the Fortress would be this quiet. He doubted he would have been invited inside.

And so he waited. And listened. And struggled with words he could say that would not damn them all.

"Segara."

The word accompanied the opening of the door and brought with it the heavy perfume of strong hemp whiskey that set Vance's nerves on edge. He had forgotten, briefly, just how long it had been since his last drink, and with that heady aroma, a drink became almost all he could think about.

Vance turned, feeling the stiffness in his too long immobile body. It was a relief to finally be able to change positions. "My apologies for the hour, I did not mean to take you away from a celebration…" He assumed it was a celebration. The only other reason for drinking that much was despair and the need to forget. Better to assume one than the other.

Lowell grunted, realizing the drunken state he must seem to be in, although he did not feel too drunk to function. He felt clearheaded, despite his inability to make a decision about the friend who lay recuperating in the infirmary alongside his son.

"Surprised you made it at all." He glanced about the room, realized this was one of the few waiting rooms without a liquor cabinet and decided with a surge of spitefulness that the man who had escorted the mage here was going to pay for that particular oversight. "Where's Ernest?"

"Yes, I know, my report is overdue. The Chief wasn't at the Protectorate when I returned, I don't know where he is. Pursuing this matter has been like a dog chasing its tail...futile...running in circles; but I do think I have a lead..."

"You think?" Lowell joined him at the window, staring into the darkness with little need or desire, it appeared, to want to intimidate the tracker with an angry stare. Vance turned again to look out the window as well. Four guards lingered in the courtyard below, hands gesticulating and punctuating whatever dialogue they were sharing, gossip or business, unaware that the Laedan was watching.

"I have a lead. I don't know what it means yet...or what will be presented from it, but..."

"What sort of lead?"

Swallowing, thoughts tumbling over themselves in a haste to form a coherent sentence that would not reveal too much, Vance replied after a cough, "There has been movement of mediplies through the neutral zone into Kennedy borough, illicit movement..."

"Kennedy? Into Kennedy?"

Vance heard the perplexed distress in the Laedan's voice, as if he could not believe what he was hearing, as if it made as little sense to him as it did to Vance. It was an honest tone that Vance tucked away for dissection later.

"There's a chance it has passed through Kennedy...that it has been delivered to HOPE...to be used in the drug trade..." Yes, he thought as he said it. Pit the Laedan against HOPE, plant seeds of doubt about whether that mighty organization was as trustworthy as the Channons believed. That seemed a reasonably wise play to make. "...but until I dig deeper..." He shrugged. "I have to get proper clearance...permits and authorization writs...before I can travel freely within Kennedy...and that could take weeks..."

Or it would fail. If Kennedy was involved in some covert theft of goods and equipment from the borough they were beginning to forge an alliance with, they would either deny a Tracker Mage free passage or else they would delay that passage long enough to hide anything obvious they would not want to be discovered. Either way, it would buy Vance enough time to investigate covertly on his own.

And if the theft was unauthorized by Hallister, Vance imagined security within Kennedy borough would get sticky while the Laedans attempted to root out traitors who worked to undermine the alliance.

"I will get you clearance."

The theft in question had no roots in Kennedy, had no ties to the Hallisters. Lowell knew that. But if Vance's inquiry of the claimed mediplies theft led to any hint of where Nik had gotten his most recent addiction from, and if Hallister was, in any way, responsible for the near death of his son, the alliance between boroughs was going to suffer sorely...marriage between families or not.

Maybe it was time to have a talk with Hallister; how fortuitous he was here. And a talk with Oasis was in order too, for Lowell had few doubts she would tell him far more than her father would.

If Francis Lord and HOPE were responsible, on the other hand, it might well take both Laedans and the combined efforts of both boroughs to force the organization into some form of capitulation and agreement. Trickier, but dismantling the might of HOPE would be in both boroughs' favor.

Or would be more easily achieved once he found Fort Hamilton.

"I will get you everything you need...you will find the proof...and you will bring it back to me at once, is that understood?"

Despite the threat that existed in those words, and the fact that Vance had no intention of doing as the Laedan requested...if the trail ended where he suspected it would...he nodded his head and said, "Understood, Laedan."

It was the only thing he could say if he wanted to get out of this, if wanted to get Jia and Roland and Kato out of this, alive.

❧*☙

It had to be done. For Lowell, for LaGuardia, and yes, Quentin admitted as he stalked the empty corridors toward his destination, for himself. He had left the duty to others, others who had failed, and was now forced to tend the matter on his own. Maybe he should have done it himself the first time, but murder in the halls of LaGuardia's Fortress would have raised an inquisition that he did not think he could have escaped…especially if that mage Lowell favored had been brought into the investigation.

This time, however, Quentin had a plan. A plan to remove the threat, a plan to protect himself. There might still be the mage to contend with, but Quentin had a plan for that too.

With the Fortress settling for the night and the residents taking dinner in whatever room they chose to dine, the bustle of the day was ending and no one was encountered on his way. The one obstacle he feared, the man's daughter, was not at his bedside and Quentin breathed a sigh of relief as he paused at the window to stare at the pair of sleeping men within the dimly lit infirmary. He listened, heard no sounds near or distant, no echo of voices or heavy soled shoes on the wooden hallway floor. He was alone, but he knew that would not last. Dinner would be over soon, and he imagined Jia would return to her father's side as soon as she could. He had to do this. Now. Quickly. Before the details of his plan collapsed.

Behind heavy lids, ignoring the rising agitation that would soon push him up off of this uncomfortable gurney to find a bathroom and something to fill his belly, Nik heard the door latch turn. The footfalls were not Jia's, the one he expected to be here, the one he wanted to see, to talk to, to share what he knew about so many things. He assumed the steps were Donn's then, the only person, beyond infirmary staff, expected to come for his night-long vigil. His brother had not come since Nik's waking that morning, but it was easy to believe that business had kept him occupied, and once the chaos of Roland's return erupted, Nik figured Donn would choose to stay as far away from the infirmary, and their father, as he could.

Every one of those in that room earlier, medistaff, Roland, even Lowell, had thought him comatose, had thought him unresponsive and unaware, had not realized Nik heard every word spoken and not spoken, every tone of voice that hinted on emotion, the true thoughts that lay beneath words one could never really trust within LaGuardia's halls. As much as Nik loved his family, he knew from experience that none could be fully trusted. The only person he trusted had not yet come back to her father's side, and Nik was growing concerned that something had happened to keep her away.

No matter what his father said, the Marrocks, father or daughter or son, were no longer welcome here. She had to get away…Roland had to get away. It could not wait until morning.

The footsteps approached the other bed. Medistaff then.

But there was no accompanying hum or heat of lights being switched on, and there was a familiar layer of synthetic cologne that Nik smelled on only one man. He cracked his eyes open to see what in the name of grubber guts his father's right-hand man was doing. Quentin's back was to him so that Nik could not see what the man's hands were up to, but the movement, the twitching of his shoulders and flexing of his upper arms, showed he was doing something.

Roland's hand came up. Caught Quentin by the wrist.

Nik was prompted to sit, to act, but the door opened again.

"What in the…?" Jia froze, disbelieving what she saw as Roland tried to push Quentin away.

The clack of the latch, the unexpected voice, spun Quentin toward the door, pulling him free of Roland's grasp, the syringe he held clattering on the planked floor in the abruptly silent room. He opened his mouth to speak, though there were no words that sprung to mind and he was struck by a potent muskiness he had not come across in a very long time.

Roland stretched his now empty hand towards his daughter. "Jia…"

Kato growled and dropped into an instinctive crouch, the itch and tickle coursing below his skin and across the surface of it demanding a change.

"Fela," said Quentin with strained, nervous disdain. His eyes reflexively shown yellow, the beast within pushed to the surface by the proximity of another member of his breed. He was solitary, separate from his kind for precisely that reason. Around them, Quentin felt challenged. Around them, he could not control it.

Jia reached for Kato's shoulder, her father's hand momentarily unheeded, the golden glow in the other man's eyes making her blink and freeze in surprise. Kato eluded her touch with an equally challenging, "Fela."

Roland gasped her name again, tremors running up and down his arm, making his hand shake and spasm.

The door opened a third time, and as the weight of knowledge tangled around Jia's chest, cutting off the flow of air, the newcomer stood in the doorway, jaw slack, his legs weakening beneath him.

Quentin had known.

Quentin was a liar, a traitor.

Quentin was a monster too.

Upon the bed, Roland seized, blood pinked foam rising to his lips, his eyes rolling to expose only bloodshot whites, his hands clawing into the thin mat with a strength that tore the hempcanvas fabric as though it was filmy gauze.

Two men rushed forward, one in indignant fury, one with a roar and the anger born of witnessing a murder. Jonni had not seen the syringe, knew nothing of what Quentin had done, but what he knew now could destroy too many lives and was a deeper betrayal to his father's vision and work than Roland Marrock could ever be.

The roar, beastly in nature, unnatural in volume, brought the wail of first one alarm and then another blasting throughout the Fortress.

Jonni reached Quentin first as Jia shouted, "Father!" and lurched to Roland's side to hold his body still, as if stillness could counteract whatever Quentin had done. Fueled by Fela rage and the surge of hormones that precipitated a change, Quentin lashed out, more concerned about the other Fela whose form changed mid-leap, then he was with one meager Normal. His forearm cracked across Jonni's ribcage and flung him with such force into the metal supply cabinet that the doors buckled and the entire thing toppled down upon Jonni's crumpled form.

Roland's body stilled but the spittle continued to bubble forth, ever redder, to dribble down his cheeks, his chin.

Quentin's move meant that Kato struck him sideways, the swing of claws ripping across the unchanged Fela's arm, shredding fabric and skin alike. Off-balance, Kato twisted and prepared for another leap but Quentin, yowling in pain, leaped first.

"Father!" Jia shook his shoulders as the bubbles turned into a meager trickle of blood and his chest refused to rise again.

The two Fela collided, the mass of their forms creating a ricocheting that crashed both broadside against Nik's bed.

Nik took the only opening he would have against such a pair and swung the iron bedside tray. The reverberating twang as it struck separated the combatants and drove Quentin to his knees before he toppled to the floor.

The sirens brought with it the distant thunder of boots.

"Run," hissed Nik.

Kato rolled to his feet and wrapped an arm around Jia. They would never make it through the door. There was only one chance.

"My father..." she cried, her hand clutched around Roland's ripping free as Fela strength pulled her away.

"Run!" Nik hissed again.

The leap took them both from the infirmary window across the ten-foot expanse to a precariously balanced moment on the outer wall of the Fortress. Shards of glass sprayed across the vacant courtyard, the only evidence remaining as Fela and Cana disappeared into the black borough streets.

End Part 1

About the Author

Unsatisfied with 'how the story ends' as a young reader, Tamara took on the challenge of crafting endings to the tales of others to better suit her vision of the world. That desire to mold reality into how she imagined it should be gave birth to a life-long fascination with the written word, and its capacity, particularly through realms of fantasy and science fiction, to foster an understanding of the people, events, thoughts, and emotions that make us who we are.

A long-time resident of Clearlake, California, after a life that took her back and forth across the country, Tamara is owned by a pack of papillions, a pride of cats, and an eclectic arsenal of films she enjoys in her off-moments.

Scratch The Sky is Tamara's fifth novel.

Scratch the Sky